DON'T STOP

Conn eased back to look at her. "You're a real handful of trouble, you know that?" And then he kissed her, very tenderly, very thoroughly. Hope didn't mean to kiss him back quite so passionately. She knew what would happen if she did. But her mouth parted and his tongue slid in and her own tongue slid over his. Conn groaned.

"We can't do this," she whispered, drawing away. "We might reopen your wounds."

"There's a risk in everything." Conn kissed her again and her body began to melt at the same time her brain screamed a warning. There was a chance she'd been responsible for getting him shot in the first place. She wasn't about to be the one to hurt him again.

BOOK YOUR PLACE ON OUR WEBSITE
AND MAKE THE
READING CONNECTION!

We've created a customized website just for our very special readers, where you can get the inside scoop on everything that's going on with Zebra, Pinnacle and Kensington books.

When you come online, you'll have the exciting opportunity to:

- View covers of upcoming books
- Read sample chapters
- Learn about our future publishing schedule
  (listed by publication month and author)
- Find out when your favorite authors will be visiting
  a city near you
- Search for and order backlist books from our
  online catalog
- Check out author bios and background information
- Send e-mail to your favorite authors
- Meet the Kensington staff online
- Join us in weekly chats with authors, readers and
  other guests
- Get writing guidelines
- AND MUCH MORE!

**Visit our website at
http://www.kensingtonbooks.com**

DEEP BLUE

KAT MARTIN

ZEBRA BOOKS
KENSINGTON PUBLISHING CORP.
http://www.kensingtonbooks.com

ZEBRA BOOKS are published by

Kensington Publishing Corp.
119 West 40th Street
New York, NY 10018

All Kensington titles, imprints, and distributed lines are available at special quantity discounts for bulk purchases for sales promotion, premiums, fund-raising, educational, or institutional use.

Special book excerpts or customized printings can also be created to fit specific needs. For details, write or phone the office of the Kensington Special Sales Manager: Attn.: Special Sales Department. Kensington Publishing Corp., 119 West 40th Street, New York, NY 10018. Phone: 1-800-221-2647.

Zebra and the Z logo Reg. U.S. Pat. & TM Off.

ISBN-13: 978-1-4201-2398-2
ISBN-10: 1-4201-2398-X

First Printing: April 2005

10 9 8 7 6 5

Printed in the United States of America

Chapter 1

"Oh, my God! Look at this place!" Standing in the hall outside the door of her Manhattan apartment, Hope Sinclair stared in horror at the wreckage that had once been her home.

The door stood open and two uniform policemen prowled the destruction, which pretty much included everything in the room. In the cozy living area, her overstuffed pale-green sofa and chair were turned upside down, the pillows violently ripped open, the stuffing spewed onto the floor. The coffee table had been upended, breaking the beveled glass top into a dozen pieces. Her leafy green philodendron lay on its side, dirt all over the deep beige carpet.

Hope's disbelieving gaze swung to the mahogany book-shelves she had saved up to buy and only just purchased, the items there raked onto the floor. She had sublet the apartment from her sister almost two years ago, when Charity had set off for a summer adventure that turned into marriage and a permanent move to Seattle. It had only been in the past several months that Hope had begun to make the place her own.

She moved toward the pile of novels and reference books that had once sat on the bookshelves and now lay in a heap on the carpet, along with her prized collection of jazz CDs.

Some of the plastic cases were broken, but fortunately it looked as though most of the disks had survived.

The small dining area looked as if a Scud missile had landed, the table and chairs upended, one of the wooden legs hanging loose.

Both policemen started in her direction when they spotted her standing just inside the doorway in her navy wool coat and cashmere scarf, a concession to the icy January weather. Hope moved farther into the room and closed the broken door.

"Are you Charity Sinclair?" The cop was young and blond and she could tell he felt sorry for her.

"Um . . . no, I'm not. I'm Hope Sinclair. Charity is my sister. I took over her lease when she left the city."

"I see." He scribbled something in his notebook as the second officer walked up, older, with thinning black hair going gray and a slight paunch around his middle.

"Your next-door neighbor heard the commotion and called 911," the second policeman said. "Whoever did this was gone by the time we got here." The tag on his chest read "Buckley." "Looks like they broke the lock on your door. Which wasn't too hard. You haven't got much of a lock."

"You'll need to take a look around," the blond cop said. "See if you can figure out what's missing."

Hope swallowed. "Yes . . . yes, of course." Her initial shock was wearing off, replaced by a growing anger. Who the hell would do something like this? She didn't own anything of any real value.

Which the intruders must have discovered, since they seemed to have gone through every inch of the apartment. In the bedroom, her feather pillows had been slashed open, and all of the clothes in her drawers had been pulled out. In the bathroom, the shower curtain had been ripped down and her toiletries shoved off the counter onto the floor. The medicine cabinet stood open, everything scooped out into the sink.

Ignoring the sick feeling in the pit of her stomach, Hope made a fairly thorough search of the rooms, but couldn't find a single item missing. Which, she suddenly realized, might be bad news instead of good.

"Do you have any enemies, Ms. Sinclair?" the blond patrolman asked, sending a chill down her spine. "Anyone who might do something like this?"

"No one I can think of. I can't imagine why anyone would want to do this kind of damage."

"The world is full of nuts," Officer Buckley said. "There's no telling why some people do the things they do."

She surveyed the mess, thinking of all the hours it was going to take to put the place back in order and how much it would cost to replace the things that were broken. The chill returned as she remembered the feather pillows in her bedroom, violently ripped apart.

Her gaze shifted to the older cop. "You don't think I might be in any sort of danger? Is there a chance whoever did this might come back?"

"There's always a chance," Buckley said. "You're gonna need to replace your door locks. I'd suggest you get something a little less flimsy. And keep that window by the fire escape securely locked down."

"Yes, I certainly will."

They gathered a little more information: where she worked, where she had been at the time of the break-in, whether she was routinely away at this time of day. Then the blond cop handed her a card with the precinct number printed in the corner.

"If you think of anything that might be of help," he said, "you can reach one of us at this number."

"I'll do that. Thank you, officers." She closed the broken door behind them just as her cell phone started to ring. Hope hurried over and grabbed up her big leather purse. Tossing up the flap, she frantically dug out her cell and flipped open the earpiece.

"Hello?"

"Hope, this is Artie. One of the guys heard the 911 call

come over the police scanner and recognized your address. You okay?"

"I wasn't here when whoever did it broke in. But God, they trashed my apartment."

"What'd they take?"

"Nothing. That's the weird part."

A long silence fell on the opposite end of the line. "We need to talk, Sinclair."

"I have to buy some new locks and have them put on. I've got to get this place in livable condition again."

"I said *we need to talk*. That means now. Get in here, Sinclair, on the double."

His tone left no room for argument. She had only been working for the small Manhattan paper, *Midday News,* for the last couple of months and she needed the job. "I'll be right down, sir."

The line clicked off without a good-bye, and Hope took a last look at the destruction all around her. With a sigh, she walked over to the telephone book lying in a heap next to her desk. She rummaged through the Yellow Pages and found a locksmith, got back on the phone and dialed him. She gave him her address, along with instructions to replace the broken locks with new ones, the heavy-duty kind, paid him with a credit card, then went to see the superintendent.

Charlie, one of the more dependable supers she'd had, agreed to watch the place while she was at work. He said he would get the new keys from the locksmith and told her not to worry—he would "deal with the perps if they have the nerve to come back."

Since Charlie was well over sixty and hardly in prime condition, she prayed the man or men would not return.

With a thank-you to Charlie, she went back to her apartment, pulled on her heavy wool coat, and wrapped the cashmere scarf around her neck. Slinging her purse over her shoulder, she took the elevator down to the lobby and walked out into an icy wind. Slushy snow crunched beneath her boots as she hailed a cab and gratefully climbed in out of the chill.

As she leaned back against the cracked leather seat, she thought of her apartment, and a fresh shot of anger swept through her, mingled with a trace of fear. Who would do something so heinous? Why her place and not someone else's? What were they after?

The questions plagued her as the cab wove through the traffic on Lexington, all the way down to the offices of *Midday News* on Twenty-second Street, not far from the Flatiron Building.

Her editor, an overweight, balding man in his fifties named Artie Green, spotted her the minute she pushed open the door leading into the main office behind the reception area and motioned her toward his office. Once there, he held open the half-glass door while she walked in, then closed it firmly behind her.

In the cluttered newsroom outside, reporters sat at their computers surrounded by messy stacks of paper next to half-full mugs of cold coffee. At least the overflowing ashtrays were gone—thanks to a new city ordinance that banned smoking, the one bad habit she hadn't acquired over the years.

"Sit down, Sinclair." He was wearing his usual dark slacks and rumpled shirt with a tie that was way too narrow to be stylish.

Beneath her coat, which she hung on a hook beside the door, Hope wore slacks, too, dark brown with a light beige sweater. She sat down in one of the metal, vinyl-covered chairs on the opposite side of Artie's desk.

"Sorry about your place. That's got to be a real bummer."

Hope held back a sigh. "That's putting it mildly."

"The cops got any idea who might have done it?"

"Like I said earlier, nothing was taken, so they really don't have a clue."

"I hate to say this, but you pissed off a lot of people with that article you wrote on old man Newton and Hartley House. Maybe someone was sending you a message."

Goose bumps ran over her skin. She had thought of that

herself. Over the last few days, she had gotten several nasty calls at the office, but nothing she considered a serious threat.

"All I did was give the tenants' side of the story. They don't think the building should be condemned. Those old people love that place. They've been living there for years. It's their home and they don't want to leave." Hartley House was a retirement home on the south end of Manhattan. There were thirty-five units, each occupied by a tenant over sixty-five, most of them older than that.

"The building inspector says the place isn't safe," Artie said. "A lot of the people in the neighborhood agree. They think the building's an eyesore. They want to see something new go up, something more classy that will add to the value of the area."

"Buddy Newton thinks it's just a scheme to force him to sell." Buddy was the owner of the building, one of the occupants himself.

"Newton's an old fool, just like the rest of 'em. The place needs to come down. He might as well get as much money as he can and get on with his life—whatever's left of it."

"Even if the neighbors believe that, surely no one was mad enough about the article to break in and vandalize my apartment."

Artie just shrugged. "It's a hot issue and tempers are running high. Which is why I'm pulling you off the story."

Hope shot out of her chair. "What are you talking about?"

"You heard me. The publisher's taken an editorial position in support of the condemnation." Meaning the advertisers were screaming and the paper was caving to their demands. "We're winding this one up," Artie said. "If something interesting develops, Randy Hicks will handle it."

"Randy Hicks! You've got to be kidding. That guy hasn't had a fresh idea in years."

"In this case, we don't need fresh ideas. Fortunately for you, an assignment's come up that's a whole lot better."

She eyed him warily. "I'd rather keep working on Hartley

House." In the weeks since she'd been on the story, she had grown fond of a number of the tenants. Old Mrs. Eisenhoff was Aunt Bea come to life, right out of Andy Griffith's *Mayberry*, and one of the sweetest old ladies Hope had ever met. Mr. Nivers, on the third floor, always had a joke for her, and Mrs. Finnegan, completely alone in the world, would be utterly bereft without her slightly whacky friends and weekly bridge games.

None of them wanted to lose their homes.

And she thought that maybe Buddy Newton might be right.

"Yeah, well, you're off, kid. That's just the way it is. Like I said, you're gonna be doin' somethin' better. You're gonna be writing a series for *Adventure* magazine."

"That's crazy—I don't work for *Adventure* magazine."

"Doesn't matter. The magazine's owned by McLaughlin Media Corp, same as *Midday News*. You work for them, you go where they need you. Besides, you were requested to do the piece."

Hope was having trouble digesting all this information at once. She knew the newspaper was owned by a huge corporation that owned a string of magazines and newspapers across the country. *Midday News* was one of the smallest in the group.

"So who requested me for the story?"

"Actually, it's scheduled to be a series. And the guy's name is Brad Talbot—you know, the 'Doormat King'? You interviewed him for some kind of freelance article a couple of years ago. At least that's what he said."

She had written the piece, "Movers and Shakers," for *Young Executive* magazine. Talbot, a multimillionaire New Yorker, was the grandson of the man who invented rubber doormats back in the thirties. His father had expanded the company holdings and made profits into the ionosphere; then he died and left the entire family fortune to his son.

"So what does Brad Talbot have to do with *Adventure* magazine?"

"Talbot's one of the partners in a treasure-hunting venture. He's the moneyman in the deal. There are three other guys involved—an archeologist named Archibald Marlin, a guy named Eddie Markham, and the operations man, Conner Reese. You're going to the Caribbean, Sinclair. No more shitty snow and freezing wind, just warm, tropical sun and sandy beaches. A place called Pleasure Island."

"Pleasure Island. Sounds like someplace in Disney World— or a porno flick."

"Hey, what have you got to complain about? The magazine wants at least three articles. They'll probably take weeks to write, and while you're gone, all your expenses are paid. You're goin' on a dream vacation, kid."

"I don't want a dream vacation. I want to continue working the story I'm on. What if I refuse the assignment?"

Artie frowned. "Then you'll be looking for a job."

Hope opened her mouth, then clamped it tightly closed. She needed this job. Magazine articles were more fun to write, but they didn't come with a regular paycheck. And she did have some expertise.

Several years back, she had done some freelance articles for *Travel and Life* magazine; one of them, "Sexiest Places to Dive," dealt with islands in the Caribbean, mostly the accommodations, but during the time she spent there, she *had* learned to dive. She was still a novice, but she enjoyed the sport, and she had fallen in love with the islands. If she weren't so caught up in Buddy Newton's problems, an assignment like this would be the nearest thing to heaven.

Hope looped a hunk of thick red hair over her ear, not quite used to wearing it longer than the jaw-brushing length it was before.

"So when do I leave?"

"You've got two days to get your apartment back in order, then you're out of here."

"Two days!"

"That's what I said. Since time appears to be of the essence, I'd suggest you get moving, Sinclair."

Hope knew better than to argue. Instead, she grabbed her leather purse, her coat and scarf off the coat tree and headed out the door. On the cab ride back to her apartment, she phoned her best friend, Jackie Aimes, and told her about the vandals that had ransacked her place, about losing the story, and her upcoming trip to the islands.

"Sounds like a godsend to me," Jackie said. "I can't think of anything better than spending a few weeks in the Caribbean." Jackie was a would-be novelist who looked more like a model, standing nearly six feet tall in her stocking feet. She was black, svelte, and beautiful, a woman who made her living by writing ad copy for a small-time advertising firm on the lower west side of the city.

"When do you leave?" Jackie asked.

"Day after tomorrow."

"Mercy, girlfriend. You're gonna need help if you want to get your place in shape before you leave. I'll meet you at your apartment."

Hope breathed a sigh of relief. "Thanks, Jackie." Aside from her two sisters, her dad, and stepmom, Jackie was the one friend she knew she could count on.

Jackie was already there when Hope arrived. She had wangled the keys to the new locks from the super and let herself in. She was busily at work when Hope knocked on the locked door.

Jackie blew out a breath as she pulled it open to let Hope in. "You weren't kidding when you said this place was trashed."

"I guess that was a bit of an understatement."

"No kidding." She grinned. "At least the CD player still works and most of your disks are okay." Bernie Williams, one of Hope's favorites, played soft jazz in the background. "Take your coat off, girl, and let's get to work."

Cleaning up was even harder than Hope had imagined. It was an exhausting, depressing job, but by the end of the following day, her apartment was back in order and at least passably livable again. She didn't have time to replace the items that had been broken, but she could handle that when she got back home.

The clothes hanging in her closet—thank you, God—had been left untouched. She still had most of the loose pants and sundresses she had bought for her first trip to the islands, but she stopped by Bloomies and bought a new two-piece purple swimsuit, one that was less revealing than her yellow flowered bikini, though she tossed that one in for good measure.

By Friday morning, she was heading to the airport, a ticket on Air Jamaica in her hand. A private plane would carry her the rest of the way to Pleasure Island, about ninety-five miles off the coast.

If she hadn't felt guilty for abandoning poor old Buddy Newton, she would have been excited. As it was, she was mostly just resentful she had lost what might have been a really great story to that slug, Randy Hicks.

Conner Reese knocked on the door to the office Professor Archibald Marlin had been assigned during his stay in Jamaica. The seventy-three-year-old professor was doing a series of lectures at a small, private college on the outskirts of Port Antonio, a beautiful old harbor that was once a banana shipping port. The professor had accepted the invitation to speak because he enjoyed talking about the subject he loved—the Spanish treasure fleets—and because it put him in close proximity to the expedition going on just ninety-five miles from the island.

Dr. Marlin opened the door. "Right on time, as usual. Good to see you, Conner, my boy."

"You, too, Doc. Looks like island life agrees with you."

The professor smiled. "Perfect weather. Views of the sea that go on forever. Except for missing Mary, how could it not?"

"How's she doing?"

A cloud passed over the professor's face. He was as tall as Conn, a little over six-foot-two, but bone-thin and pale-skinned with a leonine mane of thick gray hair. His pant legs were always perfectly creased but so loose over his thin legs that when he walked, Conn always got an image of Abraham Lincoln.

"I'm afraid Mary's pretty much the same. My daughter is staying with her. They may come for a visit while I'm here." Mary Marlin, the professor's wife of nearly fifty years, was a victim of Alzheimer's. It was a hard, hopeless disease that took its toll on everyone it touched.

"I've spread the map out," Dr. Marlin said, changing to a less painful subject. "Come over and have a look."

Conn paused long enough to pour himself a cup of coffee from the half-full pot on the hot plate of the machine against the wall. Then he walked over to where a map of the Caribbean lay open on the table, this one plotting the location of shipwreck sites as far south as Trinidad, as far north as the Florida coast.

Though the office was nicely furnished, with a desk, a table, four wooden chairs, and big windows looking over the distant harbor, the professor had cluttered the place up. Old maps and drawings, stacks of reference books, and endless sea charts made it look like his office back in South Florida, where Conn had first met him.

The professor looked down at the map. "If you recall, it was January when the seven galleons of the 1605 Terra Firma Fleet left Cartagena."

"That's right. And each ship in the line was heavily loaded with gold and silver bars and trunks full of gold and silver coins."

The doc nodded, as if pleased that his student was learning. "And there were passengers, as well. Some of them extremely wealthy. The hurricane season was past. They thought they were safe. Then, when they were halfway between Jamaica and the now-Honduran coast, a freak storm came up. Two of the ships pressed on to safe harbor in Jamaica, one made it back to Cartagena, but four of the ships went down."

He flicked a glance toward the blue-green sea outside the window. "Hundreds of millions in treasure was lost, and thirteen hundred passengers drowned in the violent seas off the treacherous Serranilla Banks."

He turned back to Conn and a faint smile curved his lips. "At least that is what most of the academic community believes." Marlin was an archeologist, an expert on the Spanish treasure fleets that sailed from Spain in the seventeenth and eighteenth centuries. Conn had heard this recitation before, but it never seemed to bore him.

He took a sip of his coffee, then grimaced at the bitter taste of the hours-old brew. "According to the history books, most people think all four ships were lost in the shallows, but you think one of them—the *Nuestra Señora de Rosa*—was making for Jamaica when she was blown off course. Your theory is she survived as far as what was then called *Isla Tormenta,* and went down on. the reefs around the island."

"Exactly. Which brings us to the point of your visit. You want to know if the ship could have gone down somewhere along the southern shore instead of on the reef to the north."

"I'm concerned that it might be possible, and if it is, we might be looking in the wrong place."

The professor leaned over the map and pointed to the tiny speck of land lying south of Jamaica. The Spanish had called it *Isla Tormenta*—Storm Island. Eddie Markham, its latest owner, had renamed the place Pleasure Island to give it a better image.

"You're discouraged because the reef is so thick," Doc Marlin went on. "You think it could be hiding the ship and you might never find it."

"It seems like a good possibility. We've been out there for weeks and haven't found a thing. I was thinking maybe we'd do some side-scanning along the southern shoreline."

"I think you should stick with the reefs a while longer. Leasing a boat the size of the *Conquest* isn't cheap. We need to make the most of the time we have use of it."

"We aren't paying for the boat—Brad Talbot is. And he doesn't seem overly concerned with the cost. But you're right. We need to concentrate our efforts where they'll most likely be rewarded. For now, we'll stay near the reef."

"Maybe you'll pick up a signal from one of the cannons or maybe an anchor." He was talking about the magnetometer, a device that could detect undersea metal objects. So far it had only found a couple of rusting oil drums.

"Yeah, maybe we'll get lucky. Thanks, Doc. I'd better get going. I need to catch that plane heading back to the island."

"Call if you need anything else."

Conn just nodded.

As he left the office, he reached into the pocket of his khaki shorts and pulled out the single gold coin that was his good-luck piece. He had been managing a dive school on Key West but visiting a friend, diving off a place just north of Vero Beach, when he had found the coin. A couple of galleons had gone down in the area, his best friend, Joe Ramirez, had told him, and occasionally after a storm, artifacts turned up.

Joe was one of the guys on his former Navy SEAL team, a Cuban-American, the cliché of a hot-tempered Latino, but bigger than most. Both of them had left the SEALs some years back but were using their diving skills to make a living.

When the coin turned up, Joe had been nearly as excited as Conn. And both of them were determined to discover which ship it had come from.

"I know this guy," Joe had said. "My archeology professor in college. He's an expert on this kind of stuff."

Professor Marlin had retired from teaching, but the old man had never lost his fire when it came to Spanish treasure. He'd told Conn the coin came from a shipwreck of the 1715 treasure fleet, which was lost to a hurricane off the Florida coast. He also said much of the treasure had been recovered and that salvaging the wrecks was growing more and more difficult.

But the conversation had sparked Conn's interest, and over the next few years, he and the professor had become close friends.

Conn thought of those early days as he continued along the path to the car he had driven from the airport, an old blue Toyota Corolla with a left-hand drive they had bought to get them around the island. He looked down at the coin in his hand, remembering the incredible tale that had led them to the Caribbean and the search for Spanish gold.

He knew finding it was a long shot—all of them did. And they knew how dangerous this kind of search could be. Mel Fisher had lost his son and daughter-in-law trying to locate the galleon, *Atocha*. Even the four-hundred-million in treasure Fisher had finally found couldn't make up for that kind of loss.

Still, if the *Rosa* was out there, hidden in the waters off Pleasure Island . . .

Conn tried not to think of the problems he and the crew had already faced during the weeks they had been searching the reef. He had known it wouldn't be smooth sailing. He shoved the coin back into his pocket and wondered what kind of trouble would find him next.

Chapter 2

Hope disembarked from the Air Jamaica jet that had flown her from JFK to Kingston International Airport and headed for the baggage claim, making a brief stop first in the ladies' room along the way.

As she left the bathroom, she paused in front of the mirror. She looked tired, no doubt of that. Her eyes were a little puffy and her lipstick long gone, but her hair looked pretty good. She liked the slightly longer style, swinging smoothly just above her shoulders. It was a really great cut, straight but curling under at the ends, even when she'd just gotten out of the shower. The deep red color had always suited her, different from her two blond sisters, as different as Hope felt she was from her siblings.

Both Charity and Patience were younger and a lot more naïve. Hope had been eleven when their mother had died. With her father grieving and barely able to function, Hope had stepped in to help raise the two younger girls. Her father had remarried by the time Hope was ready to leave for Columbia University, one of the best schools in the country for journalism, but still she felt she was abandoning her siblings.

As she got older, recently turned thirty-one, she discovered she was what they call a nurturer. She missed living with a family, taking care of the people she loved. She had always thought she'd have a husband and children of her own by now.

Hope felt a quick stab of pain. In the years since her disastrous engagement to Richard, Hope had decided marriage was not for her. She would make the most of her career, find fulfillment in that direction. It was certainly the safer road to the future.

She sighed as she walked out of the airport, into the hot island sun. There was activity all around her: a row of battered taxis, their black Jamaican drivers pressing for passengers to fill the empty seats; an assortment of other men promising guided tours of the island. A makeshift art fair had been set up along the road, artists displaying their paintings on a string of easels, potters selling colorful handmade jars, woodcarvers displaying their work. An open-air food booth sold hot dogs and Jamaican Red Stripe beer.

A black man neatly dressed in black pants and a white shirt held up a sign with her name on it, and Hope walked in his direction.

He smiled, his teeth neon-white in a face so black it glistened. "You be Miss Sinclair?" he said with a thick Jamaican accent.

"Yes . . ."

He grinned. "In Jamaica we say *yeahmon*. It mean *yes* in Patois."

She remembered from her last trip that islanders were extremely friendly and very proud of their country.

"I be George Green. I will take you to de Pleasure Island plane."

"Thank you."

"No problem. Just follow me."

It didn't take long to reach the private airstrip, Million Air, where the expensive-looking twin-engine plane Eddie Markham, one of the partners in Treasure Limited, had sent sat waiting to pick her up. Hope waved good-bye to George, who stood on the asphalt, still grinning as she strapped herself into the deep gray leather seat.

"Welcome, everyone," said the pilot, an American in a spotless white uniform. "We'll be getting under way in just a few minutes. Just relax and enjoy the flight."

Now there was an oxymoron. There was no such thing as an *enjoyable flight*.

Hope glanced around the luxurious cabin. There were two other passengers aboard, a newly married couple with eyes only for each other. She didn't think they realized that the plane had left the ground until it was flying out over the water, winging its way toward Pleasure Island.

Interesting name, Hope thought. She wondered what the place would be like and couldn't resist an image of nude sunbathers, late-night bars, and reggae music.

As the plane flew over the coast, she saw that it was a small volcanic island, half-moon shaped with mountains sticking up in the middle. There was a long, private landing strip. The plane circled to make the approach, touched down gently, then rolled to a stop in front of a newly constructed white plaster building that appeared to be a mini-terminal of sorts.

A man in a cream-colored suit walked toward her, olive complexioned, medium height and build, slicked-back, jet-black hair. He looked a little like a Columbian drug dealer, but then, half the population of Florida looked that way.

"Ms. Sinclair?"

"Yes, that's right."

"I'm Eddie Markham. Welcome to Pleasure Island."

She hadn't expected to be met by the owner himself, but it was a very nice touch. "Thank you. Do you greet all your guests personally, Mr. Markham?"

"It's Eddie, and only the more important ones. Come. I'll help you get settled in."

"Thank you, but I don't expect to be here that long. I need to get out to the boat."

"All in good time. Meanwhile, I've arranged for you to have the use of one of the private villas whenever you're on the island. We can go there now. You'll have time to shower and change out of your traveling clothes before you leave for the *Conquest*."

A shower sounded heavenly. And God knew what sort of accommodations waited for her onboard a salvage ship.

She smiled. "Well, I can certainly make time for that." She reached for her wheeled carry-on, but a young black man raced over from a few feet away and grabbed the handle, along with the briefcase she was carrying.

"That's Gerald Chalko. Everyone just calls him Chalko. If there's anything you need while you're here, he's the man who'll get it for you."

Chalko smiled and nodded, and Hope smiled back. Like a lot of the islanders, his skin was very dark, his features refined and attractive. Jamaicans of both sexes, she had discovered, were extremely handsome people.

There was a pair of green-and-white, fringe-topped Jeeps waiting on the tarmac. The newlyweds and their driver climbed into one, and Hope, Eddie, and Chalko climbed into the other. Chalko fired up the engine and they zipped across the asphalt onto a road lined with palm trees and ferns. Huge-leafed philodendrons snaked up the sides of the palms, and the ground bloomed with flowers—yellow hibiscus, wild white orchids, orange bird-of-paradise.

It wasn't far to a gate marked by a sign overhead reading *PLEASURE ISLAND VILLAS*. The Jeep zipped through, and she saw that a dozen villas had already been constructed; it was obvious Eddie planned to build a whole lot more.

They were grouped in pairs, very attractive, with white plaster walls, red-tiled roofs, and ornately carved, heavy wooden front doors. Lush foliage surrounded each unit, and pink bougainvillea climbed up the stucco walls. They passed a sales office, and Hope began to see why Eddie was being so amenable.

A series of articles in *Adventure* magazine would bring a lot of notoriety to Pleasure Island. It was a beautiful spot with miles of white sand beaches, lush green tropical plants, and beautiful exotic flowers. Some of the visitors—the ones with a pot-load of money—would definitely be impressed, perhaps enough to purchase one of Eddie Markham's elegant Pleasure Island villas.

And *villa* was exactly the word. At least five thousand square feet of luxury living, exquisitely furnished in the Caribbean style, with net-draped four-poster beds, cool tile floors, and glass walls that slid open to let in the sounds of the surf and the soft island breezes.

"Take your time," Eddie said. "I'll be back for you in an hour. We'll have a boat ready to take you out to the *Conquest*."

"Great."

"You'll find food and drinks in the refrigerator. The bar is fully stocked. If you think of anything else—"

"I know—just call Chalko."

Eddie smiled. She noticed he had a few too many, very white teeth. "His cell number is next to the phone in the living room."

Eddie didn't miss a trick. "Thanks. I'll see you in an hour."

Conner Reese stood in the chart room aboard the salvage vessel *Conquest,* studying the maps spread open on the teakwood table in front of him. Pleasure Island was seven miles long and two miles wide, volcanic in nature, with lush tropical rain forests and beautiful, cascading streams. A small chunk of privately owned paradise ruled by a man who had proclaimed himself emperor of his tiny domain.

Emperor Eddie was one of Conn's partners in Treasure Limited, along with Archie Marlin, who, for more than twenty years, had researched the Spanish galleon they were hunting. The third man on the team was the moneyman, Brad Talbot, a spoiled playboy pushing forty.

They called Talbot the Doormat King, a name he despised. Conn figured part of the man's motivation for joining the venture was to change his image. Talbot seemed to think that by doing something dangerous and romantic—like finding sunken treasure—he would actually be thought of as dangerous and romantic.

Instead of just a guy who'd inherited his money and now had too much time on his hands.

"So what do you think?" Conn asked the silver-haired man next to him in a tee shirt that read "Salvage Guys Do It Deep" and a pair of navy blue shorts, the skipper of the *Conquest,* Bob Gibson.

"I don't know. These reefs are damned tricky. And they've grown a good deal in the past four hundred years. Marlin believes the ship blew in from the west. The reef protects the north end of the island, but the beach extends around the whole southern end. Maybe we should start doing a little searching—"

He broke off as he spotted the flashy white Pleasure Island speedboat racing toward them. "Looks like we've got company."

Conn followed his gaze out the window and saw the boat skimming over the waves, forty-two feet of luxury sitting on a pair of twin diesel 700-horsepower engines that could blow other boats its size out of the water. There were two people aboard. Conn recognized Chalko's smiling dark face at the helm. He reached for the binoculars sitting on one of the built-in teakwood shelves and leveled them on the person standing beside the driver.

"He's got a woman aboard. I wonder what they want."

It wouldn't take long to find out. The boat ran like lightning, and Chalko liked speed. As the vessel drew near, Conn saw that the woman was grinning. Apparently she liked a fast ride, too.

As one of the deckhands helped her aboard, he noticed she had not-quite-shoulder-length hair, the most glorious rich, deep red he'd ever seen. She was shorter than average, maybe five-foot-three, and petite, with what appeared to be a great set of legs showing below her crisp white shorts.

She wore a gauzy white shirt unbuttoned over a bright orange tank top, and when the wind whipped the tails apart, he could see she had a nice set of breasts.

His groin tightened pleasantly. He hadn't been with a woman in months, and this one had all the right equipment in just the right places. Still, he wondered why she had come, and when he saw Chalko toss up her bag, rev up the engine, and turn the boat back toward shore, leaving his passenger behind, he silently vowed he would kill Eddie Markham if he'd sent out some rich tourist he was trying to sell one of his overpriced villas.

Conn's jaw tightened as he fell in behind the skipper, heading for the ladder to the deck.

Hope felt the deck sway beneath her feet and shifted to maintain her balance. The *Conquest* was eighty feet long, Eddie Markham had told her on the way to the dock, and looked to be very well equipped. Of course, Brad Talbot would make sure of that. He would want to be viewed as a man capable of accomplishing the formidable task Treasure Limited was undertaking.

She glanced around and spotted a fiftyish, silver-haired man walking toward her while a taller, dark-haired man followed a few feet behind.

She smiled at the first man. "Hello, I'm Hope Sinclair. It's very nice to meet you. You must be Conner Reese."

He gave her a warm, inviting smile. "Actually, I'm Bob Gibson, captain of the *Conquest*." He turned to the other man who walked up just then. "This is Conner Reese."

She tried not to stare. If she'd had more time, she would have known everything there was to know about the partners of Treasure Limited. As it was, she knew Brad Talbot, and she had met Eddie Markham. This man, the head of the actual search operation, Conner Reese, was not at all what she had expected.

She extended a hand. "It's a pleasure to meet you, Mr.

Reese. I'm Hope Sinclair. I assume you've been expecting me."

"Expecting you to what?"

She didn't like his tone, or the unfriendly look in his eyes. But she had to admit they were gorgeous, the same incredible blue as the sea around them. And he was handsome. Remarkably so. He was wearing nothing but a pair of red swim trunks and white canvas deck shoes, leaving his chest bare and drawing her eyes to his deeply sculpted muscles and impressive biceps, a lean, flat, six-pack stomach, and a set of shoulders that would stretch the limits of an extra-large shirt. And he was tall, at least six-foot-two, with a very dark tan.

Still, it was obvious he wasn't pleased to see her, and that jabbed her temper. She didn't want to be there in the first place. The least he could do was be pleasant.

She pasted on a smile. "Since you weren't informed, I suppose I had better explain. I'm a writer for *Adventure* magazine. I'm here to do an article on your search for the *Nuestra Señora de Rosa*. I assumed someone from the magazine would have called you."

"Yeah, well, they didn't. *Adventure* might like to do a story, but unfortunately, we're not interested. It's a shame you came all this way for nothing, but that's the way it is. The last thing we need is a bunch of people finding out we're down here looking for sunken treasure."

She worked to keep her friendly smile in place, all the while cursing Conner Reese. "I'm afraid you don't understand. I've been assigned to do this story, and that's what I intend to do." She glanced around at all the fancy, ultra-modern equipment on the deck, most of it new. "You probably have a satellite phone out here. Why don't you call Brad Talbot? He can explain what's going on."

"Talbot? This was Talbot's idea?"

A noise behind them interrupted her answer. She turned to see one of the crew coming down from the wheelhouse, a huge black man in baggy, knee-length shorts and a blue flowered shirt that flapped open in the wind. He had a chest the size of a wine cask and arms that would rival Mike Tyson's. Hurrying toward them along the deck, he held a cell phone out in front of him.

"It's for you, boss."

Reese took the phone and pressed it against his ear. He flicked a look toward Hope, then turned and walked a couple of feet away. He was angry and getting madder by the minute, speaking louder and louder till she could hear his every word.

"Are you insane? We let her write a bunch of articles about this operation and we're gonna have every amateur treasure hunter within two thousand miles breathing down our necks. This isn't the States, Talbot, it's a private island. The only laws here are the ones they make up, and Emperor Eddie won't be able to provide much protection—legal or otherwise—if we start to have trespassing problems."

Talbot said something lengthy on the other end of the line.

"This is crazy," Reese said. Then, "Fine—have it your way. But don't say I didn't warn you." Reese ended the call and took a deep breath. He handed the phone back to the big black man. "Thanks, King."

"No problem, boss."

Reese turned to face her, a scowl on his handsome face. "I guess you're staying, since Talbot holds the purse strings." He gave her a perusal that went from her breasts to her toes and sent her hackles up another notch. "But then you probably knew that already."

Hope clamped down on a nasty retort, and the captain stepped into the breach.

"Why don't I take the lady down to her cabin?" he suggested, trying to prevent what was fast becoming a mutual dislike.

Reese gave Hope a cold, hard smile. "I'll take care of it. I want to make sure our *guest* gets properly settled in."

"I'm afraid there's one more thing," Hope said.

"Yeah, what's that?"

"There's a photographer coming. I thought he might be here already. His name is Tommy Tyler."

"Christ." Reese raked a hand through his dark brown hair. It was neatly trimmed but long enough to reveal a faint curl at the ends. "Is that it? You don't have maybe a movie crew lined up or something?"

One of her eyebrows arched. "Well, now that you mention it, there might be—" She broke off at the horrified look on his face, satisfied she had given as good as she got. "There's only Tommy and me."

Ignoring his obvious relief, Hope reached for her carry-on. Surprisingly, Reese had already picked it up. At least he knew how to behave like a gentleman, though she figured he mostly chose not to.

"This way." Turning, he gave her his back, which was wide, tanned, and muscled and looked just as good as his front. Hope fell into step behind him, having to hurry to keep up with his long-legged strides.

"Where you from?" he asked, stopping as they reached the ladder leading down to the cabins.

"I live in New York."

"Yeah? I thought I heard a trace of Boston."

"I was born there. My family still lives there."

"New York and Boston. Figures."

Her teeth clenched together. She took a calming breath. "So what about you?"

"Florida, mostly."

"Mostly?"

He shrugged those wide shoulders. "I get around some. Officially, I live in Key West at the moment."

A beach bum. She should have guessed. He certainly looked like one. Then again, there was a hardness in his features, a toughness that made her think that wasn't completely true.

"From what I've seen, it looks like your ship's very well equipped. Any chance you've got a computer on board with a satellite link? I'd like to do a little preliminary research before I start."

And she had a friend back at *Midday News* who was a major computer whiz. She'd know everything there was to know about Conner Reese and the other members of Treasure Limited by tomorrow morning.

"Yeah, we've got one. Brad said to give you anything you need. You can use it—anytime it's available."

Something in the way he said it made her wonder if he meant to keep the thing constantly in use. "Thanks."

They descended the ladder, Reese in front of her, and she tried not to notice the way the long muscles in his legs flexed when he moved. She had never been particularly interested in hard-bodied men. She preferred men with brains to those with brawn. But she had to admit, this guy made her think of sex, something she hadn't been much interested in for the past couple of years.

Even if he was rude and annoying and not the least her type, it felt kind of good to know she wasn't completely dead where men were concerned, that perhaps she was coming back to life.

"You can have this cabin. It's pretty small, but it's comfortable. We save it for anyone who happens to show up for a visit. I guess that includes you."

She gave him a too-sweet smile. "I guess it does." She glanced at the teakwood built-ins, the neatly made bunk. Through the small porthole above the bed, she could see the ocean. A door stood open in the corner, and she got a glimpse of a small, clean bathroom. *Head,* she silently corrected.

"You don't get seasick, do you?"

"Not usually. Not unless the sea gets really rough." She didn't tell him she was wearing half a scopolomine patch, just for the first few days, until she got her sea legs again. She had never really had a problem, but she would rather be safe than sorry.

"We eat in shifts," Reese said. "You'll be in the first. King puts food on the table at seven. You can unpack and make yourself comfortable till then."

"It won't take me long to unpack. How about a tour of the boat . . . say, in half an hour?"

He frowned. "This isn't a yacht, Ms. Sinclair. We've got work to do and there isn't much time for—"

"Now, now—don't forget what Brad said."

His eyes darkened. "So it's Brad, is it? That's what I figured."

She knew what he was implying. Her chin went up and her spine went stiff as a board. "I wrote an article about him several years back. Apparently he liked the job I did or he wouldn't have asked for me."

"Whatever you say." But he looked like he thought there had to be more to it than that.

Typical male chauvinist pig.

"What about the tour? Remember, you're supposed to give me everything I need."

Those cool blue eyes swept over her and seemed to heat from within. "I could probably manage that. At least I'd be willing to give it a damn good try."

Her teeth clenched. "I was talking about the boat."

He gave a long-suffering sigh. "All right. Thirty minutes. I'll see you up on deck."

The cabin door closed behind him, and Hope realized her heart was pounding. He could give her everything she needed? Oh, Lord, and he looked like he actually could. It was ridiculous. She didn't even like the guy. It was just that she hadn't been with a man since Richard.

She shuddered just thinking about him. Her ex-fiancé was a real bastard. He was also handsome, sophisticated, and intelligent. They had met at a high-society cancer benefit she was covering for one of the fashion magazines, and they had started to date. Over the next few months, she had fallen madly in love with him. Like a fool, she'd believed he was also in love with her.

Richard had proposed and they had moved in together. They were planning to have a family, to buy a place in

Connecticut. It was the reason he was always working late, he said. The reason he had to make those weekend trips. The whole time he was lying and cheating, playing her for a fool.

Two weeks before the wedding, she had come back to the apartment early one afternoon and caught him in bed with her best friend, Sherry Winters. Hope had been devastated. Completely destroyed. She had been desperately in love with Richard.

And two months pregnant with his child.

She shook her head, refusing to let her mind drift too far in that direction. She had lost the child she carried, mourned for months, and hadn't dated since. The guys at the office said she was a real man-hater, and maybe she was.

Conner Reese looked nothing at all like Richard, one of the partners of Wynn, Myers, and Daley, a prestigious Manhattan law firm.

But remembering the smug look on Reese's face, the certainty in his voice that she had slept her way into getting this assignment, it seemed more than clear they were very much alike.

Conn climbed the ladder back up to the deck and saw Joe Ramirez walking toward him, using a towel to dry the beads of water glinting on his face and chest.

"Who's the babe?" Joe asked. He was the head diver on the crew, the dive team coordinator, though Conn would be diving, too. As a SEAL, Joe had been one of the best, and he still was.

"She's one of Brad Talbot's women. This one happens to be a writer for *Adventure* magazine. Brad probably promised her the story to get in her pants. Must have worked, since she's here."

Joe grinned, gouging two deep grooves in his cheeks. "She can bunk in my cabin. I wouldn't mind a bit."

"Yeah, I bet you wouldn't. But I don't think Talbot would appreciate the competition."

"Probably not." He flashed another grin. "Then again, who says Talbot has to know?"

Conn didn't answer. Joe had a way with women. If he put his mind to it, he could probably have Hope Sinclair in his bed by the end of the week. She couldn't be much of a challenge—not if Talbot had screwed her.

Conn told himself he didn't care what Joe did. But he found himself checking his watch to see when Hope would reappear.

"How did it go?"

Recognizing the perfectly modulated voice on the end of the line, Brad Talbot gave in to a satisfied smile. "Reese knows where his bread is buttered. He gave me some crap about the article jeopardizing the search, but he'll get over it. The girl is out of your hair. She's off the story and too far away to give you any more trouble."

"You're sure about that?"

"I'm telling you, she's miles from nowhere. She'll be busy for weeks. You don't need to give her another thought."

"Thanks, I owe you one."

"Hey, no problem." But as he hung up the phone, Brad was thinking how he might collect the favor. He might not be the kind of savvy businessman his father and grandfather were, but he was no fool. He knew who his friends were.

And he knew how to use them.

Chapter 3

Hope finished unpacking. Eddie Markham had generously allowed her to leave some of her clothes in one of the villas. Apparently the place was unoccupied and for sale for a very hefty price tag. She had left her sundresses and sandals and miscellaneous items she didn't think she would have use for on the boat, taking only shorts, shirts, and tee shirts, a swimsuit, sandals, and her deck shoes.

This was a work boat, after all. She didn't think she would need anything fancy.

On the other hand, she liked to be prepared.

Which was why she could kick herself for not taking some of the money her grandfather had left her and her two sisters and bought the fancy electronics that a lot of her contemporaries used. Okay, so maybe she was a little archaic, a little resistant to all the new gadgets. She liked taking notes, liked the personal interaction, though she also used a portable tape recorder and she had brought that along.

She did have a Palm Pilot, so she wasn't completely out of touch. Since she'd started working at the paper, she had been looking at a Blackberry, a wireless, hand-held device for sending and receiving wireless e-mail, surfing the Web, and keeping track of contacts. But the darn things were expensive, and out here she'd need to have a satellite phone in order to use it, and that was something she wouldn't have much use for back home.

She had left her laptop back at the villa, since she wasn't sure what kind of power she would have out at sea, and instead brought her AlphaSmart, a lightweight keyboard with a four-line screen that did word processing and ran for a hundred hours on four flashlight batteries.

Thank God she'd be able to use the *Conquest's* computer to do the Internet work she needed and bring up her e-mail—assuming Reese didn't purposely keep the machine in use. She made a mental note to break out a little of Grandpa's twenty thousand she had stashed away and buy what she needed before she started her next assignment.

Hope checked her watch. Time for her tour. She needed to know more about the boat and the equipment aboard, and Reese looked like a guy who knew his end of the business—the operations part, according to Artie Green. She found herself wondering about him, what his background was and how he had gotten involved with Brad Talbot.

Whoever he was, one thing was clear—he didn't like her any more than she liked him. As she stepped out into the passage, she steeled herself for whatever he might have in store for her when they butted heads again.

Conn checked his watch. Thirty-three minutes. If she didn't show up in the next two or three, he was heading down to the chart room. Since Hope was a woman, he could count on a good twenty-minute wait. He might as well go down now.

"Mr. Reese?"

The sound of her voice surprised him. He turned as she walked toward him along the deck. The wind whipped her hair away from her face and he noticed the strong line of her jaw. She was pretty. Better than pretty. But there was something about her that warned a man to beware.

Which was fine with him. The last thing he wanted was to get involved with a woman.

"It's just Conn," he said. "And you're almost on time."

"Yes, I am, and it's just Hope."

"Fair enough . . . Hope." In concession to her being a woman, he had pulled a white cotton tee shirt over his bare chest. Hope had tied the tails of her gauzy white blouse together to hide the curve of her breasts.

At least they knew where they stood.

"Where would you like to start?" He was eager to get this over, mollify her a little so he could get back to work.

"Tell me about the boat. Eddie Markham said it was eighty feet long, but that's about all I know."

"Well, she's iron-hulled, powered by a pair of twelve hundred-power Caterpillar diesels. The *Conquest* carries five thousand gallons of fuel and a thousand gallons of water. Even at that, you need to keep your showers short."

He watched her jot down notes on a spiral pad. Not exactly state of the art, but then everyone had his own way of doing things.

"There are two generators on board, one that powers the equipment and one for backup."

"So I guess it's okay to use my hair dryer."

His gaze moved up to the glossy red hair brushing her jaw, not quite touching her shoulders. Man, her hair was gorgeous, sleek and shiny as a seal, and the prettiest dark red shade he'd ever seen.

"Yeah, you can definitely use your dryer."

"What about the equipment you're using?" She turned and pointed toward the stuff that was sitting on the deck.

"For starters, that yellow thing with the runners on the bottom is an underwater sled. We can use it to take us down to whatever depth we want. It provides light if we need it, and the prop can serve as a blower."

She made some more scribbles. "What about the cranes?"

"We've got a ten-ton knuckle crane and an eight-ton auxiliary winch. We find something, you can bet we'll be able to bring it up."

"Like treasure?"

"If we're lucky. That *is* what we're here for." He looked over at the wheelhouse. "That thing on the top of the boat—that's the radar bridge. And we use satellite navigation—GPS. We've got a couple of dinghies, for safety's sake, and a fifteen-foot Boston Whaler with a fifty-horse engine we use to get over to the island. A lot of the equipment's being used in the water. Let's go down to the chart room and I'll show you how it works."

"Great."

The wheelhouse sat above them, Captain Bob at the helm. Instead, Conn ducked through an open hatch and descended a ladder into the chart room that connected with the bridge through a second set of stairs. He heard Hope's feet ringing on the ladder behind him, turned to see they were slender and feminine in a pair of white sandals.

"Pretty impressive," she said as she looked over the row of monitors that relayed the messages received from below.

"The guy in front of the screen is Andy Glass," Conn said, introducing her to the small, nondescript man wearing spectacles who kept an eye on the monitors. "He's our engineer. Andy, this is Hope Sinclair. She's doing an article on the search."

"Nice to meet you, Ms. Sinclair."

"It's just Hope, and same here." She went back to her perusal of the room, pausing when she reached a television screen projecting a video picture of the reef they were searching and the area around it.

"That's a boat-deployed video camera. There's a light mounted on the front so we can see what it sees."

"And this?"

"Magnetometer. It detects ferrous metals."

"Iron?"

"Both iron and steel, among other things. The Spanish ships all carried iron cannon, fittings, maybe five or six anchors. An underwater metal detector can find them, which helps us locate the approximate area where the ship went down."

Hope shook her head, her shiny hair swinging several inches below her jaw. "I'm coming at this all wrong. Usually I'm prepared for an assignment, but apparently someone was in a hurry. They shipped me off without giving me time to do my homework. I need to know exactly what you're looking for—and why you think you're going to find it here."

Conn hesitated. He wasn't sure how much he was willing to tell her. Damn, Brad Talbot was an idiot. But then he had known that from the start.

"We're looking for the *Nuestra Señora de Rosa*. She went down with three other Spanish treasure ships in 1605."

"Four ships sank all at once?"

"That wasn't uncommon. They didn't have weather forecasts. They encountered unexpected storms, even hurricanes. About ninety treasure ships sailed every year. Ten percent of those were lost. In a two-hundred-year period, that adds up to around two thousand sunken ships. Only two hundred have ever been found."

"My God, I had no idea." Hope sighed. "I need to use your computer. I don't know enough to do this assignment properly. I need to find out about your lost ship—hell, I need to know what questions I need to ask."

Conn almost smiled. At least she was being honest. He hadn't expected that. After all, she was a woman.

"No one's using the computer right now. Be my guest."

She seemed surprised at his offer. Obviously she didn't trust him any more than he trusted her.

"This might take a while," she said.

"Hey, Talbot's footing the bill. Since he's the one who sent you, I guess he won't mind if you run up his satellite phone expenses." Of course, if they found the treasure, Talbot's entire investment would be repaid, plus his share of the profits. Talbot would make out like a bandit.

On the other hand, if they didn't find the ship or there

wasn't any treasure aboard, the Doormat King would be out several million bucks.

Conn watched Hope walk over to the computer and start clicking away on the keyboard. In minutes she was working on the Internet, digging up information on the Spanish treasure fleets. Conn left her at it. He had a dozen things to do.

And none of them included spending time with one of Brad Talbot's women, no matter how attractive she was.

It was time for supper. Hope made her way down to the galley in search of something to eat. Her stomach was growling, and it occurred to her she hadn't had a bite of food since she got off the plane in Jamaica. And what the airline had fed her could hardly qualify as a meal.

Conner Reese came down the ladder a few minutes after she arrived, followed by the captain, Bob Gibson, and a couple of members of the crew she hadn't met. One of them earned a second glance, a smiling, dark-complexioned man with huge dimples who appeared to be Latino. He was probably in his thirties, even better-looking than Conner Reese—in fact, almost pretty, and equally well-built.

"Hope Sinclair, this is Joe Ramirez, and that's Pete Crowley. Joe's head diver—Pete's part of the boat crew."

"Nice to meet you," Hope said.

"Welcome aboard, Hope," the handsome Latino said, not bothering with formality. Pete Crowley just nodded.

The big black Jamaican, King, began setting food on the table, filling the galley with the aroma of fiery spiced jerked chicken, and rice and peas. She wound up sitting next to Conner Reese, though she wasn't quite sure how it happened. With three other good-sized men also sitting in the booth, they were fairly well jammed together.

He was wearing the same red swimsuit and white tee shirt he'd had on earlier, and whenever he moved, she could feel the slight abrasion of the dark hair on his legs rubbing against her from calf to thigh. She tried not to notice, thought that she had succeeded, till she glanced over and caught the look on his face. Those blue eyes seemed to burn, and the heat there seared her bones. They were skin-to-skin, and obviously he could feel it, too.

He glanced away and began to concentrate on his food, and Hope did the same, but her appetite had left her. Though her food was only half eaten, when the men finished their meal, she shoved her dish away.

"I think I'll go down to my cabin." She rose from the built-in dinette seat. "It's been a long day and flying always wears me out." Reese got up so she could slide out of the seat, her body brushing his as she left the table. "I guess I'll, um, see you in the morning."

"Yeah, I guess so." His eyes were hot again. They made her stomach flutter.

"Good night, Hope," Joe Ramirez said, his dark eyes moving over her in a way that told her exactly what he was thinking. Unlike Conner Reese, he wanted her to read his thoughts, which clearly belonged in the bedroom.

"Good night."

It was dark outside, still warm and balmy, but it was January and even in the Caribbean, the sun set early. Once she reached the deck, she looked out over the waves toward the island. A few lights sparkled in the area around the Pleasure Island villas, and there appeared to be a small settlement at the south end of the shore. Hope took a deep breath of salty sea air and started toward the hatch leading down to her cabin.

"Have a good night," an unfamiliar male voice said.

She turned to see Pete Crowley standing not far behind her. She hadn't paid much attention to him before. Now she saw that he was tall and spare, with rough, deeply weathered skin, black eyes, and a slightly Roman nose.

"You, too," she said, wondering if he had followed her out of the galley, not liking the thought that he might have. She wasn't sure what to expect from the men in the crew.

The brief, uneasy encounter reminded her to be wary.

Hope awakened the following morning more rested than she had expected. The gentle lap of waves against the hull had been a powerful sleeping pill, and she had slept later than she meant to. She'd missed breakfast, but at home she rarely ate anything before lunch, just downed several cups of Starbuck's coffee and went to work.

Coffee sounded heavenly right now. After pulling on a pair of khaki shorts and a yellow tee shirt, applying a dab of makeup and a liberal amount of sunscreen, she grabbed a wide-brimmed straw hat that tied beneath her chin and headed up on deck. The Caribbean sun was brutal, she had learned, having suffered a painful sunburn the last time she was there. She intended to be a lot more careful this time.

On deck, some of the crewmen were already hard at work. She waved and kept walking, then darted into the galley where King was busily cleaning up after the morning meal.

"You missed breakfast," he chided in the deepest voice she had ever heard.

"I never eat in the morning. But I could sure use a cup of coffee."

"Always got a pot goin'. You be welcome to a cup."

"Thanks." She filled one of the heavy white china mugs and started toward the ladder.

"Ought to eat somet'ing," King said, his black face glossy with perspiration.

She waved to him over her shoulder. "Coffee's enough, and this sure tastes good. Thanks again." Climbing the ladder, she headed for the chart room to see if the computer was available.

She had a lot more work to do, but she wasn't as ill-prepared as she had been on her arrival. Yesterday, she had printed out a pile of information on the Spanish treasure fleets—fascinating stuff, she had discovered. As Reese had said, the voyages had continued for over two hundred years, carrying untold wealth back to Spain from the New World.

In the back of her mind, she remembered reading something about a guy named Mel Fisher, one of the great treasure salvors—that's what they called themselves, she had learned. But until yesterday, she hadn't connected him with the *Atocha*, the Spanish ship it took him seventeen years to find. In the end, his efforts were rewarded, he and his crew recovering more than four hundred million in treasure.

Obviously Brad Talbot was interested in more than just publicity when he funded Treasure Limited's search.

Assuming they could actually find the ship.

In the course of her research, she had dug up tons of information, but findings on the *Nuestra Señora de Rosa* were scarce. On a site called *TreasureExpeditions.com,* she learned that the ship had sailed with the earliest of the treasure fleets, going down in 1605, nearly four hundred years ago. Oddly, from what she read, it hadn't sunk anywhere near where the *Conquest* was searching.

A series of archeological sites confirmed that the *Rosa* was believed to have gone down along with three of its sister ships near a place called the Serranilla Banks. And those banks were a long way from Pleasure Island.

Hope returned to the chart room with more unanswered questions than she'd had before and was relieved to see the chair in front of the computer sat empty. She needed to e-mail her friend, Gordy Weitzman, at *Midday News,* something she had meant to do yesterday, to see what he could find out about the partners of Treasure Limited. She also wanted to ask him to check with the police in regard to the vandals who had demolished her apartment and get an update on what was happening with Buddy Newton and the tenants at Hartley House.

As Conner Reese had said, Talbot was the man responsible for her presence aboard the boat so she felt justified in using his equipment, including his satellite phone.

She got the ship's phone number from the engineer, Andy

Glass, pulled her Palm Pilot out of the pocket of her shorts, retrieved Gordy's office e-mail address, and sent him the cell number for use in case of emergency.

Buddy Newton's e-mail, *buddyboy@aol.com*, was also in her Pilot. She sent him a message, too, asking what had happened since she had left New York. She gave him the satellite number but asked him not to call unless he really needed her. She e-mailed a single message to her dad and stepmom and her sisters, told them she had safely reached Pleasure Island, was aboard the *Conquest*, and getting settled in. She gave them the emergency number.

Feeling less isolated than she had before, she signed off, breathing a momentary sigh of relief. She turned at the sound of someone moving around in the chart room.

"You finished?" Conn Reese asked.

Hope nodded. "I need to do a lot more research on treasure hunting—yesterday I barely tapped the surface. But I'm through for now. Thanks for letting me use the machine."

"Like I said . . . as long as no one needs it." He sat down at the computer and began to pull up his e-mail. His hair was neatly combed, but the faint wave remained.

"There's something I need to know," Hope said, drawing his attention. She tried not to notice the way his tee shirt stretched over the muscles across his chest, but the man had a very impressive chest.

"Yeah, what's that?"

"Why do you think you'll find the *Rosa* near Pleasure Island? Everything I've read so far says the ship went down on the Serranilla Banks. That's a heck of a long way from here."

Reese studied her for several moments. She thought he was trying to make some sort of decision.

"Tomorrow I'm hopping a ride on the Pleasure Island plane. It flies into Jamaica fairly often, picking up either passengers or supplies. I've got a meeting with Professor Marlin. He's lecturing at a private college in Port Antonio. He's the guy who can tell you how we got here. I guess if you want, you can come along."

He delivered the invitation with a slightly rigid jaw. It was obvious he didn't really want her to go. She couldn't tell if it was because she was writing a story he didn't want written—or if he just didn't like women in general.

Something told her it was a little bit of both.

"I'd love to come," she said, though the thought of spending the day with him wasn't really all that pleasant.

It was later in the afternoon when Conn saw the Pleasure Island speedboat heading their way. The forty-two-foot Sea Ray was built for speed, and it showed in the low, trim lines of the hull, the sharply pointed bow, and aerodynamic tilt of the windshield. Yet Conn knew that the salon below deck, with its smoky mirrors, deep pile carpeting, wet bar, and built-in TV, would impress even the most discriminating island visitor.

As the boat drew near, Conn recognized Chalko but not the man standing next to him beside the wheel, a young guy with carrot-red hair.

"That's Tommy Tyler," Hope said, walking up beside him. "The photographer I mentioned."

"He looks like a kid."

"He's only twenty-five, but he's a great photographer. You read any kind of outdoor magazine, you'll see some of his work."

"I presume that includes underwater photography."

She nodded. "Tommy's one of the best. That's how I met him. I was down here doing an article on scuba diving. Mostly it was about the hotels and nightclubs in areas that cater to the sport, but it involved a lot of underwater work as well."

His gaze swung to hers. "So you dive, too?"

She nodded. "I'm definitely a novice. But I've got my

Open Water Certification, and I really enjoyed the times I went down."

Conn didn't say more. His mind was trying to digest the fact that the lady might be more than he'd thought. Diving wasn't an easy sport. A lot of people were scared of getting claustrophobic, or scared of sharks, or just plain scared.

It took a cool head and steady nerves.

Unless you were just too dumb to realize how dangerous the sport could be.

He was beginning to think Hope Sinclair was far from dumb.

Still, he wished he hadn't agreed to take her with him to Jamaica. She was a good-looking woman and he was attracted to her, though he damned well didn't want to be. He hated the kind of women who used sex to get what they wanted.

Hell, he'd been married to one.

Kelly was blond and beautiful, with a slender, voluptuous body and legs that went on forever. The day he'd met her, he'd thought she was the sexiest woman he'd ever seen. Another SEAL's wife had introduced them and all he could think of was getting her in bed. Kelly seemed to feel the same. The second time they went out, she practically tore off his clothes.

He hadn't expected to wind up married to her. He'd figured marriage for him was still a few years away. But their whirlwind affair led straight to the altar and by then he didn't care. He had always wanted a family and Kelly seemed like she would make the perfect wife.

Two years later, she was bored with the whole idea of settling down. She didn't like his job, didn't like his traveling, though they had discussed the problem early on and she had sworn she could handle it. She didn't want kids, she finally admitted—she never really had.

What she wanted was the savings in his bank account, which, over the years, with his salary and hazardous-duty pay and not much time to spend it, had turned into a pretty good chunk.

Six months later, they were divorced. Conn was single again and Kelly was gone from his life nearly as fast as she'd come into it—financially, a hell of lot better off than she had been before she had met him. She was nothing but a schemer, he'd found out far too late, like most of the women in his life, including his mother.

His mother, his ex-wife, and marriage had left a bitter taste in his mouth, and though he had the same needs as every other male, he was a whole lot more cautious about the women he took to bed.

He might like to spend a few hot nights with Hope Sinclair. But it wasn't going to happen.

Chapter 4

Hope watched the young photographer, Tommy Tyler, climb the ladder to the *Conquest* and drop his duffel bag on the deck. He looked exactly the same as he had a few years back—like an eighteen-year-old kid with freckles on his face and a flat-top haircut.

Chalko handed him his camera equipment, stored in several padded green canvas bags, and Tommy waved as the young black man revved up the boat and powered it back toward shore.

"Hey, Hope!" Tommy walked toward her in baggy khaki shorts, a tee shirt with a photo of a dolphin on the front, and a pair of flip-flops on his skinny feet.

"Hey, Tommy!" She smiled as he enveloped her in a big bear hug.

"Good to see ya, sweet thing." He gave her a quick perusal, then wiggled his eyebrows. "Still lookin' hot as ever."

She laughed. "Thanks." She turned to Conner Reese and ignored the fact that he was frowning. "Conner Reese, meet Tommy Tyler."

"Pleasure," Tommy said, extending a hand, which Reese shook.

"Hope says you're expecting to do some underwater photography."

"That's right."

"You won't have much to do, at least not yet. We haven't found anything worth taking a picture of."

Tommy looked surprised. "I figured you'd be pulling stuff out of the water or they wouldn't have sent me."

"Yeah, well, you might want to ask Brad Talbot about that."

"Or maybe Eddie Markham," Hope said. "I think he's more than eager to get publicity for Pleasure Island. Just the idea that people are out here hunting for treasure makes the place sound exciting."

Tommy glanced around the deck of the salvage boat. "We'll take shots of the *Conquest* and all this equipment. Combined with photos of the island and surrounding reef, we'll have plenty for the first article in the series. I'll make it look good, and Hope will make it interesting."

Reese didn't reply. He wasn't keen on this project, and he didn't seem to care who knew it.

"Hope's using the empty cabin," he said. "You'll have to bunk in with the crew."

"No problem. If someone will show me the way, I'll stow my gear and get settled in."

A few feet away, Joe Ramirez set the oxygen tank he was working on down on the deck and started toward them.

"I'll take him down," Joe volunteered. The two men introduced themselves, and Joe led Tommy off toward the crew's quarters in the bow of the boat.

Hope's gaze returned to Conner Reese. She saw that he was watching her and there was a scowl on his face. Suddenly, it dawned on her exactly what he was thinking.

"Tommy and I are just friends, for God's sake! He's six years younger than I am, and even if he weren't, I don't sleep with the people I work with."

One of those dark eyebrows went up. "Not even Brad Talbot?"

"God, no. *Especially* not Talbot. Not even if he had nothing to do with my job."

"Why not?"

"For one thing, the guy only talks about one subject—himself. On top of that, he has about as much sex appeal as a dead fish."

His mouth quirked into what might have passed for a smile, then quickly faded. "That's not what most women say."

"Well, I'm not most women. I'm not interested in Talbot—no matter how much money he's got. Now, if you'll excuse me, I have work to do."

She didn't wait for his reply, just turned and started walking. Every time she was around Conner Reese, he made her angry. The man had a low opinion of women, that was for certain.

Then again, she had a pretty low opinion of men.

As she walked into her cabin and grabbed her AlphaSmart to type up some notes, Hope couldn't help thinking that maybe they had more in common than she thought.

Another perfect day in the islands. Perfectly cloudless skies, breezes that ruffled the heavy fronds on the palms that lined the road, vistas of blue-green seas that seemed to go on forever.

Conn loved the islands. He liked the heat and water, the sun and sand, the different kinds of people all thrown together. And Jamaica was spectacular.

"From Many People, One People," was their motto, and it was the truth. The country was primitive, almost third world in places, with tin shacks for houses and tumbledown, eighteenth-century buildings to house village merchants. Yet there were mansions and resorts posh enough for the filthy rich and scenery as magnificent as anyplace on earth.

Living in Florida, he was close enough to visit Jamaica and the other islands as often as he liked. If they found the treasure—the professor always said *when*, but Conn didn't want to jinx his luck, and besides, he was more realistic. But if by some wild chance they actually succeeded, he planned to use his share to buy a resort that specialized in diving, probably on one of the Florida Keys.

Before he met Kelly, he had been saving for something like that. His wife's departure—along with his money—had put an end to his plans.

Sitting behind the wheel of the old Toyota Corolla they kept at the airport in Port Antonio, Conn wove his way along the winding road overlooking the turquoise sea. Thick tropical jungle, breadfruit trees, bamboo, and a dense growth of vines and leaves covered the hills on the opposite side of the road, and an occasional bubbling stream made its way down the mountain to the ocean. Turning his attention away from the scenic vistas, Conn flicked a glance at Hope Sinclair sitting in the passenger seat beside him.

She hadn't said much since they'd left Pleasure Island. Probably still pissed about those cracks he'd made about Brad Talbot. Hell, he couldn't blame her.

But for some strange reason, he'd really wanted to know if she was involved with the guy. Hope had vehemently denied it.

The bad news was, he believed her.

She wasn't screwing Talbot, which only added to the attraction he already felt for her. As she sat there staring out the window, he surveyed her profile, the feminine lines of her face, the way her lips softly curved. They were full and a nice shade of rose. She was wearing shorts, and her legs were smooth and showing the first hint of a tan.

Even with her standoffish attitude, she attracted him. He wanted to know what kind of woman was beneath that cool façade, wanted to know if he could wring a response from those unsmiling lips. He wanted to take her to bed, he realized, as his body tightened and he started getting hard.

Conn silently cursed, knowing it wouldn't be a smart thing to do. She was there on business and so was he. He had to remember that.

Forcing his thoughts back to the road, he told himself to concentrate on his driving. They drove on the left in Jamaica and most of the other islands. He was fairly used to it, but he still had to pay attention.

He cast her another glance. "About that thing yesterday," he said as he neared the turn to the college and his meeting with the professor. "You and Talbot, I mean. It was really none of my business."

"No kidding."

"It's just, well, Talbot's the kind of guy who doesn't do anything for nothing. I figured he had a motive for sending you out to do the story."

She turned a little in the seat and he thought again how pretty she was. "Brad's definitely a quid pro quo kind of guy. If he does have a motive, I haven't got a clue what it is. Normally, I don't even write for *Adventure*. I work for a paper called *Midday News*, which is owned by the same big corporation. My boss wanted me off a story I was digging into. Maybe Talbot owed someone there a favor."

She sighed. "I really wanted to write that story. Except for getting to spend the winter in the Caribbean, I wasn't any happier to be sent out here than you were to have me arrive."

Conn didn't say more. The woman kept surprising him. Then again, Kelly had surprised the hell out of him. He was still paying the price for thinking with his dick instead of his brain.

"The professor's office is in that building at the top of the hill," he said, pointing in that direction as they pulled into the parking lot. He found a parking space, turned off the engine, and both of them got out.

When they reached the two-story structure at the top of the hill, Conn knocked on the professor's office door. Seconds later, it opened.

"Conner, my boy! Come in!"

Conn smiled, shook the older man's hand. The professor turned toward Hope and smiled. "I see you brought a guest."

"Doc, this is Hope Sinclair. She's writing an article on the search."

The professor's smile slid away. His gray brows drew nearly together in his thin, lined face. "An article? Whose idea was that?"

"Not mine, I can tell you. Both Markham and Talbot have ulterior motives. They're after the publicity. We should have known they would be."

"Yes, I suppose we should have." Marlin looked again at Hope. "I suppose their interests are none of your concern. You are merely employed to do the story."

"That's right, Professor. I didn't pick this assignment, it picked me."

"So what can I tell you, Ms. Sinclair?"

"I'd like it if you called me Hope. As you say, I'm merely here to write a story. Which is why I need to know the reason you think the *Nuestra Señora de Rosa* sank off Pleasure Island and not the Serranilla Banks."

Warming to his favorite subject, the professor slowly smiled. "Well, I suppose, once the fact we're working off Pleasure Island becomes public, the reason we're there will come out, sooner or later. You understand the ship's location is merely conjecture—a theory based on certain facts."

"They must be convincing facts or Brad Talbot wouldn't be putting up what might end up being millions of dollars to back your venture."

"Why don't I explain and you can decide for yourself?"

Hope nodded. Reaching into her purse, she pulled out a tiny portable tape recorder. She started to turn it on when Conn reached over and plucked it out of her hand.

Anger reddened her cheeks. "What the hell do you think you're doing?"

"Use your notepad. It's bad enough you're giving away information Professor Marlin spent the last twenty years digging up. Notes will keep things a little less specific."

She cast him a look that wished him to the bottom of the

sea, reached back into her purse and pulled out her spiral pad, then fished out a ballpoint pen.

"Fine, we'll do it your way. And if I get anything wrong, you'll be the one to blame."

He gave her the edge of a smile, hoping like hell she got lots of things wrong, enough to confuse anyone who might be interested in finding the treasure.

"Go ahead, Professor." She poised her pen above the pad, ready to take down whatever he said.

"Why don't we start by looking at the map." Motioning for her to follow, Marlin led the way across the room to the table in the corner. The map showing the location of sunken ships was still spread open on top.

For the next several minutes the professor explained about the treasure fleets that sailed from Spain to the New World and back each year, the Terra Firma Fleet that went to Cartagena, and the New Spain Fleet that sailed to Vera Cruz.

He went on to tell her about the four ships of the Terra Firma Fleet that sank in 1605, pointing out the Serranilla Banks and showing her how he thought the storm pushed the last ship in line *around* the banks, instead—and into the reef on *Isla Tormenta*.

"I've done a complex search of ocean currents dating back to the time of the disappearance of the fleet," he said. "Combined with survivors' accounts of the storm and their descriptions of the way some of the ships seemed to just disappear, I began to suspect the *Rosa* never hit the banks. I believe she made it almost as far as Jamaica before she went down."

"You're thinking somewhere near Pleasure Island." She jotted down the information, then looked up at him. "That seems like a pretty long stretch, Professor. There's a lot of ocean out there between those shallows, Jamaica, and Pleasure Island."

Marlin cast a glance at Conn, then reluctantly added, "It is . . . except for the matter of the jewelry."

Hope's pen went still and her head came up. "What jewelry?"

Behind his glasses, the professor's pale blue eyes gleamed. "The emerald cross was the first piece of jewelry to surface. Solid gold. Heavily ornamented. With the initials ACCHE carved into the back. You see, the passengers on these ships were often extremely wealthy. The style of the day encouraged them to wear a great deal of expensive jewelry."

He waited while she jotted down some notes. "The cross turned up in Jamaica some ten years ago—a collector by the name of St. Giles owned it. I researched the piece from here as best I could, but I didn't get very far. Then, in 1998, I went to Spain, to the Archivo de las Indias, the marine archives in Seville. It wasn't my first trip, but it was by far the most productive. The museum turned up an early passenger register from the *Rosa*. It showed a man by the name of Alejandro Carrillo Castro Hidalgo y Espinoza on board. I believe the cross that was purchased by St. Giles belonged to Espinoza."

Marlin paused for effect, as he dearly loved to do, and Hope took the bait.

"There must be a connection, but somehow I seem to be missing it."

The professor smiled. "St. Giles purchased the cross here in Jamaica, but it was originally found on *Isla Tormenta*."

"Pleasure Island."

"Exactly so. Over the years, a few other artifacts were discovered on the island that likely came from the *Rosa,* but the secret has been fairly well kept."

"How did you hear about the cross?"

"I stumbled upon a photo in a magazine and contacted the owner. St. Giles and I both had an interest in the history of the Spanish galleons and we formed a sort of friendship. Eventually he told me where the cross had been found. I began to do more and more research. In the end, I became convinced the *Rosa* didn't go down on the Serranilla Banks, but on the reef protecting Pleasure Island."

Hope looked down at the photo the professor handed her,

a picture of the emerald-encrusted cross. The piece was startlingly beautiful, even in a photo, the emeralds a clear, deep, sparkling green, the heavy gold glittering against a background of stark-black velvet. The thought of finding something as stunningly beautiful as that—perhaps even a boatload of such objects—no wonder people spent their whole lives searching for treasure.

"Thank you, Professor. You've been extremely helpful."

"My pleasure. I only hope what you write won't wind up causing Conner trouble. Where treasure is concerned, people don't always think clearly."

She looked back down at the photo. "It's easy to understand why."

They said their good-byes. Conner returned her tape recorder and the two of them left the campus. Though Hope would have liked to have seen a bit of the harbor town, they each had a job to do and instead drove straight to the airport.

Unfortunately when they got there, the plane was already gone.

"What are you talking about?" Hope said to the guard at the gate to the private airplane terminal. "They were supposed to wait for us. We have to get back to Pleasure Island!"

He was short and bald, dark-skinned and pudgy. "Sorry," he said in a heavy Jamaican accent. "Somet'ing come up and dey have to leave. Dey say dey be bock noon tomorrow. Dey pick you up den."

Hope sighed. "I don't believe this." She didn't say more, just started walking toward the car, trying to think what to do. Conner Reese fell in beside her. When she glanced in his direction, she saw that his mouth was faintly curved, his expression amused, and an unpleasant thought suddenly struck.

Hope stopped in her tracks, forcing him to stop, too. She pinned him with a look of accusation. "Did you know about this? Did you have something to do with that plane leaving

early? If you have any intention of . . . of . . . If you think
this means that you and I are . . . are . . ."

"Look, lady, I'm not any happier about this than you are.
I've got work to do, too. But out here sometimes these things
happen. We'll be back by tomorrow afternoon. This is the
Caribbean. Time here is not that big a deal."

She glanced away from him, off toward the water, feeling
like a fool. So far the man had kept his distance, just as she had
kept hers from him. He didn't approve of her being there,
and he had made it fairly clear he had no real interest in her.

"Sorry," she said. "Sometimes I have a tendency to expect the worst from people."

"By *people*, you mean men."

She sighed. "Yeah, I guess I do."

"Well, don't worry about it. I'm not the most trusting guy,
either."

She wanted to ask him why. And if, like her, his paranoia
ran mainly to the opposite sex.

Instead she got back in the car and sat there while he
climbed in and started the engine. "I guess we'll need to find
a place to stay," she said.

"Not a problem. One of Talbot's companies owns a string
of motels in the islands. Bayside Inns. There's one in Port
Antonio—nothing fancy, but it's clean and we won't have to
pay."

"Well, I like that part. But I sure wish I had a change of
clothes."

Reese made no reply, just kept driving along Route A till
they spotted the red-painted sign for the motel. As he had
said, the rooms were small but clean, with pressboard furniture and aging green shag carpeting. Instead of a queen-sized
bed, each room had only a full.

"The afternoon's almost gone," Reese said. "I've got a
couple of errands to run, then I'll be back. I'll pick you up at
five. I know a place we can have a drink and watch the sunset. Then we'll get something to eat."

Her wariness returned. "I don't think—"

"Listen, Hope. I didn't have anything to do with that plane going back without us. The fact is we're stuck here until tomorrow, so we might as well make the best of it. And we both have to eat."

She tried to look away from those blue, blue eyes, but it was impossible to do. The breeze ruffled his wavy dark hair, and for once the harshness was gone from his features, making him look even more handsome than he usually did.

"You're right," she agreed, knowing deep down she shouldn't. "We have to eat. I'll see you at five."

He nodded and turned away, heading back to the car. She watched him as he climbed in, admiring his lean, hard-muscled frame, the way the sinews in his long legs lengthened and tightened as he moved. She probably should have skipped supper and stayed in her room. Conn Reese was, after all, a virile, extremely attractive man, and she was a woman who hadn't had sex in more than two years.

Then again, she wasn't going to ravish the man and she really did need to eat.

With a sigh, she crossed the room to the telephone on the nightstand. Using her international credit card calling number, she dialed Gordy Weitzman at the newspaper.

"Hey, kiddo," he said with a smile in his voice. "You get my e-mail?"

"I'm not on the boat, Gordy. I'm stuck for the night in Jamaica. What did it say?"

"That the cops came up empty-handed. They haven't got a clue who hit your place—or why."

"Artie thinks it was a message. If it was, I guess whoever did it must be happy, since I'm no longer working the story."

"I'll tell you who isn't happy—poor old Buddy Newton. I think he feels like you abandoned him. Maybe you ought to give him a call."

Hope suffered a shot of guilt, though it was hardly her idea to come to Jamaica. "I will, but there's not a lot I can do for him from a couple of thousand miles away." At least she had helped him find an attorney, a friend of hers who did a lot of pro bono work. Matt Westland had agreed to look into the case, and the injunction he had filed had at least bought the tenants some time.

"Everything else okay?" Gordy asked.

"I suppose. No one here's too keen on my doing this story. They don't want a bunch of amateur treasure hunters getting in their way and I can't say I blame them, considering all the work they've done to put this project together."

"I guess since Talbot's running the show, at least financially, they've got to dance to his tune, and you know how he likes to bask in the limelight."

"Yeah, I know."

"Listen, I gotta run. I'll let you know if anything turns up in regard to your apartment."

"Or on Hartley House."

"That, too." Gordy signed off and Hope hung up and re-dialed the phone. First, she made a brief call to her dad and stepmom in Boston, letting them know she was all right. She was thirty-one years old, but in her family, age didn't matter. She was single and on her own and they worried about her. It was actually rather nice.

As soon as she hung up, she phoned Buddy Newton. Buddy was usually a pretty reasonable guy, but even over the phone she could hear the tension in his voice.

"They were here again today. Damned fools."

"You're talking about the guys from Americal Corp—the men who made you the offer before."

"Damned fools," he grumbled again. "I told 'em the last time I wasn't about to sell. I said there ain't enough money in the world to make me give up my home."

"The city can force you out of the building, Buddy. You know that. You have to consider the alternatives. If Americal offers you enough, maybe you should accept their deal. You could use the money to rebuild somewhere else."

"Bull-puckey! I ain't gonna leave and that's the end of it. Your attorney friend says we can hold things up for quite a spell, keep filin' petitions and such. And that's just what I'm gonna do."

"I wish there was a way I could help."

He seemed to relax a little at that. "Just callin's a help. All of us here, we appreciate everything you did for us."

Which wasn't all that much. "You've got my e-mail address. Keep me informed, will you?"

"Will do. Take care of yourself, darlin' girl."

Hope smiled. Then she thought of the vandals who had destroyed her apartment and worried that Buddy Newton might be in far more serious danger. "You, too."

She rang off the phone and forty minutes later, Conn Reese returned, walking up to her room and knocking on the door. She was reading the romantic suspense novel she had brought to keep herself occupied on the plane. She set the book on the bedside table, went over and opened the door.

Reese caught her hand and wrapped her fingers around what appeared to be a purple, tie-dyed sundress.

"You said you wanted a change of clothes. They sell these on the street. I thought for tonight you might like to go native."

She couldn't help feeling pleased, especially when she held the dress up and realized it might actually fit.

"They only come in three sizes. I figured you'd be a small."

"That was very thoughtful." Amazingly so. She went over to retrieve her purse. "How much was it? I want to repay you—"

She broke off at the look on his face. Even the vague hint of friendliness was gone.

"It was a gift, Hope. I don't want your money."

The cheaply made garments didn't cost much, she knew. Still, she didn't like being indebted. She started to argue, but the set of his jaw warned her not to.

"Thank you," she said, trying for gracious acceptance. "Give me a minute to change and I'll be right with you."

That seemed to please him and he actually smiled. "I'll wait right here."

Hope closed the door and realized her stomach was quivering. Her heart was beating too fast and her palms felt damp. *Damn.* Conner Reese was an unbelievably handsome man, but she knew a dozen guys who looked almost that good and none of them affected her like he did. She couldn't quite put her finger on it, only that the man stirred up some major chemistry in her body.

And tonight she was going out with him.

Not that this was any sort of an actual date. Just a drink and dinner, then back to the room.

She thought of Richard and wondered if, in the days before she had met her ex-fiancé, she might have considered going to bed with Conn Reese. She was an independent woman. She believed in equality of the sexes, though she had never been the sort for one-night stands. She believed in building a relationship with a man before you hopped into bed with him—not that it had done her any good with Richard.

Not that it would be important to a man like Conner Reese. Still, Conn made her feel things she hadn't felt in a very long while. She probably owed him for that.

But just like the dress, she wasn't going to pay for it by going to bed with him. Not tonight or any night in the future.

Chapter 5

Hope changed into the purple sundress Conner Reese had bought her, tying the ends of the halter top behind her neck. It was made of a soft, gauzy cotton, high-waisted, then flowing in a straight line to the ground. She had full breasts and the dress showed some cleavage—just enough to be pretty, she thought.

When she heard Conn's knock at the door, she was glad she had worn her sandals that morning instead of her white canvas deck shoes. Smiling at the frosted pink polish on her toes, she walked over to answer the knock.

Conn stood in front of the door, one hand jammed into the pocket of his pants. He looked more remote than he had when he left and she thought that perhaps he was having second thoughts about the evening ahead. He took in her appearance, his bright blue eyes going over her from head to foot.

"You look good," he said, as if he had to force out the words. "But then, I figured you would."

"Did you?"

He shrugged those powerful shoulders, making her heart start pounding again.

"Considering you look pretty damned good in a tee shirt and

shorts, it didn't require any brilliant deduction." He was wearing the same khaki pants he'd had on earlier, but had changed into a blue flowered shirt, apparently another street purchase.

"You ready?" he asked.

"As I'll ever be." As she stepped out the door, her nerves kicked up another notch. *You're just getting something to eat,* she told herself. *It's no big deal.*

She closed the door and started walking toward the car and Conn fell in beside her. She didn't expect to feel his hand at her waist, but she was only mildly surprised, since she had noticed his gentlemanly streak before. He guided her down the path to the parking lot and opened the car door and waited while she slid into the seat.

They drove along the winding road that paralleled the ocean to a restaurant called the Panorama in the Fern Hill Hotel. The place sat on the mountainside on the outskirts of the city and the views were spectacular. The dining area was covered but sat out in the open air. There were white linen cloths on the tables and a candle sat in the middle of each one next to a small glass vase holding a single red hibiscus. Conn pulled out her chair, waited till she was seated, then sat down across from her.

"So what would you like to drink?"

Hope glanced around, checking out some of the other patrons. "I think I'll have one of those fancy island drinks that come with an umbrella in it . . . a piña colada or something."

"Try the Island Punch. That's their specialty here."

She gave her order to the waiter, while Conn ordered a Scotch and water on the rocks. She had started to think of him that way, as Conn instead of Conner or Reese. In a way she wished she could retain the formality, but after he had bought her the dress, it just didn't seem possible anymore.

The waiter brought their drinks and for several long moments they sipped them in silence, looking out at the magnificent view of the harbor and the beach and the vast stretch of blue-green ocean beyond. Tiny sailboats leaned into the wind and a few stray clouds floated by overhead.

The sun didn't set over the water on this side of the island, but still it was fun to watch the colors change as it slipped behind the lush green hills to the west.

Hope toyed with the swizzle stick in her Island Punch, a mixture of fruit juices and dark Jamaican rum that tasted utterly delicious.

"So . . . how did a guy like you manage to hook up with a guy like Brad Talbot?"

"A guy like me?"

"A man with the kind of skills to know about salvage boats and underwater search equipment and how to use it to find sunken treasure. Not a social climber with an extra fifty million in his pocket—or at least that's my guess."

"Actually, Eddie Markham knew Talbot."

She swizzled her drink. "So how did you hook up with Emperor Eddie?"

Conn reached into the pocket of his khaki pants and pulled out a big gold coin. "It all started with this." He turned the coin over in his palm, then handed it to her to examine. "I began carrying it for luck when we started this project."

It was one of the Spanish coins she had seen on the Internet, a fantastically beautiful piece of treasure. Hope handed back the coin and listened for the next half-hour as he filled her in on how the venture had slowly come together. How Joe Ramirez had been with him the day he'd found the coin and insisted he show it to his old college professor.

In time, Conn and Dr. Marlin had become good friends. Together they had found out who owned the island, then went to see Eddie Markham in person. Markham had loved the idea of treasure hunting off the island. So much so, he had introduced them to Talbot, who agreed to back the venture.

"It took us three years to put the expedition together," Conn said. "But unlike Mel Fisher, we haven't got seventeen years to find the treasure."

"How long do you have?"

"Talbot's not the kind to hang in there very long. He

wants the glory—and the money. I'd say we've got till the beginning of hurricane season to come up with something solid that will prove the ship is there."

"And the season starts when?"

"Late May, first of June. The seas get rough after that. The sands start shifting. We'll have to start again after the season ends in November, and without something concrete, we'll probably have to do it with another backer."

"If you can find one."

"Yeah."

But they both knew it wouldn't be easy. Treasure hunting was very expensive, and very high-risk. And she knew he was right about Brad. He was a spoiled playboy, easily bored. The *Conquest* had already been searching for more than two months. They needed to find some evidence of the *Rosa,* and soon.

Even then, unless that evidence glittered, Brad might pull his support.

Darkness continued to fall, and a waitress came around and lit the candle in the red glass jar in the middle of the table. Conn hadn't planned to eat at the hotel. He knew a couple of local joints where the food was particularly good, and he had meant to take Hope there. But that was before they got settled and the view and the sunset had begun to weave their spell.

For the first time since he'd met her, Hope seemed to relax, and he didn't want to spoil the mood. He shouldn't have brought her with him tonight, he knew. He was completely opposed to the article she was writing. He still didn't trust her, and on top of that, he didn't like the hot jolts of lust he felt whenever he looked in her direction.

Still, he could hardly leave her in the room with nothing to eat.

The waitress reappeared and they ordered their dinners, Jamaican oxtail for him, curried chicken for her. They ate at a leisurely pace, then ordered a fruit mélange that included mangoes, sweetsop, bananas, and coconut for dessert, and a cup of Blue Mountain coffee.

As she sat across from him in the flickering candlelight, he could feel the heavy pull of his growing attraction. Tonight her smile seemed less strained, softer, more open. She had even laughed at something he said, the sound deep for a woman and richly erotic.

She had beautiful sea-green eyes and long, slightly burnished lashes. Her red hair gleamed whenever she moved, slipping softly along her jaw, and he wanted to run his fingers through it. The long purple sundress revealed the fullness of her breasts, the soft mounds and deep cleavage.

He thought what it might be like to take the heavy weight into his mouth, wondered if it would melt the coolness that surrounded her, and his body stirred to life. His pulse began to hammer and he went hard beneath the table. Inwardly, he cursed.

He didn't want to get involved with Hope Sinclair. He had just recovered from his last disastrous relationship with a woman.

And yet he wanted her. Damn, he wished he didn't.

He worked to manage a smile, to pull his thoughts back to safer territory.

"So what about you?" He reached out and caught her left hand, turned it over to note the lack of a ring. "Doesn't look like you're married."

"No." She looked down at his own ringless left hand. "I don't imagine you are, either."

He arched an eyebrow. "You don't think I'm marriage material?"

"I don't think the kind of work you do would be conducive to a happy home life."

"Actually, I was married once."

"What happened?"

"It didn't work out." He picked up his cup of coffee and took a drink, anxious to avoid the unpleasant subject. "So you're a writer. No apparent plans for marriage. Are you planning a serious career in journalism?"

Hope looked away and he wondered what that look meant.

"I love what I do and I'm pretty good at it. Mostly, I write human interest stories. Articles that revolve around families, communities, or children. The story I was working before I came down here dealt with the condemnation of a retirement home in Manhattan."

She told him that the owner of the building thought the condemnation was false, an excuse to force him to sell, and during the time she had been working on the story, she had started to believe it might be true. She said her apartment had been vandalized, perhaps as a warning to let the matter rest, and that was one of the reasons she had been pulled off the story.

"I was hoping I might be able to help them. I hate to see those nice old people lose their homes."

Conn looked at her and saw that the coolness was gone. Her eyes were flashing, her breath coming faster, her cheeks pink and glowing. She was passionate about helping those people and it occurred to him that passion might surface in far more interesting ways.

His groin tightened until his erection grew almost painful. A heavy ache built beneath the fly of his pants and he shifted, trying to get more comfortable. Several seconds passed before he noticed that Hope had stopped speaking, that she was looking him directly in the face. He wondered if she could read the desire for her that was humming through his blood.

Her gaze met his across the table and there was something in her eyes that hadn't been there before. Heat, he realized. And need. Desire, perhaps as strong as his own.

Apparently Hope Sinclair wasn't as immune to him as he had believed.

"It's still early," he found himself saying. "If you're finished, I know this little place down on the water. We can have an after-dinner drink before we go back to our rooms." He didn't know why, but he wasn't ready for the evening to end. Or perhaps he was thinking that if she continued to let her guard down, maybe they would wind up in bed.

He liked sex. He wasn't a monk. And he had a feeling Hope wasn't looking for any more involvement than he was.

They spoke little in the car on the way to the bar, a place called the Palms, a small, open-air locals' joint that faced out onto the sea. Conn knew the owner. He waved to the thin black man as they walked in, then guided Hope over to a table in the corner.

Willie came to take their drink order, smiling at Hope with obvious approval, then giving him a wink and a grin. He returned a few minutes later with two snifters of Courvoisier but had enough sense not to stay.

The jukebox was playing. There was a couple on the tiny wooden dance floor.

Conn turned to Hope. "Why don't we dance?"

She only shook her head. "No, I . . . I don't think that's a particularly good idea."

"Why not?" He stood up, sliding back his chair, reaching for her hand. Her fingers felt slim and warm as he engulfed them in his. "We'll dance, we'll finish our drink, then we'll go back to the motel."

He didn't let her hesitate again, just drew her to her feet and out onto the dance floor. The juke was playing a slow jazz number. Trying to convince himself he wouldn't regret it, Conn eased Hope into his arms.

The music soothed her. Hope closed her eyes and let the soft, slow beat wash through her. She knew she was making a mistake. She shouldn't have left her room in the first place. She certainly shouldn't have come to a place like the Palms with Conner Reese.

A place where the lights were low and couples snuggled in corners, where the jukebox played soft, slow jazz songs. All evening she had admired Conn's tall, athletically muscular body, the confident way he moved; even the smell of him turned her on. Now she was snuggled against him, her head nestled into his shoulder. He was a whole lot taller, yet they seemed to fit comfortably together.

She inhaled his scent: salt spray, a faint trace of lime, and man. His chest felt like a wall pressing into her breasts, his arms as hard as steel bands. Her heart was thrumming, her nipples tingling. It was lust, pure and simple, and it was the last thing Hope wanted to feel.

She knew where that disastrous road led.

She broke away before the song came to an end, stepped a safer distance away from him. "I think it's time we went back, if you don't mind. I've got a lot of work to do once we get back to the boat."

His gaze held hers, seemed to know that she was running, that her body was pulsing, whispering wicked thoughts.

"If you're sure that's what you want."

She didn't say more, just walked over and picked up her purse, turned, and started for the door. Conn fell in step behind her, his long strides easily matching her rapid pace. In the car, they barely spoke, but sexual tension seemed to crackle in the air between them. When he turned off the car in the parking lot of the motel, came around to the passenger side, and reached for her hand to help her climb out, she hoped he couldn't tell she was trembling.

Somewhere down the block, a makeshift reggae band played Bob Marley, *One heart, one love. Let's get together and feel all right.* Hope kept walking, making her way along the leafy path to her room.

They arrived at the door and she stiffened, praying he wouldn't press her to come in, praying if he did, she would be strong enough to refuse him. It was only lust, she reminded herself again. It shouldn't be that hard to handle.

"Thanks for dinner," she said. "I had a very nice time."

The edge of his mouth barely curved. "Did you?"

She moistened lips that suddenly felt like paper. "Yes . . ."

"So did I."

She told herself to turn away, to shove her trembling fingers into her purse and dig out her room key. She told herself to open the door and go in.

Instead she looked up at him, read the desire in his eyes. "We can't do this," she whispered, staring at his mouth, wanting him to kiss her. Praying he would not.

"We can . . . if it's what both of us want."

Hope shook her head. "You don't know what I want. Even I'm not sure anymore." It was true. There was a time she might have had the courage for this kind of brief, casual fling, but not anymore. Not until she knew she could handle it without suffering the pain she had felt after Richard.

"I want you, Hope, and I think you want me."

An image appeared of the man she'd once loved, naked in bed with her best friend. She thought of the baby she had lost, the unborn child she had wanted so badly. Hope straightened, her control returning, her mask falling back into place.

"Is that so? Well, guys like you are a dime a dozen. If I wanted you, I'd have you. Obviously, I don't." She turned away from him, started to dig through her purse. Conn's long fingers curled around her shoulders. He hauled her toward him and his mouth crushed down over hers.

It was a hard, taking kiss, a hot, wet, delicious kiss that turned soft and coaxing and left her utterly breathless. Her lips softened under his and she tasted him, opened for him. He took her with his tongue, an erotic parody of what he would do to her if she let him come into her room. A faint moan seeped from her throat as Conn broke away.

His eyes were still hot, burning into her like a brand, and filled with something she couldn't quite name.

"Thanks for the dance," he said. Turning, he strode toward the room next door and jammed his key into the lock. He turned the handle and pushed the door open, but he didn't go in, just stood there waiting until she finally found her key, fumbled it into the lock, went in, and closed the door.

Her eyes slid closed as she leaned against it. Her stomach was quivering. She was throbbing in places that hadn't throbbed since Richard.

She wanted Conn Reese.

Worst of all, he knew it.

Hope walked over to the sink on shaking legs, ran water into the basin, and washed her face.

She was tired but her body still hummed with need. The bed beckoned, but it only made her think erotic thoughts of Conn and she knew she wouldn't be able to sleep.

The man who pounded on her door the following morning was a different man from the one she'd been out with the night before. He was just as tall and male, just as handsome and virile, but this man's jaw was set, his eyes a cool shade of blue. He was different.

But then, so was she.

It was obvious both of them had their protective walls back in place. Sometime in the night, Hope's common sense had returned. So what if Conner Reese was a good-looking man with a body right out of the movies? So what if she found him sexually attractive? She was only human. It was a completely natural reaction.

The problem was, she would only be in the islands for a few short weeks. Maybe even less than that. If nothing turned up of the *Rosa,* the magazine would probably be satisfied with the first article in the series and perhaps a brief follow-up months later when the search came to a disappointing end. The last thing she wanted was a quick fling and a sad good-bye.

On the surface, Hope seemed the most self-assured of the three Sinclair sisters, the coolest in an emergency, the strongest, the one the others could always count on. Her own personal, well-guarded secret was that she was also the most soft-hearted, the most sensitive, the most easily hurt. To compensate, she put on a tough façade and kept most people at a distance.

Other than her family, Richard was one of the few who had discovered the truth. He had used that knowledge against her, taken advantage, and broken her heart.

She wasn't about to let it happen again.

Or even take the slightest chance that it might.

Which was why, on this bright Caribbean morning, with the sun beating down on her face and a soft ocean breeze blowing in off the sea, she was determined to keep her distance from Conner Reese.

"I spoke to the guys at the airport on Pleasure Island," he said. "The plane's coming in this morning. They'll be waiting for us at the airport when we get there."

He was all business this morning, and relief trickled through her.

"That's good news," she said just as mildly, stepping out of the room dressed once more in her white shorts and coral blouse, the purple dress stuffed into her oversized purse.

"I've already eaten but we've got time for you to get something if you're hungry."

"I don't eat breakfast. But I could use a cup of coffee."

He got her a cup to go from the pot in the lobby of the motel, then drove directly to the airport. As promised, the plane was there, a Beech/Raytheon Duke, Conn told her, an expensive twin-engine with The Villas logo of a palm tree over three wavy blue lines painted on the side. It sat on the tarmac, the cabin door open and the stair inviting them in, ready to fly them back to the island.

It didn't take long to reach their destination, less than a hundred miles away. Chalko stood next to the Jeep at the edge of the private airstrip, along with Tommy Tyler, who had been busy shooting photos of the lush vegetation, waterfalls, and mountains.

"I heard you got stuck in Jamaica," Tommy said, tossing a speculative glance between her and Conn. He wiggled his eyebrows suggestively and grinned. "Tough duty, but someone's gotta do it."

At the looks he received in return, the grin slid off his face.

"We had work to do," Conn growled.

"Neither of us could afford to waste the time," Hope snapped.

"Unfortunately, out here things happen on 'island time.' There's not a whole lot you can do about it."

Hope made no further comment. It definitely would have been better if they could have returned. At least it would have been safer.

They all climbed into the fringe-topped Jeep and Chalko drove them down to the harbor.

"I don't see her," Conn said, scanning the waves for the *Conquest*, which should have been visible somewhere along the reef.

The handsome young black man just smiled. "Cap'n Bob moved her a little. Joe wanted to take a look at the area south of the reef."

Conn swore softly.

"I take it that wasn't your plan," Hope said.

"Joe's always been a hothead. We're supposed to be sticking to the GPS grid. That way we cover every inch of the ocean floor and don't chance missing anything."

"Maybe he ran across something interesting."

He grunted. "One can only hope."

They didn't say more as the Jeep pulled into the parking lot. Though the day was cool, the sun was hot, and heat radiated up from the pavement as they climbed out and walked down to the dock, where the powerful white speedboat bobbed in its slip. Once they were out on the water, Chalko skillfully avoided the reef, using the channel at the entrance, then powering the sleek craft into the open sea.

"There she is!" Hope pointed toward the big, steel-hulled salvage boat anchored a little to the south, dipping and swaying in the waves. Even from a distance, she could see activity on the deck. When the speedboat pulled alongside, Joe Ramirez came over to the rail.

"Man, I'm glad you're back."

"What's up?" Conn asked, climbing onto the boarding

platform, then turning to help Tommy and Hope climb out of the boat.

Joe grinned like a schoolboy. "You won't believe it. Hurry up—you gotta see this."

Conn left to follow Joe without giving Hope a backward glance. It was as if the attraction that had sparked between them last night had never happened. It was just a dream, a little bit of island magic. The magic was gone now, as if it had never existed, and she had a job to do.

As she and Tommy started for the chart room, following Conn and Joe, she tried to tell herself she was glad things hadn't gone any further last night.

But she wasn't really certain that she was.

Chapter 6

Trailing Joe, Conn descended the ladder to the chart room. Captain Bob was there, along with Andy Glass, and both of them were grinning. They hovered around the video camera, looking at the picture projected from beneath the sea. There was something on the screen, but mixed with snatches of plant life and covered with a dense layer of sand, Conn couldn't tell what it was.

"Check this out." Joe pointed to the side-scan sonar. "What's that look like to you?"

The monitor sat next to the video camera, but the scanner itself hung from a cable below the boat. It was designed to recognize the shapes of objects lying on the ocean floor. Conn studied the screen. Though whatever was on the video screen was encrusted with corrosion and covered by a layer of sand, the object outlined on the monitor was clearly defined.

And the shape on the screen sent a rush of adrenaline shooting through him.

For the first time, he noticed the pinging sound coming from a few feet away and turned to look at the magnetometer reading. The equipment Talbot had provided was top of the line and this detector picked up both ferrous and nonferrous metals. The object on the ocean floor was definitely metal, the shape unmistakable.

Conn started to grin. "By God, you found one of the cannons!" He slapped Joe on the shoulder. "I should have listened to you sooner. You always were a lucky son of a bitch."

For nearly a week, Joe had been trying to talk him into searching the area parallel to the coast south of the reef.

"I got a hunch," Joe had said.

But Conn had been determined to be practical and stick with the grid, which moved them slowly across the reef.

"You found the cannon?" Hope repeated excitedly from behind him. Conn ignored a jolt of heat at the sound of her voice. Last night was over. Nothing had happened and this morning he was glad.

At least his brain was glad. After a sexually frustrating night and very little sleep, his body hated his guts.

"Yeah, looks like we did." He couldn't help a smile. They had all worked long and hard for this. "Of course, we'll need to bring it up, try to verify it actually came off the *Rosa*."

Conn turned to read the fathometer, which showed the depth of the bottom. "Forty-three feet. We're about half a mile offshore and three-quarters of a mile south of the western curve of the reef. Maybe she struck some coral heads near the edge, tore a hole in her hull, then drifted this far south before she sank."

"We've set buoys to mark the spot," Joe said. "So far we haven't found any sign of the ballast pile." Ballast was weight carried in the hold to keep the ships stable in the water. The English often used pig iron. The galleons usually carried stones.

"We'll recalculate the grid, use the cannon as a starting point, and work around it all the way back to the reef." He looked over at Joe. "Let's go down and take a look. If we take the sled, we can use the prop wash to blow away some of that sand."

Joe grinned. "If you're waiting for me, man, you're backin' up."

Conn chuckled. "Give me a minute to get out of these clothes." He started for the ladder and so did Joe. After a quick trip to his cabin to change into a swimsuit, Conn returned to the deck, where Joe had their diving gear laid out. Pete Crowley, one of the deck hands, was already hoisting the underwater sled up and over the rail, beginning to lower it toward the water.

Joe checked the tanks while Conn pulled on his wetsuit. He picked up his BC vest, dive computer, tank, fins, and the rest of his gear and started toward the loading ramp that also served as a diving platform. Joe sat down beside him on the platform and they both put on their fins.

As Conn adjusted his mask down over his face and prepared to go into the water, he glanced up to see Hope standing at the rail, the breeze whipping her glorious hair. She still looked good to him. Too damn good.

Conn gave the thumbs-up signal he and Joe always used, and they scissored off the platform into the water.

Standing at the rail, Hope watched the thin line of bubbles coming up from the divers' tanks as they descended into the depths below. If she closed her eyes, she could still see Conn in his swimsuit, his chest bare and rippling with muscle. She had watched him pulling on his wetsuit, his body so incredibly fit, sinews moving, shifting beneath his suntanned skin. Her mouth still felt dry.

Shaking her head to clear the image, Hope turned to Tommy Tyler and the two of them returned to the chart room to watch the video screen. The water was remarkably clear, a gorgeous turquoise color that sparkled near the surface with the brilliance of the sun, then deepened to a crystalline blue farther down in the water. Hope could see the black-suited divers descending into the sea below the boat, disappearing now and then behind a school of flashing silver fish, weaving their way through tall stands of soft gorgonian. In the distance behind them, vivid blue and bright red sponges grew next to lacy black coral.

The sled easily carried the two men down, though they paused periodically to let their ears adjust to the depth, the light in front illuminating the area around them. As they went deeper, she could see the sandy ocean floor, interspersed with underwater plant life, floating tendrils of algae mixed with waving sea grasses, and a scattering of volcanic rock here and there, but a good portion of the floor was covered with fine, white sand.

Once the men reached the cannon, they turned the sled around and used the propeller-wash to clear the sand away so they could see what they had found. For an instant, the air grew cloudy, and men and cannon both disappeared behind a thick film of debris. The minutes ticked past; then the sled propellers stopped turning and the sand drifted away, allowing the water to clear, and the men slowly became visible again.

The divers swam the length of the cannon, searching for markings of some kind, but Hope didn't think they found any. Now that the sand was gone, the weapon looked less corroded than it had first appeared.

"There were forty-two bronze cannons aboard the *Rosa,*" Hope said matter-of-factly, turning the men's attention in her direction.

"How do you know that?" Tommy asked.

"I read it on a sunken treasure Internet site. You wouldn't believe the stuff you can find. Professor Marlin mentioned a museum in Seville. As soon as I get the chance, I'm going to see what I might be able to access there."

"Even if you get something, it'll probably be in Spanish," Tommy said.

"If it is, I imagine Joe Ramirez can translate it for me."

Tommy thought the way Joe looked at Hope, the guy would be happy to do that and a whole lot more. But Tommy could already tell Joe Ramirez didn't stand a chance. Not if the hot looks passing between Hope and Conner Reese were any indication, and he figured that they were.

Tommy had never seen Hope look at a man that way. Not

even her no-good, cheating, ex-boyfriend. Hope had been engaged to the prick when Tommy first met her. He knew she'd caught the guy in bed with one of her best friends, and Tommy had seen how badly his betrayal had hurt her.

He sighed. He wished Hope looked at him the way she looked at Reese. It was never going to happen. Hope thought he was too young for her. Besides, up until now, she hadn't been interested in men, not since she'd broken up with her rotten fiancé.

Tommy wondered if Conn Reese knew what a lucky bastard he was.

Conn and Joe finished their initial examination, searched the surrounding area, and returned to the *Conquest.* Though it was one of the smaller cannons, weighing only twelve hundred pounds, it took the rest of the afternoon to haul the weapon up on deck. All the while, Tommy Tyler photographed the event, taking shots from every angle.

Conn wanted to take the artifact along when they returned to Jamaica to resupply. He was hoping Doc Marlin would be able to positively identify the cannon as coming from the *Rosa,* though Conn was convinced it must have. How many ancient cannons could be lying in the waters off Pleasure Island? His pulse accelerated at the thought of what they might find next.

It was late in the afternoon by the time the cannon was finally hoisted over the rail, and in order to preserve it, submerged in a seawater-filled holding tank that waited on the bow. The men examined the piece as thoroughly as they could, but found nothing obvious that might identify the ship it had come from.

Hope could read their disappointment, but it lasted only briefly. The crew was certain they had found the *Rosa,* and spirits were high.

For the next three days, the ship searched the area and they got several hits off the magnetometer. Conn and Joe continued to dive, bringing up several more artifacts. The pieces were corroded, but appeared to be some sort of iron fittings. Nothing else of significance turned up.

They were scheduled to return to Port Antonio for supplies the following day, but eager to show the cannon to the professor, Conn decided to leave early. They pulled anchor that night, leaving their buoys in place, though according to Andy Glass, with the sophisticated GPS equipment aboard, the spot would be easy enough to find again.

They were under way, the first shift finishing their supper, when Andy walked into the galley with the satellite phone in his hand.

"It's for you, Hope."

She flicked a slightly embarrassed glance at Conn, knowing he wasn't thrilled at her use of his equipment. "I gave the number out to a couple of people to use in case of emergencies." She took the phone from Andy's hand, and Conn got up so she could slide out of the booth to take the call.

"Hope, it's Gordy," said the voice on the other end of the line. "I wouldn't have called, but I figured you'd kill me if I didn't."

"God, what is it?"

"Last night there was a fire at Hartley House. I was out of the office off and on all day. I didn't find out until just a few minutes ago."

Her fingers tightened around the phone. "Was anyone hurt?"

"A woman named Mrs. Gilroy was hospitalized for smoke inhalation." She was one of the ladies who played bridge with Mrs. Finnegan. "They released her late this morning."

Thank God. "I'm glad it wasn't serious. How much damage was done?"

"Two of the apartments were completely destroyed. The firemen said they were lucky they got it out before the whole damned place burned down."

"Do they know what started the fire?"

"Fire captain thinks it was faulty wiring. They're looking into it."

But Hope didn't think it was faulty wiring or any other kind of accident. Though she had only worked a few months as a newspaper reporter, she had been writing magazine articles for years. Her investigative instincts were kicking in, big time, and she had learned to listen to them.

"I want you to do me a favor, Gordy. You know that private investigator friend of yours?"

"Jimmy Deitz?"

"Yeah. You always spoke highly of him. Tell him I want to hire him. I want him to look into that fire, see if he can figure out what really happened. And I want him to find out who the players are in Americal Corporation. See if he can find out what their plans are for that piece of real estate Hartley House sits on."

"Jimmy doesn't work cheap. This could get a little expensive."

Hope thought of the twenty thousand dollars she had inherited. She had been saving it in case something came up. She thought that her grandfather would approve her helping the people in Hartley House.

"Just get him on it," Hope said. "Give him my e-mail address and tell him to keep me posted." She looked over at Conn, who was watching her and frowning, the food getting cold on his plate. "Tell him to call me at this number if he thinks it's important."

She broke off and handed the phone back to Andy. Of all the crewmen, Andy was the most forgettable. Average build, average height, brown hair, mid-thirties. His horn-rimmed glasses were the only thing that distinguished him from a thousand other average-looking guys.

"Thanks, Andy."

"No problem." Turning, he quietly made his way back to the wheelhouse. When Hope returned to the booth, Conn got up so she could slide in. She ignored a little frisson of awareness as she brushed past him.

"I couldn't help overhearing. I take it there was a fire at the retirement home."

She nodded. "Two of the units were destroyed. Gordy—that's my friend at the newspaper—says they were lucky the whole place didn't burn down."

"You said the building's been condemned. Maybe it's in worse shape than you figured."

She shook her head. "I don't think so, though I suppose it's possible. The owner was going to get hold of some contractors, get estimates on how much it would cost to put the place back in good condition. I'll e-mail him, see what he's found out."

"Call him," Conn said. "Sounds to me like people's lives may be in danger. If you're right and someone set that fire, this could get deadly."

She looked up at him, surprised and oddly relieved. "Thank you."

"That part about hiring an investigator . . ."

"Yes?"

"You're not paying for that out of your own pocket?"

Hope shrugged. "My grandfather left my sisters and me a small inheritance, about twenty thousand apiece. Charity and Hope used part of their money to pay for a summer adventure. We had all three vowed to do that, to have an adventure before we settled into our careers." *Or got married,* which was now a very unlikely part of her future. "I figure helping the people at Hartley House is more important."

His gaze held a hint of respect. "That seems pretty noble."

"I just want to know the truth. And I don't want any of those nice people getting hurt."

Conn watched her a moment more. "You never know, maybe you'll still get your adventure. You're on a boat in the middle of the Caribbean, writing about sunken treasure. Out here, danger and excitement are all around you." His gaze locked with hers and the heat she had seen before flared to life. "Who knows what might happen out here."

His eyes remained on her face and suddenly she felt breathless. The danger was standing right next to her. Tall and male and unbelievably handsome. "Yeah . . . who knows?"

She didn't say more and neither did he. She just turned and tried to concentrate on eating. But her stomach was quivering once more, and she found herself remembering how it had felt when he had kissed her.

Hope had to force herself not to get up and run out of the galley.

Conn stood next to Joe Ramirez at the rail, watching the sea roll past. A bright moon lit the darkness that had settled over the water and a warm breeze ruffled his hair. The smell of the sea enveloped him and he could hear the rush of waves against the hull as the ship cut through the water.

They would reach Port Antonio tonight, dock at the harbor, and start resupplying the boat in the morning, refilling water and fuel tanks, restocking the galley with enough food to feed one woman and seven hungry men.

He amended that. As soon as they had found the cannon, Conn had phoned Ron Keegan and Wally Short, divers he had worked with in Jamaica. The men were on standby, ready to join the dive team in the event the shipwreck was discovered and more men were needed for the search.

While Joe watched over operations at the harbor, Conn intended to offload the cannon onto a truck bed and head for the maritime marine museum in Kingston. He hoped the professor had gotten the message Conn left for him on his cell phone, telling him to meet them in the morning down at the dock.

"You think we've found her?" Joe asked, breaking into his thoughts.

"I think we've found part of the trail she left. Finding the ship itself will probably be a hell of a lot harder."

"No kidding. It took Mel Fisher years to find the *Atocha*, and he was practically on top of the wreck the whole time."

"We'll do better. We've got a lot better equipment than Fisher had."

"And better information." Joe grinned, his teeth a flash of white in the moonlight. "He didn't have Archie Marlin."

The ship dove into a trough and came up the other side, throwing sea spray into the air. The mist felt cool and damp against Conn's skin, and he thought how much he loved the ocean, had since he was a kid living in South Miami. He'd spent every waking hour at the beach, a respite from the turmoil at home. Before his mother left, she and his dad were always fighting. His mom sported a black eye at least a couple of times a year and so did he. She had saved herself, run away and left him to suffer the old man's wrath until he was old enough to leave.

"So what about you and Hope?" Joe asked, grabbing his attention once more.

"There is no 'me and Hope.' What gave you the idea there was?"

"Well, for one thing, the two of you spent the night together in Jamaica." Beneath a fringe of thick black lashes, Joe rolled his nearly black eyes. "I bet that is one hot babe."

Conn's jaw tightened. "We didn't spend the night together, Joe. She stayed in her room and I stayed in mine. She's here on business. So am I."

"Okay, take it easy. I kinda thought maybe there was something going on, that's all."

"Yeah, well, there isn't."

"If that's the case, I guess you wouldn't mind if I asked her out. We could have dinner at that little place in the village on Pleasure Island . . . or, hey, we'll be in Jamaica for the next couple of days. I could take her somewhere there." He smiled. "I still think she's one hot babe. She plays it cool, but I bet I could light a fire in that tight little body of hers. Man, I'd really like to—"

"Shut up, Joe," Conn said through clenched teeth.

Joe just laughed. "Doesn't pay to lie to your old buddy,

man. I know you too damned well. You might not want to admit it, but you're hot for the lady and I don't blame you."

"She's trouble, Joe. Trouble's something I've had more than enough of already." He should have known he couldn't fool Joe. After six years in the SEALs together, they knew each other like brothers, thought of each other that way.

He didn't like the idea of Joe spending time with Hope, as his friend had known damned well he wouldn't. Conn was attracted to Hope Sinclair in a way he hadn't been to a woman since Kelly.

Exactly the reason he meant to stay away from her.

"Not all women are like your ex," Joe said softly, clearly reading his mind.

Conn just raised an eyebrow.

"Okay, so Kelly was major bad news. But you gotta live, man. Besides, we're not talkin' marriage here. We're talkin' sex. Screamin' hot, no-strings, get-your-rocks-off sex. Hope's not some twenty-year-old kid. She's a woman, Conn, and I think she's as attracted to you as you are to her. As long as you're both on the same page about that, I don't see where there's a problem."

Joe reached over and squeezed his shoulder. "Think about it, buddy."

Conn made no reply. He was already thinking about it. He'd been thinking about hot sex with Hope Sinclair almost from the moment he had met her.

But maybe Joe was right. Hope was a grown woman and there was definitely an attraction between them. As long as they both knew where they stood, maybe they could just enjoy each other for as long as the attraction lasted.

"So . . . are you hearin' me, man?"

Conn smiled. "I'm hearin' you. And if I think about sex any more, I won't be able to walk."

Conn could hear Joe's laughter all the way back to his cabin.

* * *

It was morning, the sun well up, the crew finished with breakfast and were beginning the tasks they needed to get the boat resupplied. Conn looked over the rail, pleased to see the professor walking toward them. Earlier, he had been to Ace Truck Rentals to hire a flatbed to take the cannon to the maritime museum in Kingston.

The museum was deeply involved in the preservation of Caribbean history and contained the equipment necessary to properly preserve whatever artifacts they might find in their search for the *Nuestra Señora de Rosa.* The professor had already gained their enthusiastic agreement to help in any way they could, and now he was ready to deliver the first artifact that would need to be preserved.

First, however, the piece would undergo the professor's intense scrutiny, which Conn hoped would provide the verification they needed and point them toward the treasure. He waved at Doc, then straightened at the sound of Hope's voice as she walked up beside him at the rail.

"Looks like the professor has arrived."

"He's come to see the cannon," Conn told her.

"Joe says the two of you are taking it to the museum. I was hoping I could go with you."

"More information for your article?"

"Actually, I finished the first in the series last night. I sent it to the magazine over the Internet, along with Tommy's photographic work. I would have liked to get Dr. Marlin's comments on the cannon, but yesterday was the last possible day I could make my deadline."

She smiled. "In a way, it left kind of a good cliffhanger. You know—'Has the dedicated crew of the *Conquest* really found the lost Spanish galleon, *Nuestra Señora de Rosa?* Will they discover millions of dollars in treasure?' Readers will be dying to buy the next issue to find out if you did."

Conn frowned. "Great. Now a bunch of lookie-loos will turn out to watch us diving for Spanish gold—or worse yet, try to find it themselves."

Hope just shrugged. "Everyone but you and the professor wants this story done."

"You mean Talbot and Markham want it done."

"That's right. And so does *Adventure* magazine."

Conn sighed. "Well, I suppose you might as well come along. But first let's see if the professor thinks we've found the *Rosa*."

She fell into step beside him and he tried not to notice how good she looked, her lips glossy with some pretty peach shade of lipstick, her sea-green eyes shining with excitement. Her breasts did this sexy kind of jiggle as she walked, and he started getting hard.

Cursing himself, he let her move a little ahead of him, then cursed again and tried to look at something besides her round little derriere. Damn, he wished Glory hadn't gone back to Florida. Maybe he wouldn't be so damned hot for Hope Sinclair.

They left the boat and walked along the dock to where the professor stood waiting, his pale blue eyes twinkling, thin face wreathed in a smile.

"I just got your message this morning. You found the cannon! I can hardly wait to see it."

"Good morning, Professor," Hope said, smiling.

"Isn't it, indeed? Looks like you brought them luck."

"I hope so."

"The cannon's in the holding tank," Conn said. "You can take a look at it now or we can load it onto the truck and you can wait till we get to the museum."

"Wait? What are you talking about? I've been waiting for this moment for the last twenty years! Come on—let's go see what you've found."

They made their way back aboard the *Conquest* and the professor walked straight to the holding tank on the bow of the boat. He looked inside the tank and began to frown. "One of the smaller artillery pieces."

"We weighed her in at twelve hundred pounds. She's seven-and-a-half feet long."

"A good-sized cannon will go three thousand, maybe forty-five hundred pounds." He reached into the tank, measured the size of the bore with his fingers, ran them over the barrel. "Muzzle-loader. About three-inch caliber. Handled iron shot of a little less than three pounds."

He patted the gun as if he had found an old friend, then turned away from the tank. "The trouble is, she's a wrought iron cannon."

The look on the professor's face made Conn's stomach tighten. "So is it off the *Rosa?*"

The old man shook his head. "All the cannons aboard the *Rosa* were bronze."

"All of them? Are you sure? Couldn't there have been a few—"

"According to the records from the shipyard where the *Rosa* was built, she carried thirty-eight tons of armament. She was the pride of the fleet, outfitted with the most modern munitions. Which meant her cannons were forged of bronze and not iron, as the older ships' cannons were."

"Forty-two of them," Hope said, "in various sizes. At least that's what I read on the Internet. It never occurred to me there wouldn't be iron ones as well."

The professor stared down at the cannon, looking older than he had when he had arrived. "I'm afraid the piece we have here came from a less important ship. Likely a slightly older merchant vessel. In their day, they were often ill-equipped."

"What other ship could possibly be down there?" Conn asked, his stomach feeling like a ten-pound cannonball sat at the bottom.

"I'll need to go back and recheck my research. But all along, I've been worried this might happen."

"Worried that *what* might happen?" Surely the old man hadn't kept something important from them. Then again, he wanted the search. The man just might have.

"If you remember, the *Santa Ynez* also sank during that terrible storm in 1605. It was believed she went down on the

Serranilla Banks, just like her two sister ships. While I was tracking the *Rosa,* it occurred to me that perhaps *both* the *Santa Ynez* and the *Rosa* might have missed the banks and been blown toward *Isla Tormenta.*"

For a moment, Conn couldn't think of anything to say. They had found the wrong ship and the professor wasn't all that surprised.

"What was she carrying?" he asked, praying the ship was also filled with treasure.

"I'm afraid the *Santa Ynez* was a *nao,* not a galleon. They were short, fat, rather cumbersome, square-sailed merchant ships. Sometimes they carried treasure, but this one was carrying medicines and dyes—things like spices, rare woods, and hides. Her most valuable cargo was tobacco, worth a small fortune in its day, but certainly nothing like gold or silver that can withstand the ravages of time. You might find a few of the passengers' valuables. There were more than three hundred ill-fated souls aboard."

The wrong ship! Conn could almost see Brad Talbot's eyes popping out when he heard the news. Conn wished he didn't have to ask the next question.

"You said the *Rosa* was the last ship in the line. That means she would have been sailing behind the *Santa Ynez.* If that's the case, where do you think the *Rosa* went down?"

The professor shook his head. "It's possible she missed the island altogether and was blown farther east. The next land mass she would have come to would be Haiti."

"Haiti! You think the *Rosa* might have sunk off Haiti?"

"Calm down, my boy—I didn't say that. I said it was possible. I need to go back and take another look at my records. I need to find out how far the two ships were sailing apart from each other when they were last sighted. And I need to recheck the currents. Obviously, the wind and seas moved the vessels a little farther south than I first believed."

Conn silently cursed. "How long do you think it will take before you can give us some kind of answer?"

"Not long. I should know something by tomorrow." He

smiled. "Look on the bright side, Conner. If the *Santa Ynez* didn't sink on the Serranilla Banks, then we know for certain neither did the *Rosa*."

Conn sighed. Leave it to the professor to always be optimistic. "I suppose that's something."

"In the meantime, we still need to take this artifact to the museum. The *Santa Ynez* has been missing for four hundred years. What you've found is a valuable piece of history, even if the ship wasn't carrying treasure."

Conn just nodded. He hated to tell his crew that not only had they found the wrong ship, but the one that carried the treasure might have sunk hundreds of miles away.

Hope was going to spend the day with Conn and the professor. She felt safe, knowing the older man was going along, though it was definitely a false sense of security.

She had never met a man who attracted her the way Conn did, not even Richard. It was as if an electrical current ran between them, or perhaps some fierce magnetic field. Every time she looked at him, she wanted to touch him. She wanted to kiss him the way he had kissed her that night in front of her motel room. She wanted to take off his clothes and her own and run her hands all over that magnificent body.

"Whatever you're thinking," Conn said as the crane finished loading the cannon onto the bed of the truck, "you'd better stop right now. If you don't, I'm going to haul you off this boat, carry you away somewhere private, and do everything you're imagining and a whole lot more."

Her heart thundered. Good Lord, was HOT SEX stamped across her forehead?

"I haven't the faintest idea what you're talking about."

The edge of his mouth barely curved. "I think you know exactly what I'm talking about . . . though I'll be more than happy to show you."

Hope swallowed, grateful when the professor smilingly

returned and the three of them headed down the gangway to the truck. Grateful, until they climbed in and she realized that riding in the middle, she was pressed intimately into Conn's side, that for the next several hours she was going to feel every movement of that steel-hard body.

The road was narrow, barely two lanes, and the traffic was heavy. Conn wove between the passing cars with the skill of a native Jamaican; still, she couldn't relax, not with him so near. By the time they reached Kingston, her heart was beating like a trip-hammer and a faint trace of perspiration dampened the hair at her temples.

It wasn't the only place she was damp and she wondered if Conn knew that, too.

Her face went hot as she glanced down and saw the heavy bulge pressing against the fly of his pants. At least she had the satisfaction of knowing the intimate contact had affected him, too.

At the museum, they met with Dr. Winthrop Hardy, who was expecting them. With the help of a skip loader and several museum workers, the cannon was delivered into an electrolytic reduction tank to begin the long process of stabilizing the artifact so it could be properly preserved.

"We appreciate this," Dr. Hardy said. "Perhaps Mr. Markham will agree to allow us to excavate other artifacts from the ship."

"Perhaps," the professor said. But he looked fairly skeptical, and Hope didn't think it would happen, either. Not if there wasn't something in it for Eddie. Archeology was hardly glamorous, and the emperor was mostly concerned with things that would make money for Pleasure Island.

They finished their delivery and afterward ate lunch at a little restaurant called the Fisherman's Tavern that offered seafood specialties and typical island fare. The subject of treasure came up as they finished their meal and Hope took the opportunity to gain a little information.

"I was hoping to get your opinion on the archeological ramifications of salvaging treasure, Professor."

The professor arched a bushy gray eyebrow, impressed that she had taken the time to read up on the subject.

"There are very valid archeological concerns, of course. We need to preserve the past the best we can. Still, every year, storms spread the treasure and the artifacts, and more and more of what little is left is lost or destroyed."

"I hadn't really considered that. I know the main concern seems to be that current techniques aren't sophisticated enough and valuable information is being lost."

"It is definitely a concern, one we're attempting to deal with as best we can, but the government is trying to stop this sort of salvage work altogether. Indeed, at this very moment, Spain is trying to halt operations on any Spanish vessel lying within U.S. waters."

Conn grunted. "If you ask me, those guys have a lot of nerve. The Spaniards raided the gold and silver from the South Americans in the first place."

The professor chuckled. "Exactly so. Besides, if we do find the treasure, I intend to make certain the artifacts are carefully cataloged and preserved as well as they possibly can be."

"So you think there's still a chance you'll find it?"

The professor smiled. "Of course there is."

But when she looked at Conn, his expression seemed more hopeful than convinced.

Chapter 7

It was almost six o'clock when they arrived back in Port Antonio. Conn returned the rented flatbed and they all climbed into the old blue Toyota. Hope sat in the passenger seat as he drove down to the harbor and dropped the professor where he'd parked his car.

"I'll call you in the morning," Dr. Marlin said, "give you a progress report. Keep your fingers crossed."

"Conn's got his lucky gold coin," Hope said through the rolled-down window. "Maybe that will help."

The professor waved good-bye and Conn parked the car in a space near where the *Conquest* was docked. Hope reached for the handle of the door, but Conn caught her arm.

"It's almost time for supper. If you don't have plans, I know a place the locals go that has the best Jamaican food on the island."

A little tremor ran through her. She looked up at him, saw the heat in his eyes.

"You're asking for more than supper and both of us know it. I'll admit I'm attracted to you, Conn. There's no sense lying about it. But we barely know each other. It's not my style to climb in the sack with a guy just for a little sexual relief."

She waited for the anger. Instead, the corner of his mouth edged up.

"I hadn't thought of it quite that way, but I get your point. Believe it or not, I don't climb into the sack with just anyone, either."

She wasn't sure she believed him, but she liked that he accepted the *no* without hassling her about it. She might even have changed her mind and agreed to dinner, but just then the entire crew of the *Conquest* descended on the car.

Joe Ramirez reached them first. "Hey, you two, you're back just in time. We're all heading over to Willie's. We figure the boat won't be going out again until we hear from the professor. In the meantime, we're gonna drown our sorrows with a couple of shooters over at the cantina."

Conn had told them before he left for Kingston that the cannon hadn't come from the *Rosa*. Hope didn't really blame them for being a little down.

"Why don't you two join us?" Captain Bob asked politely. It was funny how everyone thought of him that way, as Captain Bob, not just Bob or even Captain.

"Yeah, Hope," Tommy chimed in, opening her door and tugging her out of the car. "Come on. You can't work all the time."

She flicked a glance at Conn, who had also climbed out and was watching her across the hood.

"All right," she said with a smile. "Why not?"

A cheer went up and the entire gang began the short trek across the parking lot to the thatch-roofed bar on the slope above the harbor. Even King was among the crowd, the huge black man grinning, the muscles bulging in his powerful arms and thighs as he opened the wooden front door, making the bell above it jingle. All of them were there, except for Andy, who was married and didn't drink.

They crossed the wooden floor of the bar, which was crowded with the after-five work crowd and far more raucous than it had been the night she had been there with Conn. In the sunlight streaming in through the big, open windows, she could see the decorations—painted fish hanging from nets strung over the walls, old-fashioned surfboards, seashells and other ocean paraphernalia she hadn't noticed when the bar was dark.

The group walked out to the open-air deck looking down on the water. Wooden tables and benches sat on the uneven brick patio, and the guys shoved two of them together. Tommy, Joe, Pete, and Captain Bob sat down across from her, leaving Conn and King on her side of the table.

King took up so much room she was forced to sit close to Conn. His eyes turned a darker shade of blue as her thigh brushed his beneath the table. Hope wasn't sure if the hot look he gave her was a reminder of what she'd turned down— or a promise of things to come.

Whatever it meant, sexual awareness had her nerves kicking in and she couldn't wait to order that drink.

"Tequila shooters all around!" Joe called out to the waitress, but Hope just laughed and shook her head.

"No, thanks. I'm not completely insane." She turned to the tall black woman with short, curly black hair in a red sarong and halter top. "I'll have an Island Punch."

"An Island Punch, huh?" Joe Ramirez winked at Conn. "Good idea."

Hope cast a slightly uneasy look at Conn. "That's what I had at the restaurant the other night, right? It's just tropical fruit juice and rum."

"Yeah, fruit juice and rum—mostly."

He didn't mention that there were seven kinds of liquor in an Island Punch. She didn't find that out until later. Way later. By then it was too late.

They ate dinner—if you could call it that. Fried calamari, fish and chips, fried zucchini, and fried, stuffed mushrooms, bar food all of them shared.

She knew it was time to leave when they started singing karaoke, but she was having so much fun it didn't take much to persuade her to stay.

Joe sang something sexy and Latin that had half the women in the bar swooning. King belted out the old Harry

Belafonte calypso banana boat song, apparently inspired by
the industry that was once the mainstay of Port Antonio, a
tune the entire bar seemed to know.

"Your turn, Hope!" Tommy prodded, hauling her to her
feet. "What are you going to sing?"

"Are you crazy? I'm not singing anything! I've got the
worst voice in the world." But he continued to tug her toward
the small wooden stage in the corner. She stopped at the bottom of the stairs.

"All right. I'll sing—on one condition."

"Which is?"

"Conn sings with me." She cast him a challenging look
while everyone cheered, clapped, and hooted, and Joe
dragged Conn to his feet. Hope had a feeling he was as reserved as she was about this kind of thing, but he seemed to
be a good sport about it, letting them haul him up the steps
to the microphone.

"All right, now that I'm up here, what are we going to sing?"

Hope grinned. "You know 'Jeremiah Was A Bullfrog?' "

"You gotta be kidding." But he grinned. The music began
and Hope started singing. She poked Conn in the ribs and he
started singing, too. His voice wasn't all that bad, deep and
resonant, but it was the way he kept smiling at her that almost made her forget the words.

The whole crowd chimed in, drowning out the sound of
their voices, for which she was grateful, and finally the song
came to an end. Both of them were laughing when he helped
her down from the stage. As he led her back to the table, the
room seemed to tilt a little sideways and she realized she'd
had too much to drink.

"I've had it," she said. "I'm going back to the ship. That
punch packs a real *punch* and I've had more than I should
have already."

"I've had plenty, too. I'll walk you back." Conn plucked
her big straw bag up off the floor beside her chair, but Hope
took it out of his hand.

"I'll be fine. I don't want to ruin your evening."

"I'm not letting you go back alone. Jamaica can be dangerous if you're not careful. Besides, I've got work to do in the morning."

She could tell he wasn't going to let her leave by herself. His old-fashioned, protective streak was kicking in, and Hope discovered she was beginning to like it.

They waved good-bye to the men. As she and Conn headed out the door, she noticed Joe was snuggied up to an attractive, young, cocoa-skinned woman he had charmed with his singing. She didn't think he'd be coming back to the boat tonight.

They crossed the parking lot in the moonlight and she could hear the crowd in the bar singing a Bob Marley favorite, "Stir it up, little darlin'." The man was practically a god in Jamaica. His music, worshipped by young and old, could be heard everywhere on the island.

They reached the boat and Conn helped her along the gangway, across the deck, and down the ladder that led to her quarters. The corridor seemed to spin a little, but the fresh air had revived her some.

In the dim light of the hallway, they reached the door to her cabin and she turned to say good night. Before she made a sound, Conn's mouth was on hers, stealing the breath from her lungs.

Heat roared through her. Liquid warmth sank into her bones. His lips were soft yet firm, giving and greedy all at once. The taste of him was overwhelming. The erotic feel of his slick, wet tongue sliding over hers made the muscles contract in her stomach.

The smell of him surrounded her, the fragrance of the sea tinged with lime. She could feel the wall at her back, his hard body pressing against her breasts. Her nipples began to tingle, turned diamond-hard. Her arms slid around his neck and she pressed herself even closer against him. She could feel the powerful sinews in his leg where it wedged between hers, the heat burning where his thigh rubbed against her sex.

He didn't ask permission to come into her room, just

turned the knob, then backed her through the open door, kicked it closed, and kept right on kissing her. His big hands reached for her blouse, frantically began to unfasten the buttons. He slid the blouse off her shoulders and an instant later, the front hook on her lacy white bra popped free.

She had very full breasts and they spilled into his hands, seemed to swell into his palms, and she heard him groan. Kissing her all the while, he molded and caressed each one, tested the weight and roundness, and heat rolled through her. Sweet God, she had to touch him, had to know the texture of his skin, the roughness of his chest hair, the tautness of those flat male nipples. She peeled his tee shirt over his head and planted kisses across the muscles in his shoulders. Her hands slid over his rib cage, across his flat stomach, and she felt his muscles contract.

Conn kissed her again, a wild, taking, pleasuring kiss that made her knees so weak she wasn't sure they would hold her up. Then his mouth fastened on her breast. He sucked her nipple between his teeth, bit down, then lapped at the end, took the heavy fullness into his mouth. Heat washed through her, made her wet and hot, made her tremble.

"I want you, Hope. I want you so damned much."

She wanted him, too, though, dear God, her brain was screaming that this had to end, that making love with him was the worst thing she could possibly do. Instead, her body swayed toward him of its own accord, aching and throbbing, begging him to touch her where all that heat was centered, begging him to thrust himself inside her.

She was so drugged with desire, so hot and wild, it took a moment to register the determined pounding at her door.

"Hey, Hope—you still up?"

Though the words were thick and slurred from the quantity of alcohol he'd drunk, she recognized the voice as belonging to Tommy. With the blood still pounding in her ears, it took a moment to form a response.

"I'm . . . I'm still up."

"So am I," Conn said harshly, glancing down at the hard

ridge pressing against his fly, "and I'm going to wring that damned kid's neck."

"I'm gonna rent a car tomorrow," Tommy said through the door, "take a drive 'round the island. I thought you might wanna come with me."

Somehow Tommy knew Conn was in there. Hope was sure of it. She was a little drunk and Tommy was trying to protect her. In a single, sharp instant, sanity returned and she could have kissed Tommy Tyler's freckled face.

She noticed the set of Conn's jaw but ignored it. Instead, she moved a few steps farther away from him.

"That . . . sounds like fun. I'd love to go, Tommy." Reaching down, she picked up her blouse with shaking hands, drew it on over her naked breasts.

"Great," Tommy said. "I figure we oughta leave 'round ten."

"Perfect."

Behind her, Conn cursed. As Tommy stumbled away, she could hear Conn dragging his tee shirt back on, his movements stiff and angry, and suddenly she felt guilty. She had to force herself to turn and face him.

"I'm sorry, Conn. I really am. I didn't mean for this to happen. I had too much to drink or it never would have gone this far."

Hard blue eyes bored into her. "It would have happened anyway, Hope—sooner or later. This isn't over. We're going to finish what we started—it's only a matter of time. You know it and I know it. You might as well get your mind wrapped around it because your body's already there."

A little sliver of heat ran through her, but Hope made no reply. Every part of her body was pulsing, aching with unspent need. She wanted Conner Reese. But she didn't want to wind up in bed with a man just because she'd had too much to drink. She couldn't bear the awful regret she would feel in the morning.

"I'm sorry," she said again as he opened the door and stepped outside.

"If you were half as sorry as I am, I wouldn't be standing

out here in the hall. We'd be over there in your bed, and sleep would be the last thing on your mind." Turning, he strode off down the passage, his footsteps fading as he disappeared into his cabin.

Hope closed her door and leaned against it. God, she hadn't meant for any of that to happen. She closed her eyes and tried not to remember Conn's heated kisses, the feel of his powerful erection pressing against her, the wetness of his mouth on her breasts.

She tingled all over at the memory, then the room started spinning again. At least it helped take her mind off Conn and what had almost happened.

With a sigh and a shake of her head, she walked into the head in the corner of the cabin, popped three Advil, came back and took off the rest of her clothes. *I'm going to pay the price in the morning,* she thought as she climbed up in bed, but then, so were the rest of them.

Maybe she could talk Tommy out of his island tour and she could stay on the boat and recuperate a little. Once she felt better, maybe she could get some work done. She needed to go online, see if she could reach that museum in Spain. And she wanted to check her e-mail, see if Buddy Newton had returned her latest message, or if maybe that detective she had hired might have found something useful.

Hope lay down on the bunk and closed her eyes, praying the ache pounding behind her eyes would go away enough that she could sleep.

In the end, it was erotic memories of Conn's powerful body pressing against her that kept her from falling asleep.

In exclusive Palm Beach, by noon it was warm and sunny, even a little hot for this time of year. Brad Talbot leaned back in the deck chair on the ninety-eight-foot Westport he kept in a slip in front of his big Spanish-style mansion on the water.

He had left his New York high-rise apartment three days ago. He was sick of the cold, cursing himself for not leaving sooner, but he liked the city during the holidays. And there was this girl he'd been seeing, a Broadway actress named Ginger Adair who was a stand-in for the female lead in *Annie Get Your Gun*. Ginger was great in bed, but he'd been with her a lot and she'd started to get demanding.

A little time away would be good for both of them. And if she still didn't get her act together, well, he would just have to find a replacement.

Brad pushed his wraparound Armani shades up on his nose, so relaxed that when his cell phone rang, he nearly jumped out of his tanning-bed-tanned, carefully-sun-screened skin. Very few people had his private number, certainly not Ginger. He reached over to the table and picked up the phone, flipped open the receiver, and pressed it against his ear.

"Yeah?"

"It's the Sinclair woman," the familiar voice said. "She's at it again. This time she's hired a detective, a man named Jimmy Deitz. He's been sniffing around, asking questions. I thought you said the woman wouldn't cause us any more trouble."

Brad sat up in his deck chair. "I can't believe it. Are you sure she's the one who's paying this guy?"

"Looks that way."

"Well, don't worry about it. Whatever she's paying, I'll pay more. We'll get him to stop working the case and that'll be the end of it."

"If you do, she'll just hire someone else."

Stupid broad probably would.

"I want this guy to stop poking around," the deep voice said. "You told me you'd make these problems end."

"Hey, I said I'd get this handled and I will. Relax, all right? Go have a drink or get laid or something."

The line went dead and Brad redialed the phone.

"Feldman," said the man on the opposite end.

"There's another snag on the Hartley House deal. It's nothing that big, just some private dick sticking his nose in where it doesn't belong."

Jack Feldman was Talbot Enterprises' head of security,

which was a fancy way of saying he did whatever Brad told him to and got paid an outrageous sum for doing it. Anything out of the ordinary, anything the least bit unpleasant, Feldman handled.

And he was good at his job.

"The guy's name is Jimmy Deitz. Hope Sinclair hired him. Whatever she's paying him, we'll pay double. Triple, if he'll feed her a little false information. We need him to drag his feet, come up with a big, fat zero. We want him working for us, not her, but we don't want her to know it. Do whatever it takes to make that happen."

"I'll take care of it." Feldman hung up and so did Brad.

He couldn't believe Hope Sinclair was still giving them trouble. Brad made an ugly sound in his throat. He didn't like a woman interfering in men's business. He liked a woman who knew how her bread was buttered and did what she had to do to make that happen. Those were the ones that were easy to handle.

Maybe he ought to make a little trip down to Pleasure Island, check things out himself. It wasn't that far away and he could get a look at his treasure-hunting operation while he was there. If he had the time, maybe he'd take another shot at getting Hope into bed, give her a taste of what she'd missed the first time around.

At least he could find out if she was up to anything else that might cause them trouble.

Brad leaned back in his deck chair and propped his feet up on the stool. He made a mental note to have his secretary check his calendar, see if he could squeeze in a quick trip down to Pleasure Island.

Awake till just before dawn, Hope slept late that morning. She still felt miserable when she woke up. She popped a couple of Advil, got dressed, and headed for the galley, praying King might have something left from breakfast and that if she ate, she would start feeling better.

It was well past ten, with no sign of Tommy—thank God—when she descended the ladder to the galley, hoping to find something to settle her queasy stomach. Apparently, she wasn't the only one feeling the effects of last night. Joe and Pete, obviously also done in, sat quietly around the dinette.

King was working as usual, turning pancakes and frying bacon, setting heaping platters of potatoes, eggs, and toast in the middle of the table. The men heartily dug in, but the smell of the food made Hope's stomach roll.

"Looks like we all had too much fun," King said in his deep, husky voice.

She glanced in his direction. "Yeah, I guess we did."

King cracked a huge white smile. "Sure was a good time, though."

Hope managed a nod and the semblance of a smile. "Sure was." Actually, she'd had a terrific time—so much so that she'd lost her inhibitions entirely and wound up half naked and nearly in bed with Conn. She wondered if he'd be the kiss-and-tell type, but somehow couldn't imagine him in the role.

Joe moved over so Hope could sit down on the padded seat and she slid in beside him. King set a mug of coffee, a glass of orange juice, and a bowl of oatmeal on the table in front of her, food she could actually manage to eat.

Hope closed her eyes and inhaled the warm, mild, welcome scent of the oatmeal. "Oh God, King, you're my hero."

"Made some for you and dat poor kid, Tommy. He was really hurtin' this mornin'. So far the boy ain't made it outta his bunk."

At least the island tour was off. She silently thanked heaven again. And by the time she finished her oatmeal and juice and actually ate a couple of pieces of toast, she felt almost human. She wondered if Conn was still sleeping, if maybe he'd been drunker than she thought.

"Conn's been up for hours," Joe said as if he'd read her mind. "The man's got an iron constitution. Always has. I don't know how he does it."

Probably because he paced himself better than the rest of

us. She had noticed that last night. Conner Reese seemed to be a man of iron control. He was also very bad news. A diver, an adventurer, a man with no ties and no steady income. He was the kind of guy women found wildly attractive, the perfect man for a short, meaningless fling—if a woman had the nerve—but nothing that would go any deeper. The trouble would come in trying to remember that.

He walked into the galley just then, tall, handsome, healthy, suntannned, looking far too good, as usual. Which only made her think of last night and what might have happened if Tommy hadn't knocked on her door. She tried to control the flush creeping into her cheeks but didn't think she succeeded.

Conn cast her a mildly condemning glance. "I guess your friend wasn't quite up to his tour."

The barb went right through her, sending her chin into the air. "I don't think any of us are feeling quite ourselves this morning."

"I guess not." He didn't say more, just poured himself a cup of coffee, turned around, and pounded back up the ladder to the deck.

When Hope went into the chart room to use the computer, she found him leaning over a stack of maps spread out on the table, plotting the seas around Pleasure Island.

For a while she ignored him, just stood next to Andy, waiting for him to finish up at the computer. Finally, her curiosity got the best of her and she padded over his way.

"So what are you working on?"

He barely lifted his head. "I'm taking a look at the south end of Pleasure Island." He pointed toward the map, running a long, tanned finger along the line that marked the edge, then moving outward to another set of lines.

"See this?"

She nodded.

"That's a sandbar, a shallows that runs parallel to the shoreline out about three-quarters of a mile. In places, the sand's as close as five or six feet beneath the surface of the water. Be a bad place for a ship to get caught in a storm."

She shivered, thinking of all the people who had drowned when the four ships of the fleet went down. "I can imagine."

A few feet away, Andy Glass shoved back his chair and got up from behind the computer. He was the only member of the crew besides Conn who didn't look a little green.

"If you need to use this, be my guest. I'm finished for the time being."

"Thanks, Andy." Ignoring her faint, persistent headache, a continuing reminder of her folly last night, Hope sat down and went to work. With a last glance at the stack of maps, remembering the crew's disappointment in not finding the *Rosa,* she decided to do her Internet research first.

Steering her way through a maze of sites, she finally found the *Archivo de las Indias* in Seville. The site was very well put together and she was able to locate an area dedicated to the Spanish treasure fleets. The information was in English as well as Spanish, but fairly general, nothing of any particular help. Before she signed off, she e-mailed the curator, told him she was a writer for *Adventure* magazine, and asked if there was any help he might be able to give her regarding the *Nuestra Señora de Rosa.*

Once she sent the message, she went to aol.com, opened her e-mail, and began to go over the waiting messages. There was one from Charity, one from Patience, and one from her dad. She answered each one, glad for the satellite link that enabled them to keep in touch. Then she spotted the message from Buddy Newton.

Hope clicked it up.

Contractors think the building could be fixed for a reasonable amount of money, which I figure I could borrow against the property. Insurance should pay for the fire damage, but they won't cough up the dough till the condemnation is settled. This really sucks. Buddy.

Hope smiled for the first time that day. She e-mailed him back.

*Hired a detective named Jimmy Deitz. He's check-
ing things out. Will let you know if he comes up with
anything useful. Hang in there, Buddy. Hope.*

It was afternoon by the time she saw Tommy, weaving his
way along the deck, still looking pale and shaky.

"Sorry about standing you up," he said, a little sheepishly.

"Hey, no big deal. I had a ton of work to do and I didn't
feel all that great this morning, either."

He gave her a pasty smile. "I guess I made an ass of myself last night . . . coming down to your cabin, I mean. What
you do is your business, not mine."

"Actually, I've been wanting to thank you. I had too much
to drink. You saved me from making a fool of myself."

Tommy shook his head, his short-cropped red hair glinting like neon in the sun. "I don't think that's true. You're attracted to the guy and he's attracted to you. That's all there is
to it."

"That's the problem, Tommy. That's all there is to it."

"Yeah, well, I guess guys look at things a little different.
If I wanted a woman and she wanted me, I'd go for it and not
have any regrets."

"I just don't want to make a mistake."

"You're no fool, Hope. You should probably just trust
your instincts."

Hope looked out across the harbor, watched a pair of sailboats heeling over in the wind. A glass-bottomed tour boat
prowled the harbor, heading out to the site of an old Brazilian
freighter that sank in the fifties.

"If you remember, Tommy, I followed my instincts before
and look where it got me. When it comes to men, I don't
think my instincts are all that good."

They talked for a few minutes longer, then Hope went
down to her cabin to organize some of her notes for the second article in the series.

The last, if the search for the *Rosa* came to an end.

Chapter 8

The *Conquest* stayed in Jamaica three more days, while Conn waited for the professor to come up with something that might give them hope the *Rosa* could have sunk somewhere near the island.

To keep herself occupied, Hope did a little shopping at the Musgrave Market on West Harbour, which specialized in local crafts. Woodcarvings, inlaid boxes, straw hats, Jamaican dolls, shells, pottery, and colorful baskets were sold all over Jamaica. The islanders were persistent, at times even pushy, trying to get her to make a purchase, but they were also smiling and friendly. She gave a grizzled old Rastafarian man with dreadlocks past his waist a dollar to let her take his picture, bought a few items, and headed back to the boat.

In the afternoon, she did some work on a freelance article she hoped to eventually sell. The piece involved a study of women using homeopathic drugs for menopause relief instead of prescription medicines—anything to keep herself busy.

Mostly, she made it a point to stay away from Conn, who seemed to be trying equally hard to stay away from her.

It was late in the afternoon when she went down to the chart room to check her e-mail, hoping to find a reply from the Spanish museum. She was thrilled to discover that today one had arrived.

Unfortunately, as she had feared, the lengthy pages of documents attached to Señor Ortega's return e-mail message were all in Spanish. Hope printed the pages, then left to find Joe Ramirez, hoping he'd be able to translate them for her.

She spotted him on deck, working on some diving gear. "Hey, Joe!" Hope waved to him as she walked over to where he worked.

"What's up?" He set aside the tank he was adjusting.

"I was hoping I could ask you to do me a favor."

"Sure. What is it?"

"Actually, it's kind of a bigger favor than I thought it was going to be." She held up the stack of printed pages. "This is from a museum in Seville that Professor Marlin mentioned, records that deal with the *Rosa*. I thought we might find something useful."

"I imagine the professor already knows all this stuff."

"I know, but I don't, and I thought I might want to put some of it in my article. The bad news is the documents are all in Spanish."

Joe grinned, digging dimples into his cheeks. "Tell you the truth, my Spanish is pretty bad. My father was one of those guys who wanted his kid to be completely American. We only spoke English at home. I took Spanish in high school, though, and again in the service, but my French is a whole lot better."

"You speak French?"

"French and Arabic. So does Conn. And he speaks Spanish like a native. He can talk to my mother better than I can. You ought to get him to translate these for you."

Conn Reese spoke four languages. *Amazing.* Hope could speak a little French, enough to get by, but she wasn't really fluent. She envied anyone with a talent for languages and grudgingly admitted she had underestimated Conner Reese.

"All right, you both speak a number of foreign languages, including Arabic. I'm obviously missing something here. What is it?"

Joe shoved a lock of jet-black hair back from his face. "I figured you knew. Conn was my lieutenant when we were in the SEALs."

"You guys were Navy SEALs?"

"Yeah. Conn never says much about it. I figured in your case he might have talked about it, though."

Hope's mind was spinning. Conner Reese was an ex-Navy SEAL. He wasn't just some beach bum, an adventurer without much of a past and only a gambler's hope for any sort of future. It took four years of college to become an officer in the military. And becoming a SEAL required a lot more than that. From what little she knew, a man needed rigid self-discipline and no small amount of brains.

She wished she weren't so impressed.

"You know why he didn't tell you?" Joe asked.

"Why?"

"Because he likes you. He wants you to like him for who he is, not because he was a SEAL. Some women are that way, you know, impressed by the job and all." Joe grinned and the dimples appeared again. "Now me, on the other hand, I'll use whatever tactics it takes to get a woman in bed."

Hope laughed; she couldn't help it. "Utterly ruthless, are you?"

"That's me. A completely conscienceless rogue. I love the ladies and they love me. What can I say? That's just the way it is."

She studied him, the beautiful dark eyes, the high cheekbones, the mouth that curved so sensuously it almost made him pretty. "You know what? I think you talk a good game but if the right woman came along, you'd be putty in her hands."

Joe laughed. Reaching out, he brushed a finger along her cheek. "You know what? I like you, Hope Sinclair. Give Conn a chance. He's a great guy—the best. And he's had his problems, too."

"Oh? Like what?"

"I hate to end this charming little discussion," Conn interrupted, casting a hard look at Joe, "but don't either of you have work to do?"

"Sorry," Joe said without a bit of remorse. "We were just discussing this little problem Hope has."

One of Conn's dark eyebrows went up. For an instant, his cool blue gaze met hers and even that brief contact made the bottom drop out of her stomach. Why couldn't Joe Ramirez make her feel that way?

She saw Joe slip quietly off down the deck, taking the tank he was working on with him, and the thought arose that there was something lonely about him.

Hope shook her head. Guys who looked like Joe rarely lacked companionship. Which made her think of Conn, who was also incredibly good-looking.

She turned her attention to him. "I was talking to Joe about some documents I got over the Net that pertain to the *Rosa*. Unfortunately, they're all in Spanish. Joe thought you might be able to give me some help with them."

His eyes darkened. "There are lots of things I could help you with, Hope, if you'd give me the chance."

She ignored the innuendo and shoved the papers toward him. "I know the professor has probably seen this stuff, but it couldn't hurt to read them ourselves. There might be something there that could be useful, even if it's just for the article I'm writing. Would you mind taking a look at them?"

He took hold of the papers. "I'd be happy to." He eyed her a long moment more. "About the other night . . ."

"What about it?"

"You were right and I was wrong. I was taking advantage, though I didn't really think so at the time."

"Neither of us was thinking very clearly. I guess we ought to be grateful to Tommy Tyler."

She caught the hint of a smile. "I don't think I'm willing to go *that* far."

Hope laughed as he held up the papers.

"I'll take a look, see what these say. I'll translate anything that looks interesting."

"Thanks, Conn."

He made no reply, just nodded, turned, and padded off down the deck. The professor had called a couple of times, but apparently he was still working on the problem, so they weren't yet ready to leave. Which gave Hope a chance to accomplish the mission she had set for herself.

If it looked as if the search were going to continue, she wanted to join the divers, do some diving herself. True, she was an amateur, but she really had enjoyed the sport when she had been in the islands before and she thought that actually being under water might add a new dimension to the articles she was writing.

As soon as the dive shop opened the following morning, Hope was going to buy herself some gear.

Conn spotted Hope walking along the wooden dock, struggling to carry a load of diving equipment. He didn't know whether to curse his bad luck or thank his lucky stars.

Hope was an amateur and that could spell trouble—he sure as hell didn't want her getting hurt. On the other hand, he had never dived with a woman before, at least not socially, and the idea was kind of intriguing.

As long as he went with her, she would probably be all right. And it might be fun to share some of the mystery and awe he discovered every time he went beneath the sea.

He met up with her halfway along the dock, reached out and took the tank out of her hand. "I gather you plan to go diving."

"I guess that depends on whether or not you're going to continue your search, which I suppose depends on what the professor has to say. If you're not going back, I made sure I could return it. If you are, the bill goes on my expense account."

"We're going back out—no matter what Doc Marlin has to say. At the very least, I want to take another look at the area where the *Santa Ynez* went down. According to the professor, the passengers onboard carried a lot of valuables. Mel Fisher found some fabulous jewelry at a couple of different Spanish wreck sites. Who knows what we might turn up."

He hefted the tank over his shoulder, grabbed her inflatable vest, and both of them started walking. Once they got aboard, he set the stuff down on the deck so he could examine it.

"You're pretty small." He studied the vest then had her put it on. "Sometimes it's hard to get the proper fit." But the shop here, Gilligan's, was good and the vest had been properly sized to Hope's small frame.

"The face mask and regulator cause the most trouble." To check the fit, he placed the mask over her nose and eyes to see if it was tight enough to prevent any leaking. "Yeah, that looks good." He set the equipment out of the way, satisfied it was safe.

"Did you find anything useful in those documents I gave you last night?"

He turned away from his study of the gear. "There was a lot of information about the ship itself, stuff that could be useful for your article."

"Such as?"

"I don't remember all of it, but it said the *Rosa* was a four-hundred-ton galleon, made of oak and built in Viscaya, Spain. She carried six anchors and four hundred passengers. The most interesting stuff was the treasure registered aboard. The professor showed me the list when we first started the venture, and we used it to win Brad Talbot's support. But it isn't something you get tired of reading."

Hope's eyes lit up. "Can I see it?"

"Sure. I'll go get it. Be right back." He headed down to his cabin, grabbed the stack of papers, and returned to the deck. He had translated some of the more interesting stuff and written it in the margins. He hoped she could read his lousy handwriting.

"Here's the list." He looked down at his notes: "849 registered silver bars; 250,000 silver coins in boxes; 1,788 ounces of gold in disks and bars; 1,000 gold coins in boxes. It says here the ship was also carrying 10,000 pounds of tobacco and four tons of copper in slabs. The professor thinks the contraband treasure aboard was also considerable, probably mostly gold chains and gold coins."

"Contraband is treasure the ship's captain didn't report and therefore didn't have to go to the Spanish king, right?"

"Yeah. According to Doc Marlin, it was pretty common practice. On the *Atocha* it turned out to be quite a sum, to say nothing of the incredible gold-and-emerald jewelry they found. On this ship, there's also supposed to be some Inca artifacts—a gold statue called the Maiden is supposed to be aboard."

"Sounds promising."

"Finding the Maiden is the professor's secret obsession. He says it's worth millions of dollars."

Conn looked up, broke off as he spotted Doc Marlin coming toward them along the dock. His pant legs flapped in the breeze with each of his hurried steps and he was holding a sheaf of papers.

"I think he's smiling," Hope said.

"He's usually pretty cheerful. That might not mean much."

The old man hurried up the gangway, and Conn and Hope went to meet him.

"Conner, my boy! Good news! Let's go down to the chart room and I'll show you."

Conn tried to clamp down on a jolt of excitement, but with the professor practically skipping across the deck, it wasn't that easy to do. They made their way down the ladder to the chart room, Joe falling in behind them, as eager as Conn to hear the news.

The oceanographic charts of the area around Pleasure Island still lay open on the table, and the professor headed straight for them.

He turned to Conn. "See this?" He held up a printed sheet of paper.

"What is it?"

"A translation of a sailor's account of the storm that sank the four ships of the 1605 Tierra Firma Fleet. It came from a man on one of the galleons that survived the storm."

He laid the papers down on the table. "On one of my research trips to Spain, I developed a friendship with a museum director at the National Bibliothèque in Madrid. I remembered discussing this document while I was there, but at the time, I didn't pay it that much attention. Like everyone else, I believed the *Santa Ynez* had gone down on the Serranilla Banks, so the sailor's references to her seemed unimportant."

He tapped the papers with a bony finger. "After I saw the iron cannon, I remembered the sailor's account, mentioning the *Santa Ynez*. Unfortunately, I couldn't recall exactly what the man had said, but I thought it was worth another look. After I left here the other day, I got hold of my friend, Dr. Marquez, and asked him to send me the translation. His fax arrived just this morning."

"What'd it say?" Conn asked, still trying not to get his hopes too high.

"In his account, the sailor mentions his last sighting of both the *Santa Ynez* and the *Nuestra Señora de Rosa*. Apparently, it struck him how close the two ships were traveling together. He mentions saying a prayer for their safety and wondering if they would both end up facing the same terrible fate."

Conn could feel his heart beating. "You're saying that if the ships were sailing that close together, there might be a chance that *both* of them sank off the island."

The professor nodded. "*Isla Tormenta* is seven miles long. There is definitely a chance."

His pulse was hammering now, his adrenaline pumping. "Take a look at this, Doc." He moved around the chart, pointing toward the sandbar running south along the west shore of the island. "These shallows begin a mile or so south of where we found the cannon. They lie three-quarters of a mile offshore and run nearly the length of the coastline.

According to some info Hope got over the Internet last night, the *Rosa* drew eighteen feet of water, right?"

"That is correct."

"If she was running close behind the *Santa Ynez,* she could have been blown toward the sandbar and run aground. In a storm that bad, she could have hit hard enough to rip out her bottom. I think it's the place we ought to start looking."

The professor's pale eyes gleamed. "If the ship had run aground on the island itself, even with its few inhabitants, far more artifacts would have been found over the years. The sandbar could be the answer. It's far enough away that little of the treasure would have reached the shore." He smiled. "I agree—this is definitely the place we should look."

Conn flicked a glance at Hope and saw that she was grinning. "I guess we're going hunting," she said.

Conn smiled back. Treasure fever was definitely contagious. "Yeah, I guess we are."

Everyone was eager to get under way. They planned to leave as soon as their last passenger arrived.

"There he is." King pointed down the dock. "My son, Michael."

Conn stood next to Hope at the rail, doing his best not to notice how pretty she looked with the wind in her shiny red hair and an excited smile on her face. For days, he'd been haunted by erotic memories of soft lips and full, creamy breasts, of the way she had tasted, the hot little sounds she made when he touched her. Night after night, he awakened painfully hard, wishing Hope were there to soothe the ache throbbing in his groin.

It was crazy. He was working; so was she. For now, that was the end of it.

She spotted the boy an instant after King did. "Your son's going with us?"

The big man nodded. "The two of us, we live in Ocho

Rios. His mama gone. His grandmama bring him down and
sometime Cap'n Bob let him go out with us."

"What about school? Isn't he missing his classes?"

"Special school holiday. Besides, Michael is a very smart
boy. If he misses some days, he can make up de work."

She looked over at Conn as if she expected him to disap-
prove. His eyes followed the boy, tall for his twelve years
and already filling out in the shoulders. Conn wondered, as
he had a dozen times since Kelly left, if he would ever have
children of his own.

"Mike's a good kid," he said. "Someday he's going to be a
really good diver."

That seemed to throw her even more. "You're teaching
him to dive?" As if spending time with a boy Michael's age
was something he would never consider. He wondered how
low her opinion of him actually was. Or maybe it was just
men in general.

"The kid's a great swimmer," he said. "He and King have
been snorkeling for years. Michael's a natural at diving." He
flicked her a glance. "I take it you don't like kids."

"I love children."

He worked to hide his surprise. She was a newspaper reporter, a career woman. And men were definitely low on her
priority list. She didn't look like the type to be interested in
having a family. Then again, maybe she was one of those
independent-woman types who wanted the kid without the
man.

Conn turned away from her as Michael raced up the
gangway and gave his father a brief, manly hug.

"Did you tell your grandmama we would call her on our
way back?"

Michael nodded. "I told her."

"Good." King turned to Hope. "Dis my son, Michael.
Michael, this is Ms. Sinclair. She's writin' an article about
findin' the treasure."

Michael smiled. He was a good-looking boy, Conn thought,
lighter-skinned than his father, since his mother had been part

maroon and part Spanish, though Conn didn't much like his
hair, which he wore in sort of a short, dreadlocks style.

"It's a pleasure meeting you," Michael said in very proper
English. At King's insistence and though it was a definite financial burden, he was going to a private school and he was
a very good student.

Hope offered a hand, which Michael politely shook. "It's
good to meet you, too, Michael."

The kid didn't have a mother. She'd been killed in a car
wreck when Michael was eight years old. Conn could see
the yearning in the boy's eyes when he smiled at Hope. Conn
was amazed to see that same look returned.

Then again, maybe he'd only imagined it.

Father and son left for the galley, King promising the boy
a snack before supper.

The men completed any last-minute preparations necessary for their return to Pleasure Island and Captain Bob fired
up the big twin-diesel engines. They would get there late
tonight. In the morning, they would be ready to resume their
search.

Unconsciously, Conn reached into his pocket and his fingers closed over the coin. Maybe this time they would get
lucky.

It was late when they reached Pleasure Island. As she
stood at the rail, Hope could see the mountain in the center
of the island rising in the distance. Moonlight illuminated
the clouds surrounding the volcanic peak and outlined the
palm trees swaying along the distant shore.

She heard someone coming, heard footsteps striding along
the deck, but didn't have to turn to know who walked up beside her. She was attuned to Conn in a way she had never
been to a man before, as if they were connected by an invis-
ible string.

He didn't say anything, yet she could feel the tension running through him. She followed his gaze out to sea and saw

the cause, saw the lights of four other boats bobbing in the water near the reef.

"Son of a bitch."

He was angry. She wasn't quite sure why. "What are they doing out there?"

Conn's attention swung to her and she almost flinched at the icy look in his eyes. "You ought to know. You're the one who told them about the treasure."

"That's impossible. The magazine won't hit the streets for nearly two more weeks."

For the first time, she realized Joe Ramirez and Andy Glass had also walked up to the rail.

"Does *Adventure* have an online site?" Andy asked.

Hope turned her attention to him. "To tell you the truth, I don't know. This is the first time I've worked for them."

"Well, let's go find out," Andy said, and all of them trooped across the deck toward the ladder to the chart room.

Andy sat down at the computer and, using the satellite link, accessed the Internet. He typed in *www.adventuremagazine.com* in the hope their domain might be that easy to find, and sure enough, the site popped right up. Hope inwardly cringed as she recognized the title of the lead article on the screen.

Ever Dream of Finding Sunken Treasure?

She grimaced at the sight of one of Tommy's underwater photos of the cannon they had found, appearing on the magazine's front page.

"Well, now you know why all those boats are out there," Conn said darkly.

"God, I didn't realize it would bring them running like a flock of greedy geese."

He stared down at her. "You didn't think hinting there might be half a billion dollars in treasure ninety-five miles off the coast of Jamaica might attract a few people hoping to find it?"

Her chin went up. "If you read the article you'll see I never mentioned the amount of treasure that was supposed to be aboard. I said the *Rosa* was a Spanish galleon and that a lot of the galleons carried treasure. I said Mel Fisher had taken over four hundred million dollars worth of treasure off the *Atocha*. I also said it took him seventeen years to find the wreck and that he lost two members of his family in the attempt."

"People never think of the bad things that can happen. All they see are dollar signs. Those boats out there probably came from Jamaica. There are lots of other islands not that far away. Over the next few days, we're going to have even more company."

"Even if people do show up, you've got a deal with Eddie Markham. Any treasure that's found belongs to Treasure Limited—isn't that right?"

"That's the general idea. But how, exactly, would you suggest we enforce the contract? This ain't the good ol' U.S. of A."

Hope started to reply but Conn was already stalking off down the deck.

Hope ran after him. "Wait a minute! This isn't my fault! I was only doing my job. If you want to blame someone, blame your illustrious partners. Talbot is the one who suggested the article to *Adventure* in the first place and Markham thought it was a great idea. Be mad at them, not me."

Conn turned and glared at her, his blue eyes snapping with fire. He took a deep breath, let it out slowly. "You're right, okay? It's not your fault—it's theirs. But they aren't here and you are and you wrote the goddamn article. I'll say I'm sorry in the morning, all right?"

He started walking again and she just stood there staring after him, trying to fathom what he'd said.

He was mad. He knew he was taking it out on her— somewhat unjustly. She couldn't help smiling. She wondered if he'd really say he was sorry in the morning.

Across the water, lights shone from the windows of the power- and sailboats bobbing along the curve of the reef, treasure hunters drawn by her story.

The thought occurred that maybe she should be the one to apologize first.

Chapter 9

Brad Talbot descended the stairs of his small private jet, a sleek Citation he had bought just last year. He couldn't figure out how he had managed to get along without it. A warm breeze rustled the palm trees along the runway of the airstrip on Pleasure Island, and a few passing clouds floated by overhead, drifting out to sea.

Brad spotted Eddie Markham walking over to greet him, white suit, flowered shirt, black, slicked-back hair. They shook hands and the little Italian led him toward the canvas-topped Jeep. He might call himself Emperor Eddie, he might have some pretty influential connections, but to Brad he was just another greasy little wop.

"So what brings you all the way down here?" Eddie asked. "Or are you doing a little checking up on our treasure hunters?"

"Something like that, I guess. I was staying at the house in Palm Beach. I figured since I was so close, I might as well see what progress they were making. You had any news?"

"To tell you the truth, I've been so busy getting the work done on the new villas we're building I haven't paid much attention. They've been out there working, though. Except when they go back to Jamaica for supplies, they've been prowling the waters every day."

"But you haven't heard whether or not they've found anything yet."

"Chalko's been out there a couple of times. He said they found an old iron cannon, but it turned out to be off another ship."

"Another ship?"

"That's what Chalko said."

A little jolt of irritation went through him. Reese should have called him about the cannon. That he hadn't meant something was up and that something wasn't good.

"I think I'll make a trip out there, take a look for myself." Besides, he wanted to talk to Hope Sinclair, the main reason he had come.

"I'll radio Chalko," Eddie said, "tell him to get the Sea Ray fired up. You planning to stay for a couple of days?"

"Tonight at least. You got room?" A number of the villas constructed so far were luxury time-share units, privately owned, but only for a couple of weeks at a time. There was pretty much always room.

"I'll get one of the units ready."

"Thanks." Brad didn't particularly like Eddie Markham, nephew of the late Aldo Marconi, formerly a member of the East Coast mob, though that was part of his life Eddie did his best to forget.

The guy was such a glad-hander, Brad thought, always smiling, always after something. Money, mostly. Eddie had big plans for Pleasure Island. It was the reason he'd been so excited about the possibility of finding sunken treasure. The search would definitely bring attention to the island.

And there was also the chance he'd wind up with a good-sized share of half a billion bucks.

Which, of course, would appeal to just about anyone.

Brad left his luggage in one of the villas, then Eddie drove him down to the boat and Chalko took him out to the *Conquest*. As the speedboat roared through the waves, he noticed the other boats bobbing around the reef.

Adventure had e-mailed him their Internet link so he

could read the article Hope had written. People were already showing up. Eddie was probably ecstatic.

The Villas speedboat skimmed across the surface of the water. Both sky and sea were a clear, crystalline blue, and the white, foamy spray shooting out behind the boat shimmered like diamonds.

Standing at the rail, Hope pointed toward the water. "Look! Someone's coming out from the island."

"Brad Talbot," Conn said darkly. "He called from the airport, said he just got in. I guess he's coming out to check on us."

She turned and looked up at him. "What are you going to tell him?"

Conn just smiled. "Why, the good news, of course. That we've figured out where to find the *Rosa*."

He walked away and it occurred to her that neither of them had said they were sorry. But the moment was past and there were more important matters at hand. Hope wasn't looking forward to seeing Brad Talbot, though she guessed she should be grateful he'd thought highly enough of her work to request her for this assignment.

She watched the boat ease up to the *Conquest* and saw him step out on the boarding platform. He was maybe five-foot-ten, with short blond hair perfectly styled, combed back from a face that at thirty-eight years old had already undergone cosmetic surgery. He always dressed expensively. She was sure his navy blue slacks, white pullover shirt, and navy deck shoes were Ralph Lauren and not off the rack at Bloomies.

Hope took a fortifying breath, pasted on a smile, and went to greet him.

Conn spent the next few hours with his partner and one-and-only investor in Treasure Limited, explaining the progress he and his crew had made so far in the search. Brad was a little pissed he hadn't been told about finding the cannon, but Conn said they had wanted to be sure about what they actually had, and in the end, the discovery had provided a huge leap forward in their ongoing exploration.

"The good news is, we think we know more specifically where the *Rosa* went down and if we're right, the recovery will be a whole lot easier than if she had sunk on the reef."

He explained that the coral had probably overgrown the wreck of the *Santa Ynez* and that any excavation of the ship would involve a helluva lot more work, blasting to remove the rock-like substance.

"On the other hand, if the *Rosa* hit the sandbar—and we think she may have—she'll be buried mostly in sand. If there's treasure, bringing it up will be a lot less problematic."

Talbot nodded, seemed satisfied, didn't press for more information.

In fact, Brad appeared to be more interested in Hope than he did the *Rosa* or even finding the treasure. When she suggested an interview for her next *Adventure* article, Talbot jumped at the chance. Though Conn was glad to be rid of the guy for the rest of the afternoon, he found himself continually glancing toward the galley, trying to figure out what was happening inside.

He couldn't help wondering if Hope had told him the truth about her involvement with Brad, or if there was more going on between them than she had been willing to admit.

To hell with both of them, he told himself.

He just wished he meant it.

The galley was empty, giving them a bit of privacy thanks to King, who had shooed everyone out and then left himself. Brad sat across from her on the padded vinyl seat of the dinette while she set up her small, portable tape recorder and pulled out her old-fashioned steno note pad, which she actually preferred. They'd been at it for at least two hours but Brad didn't seem the least bit bored.

Why should he be? They were discussing his favorite subject—him.

"So . . . are you excited about the prospect of finding the treasure? Are you feeling reassured, now that you've actually visited the place Professor Marlin and Conner Reese believe the ship went down?"

"I've never doubted that we're going to find the ship—and the treasure. I've got a lot of confidence in those men. They've got years of experience and they're doing a really great job. Treasure hunting is a very tough business. It takes men of strong determination and iron will to get the job done. It can also be dangerous—which all of us know. We're resigned to it, willing to take the risk."

Hope fought not to roll her eyes. The only danger Brad Talbot faced was slipping on the marble floor in his bathroom when he got out of the shower in the morning.

"Well, that about winds it up," Hope said with a too-bright smile. She had kept him talking for hours, hoping to keep him out of Conn's hair. Sort of a way of making amends for the trouble she'd caused with the article. She hoped he appreciated her efforts.

"All right," Brad said, resettling himself on the seat. "Now that you've got what you need from me, let's talk about you."

Her head came up. "Me?"

"Sure. I heard you had to give up a story you were working on in order to take this assignment. I appreciate that, by the way. What was it you were doing?"

She sighed, thinking of Buddy Newton and wishing she had heard from that detective she had hired. "I was working on an article that dealt with closing down a retirement home on the south end of Manhattan . . . old people being run over by a big corporation. It was an interesting story."

"I read about that place in the paper. Hartley House, it was called, wasn't it? I didn't really notice the article carried your byline. Sorry about that."

"You read the *Midday News?* I would think that's kind of small-time for you."

Brad glanced away and an uneasy feeling started trickling down her spine.

"My secretary reads it," he said. "I pick it up off her desk once in a while." He gave her one of his practiced smiles. "The way I hear it, that old place is practically falling down. Fortunately for the owner, some big company wants the land and they've made the guy a very reasonable offer. The old man oughta take it."

"You think so, huh?"

"Yeah, I do. I think everyone would be a winner."

There was something in the way he said it that made her nerves kick up. "You don't think the people who want to buy the property would do anything illegal, do you?"

Brad leaned back against the seat. "Like what?"

"Like start the fire that burned up two of the apartments."

Brad shook his head. "Nah. You've been watching too many movies. That stuff doesn't happen in real life." He sat up a little straighter, his eyes locking with hers. "But if those guys actually *were* behind the fire . . . if they wanted the place that badly, then the people who are getting in their way had better back off. Guys like that mean business. You might want to remember that, Hope."

There was a coldness in his expression, a look of warning that sent goose bumps over her skin.

Brad cracked a smile. "But I said, those things don't really happen—except in the movies."

But his dark eyes said something else entirely. She couldn't help wondering if Brad Talbot was there to give her a message, the same message someone had tried to deliver by vandalizing her apartment.

Was it possible Brad knew she had hired a detective?

Was Talbot somehow involved?

Keeping her smile in place, Hope got up from her side of the booth and so did Brad.

"Well, thanks for the interview," she said.

"My pleasure."

Now that's the truth. "Will you be staying on Pleasure Island for a while?"

"Just overnight. I gotta go back in the morning."

He had told her he was staying at his house in Palm Beach and just flew down to check on the progress of the treasure search. But she wondered again if he hadn't really come for some other reason entirely.

His words ran through her head. *Guys like that mean business. You might want to remember that, Hope.*

"Well, it was nice seeing you again," Hope said.

"Same here. Say . . . why don't you come back with me to the island? The Villas has a great restaurant and a fabulous chef who cooks really gourmet food. We can have a nice supper, then go back to my place and listen to some music, have a couple of after-dinner drinks. Chalko can bring you back to the boat . . . if you decide that's really what you want to do."

Hope was already shaking her head. The last thing she wanted was to spend more time with Brad—or fend off his advances at the end of the evening.

"I appreciate the offer, Brad, I really do, but—"

"But you've got work to do. Yeah, I know. That's what you said the last time." It was obvious he wasn't happy with her refusal, but he didn't press her. He must have known it wouldn't do him any good.

"I'll tell Andy to radio the island," Hope said. "Tell Chalko to come and get you."

"Yeah, you do that."

She started for the ladder, had her foot on the bottom rung, when his softly spoken words reached her.

"Remember what I said, Hope. Don't get involved in something you can't handle."

Hope didn't answer, just continued up the ladder, suddenly feeling desperate to get out in the sun, away from Brad, and out into the fresh ocean air.

* * *

Hope waved good-bye to Talbot as the speedboat roared away, glad to have seen the last of him, at least for a while.

"I thought maybe you'd be going with him." Conn's voice drifted toward her as he walked up to where she stood.

"Why on earth would I want to do that?"

Conn shrugged. "You know . . . a fancy supper, expensive bottle of champagne, maybe a few after-dinner drinks in his villa. You two seemed pretty cozy. I figured—"

"Well, whatever you figured, you figured wrong. I told you before, Brad Talbot doesn't interest me. The truth is, I kept him busy as a favor to *you*. Not that you appreciate it. He's hardly fun company, and he's the last man I'd want to spend the night with—which is exactly what he'd expect if I went back to the island with him."

She started to turn away but Conn caught her arm. "All right—I'm sorry. I shouldn't have said that. I was way out of line. I just didn't like the idea of you spending time with him."

"Why not?"

"Because I'd rather you spent time with me." His eyes were blue and intense as he backed her up against the deck house, his hard body pressing into hers. One big hand slid into her hair, cupping the back of her head, tilting her mouth up to receive his kiss, which was hard and thorough, and incredibly arousing. Though it didn't last long, it made her sizzle all over.

She was breathing too fast when Conn stepped away, but then, so was he. She couldn't help noticing the thick ridge pressing against the front of his swimsuit.

She moistened her lips, tasting him there. "What was that supposed to be?"

"Just something I've been wanting to do. By the way, thanks for keeping Brad out of my hair."

"You're welcome."

He stared out over the water, following the path of the speedboat, which looked like a speck of white against the blue of the sea. "I guess he'll be heading home in the morning."

"That's what he said." She frowned, thinking of the warning he had given her. "It seemed like kind of an odd trip, even for Brad. I mean, he didn't stay very long and he didn't seem all that interested in the search."

"Actually, I was thinking that myself."

"He said something funny to me down in the galley . . . something about Hartley House. He made it sound like it was just general advice, a casual bit of conversation, but it sounded more like a warning."

Conn's dark eyebrows drew together. "What did he say?"

"He said he'd read my article in the *Midday News,* though he didn't know I was the one who wrote it. I asked him if he thought the guys who wanted to own the property would do something illegal to get it—like setting the place on fire. Brad, of course, said I'd been watching too many movies. Then he said that if they did have something to do with the fire, guys like that meant business. He also told me I shouldn't get involved in something I couldn't handle. It kind of scared me the way he looked when he said it."

Conn's frown deepened. "Are you telling me you think maybe Talbot is somehow involved?"

"I don't know. When you think about it, he's the guy who got me pulled off the story in the first place. Maybe he's one of the partners in Americal—they're the company that's been after Buddy to sell."

"It's possible, I guess. Talbot's got his nose in a lot of different things. I don't suppose you've heard anything yet from that detective you hired."

"No, but he hasn't had much time. If I don't hear from him in a couple more days, I'm going to call him."

"Good idea."

"Of course, I might just be getting a little paranoid. Brad would love nothing better than to play the hard guy, make me think he's more than just the spoiled playboy we both know he is."

"True enough. But when you talk to that detective—what's his name?"

"Jimmy Deitz."

"When you talk to Deitz, be sure you tell him what Brad Talbot said. He might not think you're being paranoid at all."

Hope checked her e-mail again two days later, but found nothing from either Buddy Newton or Jimmy Deitz. She got a message from Gordy Weitzman that included an attachment: a four-year-old article from the real estate section of the *Miami Herald*. It was a feature about Eddie Markham and the plans he had for Pleasure Island.

According to the article, Eddie had bought the expensive piece of property three years earlier. He was a developer by trade, a very successful one, or so the paper said. He had been contacted by the seller, whose not-so-grandiose plans had never come to fruition and wanted to retire. Eddie had flown down to see the island.

According to the *Herald*, Markham had fallen in love with the place, recognized its potential, and become the owner three months later. Since then, he'd spent most of his time developing the property and promoting the sale of his luxury condominiums, villas, and time-share units. But the article was four years old. The island was developing, but there still weren't many people living there, and there were lots of time-share units still for sale.

Hope couldn't help thinking that so far, Pleasure Island might not have lived up to Eddie Markham's high expectations.

Which was undoubtedly the reason he had jumped at the idea of searching for treasure off the coast and welcomed the articles she was writing for *Adventure* magazine.

She glanced up from the computer screen as a shadow moved in front of the doorway. "You about through in there?"

"Just done. Do you need to use the computer?"

Conn shook his head. "It's another gorgeous day in paradise. Joe's feeling housebound and so am I. We thought maybe we'd take you and Michael diving. That is, if you're interested."

She shot up out of her chair. "Interested! Are you kidding?"

"So you're up for it?"

"I'd love to go!"

"All right, then let's get our gear. We can take the Boston Whaler down to that area between the cannon and the reef. Who knows, we might get lucky and find something else off the wreck."

"I need to change into my bathing suit. I'll meet you on deck in fifteen minutes." Hurrying toward the ladder leading down to the cabins in the bow, Hope made her way to her quarters. She put on her conservative purple, two-piece swimsuit—though a wicked little part of her wanted to put on her very tiny yellow flowered bikini—and headed back to the deck.

Conn was waiting. His eyes widened when he saw her padding toward him and she thought he liked what he saw.

She certainly did. He was wearing just his swimsuit, not diving in his wetsuit, probably because neither she nor Michael had one, but he had told her the suits were great protection from all sorts of things in the water, including the cold deeper down, and he rarely dived without one.

He walked toward her and she tried not to notice how good he looked, but it was almost impossible not to stare at all those rippling muscles.

"Where are Joe and Michael?" she asked, trying to concentrate on anything but that flat, six-pack stomach.

"We're right here!" Joe called out, breaking into her thoughts, thank God. Michael padded along in his wake, tall and gangly now, but with shoulders that hinted at a powerful build more like his father's.

"It's a little shallower up by the reef," Conn said, "maybe thirty, thirty-five feet, and there'll be lots of interesting things to see."

"I can hardly wait," Hope said.

"You like to dive?" Michael asked.

Hope reached down and picked up the swim fins Joe was hauling out of the gear bin. "I'm pretty new at it, but I liked it the times I tried it before."

"Cuponya!" Michael said, grinning. "It means I am surprised and pleased in patois, the language of Jamaica. It comes from a mixture of English, Spanish, and African." She knew Jamaicans were proud of the language they had developed over the years. It was fun to listen to but difficult to understand unless you were Jamaican.

"You'll have to teach me sometime."

Michael seemed pleased. "I will be happy to."

King appeared on deck to help them get their equipment loaded aboard the Whaler and all of them into the boat.

"You do what Joe say," King instructed his son.

"I will, Father."

The big man only smiled. He didn't seem the least concerned about his son's safety, and when Joe and Michael went into the water, she understood why. The kid seemed at least half fish, cutting through the water with far more grace than he had on land, and way more at ease in his diving gear than Hope ever would be.

"Just take it easy," Conn said to her, drawing her attention. "Remember to breathe evenly and not to hold your breath, even if your regulator comes out or if you have a problem."

She nodded, eager to get into the sea, her lessons coming back to her. They all climbed into the boat and Conn fired up the motor. In the distance, the boats arriving from her article on the Internet had increased to nearly a dozen, some staying only a short while, others having been out there several days. As Eddie had hoped, they usually docked for a while on Pleasure Island before returning to Jamaica or wherever they had come from.

So far, none of them had given Conn any trouble, for which Hope was grateful. Still, she knew he disliked having them out there.

Today the boats were mostly off the south shore of the island, closer to where the *Conquest* was currently searching. It was quiet today along the reef.

"You ready?"

Hope grinned. "If you're waiting for me, you're backing up," she said, quoting Joe.

Joe grinned and Michael laughed. They both seemed equally ready.

"All right, then," Conn said to Hope. "Just stay close to me and you'll be fine."

Two of them sat on each side of the boat, facing inward. Hope pulled her mask down over her nose and put the regulator into her mouth. Conn gave her the thumbs-up sign, and holding their masks in place, they tipped backward into the water.

A barrage of air bubbles rushed past her. Hope felt good right away, light and buoyant, free in a way that could never happen on land. She moved her legs, stroking her fins back and forth, getting the feel of using them again. She turned to Conn and gave him the sign for everything is okay and Conn returned the gesture.

They started down through the water, Joe and Michael swimming a little ahead, taking it slowly, stopping to let their ears adjust to the pressure. Around them, the sea was a soft aqua green, the bright sun dappling the water from above, slanting down and making it easy for them to see.

This close to the main section of the reef, they swam past tall, chunky outcroppings of coral. She spotted a huge orange elephant ear sponge and saw tube sponges in blue and red and orange. High stands of soft gorgonian—sea whips, sea rods, and sea plumes—waved to and fro in the light current, and seaweed wove up through the rocky coral surface, hiding sea urchins, octopus, and an occasional barracuda. Great schools of small glassy sweepers darted past, so close she could reach out and touch them.

It didn't take long for Hope to relax, to breathe without conscious thought, to be absorbed totally by the breathtaking beauty around her.

A cluster of small, red-and-white jellyfish floated past, far enough away not to be a danger. Several large fish swam into range, but none of them looked like sharks so she wasn't concerned.

They stayed below for about thirty minutes, Conn pointing out different colorful fish and interesting coral formations. He was completely at home in the water and she could tell he was enjoying every moment down there.

So was she. So much so that it took a while before she noticed the shadow creeping over them, beginning to block out the sun. Conn took her hand and gave it a reassuring squeeze, worried as she followed his gaze toward the surface. He made the sign that everything was all right, that she shouldn't be afraid, but still, for an instant as she realized the huge shadow blocking out the sun was a fish, her heart nearly stopped beating.

A gigantic ray at least twenty-five feet wide, floated past above their heads, the most magnificent creature she had ever seen.

As soon as the ray moved safely away, its great wings carrying it farther out to sea, Conn pointed to the surface. Hope nodded and began keeping pace with his slow ascent. They came up right next to the boat and Conn tipped up his face mask.

Hope did the same. She looked at him, thought of the huge ray they had seen, and let out a big whoop of joy.

"That was incredible! I've never seen anything like it."

Conn was smiling, looking at her with undisguised warmth. "Giant Atlantic Manta. Devil ray, they call it, among other things. They can weigh up to three thousand pounds."

"Oh, my God!"

"I was afraid you'd be scared. I'm really glad you weren't."

"It was wonderful. Amazing! When can we go back down?"

Michael's wooly head popped up just then, Joe's an instant later. "Did you see that?"

"Are you kidding?" Hope's voice still rang with excitement. "I thought we were having an eclipse."

Conn chuckled and Michael grinned. "That was unbelievable. I can't wait to tell my father."

"That's good," Joe said, "because I kind of need to get back. What say we do this again tomorrow?"

Hope grinned. "Sounds good to me."

Joe looked at Conn. "There's a place a little closer to the reef I think we should try. There's a chance Mike and I may have spotted one of the *Santa Ynez* anchors."

"Great. Tomorrow we'll bring the portable metal detectors. See what else we might find."

It sounded like fun to Hope. She was here, though not by choice. She was doing all she could to help poor Buddy Newton. She might as well make the best of the situation, enjoy herself as much as she possibly could.

Conn hauled himself up into the Whaler then reached down for her hand. He took a solid grip and pulled her into the boat beside him. Skin brushed skin and a little thrill shot through her. She looked up at him, saw the heated look in his eyes, felt her heart pounding and the blood rushing through her veins.

Conn was here and so was she. Both of them were adults. Surely they would be able to accept their physical attraction for what it was. It was time to do what both of them wanted.

She cast him another glance.

Past time, Hope thought.

Chapter 10

Unfortunately, now that she had made her decision—assuming Conn really wanted her as much as she wanted him—sleeping with him wasn't going to be that easy.

She wasn't about to invite him into her cabin—not with six sex-hungry men aboard. She amended that, since Andy was married and surely Joe never went long without it. And there was Michael to consider, a curious, impressionable twelve-year-old Hope was growing more and more fond of.

Maybe she and Conn could get together when the boat returned to Jamaica to resupply. The rooms at the Bayside Inn weren't much, but any one of them would serve the purpose.

She would have to wait and see.

In the meantime, both of them were busy. The search for the *Conquest* was moving ahead, the computer plotting and replotting the grid, the sophisticated GPS system covering each section of ocean along the sandbar running parallel to the shore, but so far there had been no sign of the *Rosa*.

In the mornings, while Conn went over search coordinates, Hope checked her e-mail. A note came in from her friend, Jackie Aimes, telling her about a fantastic new man she had just met, but there was still no word from Jimmy Deitz.

Deciding it was past time to call, Hope borrowed the satellite cell and dialed his office number. A young guy answered who said he was Jimmy's assistant. Hope told him who she was and he put the call through to his boss.

"Hello, Mr. Deitz, it's Hope Sinclair. I was hoping to hear from you by now but since I haven't, I decided to call."

A long pause on Jimmy's end of the line. "Sorry, but this isn't an easy case and it hasn't been all that long. I'm working on it."

"Have you found anything out about the fire?"

She could almost see him shrug his shoulders. "Could have been arson. Fire captain doesn't think so."

"What do you think?"

Another long pause. "Like I said . . . it could be, maybe not."

"What about Americal Corporation? Have you found out who owns it?"

"Atlantic Securities, Devcon Development, and the Inverness Corporation are the owners of record."

"I *know* that much. I also know there's another layer of companies who own those three. I need you to dig deeper, find out who the real owners are."

"I told you, I'm working on it."

"So you don't know who Americal is. Have you at least found out what the potential buyers plan to do with the Hartley House property?"

"I haven't got anything solid. If I learn something, I'll call you." Jimmy hung up, disconnecting the line, leaving the phone in her hand. She silently cursed and set it back down on the table. It was only a few minutes later that the phone started to ring.

Hope flicked a glance at Conn, who gave the nod to answer it, and she picked it back up. "*Conquest.*"

"It's Jimmy. I'm calling from a pay phone in the lobby. I got a feeling my phone's been tapped."

A little shiver ran through her. "What's going on, Jimmy?"

A raspy sigh whispered over the line. "The truth is, I'm

getting a lot of pressure on this case. A guy came to see me, didn't give me his name. The people he works for want me to phony up the investigation. And they're willing to pay me— big-time."

For a minute, she couldn't find her voice. "So then it has to be true. Buddy Newton's getting shafted. The condemnation's nothing but bull. Somebody's paying off somebody to make sure he's forced to sell. It has to be that or they wouldn't be trying to stop you from doing your job."

"That's what I figure. I don't like the way these guys operate. I've never worked both sides of the street and I'm not going to start now. But the smart thing to do is not to let them know. They think I'm working for them and for now that's the way I'm gonna leave it."

"You think you might be in danger?"

"I don't think these guys are kidding around. But I'll keep after this, just the way I promised. Only thing is, I'll have to go slow so they don't find out what I'm doing."

Her heart was beating, thumping almost painfully inside her chest. "I think Brad Talbot is somehow involved."

"Talbot Enterprises? The Doormat King? *That* Brad Talbot?"

"Yes. He was down here a couple of days ago. I think he came to give me a warning."

"Yeah? What'd he say?"

She repeated Talbot's words, the phrase that kept running through her head—*guys like that mean business . . . you might want to remember that.* As Conn had suggested, Jimmy didn't seem to think she was paranoid at all.

"Like I told you. I'll keep after it, but don't expect miracles. Tell Newton if he's determined to fight these guys, he'd better be prepared. Whoever this is, they're playing hardball."

Hardball. The shiver struck again. "Thanks, Jimmy. I'll let Buddy know what you said."

"Keep my name out of it. Otherwise, I'll be dead in the water."

She hoped he didn't mean that literally. "If you've got something, call me. Otherwise, I'll phone your office once a week and you can feed me whatever false info you need to."

"You got it." Jimmy hung up, ending the call. As she set the cell back down on the table, Hope saw that her hand was shaking.

Conn saw it, too. He caught her fingers and wrapped them tightly in his. "I heard what you were saying. I guess you and Buddy were right all along."

"I guess so."

"I don't like this, Hope. Talbot came out here personally. He obviously has some stake in this and the guy has the kind of power to do something about it. I think you ought to advise the old man to sell. If he doesn't, something might happen. Someone might get seriously hurt, maybe even killed."

She bit down on her lip. "I'll warn Buddy. I just won't tell him how I know. But I won't talk him into selling. That place is his home. It isn't fair that someone should be able to just walk in and take it."

"Life isn't always fair, Hope. You're old enough to know that by now."

"No, it isn't. But maybe this time we can make it fair."

Conn didn't argue, but his jaw looked hard. "I don't like this," he repeated.

And she thought that for once they agreed.

They dived together again the next day and, as Joe had promised, found the ancient anchor, the artifact clearly stamped with the name *Santa Ynez* on one side. As exciting as it was to find something that old, they didn't bring it up. They had no real use for it and as long as it stayed where it was, the anchor would be preserved.

The time they spent beneath the surface passed quickly. Hope loved prowling the undersea world, swimming part of the time with Michael or Joe, but mostly with Conn. He always stayed close at hand, watching to be sure she was all right, so when Joe tapped him on the shoulder and motioned for Conn to take a look at something he had found, Hope didn't think much about it.

Michael was swimming nearby and she saw him dart behind an outcropping of coral and turned to follow. Michael made another turn, exploring the reef here and there, then his dive light illuminated what appeared to be an opening in the coral. Michael swam in and Hope followed.

It was a cave of sorts, she realized with awe, shining her dive light around, amazed by the beautiful coral formations and flashing schools of fish. A brilliant yellow angelfish swam past and she followed it with her light.

Michael swam to the opposite side of the cave, which was maybe twenty feet across with rough coral walls that grew together above their heads. She heard a soft sort of rumble, felt the water move around her, fanned the beam of her light again, turned—and saw Michael.

Somehow he had dislodged an outcropping of rock that formed a natural ledge about halfway up the wall. The heavy rock ledge and jagged pieces of coral sitting on top had tumbled toward him, landing on his leg and ankle and trapping him in between the rocks. Worse yet, Michael's hose had also suffered. In the small avalanche, a hole had been gouged in the tube. The air was rushing out of his tank, the hose filling with water.

For the first time since she had been diving, a tremor of fear went through her. The boy had no breathable air and he couldn't pull himself free. His dark eyes were wide behind the mask as he motioned frantically for her to help him.

Hope took a steadying breath and started swimming toward him, determined to stay calm, knowing she had to think clearly in such a dangerous situation. Michael took his regulator out of his mouth as Hope took a breath, removed hers, and held it out to him. Each of them remembered not to hold their breath and let a few air bubbles trickle out as they shared the breathing device.

Bending down, she tried to move the heavy rocks, tried to

wedge her foot under the pile, tugged and pulled using every ounce of her strength, but she couldn't even budge them. She tried to remove Michael's swim fin, even used her dive knife to try to cut it free, hoping that without it he could pull himself loose, but the fin was lodged as tightly as his foot.

She kept looking back through the cave-opening, praying Conn would show up, but he didn't appear. She set her dive light on a rock pointing toward the entrance, but there was a slight bend in the path leading into the cave and the light didn't reach the outside.

She glanced over at Michael, who seemed calmer now that he was able to breathe again. He was a good diver and he didn't panic, and with her there to help him, he was certain he would find a way out of this dilemma.

But minute by minute, Hope was growing more and more nervous. She didn't want to leave Michael, but they'd already been down quite a while and unless Conn or Joe found them soon, they were going to run out of air. She and Michael passed the regulator back and forth, both of them silently praying help would arrive, but it didn't look like it was going to happen.

Hope checked her dive computer, and seeing the time she had left, her decision was made. She would have to leave her tank with Michael and swim off on her own. She wasn't sure how far she would get on one breath of air before she would have to return for another, but maybe Conn or Joe wouldn't be that far away.

She unfastened the buckles that strapped her tank onto her back, slipped out of the harness, and signaled to Michael she was going to go for help. She would leave the dive light sitting on the rock, hoping it would comfort the boy, knowing it would be light enough to see once she got outside the cave.

Taking a couple of last, lung-filling breaths, she gave Michael's arm a reassuring squeeze and swam out through the opening.

* * *

Conn told himself to stay calm but his heart was pounding, thundering inside his chest. In the past, he'd been in some really tough spots in the SEALs and it was always his cool head and calm thinking that had helped him and his men survive.

But this was Hope, not one of his men—Hope and a twelve-year-old boy—and it wasn't nearly the same. God, how could he have lost them? He had only swum a few feet away, hadn't been gone more than seconds. But when he'd looked back, both of them were gone.

He signaled to Joe, who also seemed calm but was inwardly as frantic as he. They should have gone up by now. The cold at that depth was beginning to leach into them. Their dive computers calculated exactly how much time and air they had left and by now it wasn't much. Both Hope and Michael knew how to use the computers, knew how important it was to pay attention to the time. They had to be in some kind of trouble.

Jesus, he had to find them!

Joe moved off in a new direction and so did Conn, swimming through walls of coral, making twists and turns in the area where the four of them had been diving, fanning out a little, but not getting too far away from the place he had originally lost them. Where the hell were they?

Time slipped past. He rechecked his computer. The air in the tanks was down to the final minutes. They would have to head up to the surface for air, have to start free-diving soon.

His heartbeat pounded in his ears. He usually found the quiet around him tranquil, but now it seemed ominous and deadly. He saw Joe approaching, shaking his head. No sign of either one of them. Joe headed off, swimming even faster, his fear escalating as rapidly as Conn's. Joe disappeared behind a coral hedge while Conn made another pass through the tall alleys and plateaus in this portion of the reef.

As he swam through the rock-like terrain, his gaze continually searching, Hope's image appeared in his mind, her face glowing with the excitement of seeing the gigantic ray.

She had to be here somewhere. She couldn't die, he thought with renewed determination.

Not when he had only just found her.

Hope returned to the cave for several more breaths of air but their supply was rapidly being depleted and she still hadn't spotted Conn or Joe. They were searching for her and Michael, she knew, doing everything in their power to find them, but the cave was hard to spot and they had probably spread out to widen the search.

She swam back to Michael and saw that he knew how little time they had left. For an instant, their eyes met and held. She saw the fear in them, the heartbreaking resignation. His gaze remained on her face as he held out the tank to her, telling her to take it and return to the surface before it was too late. Telling her he was resigned to his fate.

Behind her mask, tears burned her eyes. She didn't need the tank, she told him, shoving it back into his slim hands. She could make it to the surface on her own. But she wasn't going up—not yet. She was going to find Conn this time, no matter what it took.

She reached for Michael and caught his face between her hands, letting him know she wasn't going to abandon him. That she was going to save him. But both of them knew time was up. One last chance was all she had.

She breathed in a lungful of air, whirled and started swimming. Conn was out there. She would look as long as she dared, then head for the surface for another breath of air. But she would have to decompress along the way and that would take time, and time was something Michael did not have.

Figuring her best chance was to return to the spot where the four of them had last been together, she pushed down hard with her legs, the big fins propelling her forward, and swam as hard as she could.

* * *

Joe's air had completely run out. He had headed for the surface, tossed his tank in the boat, and begun free-dive searching. Conn knew he had maybe a couple of minutes. He prayed Hope and Michael's tanks weren't already empty.

His heart rate had returned to normal, though the fear was still there, clawing at his insides, the terror that they might already be dead. It had taken sheer force of will to regain his steady control, but Hope and Michael's lives depended on it. These next several minutes would determine their fate and he needed his every thought to be sharp and calm and clear.

He tried to think what might have happened, what scenario could have occurred that would keep both of them hidden from view.

A cave, he suspected with growing dread, a place where they couldn't be seen. Had they somehow been trapped inside? It seemed more and more likely, and if that were so, odds of them dying in such a place were building with every lost second.

Conn's heart squeezed. He forced himself to ignore it. *Stay calm,* he told himself. *Find them.*

And that's when he saw her. Swimming with all her might in his direction, frantically waving her hands. She wasn't wearing her tank and he could see by the desperation in her face that she was completely out of air. He shoved toward her, forcing the powerful muscles in his legs to propel him closer, determined to get to her before she fell unconscious.

She realized he had spotted her and it seemed to give her a last shot of strength. She pushed the last few feet between them and then he was shoving his regulator into her mouth, praying he had enough air left for both of them to reach the surface.

Hope took a couple of reviving breaths, pulled the regulator out, turned, and started madly swimming away. She was leading him to Michael and though he wanted to keep her by his side, to keep sharing his air with her, he let her go, allowing her to swim as fast as she could.

They reached the cave just seconds later and the minute

they were inside, he gave her another breath of air. She breathed at his side as he moved toward the boy, instantly spotting the rockfall that had trapped him in the cave.

Hope took a breath and together they moved the rocks that were holding Michael's foot and flipper in place. The instant he was free, they all started swimming for the entrance to the cave. Hope picked up her dive light on the way out and Michael swam, holding onto her tank, while Conn and Hope shared the last of his air.

Though the dive was shallow, the surface seemed miles away. Both tanks went dry a few feet from the top, but they were close enough to make it now without a problem. Their heads broke the surface at the same time and a few seconds later, Joe's black-haired head popped up.

"Thank God," he said when he saw them, and there was no disguising the mist that sprang into his dark eyes.

No one said anything as they climbed into the boat, Joe helping Michael, Conn hauling Hope aboard. The gear came off, got tossed into the bottom of the Whaler.

Conn cast a glance at Michael, saw Joe pull the boy against him and give him a man-sized hug. Conn turned and pulled Hope into his arms.

"I thought you were dead." It was true, though he had refused to let the idea form in his head until now.

"I tried to find you," she said. "I swam and swam, but the coral all looks the same and I had to keep letting the air out of my lungs." She clung to him and he just held her. He was shaking, he realized. He had never reacted this way to a close situation before.

"Are you sure you're all right?" he asked, still holding onto her, refusing to let her go.

He felt the nod of her head against his chest. "I'm all right." She looked up. "I don't . . . I don't know about Michael."

Reluctantly, he released his hold, sat back, and turned to the boy. Joe was examining Michael's ankle. The skin was broken and torn, bloody in several places, but the cuts didn't look too deep.

"Anything broken?" Conn asked.

Joe continued his exam, moving the ankle around, checking the shinbone upward toward the knee. "Doesn't look like it."

Michael was okay. Hope was alive and safe. A sweep of relief went through him, hitting him so hard it made him dizzy. It was followed by a rush of anger.

He turned a hard look on Hope. "What the hell happened down there? You two were supposed to stay close to Joe and me. What in God's name possessed you to go off on your own?"

Hope swallowed and shook her head. "It all happened so fast. We only swam a little ways away and Michael saw this cave and I followed him in, and he must have hit something and the rocks fell, trapping him, and . . ."

She looked up at Conn and her eyes were bleak and filling with tears and he knew she was thinking how close both of them had come to dying.

He tried to hold on to his anger, but it was no use. Instead he hauled her back into his arms. "God, I was so damned scared. I've never been that scared. Don't you ever—ever do anything like that again."

"It was my fault," Michael said softly from behind them. "I knew better. I led Hope into that cave and I almost got both of us killed."

Hope moved next to the boy, leaned over and wrapped her arms around him. "It was an accident. It never occurred to me something like that could happen. We'll both be more careful next time."

Next time? Conn recoiled at the thought. Would she really go down there again? He wasn't sure he could let her.

"You saved my life," Michael said to her. "If you hadn't gone out and found Conn, I'd be dead."

Hope gave him a falsely bright smile. "We made it." She hugged him again. "That's all that counts."

They didn't say more as Joe fired up the outboard engine and headed the Whaler back to the *Conquest*. Conn dreaded facing King, but there was no way he was going to keep what had happened a secret from the boy's father.

In the end, after a long, fatherly hug and telling him how much he loved him, King grounded the boy for not staying close to Joe and indulging in the rash behavior that could have gotten both him and Hope killed.

Michael was safe. Eyes glinting with tears, the big man thanked Hope for saving the life of his son and it was obvious she had made a lifelong friend.

Once everyone was settled back aboard the *Conquest* and Michael was returned to his father's care, Hope slipped away from the galley and headed down to her cabin. She was closing the door when a big hand wrapped around the edge and pushed it open.

Conn walked into the room and the next thing she knew he was kissing her. Kissing her and kissing her and she was kissing him back as if she couldn't get enough.

"I almost lost you today," he said against the side of her neck. "All I could think of was how much time we'd wasted."

The top of her swimsuit came off as if by magic and his mouth fastened on her breast.

"Conn . . ." she whispered as he pulled and tugged, bit down on her nipple, took the fullness into his mouth. Hope's head fell back and her fingers dug into his wavy dark hair. "We . . . we can't do this here. Someone . . . someone might hear us."

"I don't give a damn who hears."

And suddenly neither did she. She wanted Conner Reese. And after what had happened, she needed to feel alive. She wanted to feel the beat of her own heart, the sweet pull of air into her lungs. What better way than making love to a man she desired?

Mercifully, Captain Bob fired up the engines just then, covering the little panting sounds she was making.

"There really is a God," Conn whispered, nipping the side

of her neck, his palms cupping her breasts, kneading them, gently pinching the ends. Pleasure rolled through her, hot and wild and sweet, and she wanted more.

She ran her hands over his body, exploring the muscles and sinews, the heavy cords in his shoulders, the ridges of muscle across his ribs. His nipples intrigued her. She bent her head and pressed her mouth against the flat copper disk, worked the tiny crest that hardened beneath her tongue.

Conn made a low, growling sound of pleasure and she felt his hands in her hair. Tilting her head back, he kissed her again, taking her deeply with his tongue while his hand moved lower, inside the elastic band on her bathing suit bottom. Long fingers skimmed over the thatch of burnished curls at the entrance to her core, slipped between the soft folds of her sex.

"God, you feel good."

She was wet. Slick and hot and on fire for him. She moaned as he began to stroke her, pressed herself against his hand. He slid the swimsuit over her hips and it slipped down her legs, pooled in a damp lavender heap at her feet.

Hope reached for his suit, urged it down those long, hard-muscled legs, then tentatively reached out to touch him. He was big. Thick and hard, smooth skin over steel. Her hand trembled as it skimmed over the heavy length jutting toward her.

"I want to be inside you," he said. "I can't think of anything I've ever wanted more."

"What about . . . ?" *Protection?*

"I'll take care of it."

She whispered a soft little word of agreement that still hovered on her lips as he scooped her up and carried her over to the bed. He settled her in the center of the bunk, then followed her down, kissing her all the while. His mouth was hot and fierce as it moved over hers, sending liquid heat surging through her. His skillful fingers found her again, slid deep inside.

"You're tight," he said, stretching her, preparing her to accept him. "How long has it been, Hope?"

She wanted to lie to him, make him believe there was nothing unusual in this wild mating. She simply could not. "More than two years."

The admission seemed to please him. He settled to his task like a man with a mission, and in minutes she was writhing beneath him, begging him to take her.

Conn just kept tasting and teasing, kissing and nipping, his big, clever hands bringing her nearer and nearer the peak.

"Please . . . " she whispered. "I need you, Conn."

His tall frame straightened above her. His eyes met hers, the most intense blue she'd ever seen. She felt his hardness at the entrance to her passage, and then he was surging forward, thrusting hard inside her. Hope's breath caught. For an instant, neither of them moved. Then Hope arched upward, wanting more, taking him deeper still.

She heard Conn groan.

They started moving together, their bodies in perfect sync, the pleasure so sweet she knew she wouldn't last long. She tried to hold back, wanting to heighten the moment, but Conn was relentless, pounding into her again and again. He filled her completely, seemed to absorb her into his very skin. It was as if he claimed her in some way, made himself a part of her. It was frightening, but also fiercely erotic. Her body responded as it never had to another man and she tumbled over the edge.

Her release hit hard, washing over her in wild, nearly unbearable waves of pleasure. She pressed her mouth against his skin as she cried out, but Conn didn't stop. Not until she'd reached another towering climax. Only then did he allow himself to reach his own powerful release.

Conn eased himself off her. He kissed her softly one last time, eased onto his side, and curled her against him. For long moments, neither of them moved. "I knew it would be like this."

She didn't ask what he meant. She had suspected such a

strong physical attraction would make for a powerful sexual congress.

Conn lifted her hand and pressed it against his lips. "What happened out there today . . . I've been on dozens of missions. I've lost men in the line of duty. I've never felt like I did today."

"Michael's just a boy, not a soldier, and I'm a woman. I suppose to you that would make a difference."

He stared up at the ceiling. "Maybe." Conn came up on an elbow to look at her. "You were amazing down there. You stayed cool in a really bad situation. And because you did, you saved that boy's life."

She shrugged, but she couldn't help being warmed by his praise. "I got lucky. I found you in time."

His eyes darkened. "Yeah, you did. But you went way too far. You should have headed for the surface before you ran out of breath. You were only seconds from drowning."

"I was just going up when I spotted you. I thought I could make it that much farther. I figured you wouldn't let me drown."

"Yeah, well, you took a damned big chance." And then he was kissing her again, ravishing her mouth as if he might devour her.

They made love two more times before Conn left her bed.

Later that night, the boat would be making its near-weekly trip for supplies. Hope pled a headache and skipped the evening meal, not prepared to face the rest of the crew after what she and Conn had been doing all afternoon.

She thought that he might return to her cabin sometime during the night but prayed that he would not. She didn't want the men talking about an affair that might end in a day or two. She didn't want them gossiping about her at all.

But Conn didn't return, and though part of her was relieved, another part wondered if he might be having the same second thoughts that she was having.

Chapter 11

The *Conquest* was docked in Port Antonio when Hope awakened the following morning. Outside the porthole, she could see activity all around her: a pair of local fishermen selling their catch of the day, American tourists taking pictures along the pier, an old man dangling his fishing line in the water. Several small black children ran alongside their mothers, who held up their handcrafted items for sale.

Michael's grandmother, a stout, gray-haired black woman wearing a bright-colored housedress, arrived late in the morning, happy to have her young charge returned. It went unsaid there would be no mention of yesterday's near-disaster. Instead, the boy told the plump older woman about the giant manta ray he had seen and how much fun he'd had during his stay on the boat.

Michael waved good-bye to his father and the crew, and Hope and the others waved back. "You do good in school!" King called after his son. "And do what your grandmamma say."

Watching him cross the parking lot to the old car his grandmother was driving, Hope thought of the young boy's brush with death and a soft pang rose in her chest. She had wanted children so badly. She thought she had found the ideal mate in Richard. Instead, Fate had a bitter lesson in store for her, one she had yet to truly get over.

"He's a good boy," Conn said, walking up beside her, his gaze following Michael's slim, brown figure as the youth disappeared into the battered old car. "I still can't believe how close we came to losing him."

"You were great with him. I didn't think you'd be a kid sort of guy."

One of his dark eyebrows went up. "Why not?"

"Are you saying that someday you'd like to have a family?"

He shrugged those wide shoulders. "There was a time I wanted one. Back when I was married."

"But not anymore."

He glanced off toward the water. "I'm not interested in marriage. I don't want to go down that road again."

Hope couldn't agree with him more. She had almost been married, almost had a child, but wound up with neither. She didn't want that kind of pain again.

"You could still have kids," she said. "You could adopt or maybe pay a surrogate mother."

He snorted a laugh. "Sorry. I believe a kid deserves both a mother and a father."

"Hey, a lot of people raise children by themselves. Ever hear of single parenting?"

"Yeah, but most of those people wind up that way after a nasty divorce. I still don't like the idea."

Hope didn't answer. Before Richard, she had considered having a child by herself. Women did it all the time. But she had kept thinking of her parents and what a happy childhood she and her sisters had been blessed with. True, her real mother had died, but her stepmother was terrific. As children, they had been lucky to be raised by such a wonderful couple.

She felt Conn's gaze on her and looked up at him. "What?"

"About yesterday afternoon . . ."

"That sounds like a movie title. So what about yesterday afternoon?"

Conn shook his head. "I don't exactly know what happened. I was just so afraid you were going to die. And so damned glad you didn't. I needed to touch you, to know for sure you were all right. I think you needed me, too."

"We were definitely good together."

"Regrets?"

"Lots of them. What about you?"

"I'm not sure."

She looked out over the turquoise sea, watched a big brown pelican plunge into the water after a fish. "I think we ought to slow things down, give ourselves some time."

"We don't have much time. That's the problem."

"True. But that's the way life is sometimes. Whatever we decide, both of us have jobs to do. We need to worry about that first."

Conn nodded, knowing she was right, but he didn't look too happy about it. As if to prove the point, Andy Glass walked up just then.

"Captain Bob's looking for you, Conn. We got a problem with the aft capstan. I thought maybe you'd take a look."

"Sure." Conn cast her a last, lingering glance. "I've got to go. We'll play this by ear. For now."

That sounded like a good idea. Even if the *for now* held a note of authority she wasn't sure she liked.

The day slipped past. Eager to resume their search, the crew finished resupplying the boat in record time and by the end of the afternoon, they were headed back out to sea. She didn't see Conn again until the crew started casting off lines and the boat began easing away from the dock. He'd had errands to run in Port Antonio. He had a job to do and a lot of men and equipment he was responsible for.

She thought of him as she stood at the rail on the way back to the island. Her body still felt pleasantly sore in intimate places, tingling when she remembered some of the things they had done. She'd been way overdue for some recreational sex and Conn had certainly filled the bill. She had been taking birth control pills for years, ever since her miscarriage, just to keep her periods regular, even if they hadn't used protection there wouldn't be a problem.

But any sort of relationship would be short-lived, a few more weeks at most. Neither of them was interested in marriage, or any sort of long-term relationship, yet saying good-bye to a man like Conn might not be that easy to do.

Not if she let herself get even more involved with him than she was already.

She would give it some thought, Hope decided, wondering if "playing it by ear" meant he would show up in her cabin that night. She wasn't sure what she would do if he did.

But knowing the way he could make her body sing, she would probably weaken and let him in.

They resumed their hunt for treasure, taking up the GPS grid pattern that marked the spot where they had left off. In this area of the ocean, the currents that ran along the island had sheared the underwater sandbar so it dropped off steeply. Hidden below the surface, for a helpless, storm-tossed ship it would be like hitting a solid brick wall. Though they were searching three-quarters of a mile offshore, the water along the edge of the shoal was only about forty feet deep, making it easy to reach anything they found.

Conn gave Andy a break and took a turn watching the monitors, checking the video camera and side-scanner, listening for the ping of the magnetometer that would signal a hit, alert for any clue as to where they might find the *Rosa*.

Assuming she was actually there.

They were moving south along the shoal toward the far end of the island, but taking it slow so they wouldn't miss something. Conn had been in the chart room a little over an hour when Joe came in to spell him.

"Why don't you go get a cup of coffee or something?"

Conn shoved back his chair. "Thanks, I could use a cup."

Joe had never mentioned the hours Conn and Hope had been missing below, but Conn figured his friend knew what was going on. The fact that Joe wasn't razzing him about it meant he knew the interlude had meant more to Conn than just a mindless round of sex.

Which worried the hell out of him.

As he left the chart room, his mind returned to the hours he'd spent in Hope's bed. As usual, Joe had been right. Hope Sinclair was one hot lady.

But Conn was right, too. Hope was trouble. With a capital T.

He replayed the nearly ill-fated dive that had sparked the encounter, how frantic he had been when he hadn't been able to find her, how terrified that she and the boy would drown. He had held those feelings in check and kept his head, knowing if he didn't, Hope and Michael's chances would be even slimmer.

Then both of them were safe and all his calm control flew out the window. When he'd hauled her into the boat and into his arms, something had broken loose inside him, some animal instinct that said she was his and clawed at him to have her. He had followed her down to her cabin and the minute he had touched her, kissed those soft, slightly trembling lips, he was lost.

He had needed to put his mark on her, imprint himself on her in some primal way.

It was frightening.

Terrifying.

Not even Kelly had affected him that way. Of course, Kelly had never come close to dying.

Conn told himself it was nothing more than that, an instinctual need to reaffirm life after a close brush with death. But even now, he wanted her. Through the open hatchway, he saw her standing near the rail and his groin tightened. Inwardly, Conn cursed.

"Hey, man! Come over here! Take a look at this!" The excitement in Joe's voice brought him back to reality. With a

Joe had never mentioned the hours Conn and Hope had been missing below, but Conn figured his friend knew what was going on. The fact that Joe wasn't razzing him about it meant he knew the interlude had meant more to Conn than just a mindless round of sex.

Which worried the hell out of him.

As he left the chart room, his mind returned to the hours he'd spent in Hope's bed. As usual, Joe had been right. Hope Sinclair was one hot lady.

But Conn was right, too. Hope was trouble. With a capital T.

He replayed the nearly ill-fated dive that had sparked the encounter, how frantic he had been when he hadn't been able to find her, how terrified that she and the boy would drown. He had held those feelings in check and kept his head, knowing if he didn't, Hope and Michael's chances would be even slimmer.

Then both of them were safe and all his calm control flew out the window. When he'd hauled her into the boat and into his arms, something had broken loose inside him, some animal instinct that said she was his and clawed at him to have her. He had followed her down to her cabin and the minute he had touched her, kissed those soft, slightly trembling lips, he was lost.

He had needed to put his mark on her, imprint himself on her in some primal way.

It was frightening.

Terrifying.

Not even Kelly had affected him that way. Of course, Kelly had never come close to dying.

Conn told himself it was nothing more than that, an instinctual need to reaffirm life after a close brush with death. But even now, he wanted her. Through the open hatchway, he saw her standing near the rail and his groin tightened. Inwardly, Conn cursed.

"Hey, man! Come over here! Take a look at this!" The excitement in Joe's voice brought him back to reality. With a

"I know, I'm backing up."

"I wanna go with you guys," Tommy said. "If the anchor's off the *Rosa,* I want some pictures of your first discovery of the ship."

Conn just nodded. The kid was all right—once you got used to him. And he was conscientious about his work, which gave him solid marks in Conn's book. "If you're coming, you better get moving."

Tyler took off like a shot, and Conn and Joe went to collect their gear.

They took a hand-held blower with them to move the sand out of the way, but as nearly as they could tell, the anchor had no markings on it of any kind. They dived the area all afternoon while the boat continued to search in a tight grid pattern around the artifact, but the only other thing they found was a length of iron chain completely oxidized and corroded.

Conn was tired by the end of the day and a little discouraged. He shed his gear and his wetsuit and put the stuff away, then went down to the chart room.

"Anything else turn up?"

"Not a thing," Andy said.

"Well, we found something, at least. That's more than we had yesterday."

Joe walked in just then. "Did you get any more hits?"

Andy shook his head. "'Fraid not."

"What say we call the professor, get his take on this?"

"Good idea." Conn reached over and picked up the phone.

Hope was standing on the deck of the *Conquest* the following day when the Pleasure Island yacht arrived with Professor Marlin. Ron Keegan and Wally Short came with him, two additional divers Conn had hired to help with the search. The men had hopped the island plane, then Chalko ferried them out to the boat on the Sea Ray.

"Glad to see you, Doc," Conn said to the professor, shaking his hand.

He turned to Ron and Wally. "Welcome aboard." The three men shook hands with obvious warmth.

Ron Keegan grinned. "I wasn't sure you'd really find anything out here. Looks like you did."

"We aren't exactly sure what we found, but after talking to the professor, we decided to bring you guys out."

On the phone, the professor had agreed with Conn that logically the anchor they had found was too far south to belong to the *Santa Ynez*. He was excited, convinced the artifact belonged to the *Rosa*. Still, the winds of time and fate were fickle, and in the ocean anything could happen.

"Ron Keegan and Wally Short, meet Hope Sinclair. Hope's doing a series of magazine articles for *Adventure* magazine."

"I guess that explains all those boats," Ron said, cocking his head toward the half-dozen sailboats and powerboats floating several hundred yards away.

Hope ignored the dark look Conn tossed her way. "It's nice to meet both of you." Ron was a tall, lanky, sandy-haired man in his thirties, obviously excited about the prospect of finding treasure. Wally Short matched his name, barrel-chested, short and stout, in a pair of baggy Bermudas that showed the hairiest legs Hope had ever seen.

"You already know Joe," Conn said to them. "You can meet the rest of the crew once you get settled in. Joe can show you where to stow your gear."

"Sounds good." Wally looked nearly as eager as Ron. Treasure hunting was contagious and these two appeared to have caught the bug. They took off after Joe, trailing him along the deck, while Hope followed Conn and the professor down to the chart room.

"I could be wrong," Dr. Marlin said as he looked at the video screen. "It might have come off the *Santa Ynez*."

"It could have. I have a hunch it didn't. Scatter pattern isn't right. Unfortunately, there were no distinguishing marks on it." Conn reached over and pulled out a stack of photos. "Tommy Tyler took these pictures." He slid the stack in front of the professor and spread them out on the table. "In this one, Joe is standing next to the anchor so you can get an idea of the size. It measured fourteen feet."

The professor tapped a bony finger on the edge of the photo. "Looks like a sheet anchor. They weigh up to two thousand pounds."

"We've searched the area, but haven't found any cannons yet. We're going to move farther along the shoal, see if we can get some hits."

"We need to start plotting the scatter pattern," Dr. Marlin said. "There are probably other anchors leading toward the sandbar. The stream anchor would have been dropped. It would have had a very long line. The anchor would have started bouncing along the bottom once the depth came up to two hundred feet. The captain knew the island was here, knew the reef protected it. He might have seen what happened to the *Santa Ynez* and tried to avoid that same fate."

A little shiver went through her. It was hard not to think of the people who had died in that terrible storm.

"They probably dropped their two bower anchors," the professor went on, "trying to keep the ship from being driven up on the shallows. You will probably find them scattered along the bottom in a line that points this way." He pointed to the anchor visible on the screen.

"There were six anchors in all. Let's back up, try to find another, or perhaps something else, a few more clues that will point us toward the ship's final resting place. If she was taking on water, they might have jettisoned the cannon. Anything we find will be a marker pointing the way to where we should look."

"I'm not crazy about backing up," Conn said. "Not when we seem so close. But I know you're right. Tomorrow we'll plot a new grid, try to pick up a cannon or something a little farther out to sea."

The professor just nodded. For the moment he seemed

satisfied. Hope glanced over at Conn. She could clearly read his impatience. He was eager to find the ballast pile, the actual spot where the hull had cracked open and the ship had gone down, but he knew their chances for success would be greater if they had more to go on.

His gaze snagged hers, caught and held, and she watched that impatience transform itself into something hot and clearly sexual. Her stomach lifted and her pulse kicked up. She wanted him, too, but she still wasn't sure of the consequences, wasn't sure that she could handle them.

"I need to make some notes," she said. "If you men will excuse me . . . " Turning away, she headed back to the deck for a breath of cooling air and a chance to clear her head. It wasn't until some time later that she went down to her cabin and went to work.

As usual, Conn thought, Doc Marlin was right. In the deeper water farther out to sea, the magnetometer started pinging. Beneath a dense layer of sand, the side-scanner outlined the shape of another anchor, not as big as the first, but with the shaft pointing in the same direction as the sheet anchor they had found.

Conn and Joe went into the water to examine it. It appeared to be brass, like the first, and was lying on its side. The end that had once been attached to the ship pointed toward the shallows, a marker of which way the boat had been traveling when the anchor was lost.

The ocean was crystal clear. Manatee grass and tall stems of algae swayed in the current, and several schools of French grunt darted past. A couple of big reef sharks circled around the men as they swam, but the sharks kept their distance and seemed mostly just curious.

Using the handheld blower, Conn cleared quantities of the heavy, deep sand, then worked some more, finally uncovering the anchor enough that they could get a good look at it. They made a cursory exam, then took another, more thorough look. And there is was, cast into one side of the long, brass shaft—*Nuestra Señora de Rosa!*

He couldn't believe the thrill that shot through him. He knew the guys were watching on the video screen and that they must be wildly excited, too. They had found their lost ship! Or at least definite remnants of it. The *Rosa* was there. Conn could almost feel her.

And he was determined to find her.

They finished their dive and returned to the ship, coming aboard to find a grinning professor popping open an icy bottle of French champagne. Several more corks made loud, popping sounds as Andy, Captain Bob, and the rest of the crew joined the party. Conn and Joe set their tanks and vests aside, stripped off their wetsuits, and joined Hope and the crew.

Conn took a long pull straight from the bottle and passed it to Hope. Her pretty green eyes were smiling as she lifted the bottle in silent tribute, then held it to her lips and took a big drink.

"You did it, my boy!" the professor said, slapping him on the back. "My God, the *Rosa* . . . after all of these years." Conn knew the professor had made the *Rosa* his lifelong study, though until the two of them had met, Marlin had never really dreamed of actually finding the vessel.

The professor stared out across the water along the trail where the anchors had been found. "She was probably in very bad shape after being blown so far off course. Leaks in the seams—perhaps the mast was gone. The captain would have known the island was here. He might even have tried to make landfall. Instead, she must have hit that hidden shoal and it was her death knell."

Unconsciously, he gazed off toward the island. "Those poor, tortured souls. How terrified they must have been. The ship must have sunk very quickly, since no survivors were found."

Conn cast a glance at Hope, whose features had gone from radiant to pale.

"It didn't seem real," she said. "Not until this moment. That huge galleon sinking, four hundred frightened people dying."

"It was a long time ago," Conn said gently, passing the champagne bottle back to her in an effort to steer her attention in a less painful direction. For all her bravado, there was a tender side to Hope he was just beginning to see. He wondered how deep it went and thought that it made her even more appealing.

She shook her head as if to clear it, forced a slightly too-bright smile to her face. "You're right—that was a very long time ago. We should be thinking about what you've accomplished—and what you might find down there. Today's a day of celebration."

That it was.

Conn had learned a long time ago to celebrate the little victories in life. In the long run, they were often more meaningful than those that seemed larger. They were on the track of the *Rosa*. They knew that now for sure. That in itself was incredible.

Still, they could be a very long way from actually finding the treasure.

The celebration continued into the evening. King prepared a meal of red snapper and rice, Indian kale, and roasted vegetables. The crew all ate together, crammed into the galley wherever they could find room, drinking Red Stripe beer and cheap red wine and laughing at the silliest jokes.

Spirits were high. The crew of the *Conquest* had already done something no one had been able to do in four hundred years.

Hope ate more than she usually did, but so did everyone else. Her ribs were aching from the quantity of food she had consumed and from the laughter. Tommy kept making groaning sounds, as if his stomach were going to pop, but when King started handing out homemade chocolate chip cookies for dessert, he was the first to grab a handful. The cookies disappeared in seconds, then Joe got out his guitar.

Perched up on the back of the dinette, he strummed away, playing a sort of Latin version of "Yo ho ho, it's a pirate's life for me," which the men began to sing with him.

All but Conn, who, along with the professor, had excused himself and gone down to the chart room to pore over the charts and maps of the area.

Needing a breath of fresh air, Hope slipped away from the others, left the crowded galley, and made her way up to the bow of the boat.

A cool breeze whipped across the deck. A quarter moon cast a silvery path over the water, making the sea look ink-black. Around her, she could hear the quiet scrape and occasional clank of the halyards, the squeak of the crane, the jangle of small brass fittings. It was peaceful out here, a place that helped quiet the thoughts running through her head.

They had found the *Rosa*. She would have to give the details in her next article, which might mean problems for Conn. But after they had found the anchor, Conn had felt obligated to call his partners and relay the news. Both Brad Talbot and Eddie Markham now knew about the discovery. Brad would want the publicity that came with the find and so would Eddie.

In a few more days, the world would know that evidence of a four-hundred-year-old galleon—once heavily laden with treasure—had been found off Pleasure Island.

The newspapers would speculate as to whether or not the ship itself would be found, whether the treasure was still there, and if it would be discovered. The world would know and not because of her. It soothed her conscience a little, and she couldn't help being excited to be the journalist covering what might turn out to be the find of the twenty-first century.

Footsteps sounded on the deck behind her. She didn't think it was Conn. Instead, Pete Crowley appeared out of the shadows.

"Nice night." He gazed at the sky as he walked up beside her.

"Yes . . . yes, it is."

He was taller than she had realized, and spare to the point of being gaunt. His eyes were as black as the sea and they sharpened as they ran over her. "You look real pretty tonight."

Unconsciously, she took a step backward. She could smell the peppery fish he had eaten, mixed with the odor of tobacco. "Thank you."

Pete moved closer, drew out a pack of unfiltered Camel cigarettes. "Mind if I smoke?"

"I thought Captain Bob didn't allow any smoking on-board."

He shrugged his shoulders. "We're celebrating, aren't we? Won't hurt nothin' "

But she knew neither Conn nor the captain would approve, and so did Pete Crowley.

Still, he lit up, took a long, lung-filling drag, let the smoke drift out through his nostrils. She felt his eyes on her again and unconsciously she shivered.

"I'm getting cold." Not the truth, but a good excuse to get away from him. She didn't really like Pete Crowley. The night she had accompanied the crew over to Willy's, Pete had gotten drunk and made a couple of lewd remarks. He managed to say them when none of the other men were around, then apologized the following day. She had chalked it up to the buckets of booze he'd consumed and the disappointment all of them were feeling, but she still didn't like him.

"Enjoy your smoke." She started to go around him but Pete tossed his cigarette over the rail and caught her arm, forcing her to turn and face him.

"What's your hurry? Why don't you stay a while and keep me company?"

Irritation trickled through her. "I told you I was cold."

"Yeah, well, maybe I can warm you up."

Anger tore through her as he jerked her against him and tried to press a sloppy kiss on her mouth.

Disgusted, Hope turned her head and pushed hard at his chest. "Let me go, dammit."

"What's the matter? Not good enough for you?"

"I'm just not interested." She shoved again, but his arms remained locked around her. "Let me go, Pete. I mean it."

It wasn't her threat but the sound of someone coming in their direction that convinced him to release her. His long arms fell away and she stepped out of his embrace just as Conn rounded the corner and came toward them.

He must have seen something in her face. His glance moved from her to Pete and back again. Hope said nothing. She didn't need Conner Reese to protect her. She could take care of herself.

"Hey, boss."

"Pete."

"Nice night."

"Yes, it is."

"Gettin' kinda late, though. Think it's time I turned in. Have a good evenin'." He cast a last glance at Hope and started off down the deck, whistling as he went along.

"I'm not sure I like that guy," Conn said.

"I'm pretty sure I don't."

"He's a good hand. Good help is hard to find."

When Hope made no reply, his eyes narrowed. "He wasn't giving you trouble."

"Nothing I couldn't handle."

Conn's gaze followed Pete until he disappeared through the hatch leading down to the crew's quarters. "I'll keep an eye on him."

"Like I said, it was nothing I couldn't handle."

Conn looked into her eyes for several long moments. Reaching out, he caught her chin. "How about this? Can you handle this?" Bending his head, he kissed her.

She'd expected fierce and hot. She got soft and coaxing, sexy, long, and deep. Damn, the man could kiss. Her insides melted like butter and her legs turned to taffy. God, she had never known a man who could slip beneath her defenses so easily.

For a while, she returned the kiss, savoring the fire, the heat that curled in her belly, the pleasure that spread out through her limbs.

"Let's go down to my cabin," he whispered against the side of her neck, taking nibbling little bites as he went along.

She could feel his arousal, iron-hard and tempting, making promises she knew he could keep. Her body softened even more, turned liquid and pliant. But her mind kept shouting a warning.

Don't do it! Protect yourself while you still have a chance!

"I don't . . . I don't think that's a good idea."

Conn's dark head came up. "Why the hell not? You want me, dammit—I can feel it. Let me make love to you."

She stepped a little away from him. "I need more time. I need to be sure I can handle this."

"That's what this is about? You're afraid?"

Her defenses went up. "Afraid? Are you kidding? I'm not afraid of you or any other man. I'm just not sure this is what I want." But she *was* afraid, and she knew it. And every time he kissed her, she was more afraid than before.

"I'm getting cold," she said. "I think it's time I went in." She turned away from him and started walking, her canvas shoes making a soft sound on the deck. Conn made no move to stop her. He was angry, she knew. He thought she was playing with him, using her sexuality to get under his skin.

She hoped he stayed good and mad. It was a whole lot safer that way.

Chapter 12

A storm blew in. The kind that only happens in the tropics. Great sheets of water dumped out of a hostile gray sky and the ocean rose up in huge, curling waves that crashed over the deck of the *Conquest*. As the boat dipped into a trough, a swath of foamy water sloshed over the bow and slid along the deck, making it nearly impossible for Hope to stay on her feet.

She clung to the rail, gripping it to steady herself, while she watched the fury of the storm around her. Lightning cracked somewhere in the distance, followed by the low roll of thunder. Still, she jumped at the unexpected sound of Conn's voice.

"What the hell are you doing out here?"

She hadn't heard him coming. Hope stiffened at the angry tone, nearly as harsh as the screaming wind. "I'm watching the storm. What does it look like I'm doing?"

"It looks like you're trying to get yourself washed overboard. Get back inside where it's safe."

A barb of irritation went through her. Hope forced herself to ignore it. "I thought we'd be heading in somewhere when it started to get this rough."

"There's a cove on the other side of the island. We would

have gone there, but the fuel pump is out. Apparently there was a problem with the diesel because the line to the second engine is also clogged. Until we can get rid of the blockage, get the other engine back up and running, we'll have to ride this out." He frowned. "You're not getting seasick, are you?"

"I'm all right so far. I've had a while to get my sea legs."

He used his body to block the next wash of water boiling over the deck. "Sea legs or not, I want you inside, out of danger."

It was hard to be mad when she knew he was acting out of concern. Besides, he was right. It wasn't safe for her out here. The argument on her tongue stayed where it was, but both of them turned as they spotted Joe walking toward them.

"Andy's making progress with that line, but so far, no luck with the fuel pump. Once we get the line unclogged and the second engine running, we can head for that cove on the other side of the island."

Joe's dark glance fell on Hope. "You ought to be inside. These waves can be dangerous."

"So I've been told."

"She's on her way down to the galley right now." Conn took a firm grip on her arm as another big wave sloshed over the bow and soaked her already-drenched canvas deck shoes. "You guys keep at it," he told Joe, beginning to lead her away. "I'll be down to help in a minute."

They made their way to the galley and King handed her a cup of coffee out of the Thermos he had filled before the weather had gotten so bad. With the violent motion of the ship, the stove was turned off. There was nothing hot in the galley and wouldn't be until the weather improved.

"I could use some help makin' these sandwiches," King said, and she figured he was trying to keep her busy enough to forget about the storm.

"No problem. I'll be glad to help." Working together, they whipped up thick bologna sandwiches slathered with mayo, country mustard, lettuce, and tomato. King kept a happy crew by serving tasty food.

Still the storm didn't lessen and the engine wasn't working. Hope poked her head outside often enough to keep her seasickness away, but with the ship wallowing in the waves like a cork in a bathtub, she was feeling worse and worse.

She wasn't the only one. Tommy staggered in looking pasty and gray, asking King if he had any soda crackers. The huge black man pulled out a box big enough to tell her this wasn't his first request.

"Man, this sucks." Tommy sipped at a glass of cold tea and nibbled on the crackers. "I wonder how long we're gonna be stuck out here in this."

"Too long, I'm afraid," Hope said.

Conn arrived in the galley just then, definitely looking unhappy. "We're going to need some parts for that pump. It may take a couple of days."

Tommy and Hope both groaned.

"I've radioed the island. As soon as the sea settles down, they're going to send out the Sea Ray. Eddie has graciously extended an invitation for us to spend the next few days at The Villas."

"Jeez, I hope I'm included in that invitation," Tommy said.

"You and Joe, both."

He glanced at Hope, who looked far better than Tommy. "Hang in there. If we're lucky, this'll blow over in a few more hours."

She nodded. "I'll make it."

"I think I'll just put a gun to my head," Tommy said, hurrying out of the galley and running for the rail.

As the day progressed, Hope got more and more queasy but she didn't throw up. Eventually, the storm began to abate and when Conn returned to the galley and saw that she was still on her feet and didn't look too shaky, he seemed impressed.

"You're a pretty good sailor, Sinclair."

She tried not to feel pleased. "Thanks, but I'll still be glad to get off this boat and onto dry land for a while."

"I don't blame you."

That night, the sea calmed enough so she could actually get some sleep, and in the morning the Sea Ray arrived. Joe and Tommy climbed aboard. Conn helped Hope into the boat and then climbed in himself. When they reached The Villas, the men were given one of the big five-bedroom, five-bathroom units to share, while Eddie Markham had given Hope the unit next door that she had used before.

"The part we need to fix the pump won't get here for a couple more days," Conn told her. "Once it arrives in Jamaica, they'll send it over on the plane. In the meantime, we might as well enjoy the island. How about a tour?"

It was late in the morning, the day stretching out ahead of her. She knew she should say no. She knew the chance she was taking if she spent the afternoon alone with him. Conn made no effort to hide the desire he felt for her. *I want you,* those hot blue eyes said, and the wanting never seemed to leave him. Hope felt it, too. Which only made matters worse. Still, as dangerous as it was, she wanted to be with him.

She gave him a smile that hid the uncertainty she was feeling. "I'd love a tour," she said and saw those blue eyes darken.

"Go ahead and get settled in. I'll pick you up in fifteen minutes."

"Eddie loaned you one of his Jeeps?"

"Finding the *Rosa* put him in a really good mood."

"Give me time for a nice, long shower. Thirty minutes and I'll be rarin' to go."

"Bring your bathing suit," Conn said. "There are some great pools not far off the road."

She thought of her tiny yellow bikini, imagined Conn seeing her in it, and her stomach contracted. "I'll see you in thirty minutes."

She knew she was asking for trouble. God help her, today she simply did not care.

*   *   *

Brad Talbot sat on the terrace of his impressive Spanish-style house in Palm Beach holding his cell phone against his ear. It was sunny, as usual, but a little too hot so he was running his misters, putting out a fine sheen of spray that cooled the air.

"Take it easy, okay? There's no way anyone could have known the old fart would hold out this long. I'll see what I can do to shake things up a little. Once things get handled, I'll get back to you." Brad flipped the phone closed, disconnecting the line, and muttered a curse. *Can't anyone do anything right anymore?*

If he'd known what a pain in the ass this would turn out to be, he might not have gotten involved. On the other hand, it was always good to have friends in high places, and the long-term benefits would more than make up for the trouble.

He flipped open the phone and dialed Jack Feldman's number in New York.

"Feldman."

"Listen, Jack, that old geezer is still holding out."

"Why don't they just up the ante?" Feldman asked.

"In his case, I don't think more money would work. I figure giving the old boy a little taste of what's going to happen if he doesn't start playing ball might do the trick."

"No problem. I'll have the boys rough him up a little. Give him the message in terms he'll understand."

"That's the idea, but you've got to be careful with this one. There can't be any connection to Hartley House or the offer that's pending. The old man just happened to be in the wrong place at the wrong time—at least as far as the cops are concerned."

"Not a problem."

"I didn't figure it would be." Brad signed off and clicked the phone closed. He was tired of this whole gig. He just wanted the old man to sell and the deal to go forward. He wanted his newfound friend to be happy.

And indebted.

There was a lot of money to be made on this. The more money, the bigger the debt.

Brad found himself smiling.

He would wait patiently for just the right moment to collect.

Pleasure Island definitely lived up to its name. The place was a miniature Jamaica, with lush green foliage and beautiful exotic flowers: water lilies, bird-of-paradise, bright red bougainvillea. The same high, rugged mountains rose out of the center of the island, covered by dense rain forests, and near the top, a circle of clouds cooled the air around the peak of a dormant volcano. Tiny iridescent hummingbirds darted between the branches of ancient banyan trees, and great cascading falls formed deep, secluded pools surrounded by delicate orchids.

Conn drove the Jeep along a narrow dirt road off the main route around the island and parked near what appeared to be a trail.

"Come on," he said, tugging her out of the Jeep. "You're really gonna like this."

It didn't take long to reach their destination. Walking next to Conn, she traversed a forest path spongy with moss and overgrown with leafy ferns. She could hear the twitter and chirp of dozens of birds and the low, steady roar of a nearby stream. They rounded a turn in the path, and the spot they came to was so lovely Hope sighed. The sound of frothy water rushing over the slick gray rocks at the edge of the secluded pool muffled the sound of the stream.

Conn carried a picnic basket on his arm, lunch prepared by The Villas' restaurant, Trade Winds. A white linen tablecloth was draped over the top and a blanket rode under his arm. Delicious smells rose out of the basket as he spread the blanket on the ground beside the pool, laid the tablecloth on top, and began setting out matching napkins, crystal wineglasses, and a bottle of chilled white wine.

"Looks like you thought of everything. I appreciate a man who plans ahead."

His mouth edged up at the corner. "Wait till you find out what else I've got planned."

She had a hunch she knew what it was. In fact, she hoped he planned an afternoon of seduction. She was tired of fighting her craving for him, tired of denying herself the pleasure he could give both of them.

They kicked off their shoes and sat down on the blanket. Conn set the basket on top of the tablecloth, reached inside, and took out cold fried chicken and potato salad, big, ripe strawberries, soft, freshly baked buns, and a pot of thick yellow butter. Two huge slices of white coconut cake with raspberry filling appeared for dessert.

"This looks delicious."

"Markham's chef is damned good. Eddie doesn't chintz on much of anything when it comes to the island."

She sipped her wine while Conn filled two china plates with food and handed one of them to her. In shorts and a tank top, he stretched out on the blanket, munching on a chicken leg, but neither of them was in a hurry.

Instead, they drank their wine and picked at the chicken and strawberries, relaxing more and more in their glorious surroundings. They talked about the treasure for a while, and then they talked about her job. Somehow she found herself telling him about Richard, though she wasn't quite sure how it happened.

"I can't believe I fell in love with such a jerk. I should have seen the truth. I can't believe I bought into his line of bull, but I did—lock, stock, and barrel."

"What did he say?"

"Oh, the usual. How much he loved me, how happy we were going to be. I pictured a house in Connecticut—you know, the white picket fence, the whole bit."

"Kids?"

The bite of chicken she had taken lodged in her throat. She had never told anyone about the baby she had been carrying, not even her sisters. She wasn't sure she ever would. "We both wanted children—or at least that's what I thought."

She managed to muster a smile. "At least two-point-three of them."

Conn laughed, easing the pain she was feeling. "So what happened?"

Hope began to clear their empty plates, putting them back into the basket along with the leftover food. "About two weeks before the wedding, I was supposed to go to New Jersey to do a family living piece centered around this quaint little town called Ridgewood, sort of a what's-it-like-to-raise-a-family-in-an-all-American-city kind of thing. Richard and I were living together by then. At the last minute, the interview I was going to do was cancelled and I went home early."

"I'm getting a very bad feeling here."

"I wish I'd had one. I might have been better prepared. Instead, I walked into our apartment and found him in bed with my best friend. I was so astounded, so totally unprepared, that for a couple of minutes I just stood there watching them."

"What did good ol' Richard do when he saw you?"

"He jumped out of bed stark naked. He was so flustered he didn't even think to reach for his robe. He said, 'Oh, my God—Hope, what are you doing here?' Like I was in the wrong place or something. He started saying he was sorry, that it was just pre-wedding nerves. But I could tell by the way they looked at each other that this wasn't the first time they'd been together, and it likely wouldn't have been the last."

Conn wiped his hands on his napkin. "At least that explains what you've got against men."

"I never spoke to him again. I never took one of his phone calls or anything else. I won't make that kind of mistake again." She took a drink of her wine and realized her hand was shaking.

"So what about you?" she asked, trying to shift the conversation away from herself and ease the tightness in her chest. "What have you got against women?"

"What makes you think I have anything against women?"

Hope laughed. "All right. I was honest with you, but I can see that you aren't quite ready to come clean. So . . . what will you do with your share of the money, if you actually find the treasure?"

Conn took a drink of his wine. Hope noticed the way one of his long fingers absently played with the glass, and her stomach muscles tightened. She couldn't believe just looking at a man's hands could do that to her.

"Even if we got lucky enough to find the mother lode, like Mel Fisher did, the money wouldn't come all at once. First you've got to bring the treasure up, bit by bit, and that can take a good, long time. You've got to get the artifacts cleaned up and identified and find people who want to buy them."

"Yes, but if you wound up with, say, even a couple of million, what would you do?"

"I'd buy a resort on the beach. I'd want a good-sized complex that includes a hotel and restaurants. I want to specialize in diving, have a diving school and boats that take people out. Someplace nice, maybe in the Florida Keys, or maybe down here in the islands."

"Sounds like you've given this some thought."

"It's always been my plan. I had a good bit of money saved up before I got married. Unfortunately, my wife managed to wind up with most of it."

"Didn't you have a prenup?"

Those intense blue eyes lasered in on her face. "Don't tell me that creep, Richard, asked you for a prenuptial agreement?"

Hope shrugged her shoulders. "That's the way it's done these days. Richard worked hard for his money. If things didn't work out between us, he wanted to protect himself."

Conn snorted a laugh. "He was setting you both up for failure from the start. Marriage is supposed to be a partnership, two people working together to build a future. If either party isn't willing to do that, why bother getting married?"

He had a point. It was certainly what she had always believed, and at the time, though she never let Richard know, his asking for that kind of agreement had hurt her very badly.

"You may be right. I kind of thought so, once. Still, if you'd had one, you might not be so bitter about your divorce."

"I'm bitter because Kelly went into the marriage with the same attitude Richard did. She was never really committed. Mostly, she wanted what she could get for herself and in the end, she did pretty damned well."

"So now we know what you've got against women."

His mouth edged up. "Not all women." Reaching over, he caught her wrist, hauled her down on the blanket, and came up over her. He started kissing her and she sighed into his mouth. The kiss went on and on, his tongue sliding over hers, their lips melding, teasing and coaxing and sexy.

The tank top left his shoulders bare. Her fingers dug into the muscles there and she felt them tighten. His hands found her breasts, softly cupped them. He unbuttoned her blouse and pulled it open, then looked down and saw the minuscule top of the yellow flowered bikini underneath.

Conn hissed in a breath. "This I've got to see."

She laughed as he helped her shed the blouse, unsnapped her shorts and buzzed down the zipper, then urged her to lift her hips so he could slide the shorts down over her legs.

He surprised her by coming to his feet and tugging her up beside him, then taking his time with a long, thorough perusal of her body.

"Sweet God have mercy. You're practically naked. If you wear this in front of Joe, I'll have to kill him."

Hope laughed, enjoying the desire she read in those fierce blue eyes. "You're drooling a little. Let's see if you like the view from the back." She turned around, flashing the tiny square of fabric that didn't quite cover the crack of her behind.

"Oh, yeah," Conn said. "I like it just fine. Why don't we see how practical it is?"

He stripped off his tank top and shorts and she saw that

he was wearing a Speedo, smaller and more comfortable, under his shorts. God, he had a body to die for, a swimmer's body, vee-shaped and solid muscle. The sinews across his stomach rippled as he swept her off her feet and into his arms. Hope shrieked as he waded into the pool.

The water was cool, but not cold. When he let go of her legs, she slid the length of his body and her toes curled into the sandy bottom. In this spot, the water came just above her waist.

"I love your bathing suit," Conn said, his eyes fixed on her breasts. "As long as you only wear it for me."

She gave him a flirty smile. "I'll think about it."

"One more thing." He lowered his head and started to kiss her.

"What's that?" She let her head fall back as his mouth drifted over the side of her neck.

"Don't expect to have it on long."

She laughed as he pulled the string on her top and it fell into the water. Conn plucked it up, tossed it up on the bank, then replaced the fabric with his mouth. Hot, tugging pulls on her nipple made her quiver. His tongue slid out, curled around the end, and she moaned.

She tested the muscles on his chest, ran her fingers through his softly curling chest hair, moved lower till her palm covered the thick bulge barely contained by the tiny swimsuit.

"That can't be comfortable," she said. "I think you had better take it off." She slid her hand inside the elastic band and pulled it open, freeing his arousal, and Conn made a low, hissing sound in his throat. She slid the suit down over his hips and a faint tremor ran through him. He tossed the swimsuit up on the sand next to her top and zeroed in on her bikini bottom, pulling the strings on the sides, yanking it off, and tossing it up with the rest.

Hope moaned as his hands moved over her flesh, cupping her breasts, moving lower, testing the springy curls between her legs, his fingers parting her sex and sliding inside. He stroked her all the way to a crushing climax; then, as she spiraled down, lifted her up, wrapped her legs around his waist, and filled her with a single penetrating thrust.

They made love there in the pool, a fierce mating that built swiftly to climax. Afterward they climbed out of the pool, up on a mossy bank, and lay down side by side. Overhead the sky was as blue as Conn's eyes, and not a whisper of a cloud to block the heat of the sun.

From beneath her lashes, Hope studied the man beside her, the beautiful golden-brown tan, the curly dark chest hair barely hiding the slabs of muscle underneath. Her gaze moved lower and she saw that he was as hard as he had been before.

"I think you need a cold shower," she teased.

Conn smiled. "Good idea." Taking her hand, he tugged her toward the pool and both of them slid back into the water. Naked, they swam toward the falls on the opposite side and Conn climbed up on a rocky ledge beneath the misty spray. Reaching for her hand, he pulled her up beside him and straight into his arms.

His kiss was slow and deep, a long, wet kiss that had her moaning. The waterfall thundered in her ears, even louder than the rapid beat of her heart. A cool spray washed over her and yet she felt on fire. She kissed him and kissed him, couldn't seem to get enough and neither could he.

She felt his mouth on her breasts, lapping, tasting, teasing. He lifted the fullness into his palm, suckled and tugged until her knees felt shaky. His hands slid down her body, through the thatch of reddish curls at the juncture of her legs. Beads of water sparkled there, glittering in the sun slanting down through the lush growth of trees.

She was damp inside as well, as Conn soon discovered. She wasn't sure how it happened, but she found herself turned toward the slick rock wall, Conn's hard body pressing against her back. Catching her wrists, he lifted them above her head and flattened her palms against the wall.

Hot kisses rained over her shoulders and along the side of her neck. Nudging her legs apart, he stroked her until she was trembling. She felt the head of his erection replacing his talented hands, then he was filling her, surging deep inside.

Dear God! Hope arched her back, lifting her hips, taking him deeper still, and heard him groan.

Conn set the pace and his rhythm caught her up, the heavy thrust and drag, the feel of his hardness inside her. The heat was overwhelming. The power of him seemed to surround her, absorb her into his very skin. One of his big hands slid around her waist, moved down to part the soft folds of her sex. He stroked her in rhythm with each of his heavy thrusts, his hips pounding into hers, skin against skin, the pleasure building until she wanted to scream.

Her body shook. Her womb contracted and she started to come. *So sweet,* she thought. So incredibly sweet she couldn't seem to stop.

She was calling his name, she realized, as her senses slowly began to return, repeating it over and over like a prayer, and Conn was whispering soft words in her ear.

"Easy. I've got you."

Tears welled in her eyes. It was ridiculous. Their mating had hardly been tender. It was wild, almost primitive. Perhaps that was the cause. He had reached deeper inside her, claimed more of her than any man ever had.

"It's all right," he said softly. "I'm not going to hurt you. You're safe with me."

The words slithered through her head like a snake in the garden, bringing a cold wash of reality. Men said those things to women all the time. They didn't really mean them. She closed her eyes, tried to close herself off from him, but Conn turned her around and gathered her up in his arms.

"You don't have to be afraid. We're good together, that's all. It surprised me a little, too."

She swallowed past the tears in her throat, began to feel like a fool. He was right. It was just that the sex was so good, so powerful. She had never experienced anything like it.

"I'm sorry." She managed a wobbly smile. "It was just . . . I wasn't quite prepared, is all."

Conn caught her chin, lifted it, and very softly kissed her. "Neither was I."

He slipped down off the ledge, back into the water, reached up to help her down. They swam back across the pool and climbed out on the mossy bank.

"I didn't think of everything," he said, looking down at the blanket. "I forgot to bring towels."

Still trying to get back on track, she made a feeble attempt to smile. "That's all right. We'll sun-dry, just like tomatoes."

Conn laughed. "That sounds good to me. But if you don't put something on––something more than that tiny bikini, I can't be responsible for my actions."

Her gaze swung toward him. "You don't mean you could—" She broke off as she realized he was already hard again.

"Yeah, I could. I can't exactly figure out what you do to me, but it's pretty amazing."

Hope felt a wave of relief. Okay, so maybe she wasn't the only one who was caught a little off guard by the incredible attraction between them.

After they had dried a little in the sun, she put on her shorts and blouse and began to feel a little better.

Then she thought of the intense emotion she had felt when Conn had made love to her beneath the falls, and all her old fears rose up again.

Chapter 13

The Jeep carried them back to The Villas. The roads around the island were narrow but mostly paved and the views were spectacular, turquoise water rolling up on white-sand beaches, the sea darkening to a crystalline blue farther offshore. As they pulled through the gates of The Villas, there were more guests than usual milling in front of the lobby, pool area, and restaurant, the beaches dotted with more people than Conn had ever seen before.

He wondered if the article Hope had written in *Adventure*, now out on the stands, combined with the stories of finding the *Rosa* that had started appearing in the newspapers, were responsible for the increase.

If so, he imagined Emperor Eddie would be pleased.

Conn sure as hell wasn't.

He flicked a glance at the woman sitting next to him. She hadn't said much on the ride back to The Villas. He had a hunch she was running scared again. In a way, he didn't blame her. He couldn't remember having a more powerful sexual encounter with a woman.

And he was afraid it wasn't just body chemistry that made the attraction between them so strong.

He was pondering the notion when he pulled down the

lane that led to the units they were occupying and noticed another of the island Jeeps driving up in front. Hope's villa sat next to his. Conn pulled up there and turned off the engine.

"Looks like you've got company." Hope was staring at the Jeep.

Conn followed her gaze to the tall, statuesque blonde who climbed out of the passenger side and started walking toward him. For an instant, he figured she was one of Joe's numerous conquests. Then she turned, flashed a perfect white smile and an astonishing set of dimples. Conn cursed.

"Conn! Conner! Hey, Conn, it's me!" The blonde started toward them, waving and smiling, obviously glad to see him.

"Old friend?" Hope asked, a burnished eyebrow arching up. Her expression, stiff before, had turned completely to stone.

"I guess you could say that. Listen, Hope—"

"Conner!" Gloria Rothman rushed toward Conn's side of the Jeep. Hoping to head her off, he climbed out as she approached.

"Oh, Conn, I'm so glad to see you!" Glory threw her arms around his neck and gave him the female version of a body slam. "I missed you so much!" Then her lips covered his in what was meant to be a steamy kiss. Conn grabbed her arms and tried to pull himself free, but she hung on like a leech.

"Cut it out, Glory!" He was finally able to extricate himself by holding her arms down to her sides. "For God's sake, what are you doing here?"

She looked crestfallen. "Aren't you glad to see me?"

"Well . . . sure I am, but . . . " From the corner of his eye, he saw Hope walking rigidly toward her villa, and he swore a silent oath. "The problem is, since I didn't know you were coming, I made plans with someone else."

"Someone else?" Her big brown eyes went huge. "What do you mean, *someone else?*"

"Listen, Glory, there was never anything exclusive about

our relationship—you know that. We only went out for a couple of weeks, just while you were in Jamaica on vacation. We had a lot of fun, but I wasn't even sure I'd ever see you again."

Fun meaning they had spent most of the time in bed. Glory was twenty-seven, beautiful, and bored. She came from a wealthy Jewish family who lived in Florida. By the time he met Glory, Kelly had been gone for months and he had badly needed some sexual relief. Glory was definitely good for that.

He heard the front door of Hope's villa open and slam closed. *Son of a bitch.*

"I thought you'd be glad to see me," Glory said, her bottom lip quivering. "I thought I would surprise you."

He took hold of her slim shoulders. "Look, Glory. I never meant to hurt you. If things were different . . . if I'd known you were coming, I could have made other plans. As it is, at least for the time being, I'm committed somewhere else."

She sniffed, stuck her perfect little nose into the air. "I can't leave until tomorrow. I'll have to stay with you until then."

"I'll talk to Eddie, find another place for you to stay."

"All of the units are full. They told me so when I called. I didn't think I'd need a place to stay. I was planning to come out to the boat."

"The boat's under repair." He looked at Glory, but his mind was on Hope. *Damn.* After that bastard, Richard, she was bound to be thinking the worst.

Glory's eyes welled with tears. "What am I going to do? I can't believe you don't want me anymore."

Conn sighed. He cast a glance toward the unit he was staying in. There were five big bedroom suites. They were only using three. "All right, you can spend the night. But you're going back on tomorrow's plane."

The tears were gone in a heartbeat, replaced by a bright, triumphant smile. "I knew you'd change your mind. I'll just go unpack." She grabbed the handle of the carry-on Chalko had set on the sidewalk in front of the villa and started wheeling it toward the house.

Conn swore under his breath and started walking toward the unit next to his.

Hope heard the determined pounding. For a minute she thought the sound was the ringing in her head. She had a monster of a headache, getting worse by the minute. It had started when she'd seen Conn kiss the blonde.

The noise grew louder, more insistent. "I'm not going away until I talk to you, so you might as well let me in."

It was Conn. She didn't want to talk to him. She knew the kind of things he would say, the things men always said. "Go away!"

Conn said a dirty word she would rather not have heard.

The pounding stopped. Several seconds passed. She heard the thud of his deck shoes hitting the ground on this side of the patio wall, then the whoosh of the sheer white curtains as he strode into the living room.

"I've got something to say and you're going to listen."

"Get out of here before I call security."

His mouth curved into a nasty smile. "Go ahead. Right now I can't think of anything I'd like more than to get into a good, old-fashioned brawl with a couple of security guards."

A thread of uneasiness slid through her. He was an ex-Navy SEAL. He could certainly handle any of the men who worked on the island.

She turned her back on him. "Say what you have to say and get out."

Conn moved behind her, took a solid grip on her shoulders, and forcibly turned her around. "I went out with Glory when I first got to Jamaica. We dated for a couple of weeks while she was here with her girlfriend on vacation. That's all there is to it. She went back to Florida and I stayed here. I had no idea she was going to show up on Pleasure Island."

"Fine. Unfortunately, that doesn't change the fact that

she's here now and she expects you to . . . to . . . *entertain* her."

"I don't want to *entertain* her. She's going back where she came from and that'll be the end of it."

"She's leaving?"

"Yes."

"When?"

"On tomorrow's plane."

She gave him a tight, knowing smile. "And in the meantime, I'll bet she just has to stay with you. Right?"

"Goddamn it, Hope! I don't want her here at all, but the rest of the villas are full and she has to stay somewhere. Unless you want her staying with you."

"Oh, no. No, thanks. She's *your* friend. You deal with her."

"Fine. I'll remember you said that." Turning, he stalked toward the door. When he reached it, he stopped and turned. "I'm not interested in Gloria Rothman. I'm interested in you. Maybe that's what you're really worried about."

Lifting the wrought iron latch, he strode out, slamming the heavy wooden door behind him.

Hope just stood there. This afternoon Conn had made passionate love to her. Now he was spending the night with another woman. She told herself she should have known something like this would happen. That was just the way men were.

But her chest was aching, her stomach twisted into a baseball-size knot.

Hope swallowed the tears in her throat and willed herself not to cry.

Women. Joe Ramirez watched the blond bombshell throwing herself at Conn and shook his head. Conn wasn't interested. Couldn't she see that? She was a beautiful girl. Spoiled, for sure, a little bit selfish. But there was something sweet about her.

Angry when she wouldn't leave him alone, Conn had

slammed out of the villa. Joe figured he'd go off someplace where he wouldn't have to think about anything remotely connected to the opposite sex. Across the room, the girl, Glory, sat in a wicker chair staring out the window toward the beach. She was pouting, furious she hadn't gotten her way with Conn.

Joe inwardly grinned. A Cuban man would probably put her over his knee. He got up from his chair and sauntered toward her, propped his shoulder against the wall a couple of feet away.

"Odds are, he won't be back till late—if he comes back at all. You want to go get something to eat?"

She shook her head, blond hair swinging from her make-shift ponytail.

"You know, you two only dated for a couple of weeks. He doesn't owe you anything. You don't owe him anything, either."

Her attention lifted to his face. "What do you mean?"

"I mean, I think you're a beautiful woman and if I were Conn, I'd love to spend the night with you. But Conn's met someone. He's involved with a woman he cares about. Sometimes things like that happen."

"But we had so much fun together. I thought he really felt something for me. That's why I came to see him."

Joe shook his head. "I don't think so. I think you just got bored. You wanted to play and you thought Conn would want to play, too."

He reached down and caught her hand, tugged her to her feet. "Why don't the two of us play instead? It's going to be a fabulous night. They'll have a steel band playing on the terrace. We could get some supper, then take a walk on the beach."

She bit her lip, plump and a pretty pink color. Joe felt a tightening in his groin.

"I don't know . . ."

"There's a little sailboat out there on the sand. I could take you out for a midnight sail if you like."

Glory looked at him and for the first time she actually

seemed to see him. "You're a really good-looking guy, Joe. Maybe if I went out with you, it would make Conn jealous."

She seemed so hopeful he almost smiled. "I don't think so." He lifted her hand to his lips, pressed his mouth against her fingers. "But I do think we'd have a good time. I bet you wouldn't even think about Conn. You might even be glad you came here."

She eased her hand away, looked at the spot where his lips had been, then gave him a tentative smile. "I think, Joe Ramirez, you could be even more of a heartbreaker than Conn."

Joe looked into those deep brown eyes and felt as if he could get lost in them. "You know what I think? I think if you tried, you could break any man's heart you wanted."

Glory studied him for several long moments, took a long, deep breath and let it out slowly. When she smiled, he felt this funny little pinch in his chest.

"All right, Joe, let's go out and play."

Conn spent the night on the beach. It wasn't the first time, probably wouldn't be the last. He told himself it had nothing to do with Hope, nothing to do with the fact that he didn't want her thinking he had spent the night with Glory. It was just that he was pissed at women in general and he needed a little space.

By the time he got back to the villa the following day, Joe was up and gone and so was Glory. Tommy Tyler came stumbling out of one of the bedrooms, scratching the curly red hair on his skinny chest.

"You just get in?" Tommy asked, yawning.

"I figured I was safer on the beach than I was in here."

"I think Joe kept her occupied."

"Sounds like Joe."

The telephone rang just then. Conn picked up the receiver, heard the voice of the woman at the front desk on the other end of the line.

"I'm supposed to tell you the new part you needed for the boat came in early. The plane is bringing it back with them this afternoon."

Well, at least there was some good news. "Has the plane left yet for Jamaica?"

"They'll be taking off in just a few minutes."

"Thanks." Conn hung up the phone, thinking of Glory, hoping she was with Joe and he was putting her on that plane.

Instead the front door slammed open and the laughter of a familiar female voice floated into the living room. Glory and Joe walked through the foyer, past the big, leafy planter overflowing with tropical greenery, across the deep cream carpet, stopping right in front of him.

"Morning," Joe said.

Conn looked over at Glory, who was staring up at Joe with that same doe-eyed expression she had formerly reserved for him. "I thought you were leaving."

"I talked her into staying one more night," Joe said, looking damn near as starry-eyed as Glory.

"Yeah, well, the part we need for the fuel pump is coming in on the plane this afternoon. We'll be taking it back to the boat as soon as it gets here."

"We're about due to resupply. When do you plan to head back to Jamaica?"

"I'd like to get in at least another day's work before we leave." He looked at Joe, clearly reading his mind. "And we won't be in Jamaica overnight."

Joe turned to Glory. "If you stay here tonight, you could ride back on the boat when we go. And we'd have most of today together. What do you say?"

Ride back on the boat? Conn wanted to strangle Joe.

Instead, he left them to work out the details and went in to shower and shave. Once he had dressed in a clean pair of navy blue shorts and a loose-fitting shirt, he felt better.

Which was good, because there was something he needed to do.

Conn left his villa and headed for the villa next door.

* * *

Hope turned at the sound of the front door opening and closing, saw Conn walk into the entry. "You left the door unlocked. I don't care where you are, it's not a good idea."

"No kidding. You never know what kind of lowlife might come waltzing in."

His jaw hardened. "If that crack is supposed to piss me off, it does. I don't know what you're thinking, but I can pretty much guess. The truth is, I've been straight with you from the start, Hope. I've never lied to you about anything and that includes Glory Rothman."

"Speaking of whom, did the two of you enjoy yourselves last night?"

His gaze sharpened. She knew she was making him angry but she didn't really care.

"For your information, I didn't see Glory last night. She spent the evening with Joe. Apparently, she's over her crush on me and now she's after him."

"Jealous, are we?"

Conn's blue eyes hardened. He stalked toward her, caught her shoulders and hauled her against him. "I'm not a damned bit jealous of Joe and Glory. If anything, I'm grateful. The only thing I did wrong last night was not come over here and haul you into bed. You would have known exactly where I was and you wouldn't have been thinking about anything but how good it feels when I'm inside you."

Conn's hands slid into her hair. Hope gasped as he tilted her head back and his mouth crushed down over hers. It was a wild, possessive kiss that still held a trace of anger. She was angry herself, furious that she cared what Conner Reese had done last night.

She tried to pull away, pushed against his chest, but he didn't even budge. Instead, his mouth moved over hers, the kiss softened, and heat enveloped her. She found herself clinging to his shoulders, kissing him back as wildly as he was kissing her.

She didn't resist when he lifted her into his arms and carried her into the bedroom, settled her in the middle of the king-size bed. They made passionate love, then made love again. Afterward they lay naked, their legs entwined on the white eyelet comforter, watching the ceiling fan go around.

She felt pleasantly sated, her body completely relaxed. Sex with Conn was amazing. Incredible. Still, she couldn't stop thinking of the woman who had rushed into his arms the day before. She kept seeing Richard with Sherry, thinking of the lies he had told, the awful betrayal she had felt.

The baby she had lost.

Conn was a man and he was only human. How long would it be before the same thing happened with him?

"I wish I could stay here all day," he said, running a finger along her cheek. "But I think I hear the plane coming back, which means I've got work to do." He leaned down for a last, lingering kiss, climbed out of bed, and padded naked into the bathroom. She heard the shower running. He was dressed when he came back out.

"You can stay in the villa another night if you want. Eddie doesn't have anyone booked for this unit until tomorrow. The boat should be up and running this afternoon. We'll work the rest of the day and all day tomorrow, then leave for Jamaica tomorrow evening to resupply. You can have Chalko bring you out before we go."

"All right." She smoothed the comforter, which she had climbed beneath. "Since this is possibly the greatest bed I've ever slept in, I'll stay right here." Besides, she needed some time away from him, needed to get her head on straight about where their relationship was going.

Nowhere, she reminded herself. This was only a fling. She wasn't interested in a long-term relationship and neither was Conn.

She watched him leave, heard the door close, and headed for the shower. She had work to do herself. She needed to get back to writing the second article in the series for *Adventure* magazine. A beautiful villa overlooking the Caribbean Sea was the perfect place to do it.

As long as she could keep her mind off Conn.

* * *

The boat was running again, the fuel problem solved. They ran the grid pattern all of the following day, but got no interesting mag hits, so that night they headed for Jamaica. Since Joe bunked in with the crew, Glory had decided to return on the plane—Conn silently thanked God for that—but she was meeting Joe when the boat got in.

Hope was back aboard, but it was clear he wouldn't be spending any time in her cabin. It didn't take a Rhodes scholar to sense her change of attitude where he was concerned, the distance she was determined to put between them.

Considering it would be a whole lot better for him if their relationship cooled down a little, the brain part of him should have been glad. But neither his body nor his brain was pleased, which had him worrying again.

Fortunately, he had plenty of work to do to keep his mind off Hope Sinclair.

They finished restocking the boat in Jamaica and returned to Pleasure Island late in the day. The following morning, they resumed their search, beginning at the spot on the grid where they had left off, moving south along the sandbar.

It was late in the afternoon when the magnetometer started pinging. Andy Glass came up on the deck to bring Conn the news.

"I can't tell for sure, but I think we've found one of the cannons . . . maybe more than one."

His adrenaline kicked up. "Let's go take a look."

They returned to the chart room, walked over to the sonar scanner, and sure enough, outlined on the monitor was an image shaped remarkably like a cannon. On the video screen, zeroed in on a spot a few yards away, there appeared to be another.

Cautious excitement filled him. "I'm going down."

Leaving the chart room, Conn went in search of Joe. "Looks like we found something. Let's get suited up and take a look."

"Great. Any idea what it is?"

"Cannon, looks like."

"How deep?"

"Just under sixty feet."

"All right!" Joe smiled for the first time since they had left Jamaica. Conn didn't ask what had happened to put him in such a dismal mood, but he figured it had something to do with his newest lady love.

Conn was standing next to Joe in front of the diving locker pulling on his wetsuit, when Hope and Tommy appeared on deck.

"I hear you found a couple of cannons," she said.

"Could be. We'll know more after we get a look."

"I'll keep my fingers crossed."

"Thanks." Conn turned to Ron Keegan, who had come up on deck with Wally Short. "If those cannons turn out to be bronze, they're likely off the *Rosa.* If that's the case, I want you and Wally in the water as soon as we come back up. I want us to make a thorough search of the area."

Ron grinned, obviously eager to look for treasure. Andy, Pete, and King worked directly for Captain Bob, who was paid a set amount of money per day for use of the boat and crew. The divers received a salary plus a percentage of any treasure they found.

"We'll be ready," Wally said. "Can't wait to get my feet wet."

The two men helped Joe and Conn put on their diving gear, using double tanks so they could stay down longer. Once they were set to go, Conn grabbed a handheld blower and the men made their way to the loading platform. Seconds later, they disappeared into the sea.

Chapter 14

It was a scorching day, the hottest they'd had so far, the sun beating down relentlessly, not a cloud in the azure sky. Even the usual cooling afternoon breeze had deserted them. Hope stood at the rail, a wide-brimmed straw hat shading her face, protecting her head and neck, anxiously watching the flat, gleaming surface of the water.

Conn and Joe had been below for nearly an hour. For a while she had watched the video screen in the chart room, seen Conn use the blower to remove deep layers of sand from one of the cannons. The artifact seemed to be in surprisingly good condition, a huge artillery piece at least twelve or thirteen feet long. But the minutes had been slipping away and it was time for the men to surface.

Hope looked down at the water, saw the telltale air bubbles rising, and her heartbeat quickened. Conn's snorkel broke the surface, his head and mask, then Joe popped up beside him. The men pulled out their regulators, raised their masks, and set them on the back of their heads. Hope's excitement built when she saw both men were grinning.

"Wait till you see what we found!" Joe shouted, following the words with a great whoop of glee.

Hope, Tommy, Captain Bob, and the other two divers all raced toward the diving platform. Pete, Andy, even King poured out on deck to see what the men had found. Conn was still grinning as he held up his hand, and Hope could see the bright, unmistakable glitter of gold.

"Oh, my God!"

"Gold!" Pete shouted. "That's gold he's got there!"

There was excited conversation among the crew as Conn and Joe climbed up on the platform. They shed their fins, tanks, and the rest of their gear, then Conn held out his hand to reveal the most beautiful emerald cross Hope had ever seen.

"Incredible," Captain Bob said.

The men came up on the deck and walked over to a spot on the stern where King laid out a dark green plastic tablecloth he brought up from the galley. All of them gathered round to take a closer look.

From a bag at his waist, Conn drew out a length of solid gold chain and a clump of gray, lead-looking matter Hope figured must be oxidized silver coins. He set them down on the plastic tablecloth and Joe set three gorgeous gold coins beside the rest of the treasure.

"Unbelievable," Ron Keegan said almost reverently.

"Do you think you've found the mother lode?" Hope asked, using salvors' jargon for the heart of the treasure.

"I don't know." Conn set the beautiful golden cross down next to the coins. "There wasn't any sign of the ballast pile. But I think, once we put the suction dredge to work, we're going to find a whole lot more stuff down there."

"We saw lots of pottery shards," Joe said excitedly, "olive jars, iron fittings, barrel staves, stuff like that."

"I still can't believe you actually found treasure," Andy Glass said. "To tell you the truth, I never really thought you would."

Tommy Tyler squeezed in between Hope and Ron Keegan, panning his digital camera over the artifacts set out on the table. Against the dark green background, the gold coins glittered in the sunlight as if they had a life of their own. The emeralds seemed to shimmer.

"I got a great shot of you coming out of the water holding up the cross," Tommy said. "Jeez, what a fabulous piece that is."

Hope looked down at the magnificent piece of jewelry, an ornately carved cross about five inches long, inset with huge emeralds interspersed with diamonds. The cross looked just as beautiful as it had the day it had gone into the water.

"I wonder whose it was," she said, thinking of the people on the ship who had died that day.

"Someone with plenty of money." Conn picked the cross up to examine it more closely. "This is sure going to make the professor's day."

"He'll want to come out to the site," Hope said.

"I don't blame him. He's put a lifetime into studying this ship. If it weren't for Doc Marlin, none of us would be here right now."

Conn phoned the professor, who was apparently over the top with glee, then phoned his partners, Eddie Markham and Brad Talbot. Markham had left the island on a business trip, but he was due back home in a couple of days.

Brad Talbot was ecstatic.

"I've got to admit, I'm surprised," he told Conn. "I figured we had a shot, but I knew it was a definite gamble."

"We haven't found the ballast pile yet." And since the real treasure, the heavy gold and silver bars and boxes of valuable coins, would have been stored in the hold, the ballast pile would likely be the site of the true mother lode. "But we're bringing up some really good stuff. I'll call you in a couple of days, give you an update."

"The press is going to love this."

A muscle flexed in Conn's jaw but he made no reply. It was obvious Talbot couldn't wait to spread the news, which was the last thing Conn wanted.

At the moment at least, Emperor Eddie wasn't on the island, and Hope figured Talbot wasn't likely to fly down unless they found a lot more than they had come up with so far.

Professor Marlin, however, arrived on the Pleasure Island plane the following afternoon. He was practically beaming when he came aboard the *Conquest*, pant legs flapping, so excited his thin feet barely touched the deck.

"You've done it, my boy. You found the ship and now you've found the treasure."

"Some of it," Conn corrected. "We aren't sure just how much."

"What they brought up so far is beautiful, Professor," Hope said. "It's absolutely amazing."

"Still no sign of the ballast pile?"

"Not yet. This morning Ron found a small gold box that held a couple of gold-and-ruby rings. We've been finding some interesting artifacts as well. Joe brought up an olive jar that's in nearly perfect condition."

Conn led the professor along the deck to where the treasure had been laid out for him to examine, and Hope walked up beside them.

"You're right, my dear. It truly is amazing." Dr. Marlin spent the balance of the afternoon studying, cataloguing, and diagramming the treasure, then plotting where each piece had been found.

Meanwhile, the divers continued to search. Joe found another gold coin and so did Conn, but there seemed to be no rhyme or reason, no real pattern to where they were discovered.

With the professor aboard, that night they celebrated their recovery of the first treasure off the *Rosa*. They were out of champagne, so they drank red wine and Red Stripe beer, and King came up with one of his usual great meals. The men were still laughing and joking when the professor slipped away, tired after such an eventful day.

Hope slid quietly out of the booth and left the galley. Sitting next to Conn was always a strain, more so after sharing his excitement all day. She had done her best to ignore him, fixing her attention mostly on the professor. But her glance kept straying and every time it did, he was watching her. He knew she was avoiding him, had been since her return to the boat. He wasn't happy that after their time together on the island, she had decided to end their brief affair.

Conn wanted more of the hot, incredible sex they had shared, and part of her wanted that, too. But the other part kept seeing Conn with the blonde. He had said there was nothing between them, and she supposed it was true.

But the sight of him with another woman and its painful impact on her had forced her to see things the way they really were. She was getting too involved with Conn, getting in far too deep. He was making her feel things she didn't want to feel, and the sooner she cut herself off from him the better.

In the darkness, heavy footsteps moved along the deck behind her. She turned at the sound of Conn's deep voice speaking softly beside her ear.

"Out here wishing you were back in New York?"

Her guard went up at how close he was to the truth. She forced herself to face him. "Now, why would I be wishing that? According to the e-mail I got from my friend Jackie Aimes, it's snowing and twenty-five degrees."

"True, but if you were back there, you'd be safe. You wouldn't have to deal with me."

Her stomach instantly knotted. She hated his ability to read her so well. "What makes you think that's a problem?"

"If it weren't, you wouldn't be trying so hard to stay away from me."

"Really? You know, your ego is amazing."

Conn just laughed. "Always so tough. You know what? I'm beginning to think you aren't tough at all."

She could feel herself going a little pale. The last thing she wanted Conner Reese to know was how vulnerable she really was.

"Look, Conn, we had a fling. We had a good time—now it's over."

"It doesn't have to be over. You're still here and so am I."

He ran a finger along her jaw and goose bumps ran over her skin. "I want you and I think you still want me."

Hope turned away from him, hoping he wouldn't see that she was trembling. "This isn't the time, Conn. It never has been."

"No, I don't suppose it is. But you can't always pick the right time. Sometimes something special happens in our lives and we have to reach out and grab hold of it. If we don't, if we let those special times pass, we miss out on some of the best parts of living."

"Maybe. Or maybe letting them pass is the way we keep from getting in too deep." She started to walk away, but Conn caught her wrist.

"I could make you want me. You know I could." His eyes were blue and intense and they reflected the desire he felt for her. Her pulse quickened. Arousal swept through her. With it came a faint stirring of fear.

"Please don't," she said softly, feeling the unexpected sting of tears. "Please don't, Conn." Hope turned away, her chest squeezing.

In the darkness behind her, she heard Conn softly curse.

They searched the waters near the shoal for the next three days, recalculating the grid to stay in the area around the cannons. The professor had lectures scheduled at the college and was forced to return to Jamaica, but Eddie Markham appeared that third day, back from the States and grinning from ear to ear at the news of their discovery.

"I got your message. Congratulations." He was wearing perfectly creased white Bermuda shorts, a flowered shirt, and a flat-brimmed Panama hat. A pair of Gucci sunglasses hid his dark eyes.

"Thanks."

He turned to Hope. "Well, I guess you got your story."

"Yes, I guess I did."

"I can't wait to see the treasure. Up until now, I've only seen pictures of stuff like that."

"Come on, then. Follow me." Conn led the way to the chart room, Hope and Eddie walking along behind him. The treasure was locked in the captain's small safe. Conn took it out and spread it on a soft cloth on top of the teakwood table.

Eddie stared down at the beautiful artifacts they had found, his hands slightly trembling as he picked up the golden cross.

"The public will want to know about this." He reached into the pocket of his shorts and pulled out a newspaper clipping. "I saw this in the *Miami Herald* when I was at the airport. I figured you'd want to see it."

It was only a small article relaying news of the discovery; there weren't any photos.

"Once they see a picture of this cross, the story will spread all over the globe."

"I'll be turning in my second article this week," Hope said. "The photos Tommy took will be on *Adventure*'s Internet site a couple of days after that."

A muscle tightened along Conn's jaw. He didn't like the idea, she knew, but she was there to do a job and she intended to do it.

At least Eddie Markham looked pleased. "That's certainly a start. Where's the Tyler kid now? I imagine he's got some great stuff, right?"

"I heard that." Tommy descended the ladder to the chart room. "And yeah, I've got some really great stuff, if I do say so myself. As word gets out, the wire service will probably be after some of it."

"I'd love to see what you've got."

"No problem. Come with me and I'll show you."

Eddie and Tommy left the chart room, leaving Hope alone with Conn.

"The more this story gets out," he said darkly, "the more people we'll have poking around here. I hope to hell this doesn't bring us a shitload of trouble."

Hope said nothing. For Conn's sake, she hoped so, too.

* * *

Conn invited Eddie Markham to stay for supper but he declined. As good a cook as King was, it appeared the emperor preferred the gourmet food in his restaurant on the island. Conn watched the Sea Ray disappear across the water and turned to see Joe standing at the rail a few feet away. Joe also watched the boat, but he didn't really seem to be seeing it.

Conn walked over and braced his hands on the rail. "You look like your best dog died. You must be having trouble of the female sort."

Joe sighed. "Yeah, how'd you know?"

Conn pinned him with a look.

"Okay, so you know me as well as I know you."

"Glory?"

"Yeah. It's weird, man. I've been with so many women I've lost count, but those days we spent together—somehow it was different. I keep thinking about her, you know? I can't get her out of my head. She's just another woman. I don't get it."

"Glory wasn't right for me, but I have to admit there was something about her. She struck me as kind of naïve, a little lost somehow, but really very sweet. Her family's rich, but as a kid, I think they mostly ignored her. They travel all the time and none of them are close. I had the feeling she was looking for something—or someone. I wasn't it. Maybe you are."

"God forbid." But Joe stared back out to sea and Conn figured he was still thinking of Glory.

Imagining the two of them together, Conn thought they might not be such a bad match. Deep down, Joe was kind of a loner, maybe even a little lonely. Glory seemed to need someone very badly and if Joe actually felt something for her, maybe it could work.

Of course, there was the problem of Joe being Cuban and Catholic and Glory's family being Jewish. Her parents wouldn't be keen on their daughter getting seriously involved with someone not of their faith.

Conn mentally shook himself. Glory and Joe had only

spent a few days together. It was highly unlikely the relationship would ever get off the ground, and even if it did, anything of a serious nature was going to be way down the road.

Thinking of relationships—or lack of them—returned Conn's thoughts to Hope and a memory surfaced of making love to her at the pool. He'd told her that he wouldn't hurt her. It was odd how important that had become to him.

Maybe she was right. Maybe it was better if he just left her alone.

Hope was sitting in the galley drinking a cup of King's thick Blue Mountain coffee when Andy came in with the satellite phone.

"It's for you. He says his name's Deitz."

"Thanks, Andy." Hope took the phone and pressed it against her ear. "Jimmy?"

"It's me, all right. I'm afraid I've got bad news."

Her fingers tightened around the phone. "What is it?"

"Buddy Newton's in the hospital. Got a concussion, broken ribs. He's busted up real bad."

She sank back down on the seat of the dinette. "What happened?"

"Story I got, he was coming into the building pretty late. I guess he likes to walk his dog in the evenings. He's got some kind of terrier or something."

"Skolie," she said, thinking of the fuzzy little brown mutt that Jimmy was so crazy about.

"Looks like a couple of thugs jumped him. Beat the crap out of him and stole his wallet."

Her hand shook. "So you're saying this was a mugging? The men were after his money?"

"Buddy doesn't think so. I went to see him in the hospital this morning. He said one of the guys told him he had better take the offer on his place or he wouldn't have to worry about selling. He wouldn't have to worry about anything at all."

"What do the police say?"

"To put it bluntly, they think Buddy's full of shit. They figure he'd say anything to get the public behind his cause. His wallet was stolen. That's enough for the cops. They're looking for the guys who did it, though. I think they're seriously concerned about an old man being beaten up like that."

"He's going to be all right, isn't he?"

"Like I said, he's busted up pretty bad, but it looks like he'll recover."

Hope's throat felt thick. "Anything else turn up?"

A pause on the end of the line. "I had a friend take a look at that apartment fire at Hartley House. He's an ex-arson investigator. He says he thinks someone may have tampered with the wiring, messed with it enough to make it look like the wiring was faulty. He's pretty convinced it wasn't."

"You think we should go to the police? Maybe after what happened to Buddy——"

"We haven't got any real proof. Like I said, my friend's retired. He's making an educated guess. Still, between the two of us, I'm betting he's right."

"Have you heard from the men who came to see you about throwing the investigation?"

"No. I just got a check. I haven't cashed it and I don't intend to."

Hope took a long deep breath. "Thanks, Jimmy."

She hung up the phone but it rang again almost at once. This time it was Gordy Weitzman, giving her his version of the same information. He pretty much agreed with Jimmy, that Buddy's attack was probably a warning.

"I'm coming back to New York, Gordy," Hope said, making a sudden decision. "I want to see Buddy, make sure he's going to be all right."

"I wouldn't do that if I were you. You don't want to get involved in this any more than you are already. Way out there, you're safe. Here, anything could happen."

But Hope was determined. As she hung up the phone, she was already mentally planning her trip back to New York.

She would go on the Net, find a reasonable fare. If she got lucky, she could be there by tomorrow night.

Conn stuck his head into the galley just then. "Andy said you got a call from some guy named Deitz. That's the detective you hired, right?"

"That's him."

"What'd he say?"

Hope told Conn about Buddy being in the hospital. She told him about the arson investigator and that it looked almost certainly like the fire had been set.

"I'm going to see him. I want to let him know there are still people who care about him. I want to be sure he's okay."

"Going back is not a good idea, Hope. You're getting involved in something way too dangerous. I know you want to help that old man, but this really isn't your problem."

"I'm going, Conn. I'm going to get on the Internet and get a ticket, then I'm going to call Eddie and ask him to send the Sea Ray out to pick me up in the morning."

"Fine. If you're that determined, then I'm going with you."

"Don't be absurd. This has nothing to do with you."

Conn's jaw hardened in a way she was coming to know. "Maybe not. But I'm going anyway."

"What about the treasure? You're making important discoveries every day. You're needed here, Conn, and you know it."

"Just get the damned plane tickets. I'll call Eddie and set things up for us to leave in the morning."

She started to argue but the look in his eyes warned her not to. And the more she thought about it, the more she figured, under the circumstances, having an ex-Navy SEAL along might not be such a bad idea.

"Are you sure?"

"I'm sure you're doing something crazy. Maybe if I come along, I can keep you from getting into even worse trouble."

Hope opened her mouth to tell him she could take care of herself, but Conn was already gone.

Chapter 15

After a three-hour-and-forty-minute Air Jamaica flight out of Kingston, the plane landed at JFK a little after eight in the evening.

Hope worried most of the way, first about Buddy, then about what her boss would do if he found out she was back in New York and involving herself in the Hartley House story again. The last hour of the flight, she worried about Conn spending the night in her apartment.

"I don't suppose you'd consider getting a room," she said to him as the yellow taxi they caught at the airport wove its way through the traffic in the busy Manhattan streets.

Conn fixed her with a glare. "I don't suppose."

The cab cut in and out between cars, the Pakistani driver blasting his horn and occasionally shaking a brown-skinned fist. The crosswalks were crowded, people bundled in heavy coats and woolen scarves. The recent snow had melted but a frosty mist hung in the air and a slick film of ice made the sidewalk a danger to navigate.

The taxi cut over to the curb in front of her Sixth Street apartment and Conn helped her out of the car. He paid the fare, caught her arm, and helped her cross safely to the door of the lobby. A chilling wind blew her hair back from her face and even though she was bundled in the heavy wool coat she had been wearing the day she'd left the city, after weeks in the Caribbean heat, she shivered.

"Not exactly Pleasure Island, is it?"

"Not exactly."

They took the elevator up to her twelfth-floor apartment and she used the new key she'd had made to get in. The place was neat and clean, exactly as she had left it, but even more spartan than when she had first moved in.

"I didn't have time to replace the stuff that was broken after the apartment was vandalized. I planned to do it when I got back to the city."

Conn surveyed the room, his gaze taking in the bare walls that had once been warmed by pictures, the pale green sofa that no longer had any decorative pillows. The coffee table was there, but she hadn't had time to replace the broken glass top.

"So you figure the attack on your place was a warning similar to the one Buddy Newton got."

"Similar, but not nearly as painful." She glanced around the apartment, wondering why it didn't feel more like home. Maybe it was just that it was now so austere. She turned up the heat, hoping that would help.

"You'll have to sleep on the sofa," she said. "There's only one bedroom."

Conn picked up her soft-sided black canvas carry-on and carted it through the bedroom door before she could stop him.

"I'm too tall for the sofa," he said from the other room. "You've got twin beds. I'll sleep in one of those."

"I have twin beds because my sister, Charity, and I shared this place for a while. But I don't think it's a good idea for you to—"

"Look, Hope—" Conn walked back into the living room. "I came here in case there was trouble. That's something I know how to handle. I suppose I should have known the trouble would be you."

"What are you talking about? I'm just being . . ." She let the words trail off. She was just being what? Cautious? Practical? She was only trying to protect herself, but that was something Conn didn't seem to understand.

She sighed. It was obvious arguing was pointless—she could tell by the set of those very wide shoulders. He was wearing a pair of dark brown slacks and a white short-sleeved shirt. Once they got off the plane, he had pulled on a vee-necked tan cashmere sweater he got out of his carry-on, then stopped at one of the men's stores in the airport and bought a pair of black leather gloves and a black wool overcoat—an impressive size 46.

Before they had left the boat, she had secretly wondered if he might not look like a fish out of water in his khaki slacks and deck shoes. Instead, in slacks and a sweater, he looked as if he had stepped right out of *GQ*, which irritated the hell out of her, though she had no idea why.

Maybe because he looked so good it made her itch to touch him, to run her fingers over his soft cashmere sweater and feel the muscles tighten underneath. Whatever it was, it wasn't going to happen. She wasn't here to scratch an itch. She had more important things to do.

"I know it's past visiting hours, but I'd still like to go down to the hospital, see if I can find something out about Buddy's condition. I suppose I could call, but if we went down there, they might let us in."

"Depending on who's on duty, there's always a chance."

"Sounds like you're talking from experience."

His shoulders lifted in a shrug. "I spent a little time in the hospital after one of my first missions."

"Is that the scar I noticed on your thigh?"

He nodded. "Simonov SKS—old Russian carbine. After that, I learned to be more careful."

She had seen the ragged scar on his leg when they had been in the pool. At the time, her mind had been on other, more interesting parts of his anatomy.

Now she figured he had probably gotten the scar during a

mission in Desert Storm, but figured, considering the nature of his former occupation, he would probably never tell her.

"The wound must have been pretty serious to leave a scar like that."

The corners of his mouth curved up. "Yeah. You wanna see it?"

Hope bit back a laugh. "Some other time."

Making her way into the bedroom, she changed out of her cotton pants and blouse into a warm pair of black wool slacks and a fuzzy black sweater. It was another cab ride to New York University Hospital, where Buddy had been taken. One of the maintenance people swept the walk out in front as they made their way toward the automatic doors. Conn took her arm, helping her along the slippery path, and they entered the busy reception room.

Hope walked over to the desk. "I'm here to see a man named Buddy Newton. Can you give me his room number?"

A black woman in a crisp white uniform tilted her head back to read the computer screen in front of her through bifocal lenses.

"Here it is . . . William "Buddy" Newton. Sixth floor, room 613. But visiting hours are over."

"Thanks. I just want to check on him." Before the woman could argue, Hope took off for the elevator. Conn caught up with her before the doors slid closed. They got off on the sixth floor, but when they reached the nurses' station, it was deserted. Hope could hear female voices coming from one of the rooms down the hall.

"He's in 613," she said softly. "That's this way."

Conn chuckled. "I didn't know you had such a streak of larceny in you. If you'd been a man, you might have made a pretty good SEAL. Once you put your mind to something, you don't let a little thing like breaking the rules keep you from accomplishing your mission."

Hope just smiled. They slipped quietly into Buddy's room and the heavy door swished closed behind them. He was lying in the narrow bed closest to the door. The man in the bed next to his was either deeply asleep or unconscious. From the looks of the tubes running into his arms and up his nose, she thought it might be the latter.

"Hope? Hope, is that . . . is that really you?"

"Buddy!" She hurried to his side, knelt down beside the bed, and reached for his weathered hand. Hope saw that he was hooked up to an I.V. tube and a heart monitor. The steady beep was somehow reassuring.

"I thought you'd be sleeping. I just wanted to check on you, see if you were all right."

"Hell, no . . . I'm not . . . all right." He wheezed in a breath and it was obvious it was painful for him to speak. "Those bastards . . . pounded me . . . into the sidewalk." He paused to catch his breath, then looked up at her and managed a wobbly smile. "Wouldn't have happened . . . twenty years ago. I was still . . . pretty tough back then."

Hope smiled. "Are you kidding? You still are."

Speaking of *tough* reminded her that Conn stood in the shadows a few feet away. She had never seen him in action, but from the beginning, she had noticed a hardness about him. She had no trouble believing he was a man who could handle himself in a difficult situation.

"Buddy, I'd like you to meet a friend of mine. His name is Conner Reese."

Buddy squinted toward Conn, who stepped out of the shadows so Buddy could see him.

"Nice to meet you, Mr. Newton."

"Same . . . here. Any friend of Hope's . . . and all that." Buddy was a small man, maybe five-foot-six with his shoes on. He had freckles, once-red hair now faded to gray, and a weathered, ruddy complexion. Tonight his face was sort of a pasty gray.

"Conn came back with me from Jamaica. He was afraid there might be trouble."

"Oh, there's trouble . . . all right, and don't I . . . know it." He coughed then groaned as a shot of pain jolted through his injured ribs.

"Don't try to talk," Hope said. "You need to get your rest so that you can get well and get out of here."

Buddy closed his eyes and she could see their brief conversation had exhausted most of his strength.

Hope squeezed his hand. "You get some sleep, okay? I'll be back to see you in the morning. We can talk a little more then."

Buddy just nodded. Hope waited at his bedside until he fell asleep, then she and Conn quietly left the room. The night nurse, a heavyset woman in her forties with dark hair pulled back in a very tight bun, spotted them the moment they stepped out into the hall.

"Hey, what are you doing in there? Don't you know visiting hours are over?"

Conn flashed a smile unlike anything Hope had ever seen. It made his eyes look bluer, his handsome face even more handsome. As he took in the woman's rounded features, for once he looked almost friendly.

"Sorry. We just got in from the Caribbean . . . one of those long, bouncy flights, you know? Hope's been worried sick about Buddy. We just stopped by so she could get word of his condition. We didn't see anyone when we got off the elevator. I'm glad we found you. I'm sure you'll be able to tell us everything we need to know."

The woman's face lit with a smile. A thick hand smoothed back her heavy dark hair. "Of course. If you'll just sign the visitor's sheet, I'll be happy to tell you whatever I can."

They both filled out a line on the sheet beneath the date, printing then signing their names, and the woman reached for Buddy's chart. She rattled off a list of injuries that began with a concussion, several broken and cracked ribs, a sprained ankle, a deep gash on the back of his head, and a list of miscellaneous bruises and contusions.

"My God, it's a wonder they didn't kill him," Hope said.

"He's a grouchy old cuss," the nurse said, "but he's also rather charming. He's got half the nurses running errands for him."

Hope smiled. "That's Buddy."

They left the hospital, Hope somewhat relieved, but the long day was beginning to take its toll. By the time they were headed back to her apartment, she was exhausted.

"You want to get something to eat?" Conn asked. "You haven't had anything but airline food all day and there wasn't much of that."

"I'm not really hungry. But if you are, there's a great Chinese take-out one block away."

"Sounds like a winner to me."

The cab let them off in front of her building and with Conn's help, she navigated the icy sidewalk. "I'm really beat. I think I'll go on up."

Conn shook his head. "Sorry. It doesn't work that way. While we're here, you go where I go."

"What are you talking about?"

"I'm talking about keeping you safe. If you don't like it, just remember what Buddy looked like lying in that hospital bed. I'm not about to let that happen to you." He tipped his head toward the block on the other side of the intersection. "Come on. Toughen up. We'll be out of there and back to your apartment in just a few minutes."

Hope sighed. Surely Conn was overreacting. But she thought of Buddy and the destruction of her apartment, then nodded and took hold of his arm.

Conn slept in the damned twin bed. He could have handled the tight fit if he'd been snuggled up with Hope. As it was, he tossed and turned and constantly looked over at the small lump curled in the center of the other bed.

Amazing how well a woman slept when she knew a man was lying there aching for her. Hell, he'd had a hard-on for the last two hours. He was tempted to go in and take a cold shower, but it was the middle of the night and he didn't want to wake her. Besides, he didn't really think it would do any good.

Conn shifted onto his back and shoved his hands behind his head. Staring up at the ceiling, he thought of Hope and how gentle she had been with the sick old man. His suspicions about Hope were growing. He was beginning to believe there wasn't a single tough bone in her entire luscious little body.

Except when it came to him.

Hope was steadfast where he was concerned, determined to keep her distance. Funny thing was, the more she tried to escape him, the more resolute he became that she wouldn't. It was crazy, but he was beginning to entertain some semiserious thoughts about the woman. He could hardly believe it. A month ago, getting involved with a female was the last thing he wanted.

Morning finally came and Conn climbed out of bed. Though he had tossed and turned most of the night, he had actually managed to catch a couple of hours of sleep. Since there'd been a time he ran mostly on less than none, he felt passably good.

Hope was already up, he realized, a little surprised since he was an early riser. Rubbing a hand over his night's growth of beard, he padded into the bathroom. When he came out fifteen minutes later, the smell of coffee greeted him and his stomach growled. Pulling on a pair of black slacks and a dark gray sweater, he headed into the kitchen.

"I hope you're hungry." She was frying a skillet full of bacon, doing it so well she didn't even have to dodge any popping grease.

"Are you kidding? King has ruined me. I'm starved." He looked around the cozy kitchen, which was neat and orderly: white cupboards, a couple of bright yellow dishtowels folded neatly on the light oak Formica countertop. "Anything I can do to help?"

"Just sit down and get your appetite ready."

Conn pulled out a chair and sat down at the little butcher block table in the kitchen, noticing one of the legs was held in place with clear wrapping tape, obviously another casualty of her intruders. He thought of what might have happened if Hope had come home while the men were still in the apartment and his chest tightened.

Hope walked up behind his chair. "Here. Dig into this." Leaning over his shoulder, she set a big plate of bacon and eggs down in front of him, followed by a platter of buttered toast. Her soft breasts pushed against his shoulder and his groin throbbed. The attraction he felt for her still amazed him.

Conn looked at her and smiled, forcing his thoughts in a safer direction, inhaling the aroma of the delicious-looking food.

"I don't believe this. A woman who can actually cook. And a city girl at that. I haven't met a woman in years who knew how to fix a meal. Never did know many. Not even my mother."

Hope arched a burnished eyebrow. "You can't have a mother. That would mean you were actually a child at one time. I find that nearly impossible to believe."

He laughed. "You'd be pretty much right, then. I was never really a child. I was born twenty-five years old. And I never really had a mother. She ran off with a carpet salesman when I was just a kid."

Hope looked stunned. "Your father raised you?"

"More or less. Considering he was the town drunk, you couldn't really call it that." He dug into the eggs on his plate.

"How . . . old were you when your mother left?"

"About five, I guess."

"Did you ever see her again?"

"No, and I didn't really want to." He reached for a couple of pieces of toast, wishing he hadn't brought up the subject. He sure as hell hadn't meant to. Still, he refused to avoid it now that he had.

"What about your dad? Is he still alive?"

Conn shook his head. "He got drunk and drove his car into a tree. Probably saved some other guy's life."

Standing behind his chair, Hope leaned over and wrapped

her arms around him. "Conn, that's so awful. I can't imagine a mother abandoning her child. For me it would be an impossible thing to do."

"Yeah, well, sometimes bad things happen."

"I guess that's another reason you hate women."

Conn caught her hand where it rested against his chest and pressed a kiss on the back. "I don't hate women, and if I'd known telling you the sad tale of my misplaced youth would have you holding onto me like this, I would have told you sooner."

She laughed, slapped him playfully on the back, and drew away.

Conn just smiled. Getting back to the food on his plate, he closed his eyes and sighed at the taste of perfectly cooked eggs and just-crisp-enough bacon. "Wow, this is really good."

"I love to cook, but I'm usually too busy to do much entertaining."

"Now, that's a real shame." He looked at the other placemat on the table. "Where's yours?"

"I wasn't hungry." She let out a breath. "I keep thinking of Buddy. Someone needs to convince him to sell that building before he winds up getting killed. Nothing's worth your life."

"Maybe this time he'll listen to you." He finished eating, mopping up the egg yolk with the last of his toast. "That jam was fantastic. What was it?"

"Blackberry. I canned it last year."

One of his eyebrows arched up. "Who would have guessed that beneath that tough façade lies a regular little Martha Stewart."

Instead of smiling, Hope's spine stiffened. "It's just a hobby, is all. I really don't have time to fool with it."

Conn came up out of his chair, turned, and caught her around the waist. "What is it with you, Hope? You know, it's okay to be a woman. You don't have to constantly be proving yourself. So you like to cook. What's the big deal? You know what I like to do sometimes?"

"What?"

"Paint. I like watercolor painting. There, now you know my terrible secret."

Hope's eyes searched his face. She recognized the lie for what it was and his reason for telling it.

"You are such a liar," she said, but she was smiling, her tension slowly draining away. "I keep trying not to like you, Reese, but sometimes you really make it hard."

Conn grinned. "I wouldn't touch the next line for all the gold on the *Rosa.*"

Hope laughed, and Conn thought how much he liked the feminine, slightly throaty sound. "Come on, I'll help you with the dishes," he said, though there were other, more intimate things he would far rather be doing. "When we're done, I need to call the *Conquest,* see what's going on. Then we'll head down to the hospital."

"All right. Thanks."

They finished up in the kitchen. Conn phoned the boat and asked to speak to Joe, who was in charge of the salvage operation while he was away.

"So how's it going?" he asked.

"Not bad. We had some trouble with one of the generators after you left, but we're due in for supplies so we'll have it repaired when we get to Jamaica. We're heading back tonight."

"You guys find anything interesting?"

"Ron did—a fabulous gold necklace. It was broken into sections and one of the pieces is missing, but, man, it's really gorgeous. We found a couple of gold cobs, too." Cobs were crude coins struck off the end of a gold or silver bar. They came in sizes—eight escudos, four, or two, a measure of weight for shipment back to Spain.

"There are a lot of artifacts in this area," Joe said, "but there's still no sign of the ballast pile, and I'm starting to think the mother lode is somewhere else."

"Keep after it. I'll be back in a couple days. We'll recalculate the grid and take another look around, see if we can figure out what happened to the main part of the ship."

"Roger that," Joe said. "You keeping Hope out of trouble?"

"So far."

"Good. See ya soon." Joe ended the call and Conn set the phone back in its cradle. He was thinking of the shipwreck, thinking of Mel Fisher and the Spanish galleon, *Atocha,* that had sunk a few years after the *Rosa* went down.

During the journey of the 1622 fleet, the *Atocha* had been hit by two different storms, one that sank the ship, the other two weeks later that separated the top decks from the hull. Fisher had found the top decks first, then been sidetracked by the amount of treasure they had found. It wasn't until later that he finally found the mother lode.

"Anything new?" Hope breezed into the living room, coat, muffler, and gloves in hand.

"They're still finding stuff, but no sign of the ballast pile—which means we haven't found the main part of the treasure."

"You'll find it." Walking over to the hall closet, she pulled out his overcoat and handed it over. "I don't have a single doubt."

Conn just smiled, wishing he was as confident as Hope.

They took the elevator down to the lobby. Conn flagged down a cab, which sloshed half-frozen water up on the sidewalk as it pulled over to the curb.

At the hospital, they got out and headed toward the front of the building, their breath white in the frosty air. When the door swung open, they walked through the reception room to the elevator, heading straight up to the sixth floor nurses' station.

"Good morning. May I help you?" A different nurse from the one the night before stood behind the counter, this one tall and thin, blond hair sticking out in places, and generally looking pretty frazzled.

"We'd like to see William Newton," Conn said. "He's in room 613."

The papers in her hand started to rattle. She glanced

down the hall toward Buddy's room, then back to him, and her face looked bone-white.

"I-I'm sorry. I'll have to let you speak to one of the doctors on duty."

Unconsciously, Hope gripped the sleeve of his coat. "What is it?" she asked the nurse. "What's happened to Buddy?"

"Like I said—you'll have to speak to the doctor in charge. I'll go get him."

As the nurse turned to leave so did Hope, walking in the opposite direction, down the hall toward Buddy's hospital room.

"Wait a minute!" the woman called after her. "You can't do that! He isn't even in there!" The nurse looked up at Conn, her eyes full of pity. "I'm sorry, I really am. I'm afraid Mr. Newton's injuries caused him to have a stroke sometime during the night. He passed away early this morning."

Chapter 16

"I still can't believe it. He was always so vital, so full of life." Hope paced the carpet in front of the sofa in her living room. She had done her crying already. She was fiercely angry now. "Whoever attacked him murdered him as surely as if they had put a gun to his head. It isn't right—it just isn't! I wish there was something I could do."

"Take it easy, Hope. You've already done more than most people would have. You have to let the police deal with this from here on out."

Hope sighed. "I called Jimmy Deitz while I was in the kitchen making coffee. He wasn't in, but I left a message on his machine. I'm sure he'll call me back."

In the meantime, she went into the bedroom to phone her father and stepmother. She hadn't talked to her family since she had left New York, and e-mail just wasn't the same.

Sitting down on the bed, she dialed her dad's home number and smiled when she heard her stepmother, Tracy, on the other end of the line.

"Hey, kiddo! It's about time we heard from you."

"How are you, Tracy?"

"Everyone here is fine. How about you? Are you still in the Caribbean?"

Hope told Tracy she was back in New York to attend the funeral of a friend, a shortened version of the truth. "I'm returning to Jamaica as soon as the service is over."

"It's twenty degrees here. I'm jealous."

"I don't blame you." Her dad came on the line and she repeated the conversation she'd had with Tracy. She didn't mention Hartley House, or Buddy, or any of her personal concerns; she didn't want them to worry and she knew that they would.

"You take care of yourself," her dad said. "And give your sisters a call. They're beginning to get worried."

"I'll phone them as soon as I hang up."

She started with a phone call to Charity in Seattle, then called Patience down in Texas, telling them both she was fine, catching up on a bit of family gossip, but careful to keep the calls light and fairly brief. Last, she called her best friend, Jackie Aimes.

"You're back in the city?"

"I found out Buddy Newton was in the hospital. You probably read about it in the papers."

"After what happened with your apartment, I was following the story, what little there was of it. I saw the piece about him being mugged in front of his apartment."

"Buddy died last night, a stroke caused by the injuries he received."

"Poor guy. Seems like he sure caught a lot of bad breaks."

"It's worse than that, Jackie. Buddy was murdered. I only wish I could prove it."

"Hey, girlfriend, I thought you learned your lesson when those guys busted up your apartment."

Hope sighed. "If it makes you feel any better, I'm only staying in town until the funeral is over. Then I'm heading back to Jamaica to finish my assignment."

"Smart girl."

"In the meantime, just in case, I've got my own personal bodyguard."

"Now *that* sounds interesting. I want details, girl. Fess up—I bet this guy's a major hunk."

"Actually, he is. I'd tell you about it, but right now, I've got to run. I promise I'll keep in touch—I've got your e-mail address."

"You take care of yourself, you hear?"

Hope smiled into the phone. "I will. Thanks, Jackie."

A deep voice reached her from the doorway. "You're smiling. I take it this *Jackie's* a friend."

"Of the female sort, yes. A very good friend."

"Family okay?"

"Everybody's fine." Hope looked down at the phone, thinking of Buddy and willing Jimmy Deitz to call.

Better than that, he showed up at her apartment thirty minutes later.

Conn insisted on answering the door. Jimmy said who he was and Conn let him in. Deitz walked into the living room stripping off his heavy, slightly worn overcoat, tossing it over a chair.

"You must be Hope," the detective said. "It's nice to finally meet you." He was short and stout, with heavily muscled shoulders, a fireplug of a man with a scar that bisected one of his dark eyebrows. He was built a little like Wally Short, but Deitz was a hard-looking man while Wally just looked friendly.

"Jimmy, this is a friend of mine, Conner Reese."

Jimmy stuck out a wide, scarred hand. "Reese. You're one of the guys involved in the treasure hunt. You run the dive operation."

"Among other things." Conn gripped the shorter man's hand. For a couple of seconds, the two men sized each other up, though Hope had a feeling Jimmy had already checked Conn out, probably when he first took on her case.

"You as tough as you look?" Jimmy asked bluntly.

Conn's mouth edged up. "If you want to know if I can take care of Hope, the answer is yes."

Jimmy just nodded and Hope was sure he knew Conn was an ex-Navy SEAL.

"I hated to hear about Newton," Jimmy said. "I don't

think whoever roughed him up meant to kill him. I do think whoever's calling the shots on the Hartley House deal wants that piece of property and they'll do whatever it takes to get it."

"Any idea who that might be?" Conn asked.

"Not so far. The guys who own Americal, the company that made the offer, have managed to bury their names pretty deep. The way these things work when the people involved don't want to be known, a legal firm files the corporate papers, listing a couple of lawyers in the firm as directors. Later, they amend the documents internally, change the directors, and put in whoever they want."

"Pretty tricky," Hope said.

"No kidding. Atlantic Securities, for example, one of the companies named as owning Americal, was incorporated by a law firm named Wells, Powell, and McGuiness."

"I've heard of them," Hope said. "Back when I was with Richard we attended several benefits for charities they were involved in."

"Yeah, well, the interesting thing is the name pops up again in connection with the property next door."

"How are they connected?" Conn asked.

"Back in 1986, Wells, Powell, and McGuiness defended the corporation that owns the piece of property north of Buddy's in a lawsuit brought against them for negligence. I guess somebody fell down and broke his arm or something. Seems like everybody's sue-crazy these days. The point is, out of all the attorneys in the city, these guys' names come up on the property adjacent to Hartley House."

Jimmy flashed a smile. "Even more interesting, that firm was also used in 1993 to incorporate a company called Royalty Park. Royalty Park owns the piece abutting Newton's property to the south."

"Oh, my God," Hope said.

"Amazing, ain't it? All three of those pieces front the Hudson River. Put them together, you got enough real estate for a major development."

"I thought it might be something like that," Hope said.

"What kind of development are you thinking?" Conn asked.

"Who knows? Could be anything. Residential condos, time-shares, high-rise professional office space for sale. Whatever it is, if the deal goes through, the numbers are going to run into the hundreds of millions."

Conn whistled.

"No wonder they need Buddy's property," Hope said. "Without it, they're limited in what they're able to do—maybe even blocked completely."

"That's just about it."

"So what can we do to stop them?" she asked.

"Now that Buddy's gone, we don't have much to say about it. Whoever the old man left the place to is likely to agree to whatever deal he's offered. From what Buddy told me, the offer's more than fair. It was just that he didn't want to sell."

"The building belonged to him. It was his home. He had every right to refuse to sell."

"True, but look where it got him."

Hope took a steadying breath. "You're saying Buddy's murderers are going to get away with it. They've killed an innocent old man and now they're going to be rewarded by making millions of dollars."

"The cops are on it. They don't like seeing an old man murdered any more than you do. There's always a chance they'll find the thugs who beat him to death."

"But not the real killers—the men who ordered the attack. Those men will go unpunished."

Jimmy just shrugged. After so many years in the business, he was bound to be a realist.

"So who's in line to inherit the property?" Conn asked.

"I don't think Buddy had any real family left." Hope's glance strayed out the window. In the office building across the way, people worked in little cubicles, absorbed in their own concerns. But Buddy had been different. He cared about other people. Now he was dead. "Of course there might be a distant cousin or some other relative out there somewhere."

"I guess we won't know until the will is read. I spoke to that attorney friend of yours, Matt Westland, the guy who was helping Newton. He says it might take a couple of weeks."

Jimmy gave her shoulder a surprisingly gentle squeeze. "You did the best you could, Hope. You got to think of it that way."

She only shook her head. "All those poor old people are going to lose their homes."

Conn reached down and linked their fingers together, his strong grip oddly reassuring. "Like Jimmy said, you did your best. That's all anyone can do."

"When are you two heading back?" the detective asked.

"Right after the funeral," Conn answered. "That's day after tomorrow."

Hope didn't argue, though she hadn't completely made up her mind.

"Be better if you left today. If they've figured out you're here, there might be trouble. Until this is finally over, anything could happen."

Hope let go of Conn's hand. "I'm not leaving until after Buddy's funeral. There's only so much I'm willing to take."

Jimmy cracked a brief, approving smile. "That's the spirit. But if you stay, you'd better be careful."

"I will."

He looked up at Conn. "You keep an eye on her."

"Believe me, I intend to."

Jimmy left and Hope took a weary breath, her thoughts more in turmoil than they had been before. She wanted to stay in New York and do what she could to help, but even if she did, it probably wouldn't matter. The will might not be read for weeks and even then, the new owner would undoubtedly take the Americal offer.

She was still thinking of Buddy and the tenants at Hartley

House the following morning when the phone began to ring. Hope picked it up, wondering who besides Jimmy knew she was in the city.

The voice on the other end of the line was her boss, Artie Green. "I heard you were back in town." The anger she heard in his voice made her stomach churn. "I want to see you in my office, Sinclair. Now."

He hung up before she could reply. Hope set the receiver back in its cradle and looked up at Conn. "I've got to go down to the office. I'll be back in an hour or so."

She crossed the room, heading for the coat closet, then realized Conn walked beside her.

He smiled. "I'll just keep you company."

"This is business, Conn. I've got a meeting with my employer."

"No problem. I'll wait out at the front desk."

"That is ridiculous!"

His dark eyebrows drew together over eyes that had turned an icy blue. "Yeah? That's what Buddy thought." Grabbing his overcoat, he gripped her arm and propelled her out into the hall. "You don't want to be late. Let's go."

As usual, the offices of *Midday News* on Twenty-second Street hummed with activity. Hope left Conn perched on an uncomfortable chair in the small reception area, the object of speculative glances being cast his way by Agnes Holland, the thin, gray-haired woman at the desk.

Conn bestowed one of his rare, charming smiles, and Agnes, the battle-ax of the office, returned it almost shyly. Hope rolled her eyes as she walked through the door leading into the main part of the office. Once inside, she made her way past a small sea of reporters who pounded away on their word processors, madly working to make their deadlines.

Hope waved at a couple of familiar faces but kept on walking, heading toward Artie Green, who stood in the open doorway of his office, his bald head gleaming in the bright

fluorescent lights overhead. As she drew near, she noticed
the frown on his face and the blunt hand clamped on his hip.
Not a good sign.

"Get in here, Sinclair."

"Yes, sir." Hope eased past him into the office, and Artie
slammed the half-glass door.

"Sit down."

She did as he commanded, carefully tucking the skirt of
her brown wool suit around her knees while Artie sat down
in the chair behind his cluttered desk.

"You . . . um . . . wanted to see me?"

"Yeah. What the hell are you doing here, Sinclair? Why
aren't you sunbathing somewhere out in the middle of the
ocean?"

Hope managed a smile. "I found out a friend of mine was
in the hospital. I came to see if he was all right."

"And was he?"

The fake smile slid away. "No."

"And that friend wouldn't happen to be Buddy Newton,
by any chance, would it?"

Her eyebrows went up. "Actually, it was. But how did you
know? As a matter of fact, how did you know I was even in
the city?"

"Randy Hicks stopped by the hospital to see your late
friend. The nurse mentioned he'd had out-of-town visitors.
Your name came up as one of them."

Randy Hicks, the reporter—and she used the term loosely—
who had taken over her story. "So what did good ol' Randy
have to say about what happened to Buddy?"

Artie picked up the newspaper sitting on top of the stack
on his desk and handed it over. "Here. See for yourself."

Hope took the paper, opened it, and began to scan the
pages.

"Section B. Top of the page."

It was a prime location, the headline in large, bold print:
IRONIC END FOR OWNER OF HARTLEY HOUSE. Hope
quickly read the article, which basically said that the neigh-

bors had been correct in their efforts to improve the neighborhood. After all, look what had happened to poor old Mr. Newton, mugged and killed almost in front of his own home. A new development in the area would help get rid of the unsavory element that was beginning to move into the neighborhood.

Hope smiled sardonically. "Of course, Randy didn't mention the fact that the guys who want to buy that property already own the pieces to the north and south. That whatever they're planning to build will make them millions of dollars. Or that they are undoubtedly the men behind the attack on Buddy that ultimately killed him."

Artie shoved to his feet, his face a violent shade of red. "What the hell? I told you to stay out of this!"

Hope came up out of her chair. "I am out. I'm thousands of miles away. Besides, now Buddy's dead so it really doesn't matter. Though I kind of hoped you might be interested in taking a closer look at what actually went on there."

"I told you, Hope. The paper's taken a stand. They think tearing that building down is good for the neighborhood— hell, good for the whole damned city. They aren't interested in digging up dirt that might keep that from happening."

Artie sat back down in his chair and Hope eased back down as well.

"Now here's the way it's going to be. Either you go back and complete your assignment—"

"I sent the second article in over the Net before I left to come back here."

"Yeah, well, now you can get back there and finish the third. By the time you get done, all this will be settled and you can get your ass back to work."

"I thought I *was* working."

Artie looked at her over the top of the paper he had just picked up. "Get out of here, Sinclair. Before the job I'm holding disappears."

Hope didn't argue, but Artie had just confirmed her suspicions. She had been assigned to do a story in the middle of nowhere *not* because Brad Talbot had liked the work she had done before. He just wanted her away from the city. It was a very good bet Brad Talbot was one of those nameless men trying to develop the Hartley House property.

Unfortunately, Hope didn't think there was any way to prove it.

Beyond that, the building would soon be sold and the project would go forward. The tenants at Hartley House would lose their homes and it didn't look like there was a damned thing she could do.

She had almost reached the door when she heard Artie's gravelly voice behind her. "One more thing."

She stopped and turned. "Yes?"

"Do yourself a favor, Hope. Forget whatever it is you think you've found out. One old man is already dead. I don't have any idea what's going on and I don't want to know. I do know that whatever it is, it's dangerous to be on the wrong side of this thing."

Hope made no reply, just turned and started walking, her legs a little wobbly. She felt bitter and betrayed and a little bit frightened. If Artie knew she had returned to the city, so might someone else. Odds were, her opposition to the project no longer mattered, since it appeared the developers—whoever they were—were going to get what they wanted.

Still, the deal wasn't made yet, and until she was safely back aboard the *Conquest,* she would need to stay alert. Silently grateful that Conn had come with her, she spotted him in the reception area as she walked in.

Conn saw her and came to his feet. "Everything okay?" The familiar deep voice sent a leap of awareness through her. For days she had been doing her best to ignore him. It was getting harder and harder to do.

"If you call letting the bad guys get away with murder, everything's peachy."

They started for the elevator, stood in front of the doors until it arrived on their floor. Then the bell chimed, the elevator doors slid open, and Gordy Wietzman walked out.

"Hey, Hope!" He glanced from her to the office. "I sure didn't expect to see *you* here."

"Yes, well, you can thank our friend, Randy Hicks, for that. He found out I was at the hospital visiting Buddy and ran straight back to tell Artie I was in town."

"I don't suppose that made Artie too happy." Gordy turned his attention to Conn. "Gordy Weitzman. I work with Hope." He stuck out his hand and Conn grasped it.

"Conner Reese. I guess you could say I'm her current assignment."

"Is that so?"

"Conn's one of the partners in Treasure Limited. He's heading up the search operation."

"Nice to meet you." Gordy's gaze slid over Conn with the practiced eye of a reporter. Aside from the air of competence Conn wore like a comfortable shirt, Hope wondered what else Gordy saw.

The reporter shook his head. "That whole thing with Buddy Newton . . . that really sucks. The old guy caught a really bad break." Gordy was shorter than Conn, but not much, lean, and fair-haired. He was divorced and on the prowl, but after his first *no* from Hope, he had accepted the fact they were never going to be more than friends. She thought that in a way he'd been relieved.

"I still can't believe Buddy's gone," she said.

"Be interesting to see what happens next." Gordy shifted the briefcase he was carrying into his other hand. "I know the old man had a will, but nobody seems to know who's going to inherit. Looks like whoever it is, the guy's going to make out like a bandit."

"Sounds like it," she said.

"How's Deitz working out?"

"I like him. Better yet, I trust him."

"He come up with anything useful?"

Hope explained Jimmy's theory that the properties north and south of Hartley House were actually owned by the same people, that they were trying to connect all three riverfront pieces, and that hundreds of millions of dollars were involved.

"That's something, I guess, but I don't know how much good it'll do you, now that the old man's dead and the piece will belong to someone else." Gordy tipped his head toward the door leading in to the main part of the office. "Listen, I gotta run. You need anything, just call."

"Thanks, Gordy."

Hope watched him leave and so did Conn.

"Seems like a nice enough guy." Conn's eyes remained on Gordy until the door closed behind him. "I guess you figure you can trust him."

"Gordy's helped me from the start. I'm lucky to have him for a friend."

"Is he? Just a friend, I mean?"

Hope flicked Conn a glance. "The truth is, I think there's a chance he's gay but if he is, he's fighting it and he's definitely not out of the closet. And yes, we're just friends."

Conn said nothing more, but the tension in his shoulders seemed to ease. Another elevator arrived. They walked in and rode down to the lobby. Conn hailed a cab out on Twenty-second Street, opened the door, and they slid onto the black leather seat.

"Buddy's funeral's tomorrow," Conn said as the cab roared over the slick streets back to her apartment. "That's not going to be any more fun than the rest of this trip. We'll be catching a plane tomorrow afternoon and going back to work. But tonight we'll be in New York City. I don't think Buddy would mind if we went out to dinner someplace nice, maybe listened to some jazz somewhere afterward."

Hope looked up at him. Buddy was gone. Conn had come thousands of miles just to watch out for her if she ran into trouble. She owed him something for that. An evening in the city didn't seem like much of a price to pay.

Hope smiled. "I knew you liked jazz. You took me to the Palms, and sometimes at night, I could hear the music on your CD, seeping through the wall between our cabins."

"You've got a pretty fair collection yourself. Dave Brubeck, Miles Davis. You've got Mingus and Nick Drake."

"It was better before those jerks broke in and banged up some of the albums. Fortunately, most of them survived."

"Then maybe we should just go home after dinner and listen to music at your place." She didn't miss the heat in his eyes and a soft pang went through her.

Hope forced a smile. "And maybe your first idea was best. When we get back to the apartment, I'll call and make dinner reservations. I know a great little Italian place just around the corner, very classy but quiet, and the food is really great. There's a jazz bar not too far away."

"Sounds good to me." But desire still burned in those blue, blue eyes and it did not go away.

Twenty minutes later, Artie Green was still grumbling about Hope Sinclair. When he opened his office door, preoccupied as he usually was, he was a little surprised to see Randy Hicks, knuckles raised to knock, on the opposite side of the glass.

"What's up?" Artie asked.

Randy cocked his head toward the door leading out to the reception room. "I thought I saw Hope Sinclair in here."

Artie stepped back and motioned him in. "She was here. I wanted to know what the hell she was doing in New York when she's supposed to be on assignment somewhere else."

"What'd she say?" Randy was fifty-five years old, black hair going to gray, a body still thin but had seen better days.

"The woman's all wound up in this Buddy Newton thing. She's convinced something shady's going on, gave me some crap about a project worth millions of dollars—enough, I gather, that she thinks Buddy was targeted as a way of forcing him to sell."

"It's possible, I guess." Though Hicks was only in his mid-fifties, his big goal in life was to retire. He'd started in the newspaper business when he was just a kid. Now, thirty-five years later, he was bored and lackadaisical, jaded and itching to quit. Three months from now, he would start getting his pension and it was obvious the man could hardly wait.

"It's possible," Artie repeated, "but you don't think that's the way it is."

Randy shook his head, his hair, a little shaggy, brushing the tips of his ears. "I think Newton's building is in piss-poor shape and needs to come down. I think the old man was mugged in his own neighborhood, which just proves they need to make the area safer. A new building, with more upscale tenants, would be a major benefit. That's what I wrote and that's what I think."

"Hope's not convinced. I warned her to stay out of this. I hope to hell she listens."

"I don't know . . . she can be pretty stubborn."

One of Artie's thick eyebrows hiked up. "No kidding." He glanced toward the door. "So what was it you wanted to see me about?"

"What? Oh . . . uh, I was just checking to see if you wanted any kind of follow-up on the story I did about the bookstore owner who has his entire house filled floor-to-ceiling with books."

"The guy's a kook. One piece is plenty. I thought you were working on something else."

"I am. I just . . . I guess I'd better get back and finish."

"Good idea," Artie said. He watched Randy leave, thinking how much he would love to fire the lazy bum, but with only three months to go, he just couldn't do it.

Artie grunted. And people said he didn't have a heart.

Chapter 17

The Italian restaurant, Café Fiore, was even better than Hope remembered. It was kind of expensive so she rarely went to dinner there, but with all that had happened, she needed a little lift and she thought that Conn would enjoy it.

The interior was all beige and cream, with soft lighting, soft music, small white flowers on the tables, and waiters who kept their distance while still giving patrons great service.

"You were right," Conn said. "This place is great. And the food's terrific."

"I have to say, your veal marsala really looks good."

Conn smiled. He had the sexiest smile. She wondered why she hadn't noticed.

"Want a bite?" He cut off a forkful and held it up invitingly, but the thought of him feeding her seemed incredibly erotic and Hope shook her head.

"I've got all I can handle right here." Fillet of halibut encrusted with hazelnuts, served over a bed of mashed potatoes and sautéed spinach. Lord, it was good.

They finished the meal and a bottle of good Chianti, then ordered tiramisu and cups of foamy cappuccino for dessert.

She was pleasantly stuffed by the time they argued over the bill, Conn insisting he pay and getting his way as usual. At the front of the restaurant, he helped her pull her coat on over her simple black sheath dress, dragged his overcoat on over the navy blue jacket and dark gray slacks he wore, and they stepped out onto the sidewalk.

The wind was blowing but not too hard, and the crisp, chill air was invigorating.

"I know it's cold for a sun rat like you," she said, "but I could sure use a walk. Club Seventy-seven isn't really that far away."

He cast her a heated glance. "A little exercise sounds good to me, though I'd rather do something more interesting than walking."

Hope's gaze shot to his face and she caught the faint curve of his lips. Biting back a smile, she took his arm and they started down the sidewalk.

The pavement was wet, reflecting the red, yellow, and green of the streetlights at the corner. The bar was a little bit farther away than she remembered, the night air a little colder than she'd thought. By the time they had walked six blocks, the tips of her fingers were numb inside her gloves and her toes felt like little cubes of ice in her black high heels. Conn had the collar of his overcoat turned up but he had taken off his gloves and stuffed them in his pocket.

An instant later, she understood why.

"Don't turn, just keep walking. We're being followed."

She automatically started to turn, but Conn tightened his hold on her arm and she kept on walking. "Are you sure?"

"Oh, he's back there, all right. Tall guy, black leather jacket, wool cap pulled down over his ears. The question is why?"

As they continued along the sidewalk, the darkness seemed to close in on them. The sound of their footsteps seemed louder, the click of her high heels like nails hitting concrete, the icy air even more frigid, seeping into her very bones. Most of the shops on the street were closed, the interiors dimly lit or not at all. Black vinyl garbage bags sat next to locked doors, ready for pickup early in the morning.

"Is he still there?" Hope asked softly, her pulse beating faster, beginning to drum in her ears.

"He's there. How much farther to the club?"

"Two more blocks."

Conn made no reply, but she could tell he wasn't pleased. Her heartbeat quickened even more. She started to increase her pace, but Conn held her back. "Easy."

They kept their pace even, moving rapidly along but not running. Then, at the next alley they passed, two men stepped out on the sidewalk right behind them. Both men were wearing ski masks pulled down over their faces, and a streak of fear shot through her. She heard Conn softly curse. Farther down the block, the ring of running footsteps echoed on the pavement, and she knew the man following them was hurrying to catch up with his friends.

"Get ready," Conn said softly. She felt his hand on her back. He propelled her ahead of him and spun to face the men. "Run!" he shouted. "Get inside the club!"

She didn't, of course, and everything happened at once.

The first man shot forward and Conn kicked out, his heel slamming into the man's shin, knocking him violently backward. He screamed as he hit the pavement, rolled several times, and crashed into a rough brick wall. The second man came in from behind, landing a glancing blow to Conn's cheek before Conn grabbed him and whirled him around, wrenched his arm up behind his back, and slammed him up against the wall.

Hope saw the gun in the man's hand and screamed the instant before it went flying. The pistol hit the pavement ten feet away and slid into the gutter. The man—white, she could tell from his hands—average in height and wearing jeans and a jacket, turned and kicked out, and Conn shoved his arm even higher.

"Call off your dogs," Conn warned.

"Fuck you, man!" He tried to turn, lashed out again with

his foot. The bone in his arm snapped with a crack that echoed along the sidewalk. Conn let him go and he slumped down on the walk a few feet away from his friend, whimpering in pain.

The third man raced out of the shadows behind them, making a fierce growling sound as he attacked. They traded a couple of punches, then, in the light of a distant street lamp, Hope saw the glitter of a blade flash from the pocket of the man's black leather coat.

"Conn, he's got a knife!" For a terrifying instant, his attention shifted to her.

"Dammit, I told you to get out of here!" He whirled toward the threat and Hope started running for the gutter.

In the darkness, she couldn't see exactly where the pistol had landed, but she knew it was down there somewhere. Blindly, she felt along the icy cement, ignoring frozen lumps of gum, slushy mud and muck, until she felt the cold barrel of the pistol. She gripped the handle with a shaking hand and swung the weapon toward the men circling each other on the sidewalk.

Conn had taken off his wool muffler and wrapped it around his arm. He was looking for an opening and an instant later he found it. The attacker jabbed the blade toward Conn's middle. Conn caught his wrist, stepped aside, and let the man's own momentum carry him forward. A big foot planted in the center of the man's behind slammed him hard against the wall and he went crashing down on the sidewalk. The guy rolled over and pushed to his feet, but instead of coming back at Conn, he turned and raced like a madman off into the darkness.

Conn started after him, said a dirty word, and turned back, his gaze coming to rest on her. She was standing with her legs braced apart, gripping the pistol with both hands as she had seen the cops do in the movies.

"You don't need that now. They're gone."

She looked around, her grip still tight on the gun, and saw that all three of the men had managed to get away. Conn hadn't gone after them because he didn't want to leave her.

"I'd appreciate it if you'd aim that thing somewhere besides my chest."

"Oh, my God!" She lowered the weapon, pointing it down at the sidewalk with shaking hands. "I'm sorry. I'm pretty new at this. I wasn't quite sure what . . . what I should do."

Conn walked over and gently took the pistol out of her fingers. "Would you really have pulled the trigger?"

"Of course! Those guys were trying to kill you!"

He shook his head. "You never fail to amaze me, Sinclair."

She realized she was trembling. She wasn't sure if it was the cold or the adrenaline still pumping through her veins. Conn gathered her into his arms and just held her, sharing some of his warmth. "It's all right. It's over."

She swallowed, nodded. "I guess we'd better call the police." Instead of letting him go, she clung to him and he kept his arms tightly around her.

"You got your cell phone with you?"

"No, I . . . I didn't want anyone to disturb our evening."

He laughed harshly. "I guess we should have known that wasn't going to happen."

"We'll have to use the phone at the club."

Conn raked a hand through his hair, which was longer now than when she had first met him. "It doesn't really matter. Those guys are long gone. Unless you got a really good look at one of them—"

Hope shook her head. "Two of them had their faces completely covered. The third had his cap pulled so low I couldn't really see him. Two of them were white, though. One had dark skin. He could have been black, but I don't think so. I was so scared, that's about all I noticed. How about you?"

"A few more details, maybe. Nothing that's really going to help." With his background, he could probably give the police a lot better description than she could. Still, there was no way he could manage a positive I.D.

"Come on. We'll call the police from your apartment, but it'll probably be a waste of time. There's no way they're going to catch those guys."

Hope looked up at him, wishing he was wrong, certain the attack was connected in some way to the mugging that had killed poor Buddy, hoping she could somehow convince the police. As they stepped into the light of the street lamp, she noticed the faint trail of blood running from his temple.

"My God, you're hurt! Why didn't you say something?"

He reached up and touched the gash on the side of his head, came away with bloody fingers. "It's no big deal. Head wounds always bleed like the devil." But he opened his coat, reached into the pocket of his jacket and pulled out his handkerchief, then pressed it against the wound on the side of his head just above his right ear.

"We'll call the police in the morning. Right now, we need to go home and get that bleeding stopped." Hope started shaking again. "I shouldn't have let you come here with me. You could have been killed tonight and it would have been my fault."

Conn caught her shoulder, his gaze locked with hers. "I'm here because I was afraid something like this would happen. Tomorrow we're going to that funeral, then we're flying back to Pleasure Island where you'll be safe until this is over."

She was too tired to argue. And clearly Jimmy was right—it was dangerous to stay. Besides, she didn't really think it would help if she did.

In the morning, she would call the police and report what had happened, then she was going back to the *Conquest* with Conn.

By the time they reached her apartment, the adrenaline rush was beginning to fade and Hope felt completely drained. Yet oddly, both of them remained on edge.

"I need to take a look at that cut," she said, summoning a last reserve of strength.

Conn reached up, found it still trickling blood. "All right. I'd hate to mess up your nice clean sheets."

They tossed their coats and scarves onto the back of the sofa. Conn stripped off his navy blue sport coat, red-and-yellow-striped tie, and unbuttoned the top two buttons on his white dress shirt as they walked into the kitchen. There was blood on his collar, she saw, and her stomach tightened.

"Sit here," she instructed in a take-charge voice, and he sat down heavily in one of the small wooden chairs. His knuckles were scraped, as well, oozing traces of blood, and her heart pinched sharply. His hair was mussed, curling down over his forehead. She combed it back gently with her fingers.

Determined to compose herself, she took a steadying breath and headed for the bathroom to find the peroxide and Band-Aids. They were on a shelf in the medicine chest. She took them out and returned to the kitchen.

Turning on the faucet, she dampened a paper towel and used it to wash the blood from his hands and the cut on his temple. A Q-tip dipped in peroxide helped remove the dried blood and dirt.

As she peeled the plastic tape off the Band-Aid and gently laid the pad over the gash on his head, her hand brushed the nape of his neck. His skin was still chilled, yet she could feel an underlying warmth. His hair felt silky where it curled against her fingers.

He had risked himself for her, come to her aid ignoring the threat to his own safety. Gratitude mixed with a need to touch him, to assure herself that he was all right. Her hands moved lower. Under his white cotton shirt, she knew the smoothness of his skin, the shape and texture of the muscles that moved and tightened across his back. She knew how his body tapered to a narrow waist and flat stomach ridged with sinew.

Reaching around, she began to unfasten the buttons on the front of his shirt. One by one, they popped free, revealing glimpses of springy dark chest hair. She touched him there, circled a flat copper nipple with the tip of her finger and felt his muscles bunch. She could feel the tension in his body, the sinews straining against the desire for her that each of her touches aroused.

His eyes were a turbulent blue and every line of his face

betrayed the control it took to endure her exploration. Her own desire built, spearing out through her limbs, tugging low in her belly. Her heartbeat quickened, yet seemed strangely to slow, the soft cadence pulsing between her legs, making her damp and needy.

She pressed her mouth against the side of his neck, her hair swinging forward, sliding along his jaw, and Conn made a low, strangled sound in his throat. His skin tasted salty and male. He smelled of lime aftershave and traces of the sea that was so much a part of him. Another soft kiss, pressed to the nape of his neck, and Conn erupted out of his chair. Hauling her hard against him, he fisted a hand in her hair and his mouth crushed down over hers.

His kiss was fierce and wildly possessive, a hard, claiming kiss brought on by the dangers they had faced. Desire swelled inside her, a hunger unlike any she had known. His tongue swept into her mouth and her own tongue fenced and mated. She wanted to feel him, wanted to touch him. Hope caught the front of his shirt, tearing the last button free, and shoved the fabric off his shoulders.

She wasn't wearing a bra and the bodice of her black Jersey sheath erotically rubbed her nipples. Conn pushed the narrow straps off her shoulders, shoved the dress down to her waist, and his long, dark fingers curved over a naked breast. He caressed the fullness and pinched the end, sending little jolts of pleasure-pain racing through her.

"Conn . . ." His name was a plea and a surrender. She wanted this, wanted him. She desired him as she never had another man, and tonight her need was greater than her fear. He could have been injured, even killed. He had risked himself for her and in doing so had somehow claimed her.

She kissed him wildly, erotically, took and took and demanded more. She could feel his arousal, thick and hard, pressing against her stomach, and she ached to feel him inside her. Conn seemed to sense her need. She clung to his neck as he gripped her hips and lifted her up on the table, knocking the bandages and peroxide onto the floor.

Conn kissed her as he came up over her, his hands in her hair, his tongue deep in her mouth. He shoved up her short black skirt and parted her thighs to make room for himself between them. The sight of her black thigh-high nylons and black lace thong underwear tore a harsh sound from his throat. Reaching down, he caught her panties and ripped them away, found her softness, and began to stroke her.

She was throbbing with need, aching with desire for him, flushed and hot and wanting. She arched toward him, felt his erection at the entrance to her passage. He was a big man and heavily aroused, his erection pulsing with the need to be inside her.

"Yes . . ." she whispered, her gaze on his beautiful face. "Please, Conn . . ."

His eyes turned a darker blue and in one hard thrust he impaled her, filling her completely. The blood pounded in her ears and pleasure rushed through her. He kissed her again, his tongue delving deeply, matching the thrust and drag of his shaft. Pleasure tore through her, seemed to scorch through her blood.

He's mine, her brain said, and her body agreed. Heat speared through her and the pleasure mounted, carrying her higher and higher. Her climax hit fast and hard, the pleasure rich and deep, forcing his name from her lips.

Still, she wanted more.

Conn gave it, his powerful thrusts rocking the table. Hope wrapped her legs around his hips and arched upward, taking him deeper still, feeling the sweetness begin to build a second time. He didn't stop, just kept driving into her as deep convulsions shook her. A little sigh of satisfaction slipped from her lips as he followed her to release.

For long moments, neither of them moved.

The room slowly came back into focus and his heavy weight began to become uncomfortable. Conn came up off the table, stepped back, and looked down at her, still sprawled on the butcher-block top. She was naked to the waist, her bodice shoved down and her breasts exposed, her skirt shoved up.

She still wore her thigh-high black stockings and black high heels.

"God, you're beautiful."

She started to rise, but he shook his head. "Not yet." Easing her back down on the table, he found her softness one last time. His eyes locked with hers as he touched her, explored her, stroked her to a sobbing climax. She barely noticed when he lifted her and carried her into the bedroom, wordlessly unzipped her dress and slipped it over her hips, then urged her down on the edge of the bed so he could strip off her shoes and stockings.

"I'm sleeping in this bed tonight," he said, and the look in his eyes warned her not to argue.

Instead she lay down on her side and watched him undress, admiring the beautiful muscles and sleek planes of his body, the smooth, darkly suntanned skin. He climbed into the narrow bed and lay down beside her, his hips cradling hers, spoon fashion. Big strong arms wrapped around her, one draped possessively over her hip. As Hope fell asleep, she had a final terrifying thought.

Oh, my God, what have I done?

Conn sat in the living room reading *The New York Times* he had purchased at the bakery downstairs. Mostly he thumbed through the pages, finding it nearly impossible to concentrate on anything but the sound of the shower running in the bathroom, knowing Hope was in there naked. Wanting her again.

It was insane, this constant hunger he felt for her.

And it forced him to face an unwelcome truth he'd been trying to ignore.

He was in love with her, in love with Hope Sinclair.

He had known it the moment he had seen her standing on the sidewalk holding the pistol, determined to protect him, though she was the one in danger.

Perhaps he had known it long before that but refused to

accept it. Now that he had, he wasn't exactly sure what he should do.

Hope wasn't looking for a serious relationship. She had made that more than clear. She was still hurting from Richard, the bastard she had trusted and loved—or at least thought she did.

And no matter what Conn felt for her, he was hardly in a position to make any sort of commitment. He had duties, responsibilities to his partners in Treasure Limited. He was the one who had started the salvage project. Once he had met the professor and been convinced the man knew where the *Rosa* might have gone down, Conn had been determined to find her. He had made the deal with Eddie and gone to Talbot to raise the money. He was in charge and he meant to see the job done to the best of his abilities.

Conn sighed as he got up from the sofa. After his antics on the way to the jazz bar last night, he was a little stiff this morning. He hadn't been in a down-and-dirty street fight in years. Not since Joe had dragged him into some sleazy South Beach bar a few months before he met Kelly. Joe had a knack for getting into trouble, at least back in the old days.

Conn smiled to think of the four guys he and his friend had taken on that night.

Ah, those were the days.

Conn was damned glad they were over.

At least, he'd thought they were.

His mind ran over the encounter he'd had the previous night—not really much of a fight, by his standards. The three men who attacked them were thugs, punks who brawled without much style. He had never really felt in any serious danger. Of course, Hope hadn't known that. He would never forget how brave she had been. But then, he had never doubted her courage.

The shower went off. Conn had known better than to suggest he join her. He had recognized that deer-in-the-headlights look when she climbed out of bed, her *I'm-feeling-cornered* expression. She was on the run again. He had never seen a woman so wary of any sort of relationship with a man.

Conn supposed, after Kelly, he ought to understand, and part of him did. The other part thought it was crazy to let some creep like Richard ruin your life.

The blow-dryer roared to life and Conn walked over to use the phone. Pressing the receiver against his ear, he dialed in his credit card number to call the satellite cell on the boat.

Andy Glass answered. "Hey, Conn!"

"Hi, Andy. Everything okay down there?"

"Pretty much so."

"You guys get that generator fixed?"

"Not yet. We're working on it, though. The boat's still in Jamaica—which turned out to be good because last night it stormed like crazy. We'll be here at least until tomorrow."

"We're flying back to Kingston tonight. I guess we'll just catch up with you in port." He flicked a glance toward the open bedroom door, saw Hope wearing only a towel, pulling a sweater out of one of her dresser drawers. His groin tightened. Christ, he just couldn't seem to get enough of her.

He forced his thoughts back to the *Conquest*. "Is Joe around?"

"He took off as soon as he found out we wouldn't be leaving for a couple of days. He had a date with that girl he brought aboard just before you and Hope left."

Conn frowned. "Glory?"

"That's the one."

Conn was more than a little surprised. "I figured she'd gone back to the States by now."

"Well, you know Joe. The ladies all love him."

Yeah, and Joe loved all of them. He rarely got involved to the degree he seemed to be with Glory and certainly never this quickly.

"If you see him, tell him we'll be back aboard late tonight."

"Will do," Andy said. Conn hung up the phone just as Hope walked into the living room.

"Everything all right?" She was dressed for the funeral, in a long-sleeved, high-necked black sweater, black wool skirt, and black stockings. The stockings reminded him of last night and sent his mind in unwanted directions but he yanked himself back to the present.

"The boat's in Jamaica. They're still working on the capstan, so we'll catch up with them in port."

Hope nodded. She seemed edgy this morning and he figured she was worried about the attack last night or them making love. When the doorbell chimed, she nearly jumped out of her skin.

Conn cast her a look. "Get in the bedroom." Hope didn't argue. After what had happened on the street, she was taking all of this more seriously. Conn moved to a spot beside the front door. "Who is it?"

"Police." A man's deep voice reached him from the hallway on the opposite side of the door. "Detectives Ryman and Kowalski."

"Let's see some I.D." Conn used the peephole to check the men's badges, then opened the door to let them in. Hope came out of the bedroom as the older detective, a man with thinning black hair, and his younger, slightly chubby partner walked in.

"We got your call this morning," the dark-haired cop said to Hope. "You should have called last night."

"Probably. But two of the men who attacked us were wearing ski masks and the third had his cap pulled so low we could barely see his face. We couldn't possibly identify any of them."

The black-haired man, Kowalski, looked down at his notes. "According to your phone call, you think this attack is connected to the attack made on a man named William Newton, the guy who died from a mugging in front of Hartley House a couple of nights ago."

"That's right."

"Why do you think the two crimes are related?"

"Because I'm a reporter," Hope said. "I was working on

the story." Conn cast her a glance, and her cheeks turned pink. Well, she was mostly telling the truth.

"I believe Buddy was attacked in order to force him to sell his property," she went on. "Whoever wants to buy Hartley House doesn't want anyone trying to stop them."

The detective wrote down what she said. Conn gave a similar report of the attack near Club Seventy-seven, adding that he figured the men must have been watching the apartment when he and Hope went out.

"Anything else you can tell us?" chubby Detective Ryman asked.

"That's about it," Conn said.

"Anything turns up, we'll be in touch." Kowalski made a couple more notes. "You be at this number if we need you?"

Conn didn't give Hope time to answer. "As soon as Buddy Newton's funeral is over, we're catching a plane to Jamaica."

"Vacation?"

"Work. We're involved in a salvage operation off the coast of a private island not far away."

"I'm on assignment for *Adventure* magazine," Hope added.

"I thought you said you were working on the Hartley House story."

The color returned to her cheeks. "Yes, well, I'm doing that on the side."

He cast her a speculative glance and jotted something in his notes.

"If you need to speak to either one of us, we'll be aboard the *Conquest*," Conn told him. "You can reach us by satellite phone." He gave the detective the number.

Kowalski closed his notebook and tucked it into the pocket of his coat. "Like I said, we'll let you know if anything turns up."

Hope managed a smile. "Thank you." She walked the men to the door, closed it behind them, and looked down at her watch. "We've still got more than an hour before we have to leave for the funeral."

"In that case, how about another cup of coffee?"

As they walked into the kitchen, Hope eyed her surroundings like a criminal going back to the scene of the crime. Conn couldn't resist a wicked glance at the table.

"I'm sure glad that packing tape held. If that leg had come off, we could have had one helluva rough landing."

Hope's eyes rounded. She opened her mouth but not a word came out. She followed his gaze to the butcher-block table, and her cheeks went bright red. Then her lips twitched and a soft burst of laughter escaped.

Still smiling, she shook her head. "I can't believe we did that. My sister, Charity, drank too much champagne one night and confessed that she and Call once made passionate love on the kitchen table in his cabin. At the time, I thought she was out of her mind."

Conn caught her shoulders, forcing her to look up at him. "What we have is special, Hope—surely you can see that. Stop running away from it. Let this thing happen between us, see where it leads. That's all I ask."

Her bright smile faded. He caught the faint glitter of tears.

"I can't," was all she said.

Chapter 18

It turned out Buddy was Catholic, though apparently he rarely attended services. Still, at the Church of Saint Francis Xavier on West Fifteenth Street, he seemed to have been well known. As Hope walked down the aisle between the rows of pews, grateful to be holding onto Conn's arm, she saw that the funeral was well attended and even began to recognize a number of familiar faces, tenants of Hartley House.

Mr. Nivers, the jokester of the building, sat in the middle of a pew next to Mrs. Eisenhoff, the lady Hope had dubbed Aunt Bea. Mrs. Finnegan sat two rows from the front, dressed all in black, a veil covering her face, her back ramrod straight. She had been a close friend of Buddy's for nearly twenty years. Hope had even heard rumors that they were romantically involved.

She smiled to think of it, remembering Buddy as he had been, always smiling, always full of fun. Certainly, he was a man who had lived his life to the fullest. That he might have had a lady friend didn't seem surprising at all.

The Mass began. Hope knelt when the others did, saw that Conn did as well. Neither of them repeated the prayers as the Catholic parishioners did, so she figured he wasn't of that faith and wondered, after the kind of things he must have seen during his years in the SEALs, if he believed in God at all.

Then she heard his deep voice softly repeating the Lord's Prayer and felt strangely relieved. Her family was Methodist. As a child, she had attended church often. If she and Richard had married and had a family, as she had wanted to do so badly, some form of religion would have been part of their lives.

The service continued. Six pallbearers carried in the coffin, two had faces she recognized as tenants of the building. Toward the end of the service, the priest waved burning incense over the white-draped coffin, and for the first time, Hope felt the reality of Buddy's death. Her throat closed up and her eyes swam with tears. She felt Conn's fingers link with hers and was glad that he was there beside her.

The priest's words were comforting and some of her sorrow eased. Buddy had been happy. She didn't believe he would have left this world with a single complaint. And wherever he was, she was certain he would find the same joy he had always found on earth.

The priest spoke of the body of Christ and began communion, but neither she nor Conn took part. The service finally came to a close. As she rose from the pew, she slid her sunglasses up on her nose and made her way to the door of the church. On the steps outside, Conn stood a few feet away as she spoke to some of the tenants, expressing her condolences, receiving a nod of gratitude that she had come.

"He was a good man," said tall, gray-haired Mr. Nivers, for once without a joke. He pulled out a cotton handkerchief with his initials on the corner and used it to wipe his eyes. "He always had a kind word for everyone."

"Yes, he did," Hope agreed.

Next to him, broad-hipped Mrs. Eisenhoff's round, fleshy face carried lines of unmistakable grief. "He was always there when you needed a friend. I wish someone had been with him that night."

"Skolie was there," Hope reminded her, speaking of Buddy's beloved pet.

She brightened a little. "Why, yes, he was. I hadn't thought of that. Mrs. Finnegan's taking care of him, now that Buddy's gone."

"I'm sure Buddy would like that."

"He wouldn't let them take our homes. He died fighting for us. It's just so terribly sad."

Hope leaned over and hugged her, then moved off to speak to Mrs. Finnegan, who seemed the most grief-stricken of all.

"'Tisn't right, what those men did to him. It just isn't right."

"Maybe the police will catch them." Hope turned to see Conn walking up beside her. She introduced him to Mrs. Finnegan, who, like the others, seemed pleased that they had come.

"Buddy thought you had pluck," the old woman said to her. "He said you were one smart cookie—that's the way he put it. He believed you were the kind of person who recognized the truth when you heard it."

"I know part of the truth, Mrs. Finnegan. Unfortunately, not enough to do Buddy any good."

The thin old woman took a shaky breath. "I guess we'll all have to move somewhere else."

"Maybe the person Buddy left the building to will keep fighting to save it. Do you have any idea who it might be?"

She shook her head. "Buddy was born in Missouri. From what he said, he had a couple of distant cousins back in some town called Waynesville. I imagine the property will go to them. I suppose they'll have to sell it to pay the inheritance taxes."

Hope took hold of the old woman's hand. It was liver-spotted, thin, and shaky. "I wish I knew a way to help."

"You tried. That's the most anyone can do."

Hope brushed a kiss on Mrs. Finnegan's papery cheek. "Take care of yourself."

The old woman nodded.

"It was nice to meet you," Conn said.

"You, too." Mrs. Finnegan's wrinkled face creased in a smile. "You look like a pretty smart young guy yourself. If you are, you'll hang on to this little gal. They don't make 'em like her anymore."

The edge of Conn's mouth went up. "You're right, Mrs. Finnegan, they don't."

Hope wasn't sure if that was a compliment or an insult, and she didn't ask.

"Time to go," Conn said, sliding an arm around her waist. "We don't want to miss our plane."

Hope looked back at the small group clustered together at the top of the church stairs, feeling a little of their pain, knowing there would be more to come when they were forced out of their homes.

When she still didn't move, Conn's jaw hardened. "I said, let's go." With a firm hand at her waist, he urged her down the steps toward the line of taxis waiting at the curb. There was no time to argue, no time to consider changing her mind. When Conner Reese took charge, somehow you found yourself obeying his orders.

After a stop at her apartment to retrieve their luggage, they were on their way to the airport. By tonight she would be back in Jamaica, back aboard the *Conquest,* in a cabin right next to Conn's.

Hope refused to think any further ahead.

If she did, she was afraid she might not go.

It was dark by the time they parked the old Toyota Corolla they had driven to the Kingston airport in a parking spot down at the Port Antonio dock.

"I'll take it back where it belongs in the morning," Conn said, dragging her luggage out of the trunk, unloading his own, then slamming the lid. He picked up both hanging bags and slung them over his shoulder. Hope grabbed the handle of her carry-on and they started along the pier toward the boat.

Pete was on night watch. "Welcome home, boss. Hope." His gaze slid over her, lingered a moment on her breasts. She was liking Pete Crowley less and less. Conn didn't notice. He was busy hauling the luggage aboard. Pete reached a hand down to help him.

"Thanks," Conn said. "Joe back aboard?"

"I heard Captain Bob say he'd be back first thing in the morning. That photographer took off, too. I guess he got called for another job. Said he'd come back as soon as we found something interesting."

Conn nodded. "You know if they got the gerator fixed?"

"They needed some part. I'm pickin' it up in the morning. Captain's plannin' to leave as soon as I get back with it."

Conn just nodded. Hefting Hope's hanging bag back up on his shoulder, he motioned for her to head for her cabin. Her stomach tightened as he set the luggage inside the door, but he made no attempt to stay. Hope ignored a pang of disappointment.

"Get some sleep," Conn said. "I'll see you in the morning." Before she realized what he meant to do, Conn caught her chin, bent his head, and very soundly kissed her. "Good night, Hope." And then he was gone.

The night seemed longer than it should have, considering how tired she was, but eventually she fell asleep. Bright sun streamed though the porthole when she awakened the following morning. Still a little fatigued, she went in to brush her teeth then dressed in a pair of comfortable shorts and a white cotton blouse.

Desperate for a cup of coffee, she headed for the galley. Joe's deep laughter drifted up as she walked along the deck— and a woman's voice she recognized as Glory's.

For a moment, Hope paused, not quite ready to face one

of Conn's former lovers. She shook her head. Glory was no longer part of Conn's life. She was now dating Joe.

And wildly happy about it, Hope saw as she descended the ladder to the galley below.

"Good morning." Hope glanced from the radiant pair to Conn and noticed the frown tugging his dark eyebrows together.

"Hi, Hope," Joe said, grinning like a fool. "Glory and I— we've got some incredible news."

"We're married!" Glory laughed and hugged her groom, pulled his head down for a quick, hard kiss. "I can hardly believe it!"

From the look on his face, apparently Conn couldn't, either. Still, he reached over and shook Joe's hand, pulled his friend into a big bear hug. "Congratulations." He leaned over and kissed Glory's cheek. "I wish you both the very best."

"Congratulations," Hope said to Glory, smiling in spite of the odd situation. "You're a far braver soul than I'd ever be."

"We love each other," Glory explained, hanging on tight to Joe's hand. "I think we both knew it the first time we were together."

"Glory's going back to Florida to tell her parents, then she's coming back and renting an apartment here. Until this job is over, we'll have to be content to see each other whenever we can."

"I'm happy for you, Joe," Hope said. "Happy for both of you."

"Neither of us has a lot of money." Glory smiled up at Joe. "I mean, my folks do, but I don't. It doesn't really matter, as long as we're together."

"And you never know," Joe added. "There's always a chance we'll hit the mother lode."

If they did, Conn had once told her, and the treasure was anywhere close to what the professor believed, Joe would take home a fat percentage of the profits, enough to set him up in whatever business he wanted.

"Yeah, we might get lucky," Conn said, though there was only mild conviction in his voice. Conn wasn't the dreamer Joe was. He was a realist who knew the kind of work that still lay ahead.

His gaze caught Hope's, held for a moment, and she wondered at his thoughts. An instant later, King's son Michael walked in. "Hey, Hope!"

"Michael! I didn't know you'd come aboard."

"I got a couple days off from school." He flashed a mouthful of very white teeth, his short dreadlocks framing a lean, attractive young face. "You up for a little more diving?"

Thinking of what had almost happened the last time, Hope suppressed a shiver.

"Come on," Michael urged. "The bad stuff's already happened."

Hope laughed. "You're right. I'd love to go diving again."

Conn frowned but didn't argue, since he was the kind of guy who would also go back down again.

"You hear about these two getting married?" Michael asked her.

"Are you kidding? Look at those faces. You think they could actually keep it secret?"

Captain Bob came down the ladder into the galley just then, and the wedding news and congratulations were repeated.

A few minutes later, Pete Crowley walked in and also heard the news. "Congratulations, Joe . . . Mrs. Ramirez."

"Thanks, Pete." Joe just kept grinning. It was really very sweet.

"The good news is you're married," Captain Bob said with a grin of his own. "The bad news is your honeymoon's over. The generator's fixed, working good as new. In about ten minutes, we'll be heading back to Pleasure Island."

Joe groaned. "And here I was hoping the damn thing wouldn't get repaired for at least a couple more weeks." He caught Glory's hand and brought it to his lips. "Come on, sweetheart. I'll walk you back to the car."

The pair left the galley, seeing nothing but each other, and Hope found herself smiling again. It was always a joy to see a young couple so in love.

Her smile slid away.

If only she believed there was the slightest chance it could work.

The boat was halfway back to the island, Conn standing at the rail when Joe walked up beside him. He followed Conn's gaze out to sea.

"So . . . I guess you aren't too happy about me getting hitched."

Conn turned toward him. "It isn't my life, Joe, it's yours. I don't have a damned thing to say about it."

"But you think I'm crazy. You think it was a dumb thing to do."

Conn sighed. "To tell you the truth, Joe, I can't imagine what you were thinking. You've only known the woman for a matter of days. How can you be so sure this is going to work?"

"I can't be—not for certain. I just believe it is. I love her, Conn. I've never felt like this about a woman before."

Conn thought of Hope. He was in love with her. They had known each other far longer than Joe and Glory, but he knew damned well if he was crazy enough to ask, she would refuse to marry him.

Conn stared out at the water, watching the way the sun's rays dappled the surface, feeling the roll and pitch of the boat as it cut through the sea. "I don't know, Joe . . . it just seems like maybe you rushed things a little."

"Yeah, well, maybe I did. But time isn't what's important. You knew Kelly for months and it didn't make any difference. Your marriage still didn't work."

"Good point."

"I love her, Conn, and I know Glory loves me. It's like

I've known her for years, like I've been waiting all my life for her to come along."

Conn clamped a hand on Joe's shoulder. "I meant what I said. I wish you both the very best. I hope the two of you are really happy."

Joe smiled. "I was kind of worried you might not like me marrying a woman you'd dated."

One of his eyebrows went up. "You thought I might be jealous?"

He shrugged. "Not really. You've never looked at Glory the way you look at Hope. For that matter, you never looked at Kelly that way, either."

Conn just grunted. Joe was smart enough to realize it wasn't a subject he wanted to discuss.

"At any rate, I'm glad you're okay with this because you're my best friend and I don't want that to change."

For the first time Conn realized how badly Joe wanted his approval. He smiled. "You know what I think?"

"What?"

"You're newly married—you're bound to be needing money. I think we'd better find the mother lode."

Joe grinned. "You got that right, man!"

It was late afternoon when the boat neared the island. Hope and Conn stood at the rail as they approached.

"What in the hell . . . ?"

"What is it?" But as she looked out at the water, she saw.

"Boats," he said. "A shitload of boats, all looking for treasure. Christ." The look he gave her said whose fault it was, and of course he was right. "I take it your article got posted on the Internet."

She looked at the small armada of sailboats, anywhere from twenty to sixty feet long, bobbing next to motor-powered pleasure craft and luxury yachts. A number of them were anchored south of the reef, closer to the area where the *Conquest* had been searching.

"A few of them have done their homework."

"There's nothing in the article that would tell them where you've been looking. I was very careful about that."

"They probably talked to people on the island. God knows the folks there have been watching us for days. A few of these guys are close but not in exactly the right spot. Of course, we don't know where exactly the right spot is."

"What are you going to do?"

"Put up some buoys, string some line between them, keep people out of the area we'll be searching. I doubt these are serious thieves. Just tourists and locals who want to see if they might be able to find something."

"Can't you just tell them that any treasure they find in these waters belongs to Treasure Limited?"

"I can tell them. There's no way I can force them to leave."

Hope looked out at the sea of boats. "I'm really sorry, Conn."

"I figure Talbot ought to be the one to apologize. Those articles were his idea."

"Yes, but all he really wanted was to get me off the Hartley House story."

"Maybe, but he also wanted the publicity, and so did Eddie Markham."

"Well, they ought to be happy, then."

Conn didn't say more, just turned and started barking orders to the crew. While Pete and King took the Whaler out to string line and put out buoys, Conn, Joe, Ron Keegan, and Wally Short got ready to dive.

It was lucky they did.

The storm that had occurred while the *Conquest* was in port had stirred up the sand in the area they had been searching. By the end of the day, King's dark green plastic tablecloth once more sparkled with the glitter of gold.

Using first the blower to clear out a hole, then the dredge—a giant vacuum that sucked sand and artifacts into a wire mesh basket where the objects were caught and the sand escaped—the men brought up a gorgeous, emerald-encrusted gold cup, a gold filigree brooch and matching earring, a fourteen-inch length of gold chain, and a little silver box.

The box was nearly black with oxidation but when they popped the lid, they found it loaded with emeralds.

Hope looked down at the deep green stones with awe. "My God, Conn, that big one must be forty carats." She watched as he fished the largest stone out of the box and laid it in the palm of her hand.

"Pretty, isn't it?"

"It's magnificent."

"We just keep finding stuff. Besides what we came up with today, we spotted two more cannons. We're obviously following the scatter pattern. I can't figure out why we haven't found the ballast pile yet."

"I can't say I'm disappointed," Joe said, walking up beside her. "Look what we've got so far."

"Yeah, but if you figure how much Talbot's got invested and how much we'll have to pay back, we still haven't made any money."

Conn looked down at the pile of treasure lying on the dark green cover. Michael stood over it, fingering a filigree brooch inset with lovely pink coral.

"Boy, this stuff is really something," the gangly youth said. "I never saw anything so beautiful. I'm glad I got to see it."

"The thing is, these are all personal items," Conn said. "Necklaces and earrings, gold chains, belts, and rings. This gold belonged to the passengers. It wasn't being transported back to the king of Spain. It belonged to the people aboard."

"You're saying none of this came out of the hold," Hope said.

"Exactly."

"Which means this might not be the spot where the ship went down."

Joe lifted the heavy gold chain off the table. Dangling it from the tips of his fingers, he watched the delicately carved links flashing in the sun. "I've been thinking . . . remember the *Atocha?*"

"It's hard to forget four hundred million in treasure," Conn said.

"The professor told us the *Atocha* was hit by two different storms."

"Yeah, I've been thinking about that myself. The first storm sank the ship. The second, two weeks later, separated the top decks from the hull and sent them skipping across the water until they sank about ten miles away."

"That's right. Fisher found the top decks first—that's where the passengers' gold would have been, the same kind of stuff we've been finding. Maybe that's what's happening here."

"If it is, the hull could have sunk anywhere. We haven't got a clue where to look."

Big dimples cut into Joe's cheeks. "Yes, we have. We've got the professor. And he's got all the info on the winds and currents way back then. All we've got to do is convince Doc Marlin that the *Rosa* might have been torn apart at two different times."

Conn nodded, thinking Joe was exactly right. "I'll get on the satellite cell."

Doc Marlin showed up two days later, his briefcase hanging from a bony hand. He set it on the table in the chart room while Conn went to fetch the latest batch of treasure they had brought up from the bottom.

The professor examined each piece with reverence, impressed with their findings. "It's all quite marvelous. But each piece needs to be properly charted. I've put my duties at the college on hold for a while so I can make sure the correct archeological procedures are followed."

Conn wasn't thrilled at being slowed down, but the professor was right. As salvors, they had a certain responsibility to history and the generations to come. And it was part of the terms the professor had demanded from the start.

"We logged each of the pieces we found the way you told us and mapped the spot for each recovery. There were a lot of other artifacts down there. Wally brought up some interesting pottery shards, but most of it we just left where it was."

"Good boy. From now on I'll take charge of the necessary documentation."

"All right. If you're going to stay, you can bunk in with me." Conn flicked a look at Hope. If she wasn't so damned stubborn, the professor could have the cabin all to himself. Conn would bunk with Hope—exactly where he wanted to be.

He didn't let his mind wander far in that direction. "What about our two-storm theory, Doc? Think it has any merit?"

"Actually, I do." The professor opened the briefcase and spread a layer of papers out on top of the table. "These are computer projections of ocean currents back four hundred years. I also e-mailed my friend, Professor Marquez, at the National Bibliothèque in Madrid in regard to weather conditions reported by survivors at the time."

"And?" Conn prompted.

"And Marquez says there is some evidence—accounts by fleet captains and passengers—that a second storm occurred about ten days after the first. No one paid much attention, as no other ships were lost, but apparently it was fairly severe. If the *Rosa* was already heavily damaged, the second storm could have been the one to completely destroy the vessel."

"So it's possible Joe and I could be on the right track, that the top decks could have separated from the hull, like they did on the *Atocha*."

"It certainly could have happened, and the interesting thing is the accounts say the storm blew in from the opposite direction." He turned to the map charting the sandbar running along the coast. "If that is the case, the ship may have initially struck farther south. The second storm could have torn the top decks loose and blown them *north*, into the area you've been searching."

"So the ballast pile may be somewhere near the southern end of the shoal."

"It might, indeed. The main part of the treasure would have been kept in the hold—gold bars, crates of silver coins, heavy gold disks. If you recall, the ship's register listed the Maiden as one of the prizes aboard. I believe it would have been kept with the rest of the treasure bound for the king."

The Maiden was a solid gold statue the professor had mentioned more than once. In fact, the artifact seemed to fascinate him. According to his research, the piece had been taken from an Inca temple, a prize now worth millions.

Conn hadn't given the statue much thought. Hell, he wasn't even sure they would find the *Rosa*. But he had to admit, now that they'd gotten this far, the possibility of discovering such a valuable artifact was highly intriguing.

"We'll recalculate the grid in the morning. Ron and Wally can work with King in the Whaler and continue to search this area, while we see what we can find along the south end of the sandbar."

The professor smiled. "I shall leave all that in your very capable hands. In the meantime, I wonder if King might be able to rustle up something for me to eat. All this talk of treasure seems to have made me hungry."

Conn chuckled as the older man headed off to the galley. Around him, the scanners, metal detectors, and video cameras were all retrieving information. Turning his attention to the GPS, Conn set to work, recalculating the search grid for what seemed the umpteenth time.

First thing in the morning, they would begin their exploration of the southern portion of the sandbar. They had done a cursory exam, of course, but found nothing of interest. Now a detailed grid search would begin.

Conn was eager to see what might turn up.

Chapter 19

It was a perfect Caribbean day, the sun hot but not burning, the sky so blue it hurt your eyes. The sea near the submerged sandbar was mostly flat and calm, a gorgeous shade of blue-green that turned darker as the water deepened. The wind blew across the bow from the east, wafting over the island, filling the air with the faint scent of jasmine.

Sitting on a deck box on the bow, Hope made notes for the final article in the *Adventure* series, adding to the list of discoveries that had been made so far.

And she had just finished typing up another article, as well.

Ever since she had left New York, Buddy's death and the future of the tenants at Hartley House had nagged her. She told herself to let it go, that it was too late now that Buddy was gone, and she was too far away to change what was surely going to happen. But the injustice of it all still bothered her.

In the end, she'd decided to take one last stab at trying to do something that might help. If nothing else, at least Buddy's side of the story might get heard.

Doing what she knew best how to do, she had written an article and sent it anonymously to a little Soho paper called the *Village Independent*. Newspapers rarely published anonymous articles, but she had a feeling the small, radically liberal paper just might.

If they did, maybe someone would see it. Enough someones could put pressure on the police or the district attorney. It was worth a try, and it made her feel good to make one last effort for Buddy.

She had finished the article early this morning and sent it over the Internet. On a glorious day like this, with the Hartley House article completed and her work progressing on the final piece for *Adventure,* with the sky so unbelievably blue and the temperature exactly right, she should be happy—and she was, she told herself.

Except that she missed Conn.

She knew he was mad at her. She'd been treating him as if their sexual involvement had never occurred, as if they were no more than friends. It was the way she wanted it, she told herself, the way it had to be. She didn't have room in her life for a man. She simply didn't trust them, and after the unbearable consequences of her affair with Richard, she wasn't willing to risk herself that way again.

An image popped into her head, the tiny pair of yellow knit booties she couldn't resist buying, though she didn't even know whether the baby was going to be a boy or a girl. Hope didn't care. She had just wanted the baby to be healthy. She would hold up the booties when she told Richard the wonderful news.

Hope shook her head, blotting the memories she rarely allowed to surface. But the pain was still there, reminding her of her folly. After Richard, she had made up her mind not to get involved in another relationship, never to risk herself that way again. She would build her career instead, and in doing so, secure a future that didn't depend on anyone else. It was a promise she intended to keep.

Afternoon turned into evening.

Another day passed, and another. The divers continued to bring up treasure, which was always exciting, yet there was an underlying tension aboard the ship. While Ron and Wally, Conn and Joe brought up an impressive array of gold and silver artifacts—a rosary made of onyx beads, a gold fork and spoon, an incredible claw-like gold dagger the professor said was a toothpick—the ballast pile remained hidden.

It worried the crew as well as Conn. As incredible as each find was, they had begun to get fewer, and the days began to lengthen.

And the nights . . .

For Hope, the nights seemed endless.

The longer she stayed away from Conn, the more she hungered for him. When he walked into a room, her heartbeat quickened. When he called her name, the sound stirred a tug of desire in her belly. She tried not to remember the last time they had made love, but the erotic picture crept into her mind again and again.

It was embarrassing, ridiculous, how badly she wanted him.

Worse yet, she was beginning to think he knew.

The sun was beginning to drift toward the horizon that afternoon when she heard the sound of his voice. Hope looked up, wondering if her thoughts had somehow reached him. She watched him striding toward where she sat on the bow, the muscles in his long legs flexing, those blue, blue eyes fixed on her face. Her stomach quivered and her mouth went dry.

"Sorry to bother you, but Joe's busy and the rest of the crew are all working. I could use your help, if you don't mind."

She swallowed, tried not to stare at the width of his chest. "What is it you need?"

"I want you to watch one of the screens down in the chart room while I make some adjustments."

She eyed him warily. Whether by chance or design, for the last few days, their paths had somehow crossed again and again. Still, she could hardly refuse to help. Following him down to the chart room, she seated herself in front of the video screen and followed his instructions to keep her eyes on the monitor until the wavy lines cleared and the picture came back into focus.

Conn reached up and began to adjust the knobs on the screen above. Wearing khaki shorts and a tank top that left his shoulders mostly bare, he was every woman's fantasy. Sitting as she was, every time he reached up, one of his long, muscular legs brushed her shoulder and her breathing quickened. She tried to concentrate on the screen, but her attention kept sliding up to his biceps as he fiddled with the knob on the monitor overhead, and perspiration dampened the hair at the nape of her neck.

Her composure began to unravel. "Are you finished yet?"

"How's the picture?"

"Looks fine to me, and I've got work of my own to do."

He looked down at her and a corner of his mouth edged up. "I'll be happy to help in any way I can."

She could think of a dozen ways he could help, but all of them involved sex and she was determined that that part of their relationship was over.

"Thanks, anyway." She got up from her chair. "Looks like it's working okay."

"Yeah, thanks for the help."

Joe walked in just then, seemed not to notice the tension sparking between them. He looked down at the video screen and Hope's gaze followed his.

"What's that?" Hope asked.

Joe's eyes locked on the screen. "I don't know, but whatever it is, there's a whole lot of it."

The camera displayed an image rising about four feet off the sandy bottom.

"According to the scanner," Conn said, "whatever's down there is thirty feet wide and a little over eighty feet long."

Joe tapped the screen. "Tell me we've found the ballast pile."

Conn actually grinned. "Looks like it to me."

Joe let out a whoop of joy that brought half the crew on

the run. "We found it!" he shouted to Captain Bob and Andy as they rushed in. "We found the ballast pile!"

"I'll get us anchored over the spot," the captain said, hurrying off to see it done.

Conn moved from the monitor to the charts spread open on the table. "The topography of the sandbar in this area doesn't fit the first map we made. The sands must have shifted during that storm the other night. When that happened, the ballast pile was exposed. In four hundred years, it may have been covered and uncovered any number of times."

"How deep is it here?" Hope asked.

Conn grinned. "Eighteen feet. We'll be able to use the hookah. We can work all day at this depth."

Joe explained that a hookah was a compressor that pumped air down hoses directly to the divers working below, eliminating the necessity of tanks. Hope looked up as the professor hurried down the ladder, followed by Michael and King.

"We just heard the news!"

"Looks like we found it, Doc."

"What can you see?" The professor came over to study the video screen. Michael and King peered over his shoulder, crowding the chart room.

"Not much of a picture," Conn said. "There's about four inches of sand covering the stones and whatever else is down there."

"There is sure a lot of it," Michael said.

"A galleon the size of the *Rosa* carried tons of ballast," the professor told them.

Conn tapped the screen. "The ship must have hit the sandbar so hard the bottom tore open and the stones spilled out right there."

The professor smiled. "Yes, indeed. In such warm water, the timbers will have mostly rotted away, but there may be some down there, along with the metal fittings, bronze spikes, and whatever treasure was in the hold."

"Assuming it wasn't perishable," Hope said, "like the tobacco aboard the *Santa Ynez*."

"You hear that magnetometer pinging away?" Joe stood there grinning. "That means there's more than just rocks down there. If our luck holds, it'll be treasure."

"Yeah," Conn agreed. "If our luck holds."

Everyone was eager to see what they'd actually found. Hope made a phone call to Tommy Tyler's cell, leaving a message that the *Conquest* had found the ballast pile of the *Nuestra Señora de Rosa*. She expected to see him off the portside rail at any moment, standing next to Chalko as the Sea Ray raced out from the island.

Though there wasn't much time before dark, Conn and Joe suited up for the dive—at eighteen feet, the shallowest they had made so far. The hookah lines would be rigged tomorrow. Today they were eager to see if they had found the mother lode.

"Let's get that mailbox in the water," Conn instructed Pete Crowley. *Mailbox* being salvors' terminology for an aluminum cage that swings down over the prop to convert the propeller wash into a massive undersea blower. At such a shallow depth, it was an invaluable piece of equipment.

As soon as the machinery was running, Conn and Joe carried the balance of their gear down to the diving platform.

"I'll be keeping my fingers crossed," Hope called down to them, holding her fingers in the air so they could see.

"Joe's got all the luck," Conn called back with a smile. "That's why I brought him along." So saying, the two of them scissor-legged into the water, and Hope headed down to the chartroom to watch the video screens.

There wasn't much to see at first. The blower moved so much sand, the water was a murky cloud the video camera couldn't penetrate.

Then Andy turned off the engines. The propellers slowed to a stop and the sea began to clear. She spotted Conn and Joe, two black-clad figures in their wetsuits, their long fins moving them gracefully toward the four-foot-deep ballast pile. They swam over the stones and what appeared to be a stack of rotting timbers, spread like pick-up sticks on top. They must have found something interesting because they stopped in one spot and both of them pointed down.

"Silver bars!" the professor shouted. "Dozens of them! And those thick clumps Conner is picking up—those are silver coins!"

Standing in front of the lens, Conn lifted the mass of coins that had oxidized and fused together, wiggled them in front of the camera, then put them in the sack at his waist. He went over and picked up the hand-blower he had set on the bottom and used it to move a little more sand around.

"That is gold!" Michael shouted as the unmistakable yellow gleam appeared among the rocks. "Joe is picking it up. It looks really heavy."

"A gold disk, my boy! They were listed on the *Rosa*'s manifest!" The professor's pale blue eyes welled with tears. "We've found it, by God! We've found the end of the rainbow!"

Chapter 20

They worked until dark, all four divers in the water, picking up as much as they could off the top of the ballast pile. But underwater salvage took time. Movements were slow and the pile of stones extended eighty feet along the sandy ocean floor.

Pete lowered a metal net attached to the heavy cable on the crane, which they loaded with silver bars. They found two more gold disks, blew a lot of sand around with the mailbox, and caught glimpses of enormous stacks of silver coins wedged beneath the stones. Lifting the ballast away was going to take time, and the day was rapidly waning.

They would start again in the morning. All of them were excited to see what the next day would bring.

A tub of ice filled with bottles of French champagne sat on the deck when Conn and Joe, Tom and Wally finished their last dive and returned to the boat. Captain Bob greeted them as they removed their gear and climbed the ladder to the deck.

The captain reached into the tub and grabbed the neck of an icy bottle. "We bought a case of this the last time we were in Jamaica. We've been keeping it chilled down in the fish tank. All of us were optimistic." The captain popped the cork and began filling red plastic beer cups, handing them out to members of the crew.

Conn reached into the tub, snagged a bottle by the neck, and hauled it out. Ignoring the cup Andy held out to him, he popped the cork and took a long, thirst-quenching drink straight from the bottle. Joe popped open a bottle of his own and they held them up and clinked them together in a silent salute. The professor was drinking from a beer cup, talking a mile a minute to Captain Bob. A few feet away, Hope drank from a cup the captain had filled.

Conn walked over and refilled her glass. "Looks like you got a great ending for your series."

"The best," she said. Turning to the others, she held up her cup of champagne. "To Conn, Joe, and the professor—and the terrific crew of the *Conquest*. Congratulations on a job well done!"

Everyone cheered. "Hear, hear!" Andy Glass shouted, and all of them took a hefty drink.

"What about your partners?" Hope said to Conn. "I suppose you'll have to call them."

"I don't have any choice. Unfortunately, as soon as I do, they'll have the news media swarming all over us."

"That'll mean more boats and more people, which could mean more trouble."

"Yeah, but a deal's a deal. They deserve to know what we've found."

"My article's not due for a while. I can hold back on the announcement I'll be doing for the Internet site if you think it will help."

Conn shook his head. "Won't matter. Talbot and Markham will break the news the minute they hear it. You might as well get the glory."

Hope smiled. "Thanks."

Conn glanced toward the chart room. "I better make those calls. Talbot and Markham find out I waited, they'll be pissed and I can't really blame them." Conn left Hope on the deck and went down to use the satellite phone. The first call went to Brad Talbot.

"I can't believe you actually found it! What have you brought up so far?"

"We only discovered the ballast pile a few hours ago. We worked till it got too dark. So far we've found a number of silver bars and coins, and three heavy gold disks the size of my hand. We'll be setting up a permanent dive site in the morning. Mostly we're celebrating, right now."

"I don't blame you. As a matter of fact, I think I'll join you. I'll come out to the island as soon as I can rearrange my schedule."

"I think you'll be impressed."

"I'm already impressed. Good work, Reese. You and old man Marlin did well." Talbot signed off and Conn phoned Eddie Markham.

"You're not kidding, right? You found the actual treasure? The thing they call the mother lode?"

"Looks that way. It's going to take plenty of work to bring all of it up, but it looks like we're the first ones who've ever been on the site. We brought up a load of stuff this afternoon that was lying right on top. We figure the rest is buried among the ballast stones."

In fact, he was planning to hire another salvage boat. If there was as much down there as it looked like, bringing it up would take another dive team or two.

"Hey, I've got an idea," Markham said into the phone. "We're having an off-night here. Why don't you and your crew come to the restaurant? We'll celebrate together. The whole thing's on me."

Conn knew he probably shouldn't. They had a shitload of work to do tomorrow. Then again, how many times in your life did you find a Spanish galleon loaded with sunken treasure?

"Sounds great." He'd have to leave a couple of men aboard,

but maybe the guys could take shifts so everyone could go to the party, at least for a while.

"I'll send Chalko out to pick all of you up," Eddie said. "Toss in your overnight bag and you can spend the night in one of the villas. Tell the professor that invitation includes him, too."

Conn thought of Hope. "I'll tell him. We may just take you up on that."

"When will you be ready?"

He looked out the window at his laughing, half-drunk crew. No one deserved to celebrate more. "Hell—we're ready right now."

Markham laughed. "Chalko's on his way."

Conn hung up the phone and made his way back up on deck. He spotted Hope in her navy blue shorts and a crisp white blouse with the tails tied up around her waist. His gaze ran over her pretty legs, lightly tanned now, and he remembered them wrapped around his waist on the kitchen table. The wind whipped her glorious dark red hair and he remembered its exact silky texture as it slipped through his fingers. Desire slammed into him with the force of a blow.

He wasn't finished with Hope Sinclair, not by a long shot. He had a strong suspicion this was the woman he had been looking for all his life and he wasn't about to let her get away, no matter how skittish she was.

She turned at his approach and Conn smiled. "Better put on your party clothes, baby. Eddie Markham's throwing us a celebration bash."

Hope laughed and the warm, feminine sound made him go rock-hard. "I'm so happy for you, Conn."

He reached down and cupped her chin, tilted her head back, and lightly kissed her lips. "Maybe the two of us can celebrate later."

She started to shake her head so he let her go. "Just think about it."

She didn't say more. Conn figured she wouldn't be able to

think about anything else. He knew her secret now, knew that she wanted him nearly as much as he wanted her. Once he'd figured it out, he'd been relentless, subtly seducing her, using their mutual attraction to lure her back to his bed. Exactly where she belonged.

The sun was well down by the time Chalko and the boat arrived to take them to the island. Captain Bob and Andy were staying aboard, but King, Michael, and Pete would be coming back early so the captain and engineer could have dinner and join the party for a while. The professor declined the invitation to spend the night on the island, preferring to stay on the boat, so he would be returning as well.

It made Conn vaguely uneasy to leave the boat so thinly manned with so much gold and silver aboard, even for a very short time. The smaller gold artifacts like the rings, belts, necklaces, and chains that had been brought up were kept in the ship's safe, but the larger silver bars, gold disks, and oxidized coins had been loaded into the hold.

It was almost time to go in and resupply, but Conn figured he could stretch their provisions a couple more days. And they would be anchored over the site, instead of having to run the fuel-guzzling diesel engines while they searched.

They all wanted to stay as long as they could, except maybe Joe, who was torn between finding treasure and getting back to his bride. Conn had already made arrangements to deposit whatever treasure they found with the Bank of Nova Scotia—Scotia Bank—in Port Antonio. An armored vehicle would be waiting when they pulled up to the dock.

The roar of an engine drew Conn's attention to the port side of the boat. The Sea Ray began to slow, sending low, rolling waves toward the hull.

Doc Marlin walked up as the speedboat eased up to the loading platform. "Been quite a day, hasn't it?"

"It sure has, Professor. Tomorrow might prove even more interesting."

"You've done a fine job, my boy."

"Couldn't have done it without you, Doc. You're the brains of this operation. You figured out where to look."

The professor seemed pleased. Making his way toward the boarding platform, Doc Marlin joined the crew climbing onto the Pleasure Island yacht. Conn helped Hope aboard, then sat down beside her on one of the padded white vinyl seats.

She was wearing a jazzy little sundress she must have brought back with her on her last trip to The Villas, white with splashy dark-pink flowers. Except for two thin straps, the dress left her shoulders bare, the bodice just low enough to show the soft swells of her breasts. Just low enough to drive him crazy.

The boat pulled away from the *Conquest,* drawing his mind in a safer direction. They had to travel farther now to reach the reef, find the entrance leading into the harbor, and cross the lagoon to the dock. The ride was great this time of evening, with the sea dark and calm and a salt spray cooling the warm, humid air.

A pair of island Jeeps waited at the dock to carry the group to the restaurant, which was in the main building next to the lobby. Like each of the villas, the restaurant, Trade Winds, was done in a sophisticated tropical motif with heavy carved furniture, candles on white linen cloths, and clusters of exotic flowers on each of the intimate tables.

In a private, equally lovely chamber off the main dining room, orchids and hibiscus decorated a long row of banquet tables overflowing with an array of fruits and cheeses, cooked and marinated vegetables, homemade breads, fresh fish, lobster, prime rib, and every kind of pastry and dessert you could name.

Conn walked into the room behind Hope. He had plans for her this evening, plans she would enjoy as much as he did, if she would just let herself. Eddie stood next to the door, personally greeting each of his guests.

"This is incredible," Hope said to him, her sea-green eyes scanning the feast the emperor had laid out for them. "I wasn't even hungry till I walked through the door and smelled all this fabulous food."

Eddie smiled, obviously pleased. He was wearing his trademark light suit, along with a blue silk shirt and flowered blue tie. His skin was even more tanned than before, giving him a George Hamilton look.

"The bar's open," he said. "There's more champagne, beer and wine, and all the fancy rum drinks you can name."

"This is great, Eddie," Conn agreed. "The guys really deserve it."

"No one deserves it more than you, Conn. If there's as much treasure down there as Professor Marlin believes, the two of you have made all of us a lot of money."

Conn had refused to let himself think that far ahead but he couldn't help hoping Eddie was right. He had plans for the future, and with enough money he could make those plans happen. "We'll know more tomorrow."

Eddie nodded. "I got a call from Brad Talbot after he heard the news. He'll be here the end of the week. He's bringing a few people with him."

A muscle tightened along Conn's jaw. "A few more people. Just what we need."

Eddie clapped him on the shoulder. "Hey, a little publicity won't hurt. The *Rosa's* been missing for four hundred years. Finding her is a very big deal."

"Finding her loaded with treasure—*that's* the big deal."

"But you're pretty sure she is."

"Yeah. Pretty sure. Like I said, we'll know more tomorrow."

Markham turned to speak to the professor, and Conn led Hope over to the bar. She ordered a piña colada and he ordered a Scotch, which he sipped slowly.

As the evening progressed, he was pleased to see that neither Joe nor the other two divers were drinking all that much.

They were looking forward to the search tomorrow every bit as much as he was.

"Are you hungry?" Hope asked, her gaze once more on the sumptuous display of food.

"Yeah," Conn said. "I'm definitely hungry." But his eyes were fixed on Hope and he wasn't thinking of food.

It was a memorable evening, one she would never forget. Hope felt an odd sort of camaraderie with the crew that she hadn't expected. The men were all so excited, so eager to see what they would find the next day. Everyone ate too much, but no one drank more than he should have. There was too much at stake. These men were on a mission and they intended to accomplish it.

All evening, Conn stayed close by, his familiar presence reassuring but at the same time disturbing. One look from those intense blue eyes and she knew she was playing with fire. Her heart raced every time he touched her. He flashed one of his sexy smiles and her breath snagged somewhere in her chest.

They sat next to the professor during dinner and Hope enjoyed the older man's sophisticated banter. He mentioned his wife, speaking somewhat wistfully. Conn had told her Mary Marlin suffered from Alzheimer's disease.

"If we find as much as we're hoping to," the professor said, "the money will certainly come in handy. I'll have enough to make certain Mary has the very best of care."

Hope reached over and squeezed the professor's thin hand. "You're going to find so much you won't be able to count it."

He laughed. "I hope so, dear girl, I truly do."

They finished the meal and Hope pushed back from the table, feeling pleasantly full.

"How about a walk on the beach?" Conn suggested, and though she knew she shouldn't, she ached to go with him.

"What about the boat? I thought you'd want to go back."

"Joe will see that the men get back to the *Conquest.* Eddie invited us to stay in one of the villas. We can go back in the morning."

Her stomach curled. So did her toes. Stay on the island. Spend the night with Conn in one of the villas. In one of those big king-size beds, naked, skin to skin, beneath a fluffy feather comforter. If she closed her eyes, she could imagine his hard body pressing her down in the mattress, feel him deep inside her.

For a moment she couldn't seem to breathe.

"You all right?"

She nodded, managed a smile. "I'm fine. Must be the champagne."

Conn flicked her a glance that said he knew exactly what was wrong with her, and Hope looked away. She wasn't sure how much more intimacy she could share with Conn and still maintain any sort of safe distance.

"Let's go." Though she hadn't really agreed, he caught her arm and urged her toward the door, leaving only a mild protest on her tongue.

They were outside in a heartbeat, heading down a winding path overgrown with big, leafy foliage, walking toward the curve of sugary white sand in the private cove below the restaurant. Hope noticed the set of Conn's jaw and the heat in his eyes, and her heartbeat thundered louder than the roar of the surf. As soon as they reached the beach, they took off their shoes and set them side by side on the sand.

Now that they were there, Conn's long strides slowed and he seemed to relax. Linking their fingers together, he led her on a leisurely stroll along the edge of the water. The foamy surf rolled up on the shore, over their bare feet as they wandered toward a secluded spot at the far end of the cove. Giant palm trees leaned out over the sand and leafy foliage hid this end of the beach from view.

Conn turned her to face him and her pulse kicked up. "I've been wanting to kiss you all evening." He touched her cheek, then his mouth settled gently over hers. Her mind shouted *be careful,* but need soon silenced the warning.

Hope kissed him back, her tongue tangling with his, her fingers sliding into his hair. Her bare toes curled into the sand beneath her feet and her body swayed toward him of its own accord. She wanted him. God, she wanted him so much.

The surf crashed around them, rolled up on the shore, splashing against their legs, dampening the hem of her sundress and the legs of Conn's navy blue slacks.

"We're going to get wet," he said softly, kissing the side of her neck.

Hope stepped away from him and gave him a sultry smile. "Then why don't we?"

Sliding the straps of her sundress down over her shoulders, she shoved the dress over her hips and stepped out of it, tossed it farther up on the shore, out of the path of the water. Her tiny white thong underwear followed. Laughing, she raced into the sea.

An instant later, Conn ran up beside her, as gloriously naked as she. He caught her up in his arms and lunged into the next wave, carrying both of them under.

They swam for a while, enjoying the water and the mild ocean breezes, kissing as they stood waist-deep in the waves. Conn was a skillful lover and not a man to rush. He kissed her until she was trembling, kissed and caressed her breasts, then lifted her into his arms and carried her up on the sand at the edge of the surf.

He set her on the sand, then stretched full-length beside her, kissing her mouth, her neck, her shoulders, moving down to the curve of her breasts. Her breath caught as he entered her, sliding deeply inside, and almost at once she started to come. His name came out on a sob that drifted away with the breeze, and he surged into her again, even more deeply.

Incredible sensations rushed through her.

"That's it, baby. Let it happen."

A huge wave washed over them as he moved inside her,

until he had her moaning. Ocean spray misted the air around them. White, foamy surf washed over their naked bodies. Conn kissed her and Hope arched upward, meeting each of his thrusts, forcing a low growl of pleasure from his throat.

His fingers slid into her slick, wet hair and his iron control seemed to snap. Driving hard and deep, his muscles tightening, he reached his release and it sent her over the edge.

They climaxed together, both of them trembling, the sensations so fierce that afterward they lay entwined, barely able to move.

The surf washed around them and they stirred. Conn came to his feet and hauled her up beside him. Wordlessly he linked their hands and they walked back into the surf to freshen themselves.

Afterward, they returned to the place they had left their clothes and silently pulled them on. Though their wet bodies dampened the fabric, neither of them cared. Walking along the beach, they made their way to the place where they'd left their shoes, picked them up, but didn't put them on.

"The crew will be back at the boat by now," he said, his eyes on her face.

"I imagine they will."

"Eddie gave me a key before we left."

Her stomach twisted. She knew they would make love again, that each time they did, he would capture a little more of her heart.

Conn must have sensed her hesitation. "I'm not letting you run this time, Hope. There's too much at stake." Words she'd thought earlier about the treasure. "We're going to find out where this is headed. You're going to sleep in my bed at night and we're going to explore these feelings the two of us obviously share."

A sliver of fear went through her. A relationship with a man like Conn—wildly handsome, skillful in bed, smart and sexy and infinitely male. She wasn't a risk-taker like her sisters—not anymore.

Still, she had never felt the turbulent mix of emotions she

felt for Conn. She refused to call it love. After Richard, she was too much of a realist for that. But whatever these feelings were, maybe it wouldn't be so bad to use the time they had left together to explore them.

"All right. We do it your way—for a while. But if things don't work out, either of us has the right to end it. If that happens, we still stay friends." She stuck out her hand to seal the bargain before she could change her mind. "Deal?"

Instead of shaking, Conn lifted her fingers to his lips. "Deal." Still holding onto her hand, he tugged her into his arms and sealed the bargain with a kiss.

Chapter 21

Conn woke up naked just before dawn, in a huge king-size bed with a beautiful woman draped over his chest and an uneasy feeling in the pit of his stomach.

As he lay there staring up at the canopied four-poster bed, a distant noise reached him, the sound of helicopter blades whirring in the distance, the *whop whop whop* growing louder as the chopper neared the island.

Then the phone started ringing and the uneasy feeling tightened into a cold, hard knot. The phone jangled again before he could grab the receiver.

"Reese."

"Sorry if I woke you," said the front desk clerk. "Mr. Markham asked me to call. He said to tell you the press is coming in."

Conn silently cursed. The last thing he wanted was to deal with the media. "I need to get back to the boat. Can you make the arrangements?"

"I'll be happy to, sir. I'll call Chalko right away. He'll pick you up and take you back out to the *Conquest*."

Conn hung up the phone, wishing his gut had been wrong just this once. *Christ.* The locusts were already descending.

Hope shifted on the mattress beside him. "What is it?"

"Hear that chopper?"

She looked up. "I hear it. Sounds like the damned thing's landing on the roof." Sitting up in bed, she shoved back her dark red hair. "What's going on?"

"The media's here. Apparently Talbot and Markham wasted no time calling them. Christ, I figured we'd have at least a couple of days before they got here."

Both of them climbed out of bed, hurriedly showered, and dressed in the same clothes they had worn the night before.

"You ready?" Conn asked as Hope walked into the living room.

She dug her sunglasses out of her purse and shoved them up on her nose. "Whenever you are."

The moment Conn opened the door, an array of lights went on and cameras began to roll. Half a dozen reporters started throwing questions at him.

"You're Conner Reese, right? You're the guy who found the *Nuestra Señora de Rosa?*"

Conn kept walking. "I'm one of them."

A woman reporter stepped into his path. "They say you found the mother lode—that's the real treasure, isn't it? When did it happen?"

"Yesterday afternoon."

"How much treasure is there?" a blond reporter asked. "As much as Fisher found on the *Atocha?*" He shoved his microphone toward Conn.

"Could be even more." Conn turned to face the eager group. "Listen, I think you would all get a much better story if you spoke to Mr. Markham. He's the owner of Pleasure Island and one of the partners in Treasure Limited. He's in charge of media communications." *At least he's going to be from now on,* Conn thought darkly. "I think you'll find him over at the office. That's in the main building, down the hall from the lobby."

"We'd rather talk to you, Mr. Reese," said the female reporter. "We want to hear the details of how you found the *Rosa.*"

"Like I said, speak to Markham." In the driveway out front, Chalko waved and Conn urged Hope in that direction. Both of them breathed a sigh of relief as they climbed into the Jeep and the tall, lean black man fired up the engine. He roared off toward the dock before anyone could possibly catch up with them.

It was early, the sun barely up, yet when they arrived at the *Conquest* and he and Hope climbed aboard, everyone was already hard at work. Today was an important day. There was a lot to do and apparently no one had forgotten.

Preparing to dive took Conn's mind off the problems he could be facing with so much media coverage. According to Captain Bob, who had been monitoring CNN on the Internet, the story had broken late last night. By afternoon, the station was showing film footage of the *Conquest* and Pleasure Island, as well as interviews with Eddie Markham and Brad Talbot and a quick shot of Conn and Hope escaping the bungalow where they had spent the night.

The professor, and his extensive background on the subject of the Spanish treasure fleets, was a feature story, and Conn was touted as the man who had found the pot of gold at the end of the rainbow known as the *Nuestra Señora de Rosa*. So far, they hadn't figured out the name of his companion.

Though helicopters flew overhead and boats circled the search area they had cordoned off with buoys and line, so far none of the media had tried to come aboard. As Conn had planned, the hookah was rigged and the serious job of recovery begun.

With the added buoyancy of the water, most of the ballast stones were able to be lifted, but carrying them any distance one at a time just wasn't feasible. The crane was put to use, the stones loaded into the metal basket which could be swung the fifteen feet from the middle of the ballast pile to the edge, exposing whatever lay beneath.

The rotting remnants of what had once been wooden chests were revealed, containing stacks of silver bars. A silver box held a cache of gold cobs ranging from two to eight *escudos;* what had once been a series of larger chests contained thousands of silver coins. But the eighty-by-thirty-foot search area covered twenty-four-hundred square feet of ocean floor, and salvaging the area was going to take time.

With so many boats in the vicinity, Conn also worried about protecting the spot where the decks had separated from the hull. Among the beds of waving sea grasses, stacks of decaying timber, and columns of leafy algae, they were sure to find more of the valuable personal artifacts that sank when the ship was torn apart. Conn and Joe planned to go back and work the deeper site as soon as they got the chance. The finds might be fewer but there could be something even more valuable than the gold and silver in the hold.

They worked the site another day, but supplies were becoming a problem. Today was the last day they could manage to stay before returning to Jamaica. Conn didn't like to think how much money the items in the safe and the hold were worth—the eight-*escudo* gold cobs alone could go for as high as seven thousand dollars apiece. With the growing fleet of boats hovering just outside the search area, he would be glad to turn the items over to the Scotia Bank in Jamaica.

Needing a break and something to eat, he and Joe had just come up from a dive when he spotted Hope and Michael carrying their dive gear along the deck.

Hope smiled. "This is Michael's last day. The water's really shallow. We were hoping you might take us down after lunch."

Since their night on Pleasure Island, Conn had been sleeping in Hope's cabin, coming in late and leaving early, trying to keep their relationship discreet, though he had a feeling most of the guys knew the two of them were spending their nights together. Remembering how good it felt waking up beside her made him smile. It also made it nearly impossible to deny her anything she wanted.

"All right. If it's okay with King, we'll take you down after we eat. But Joe goes with Michael and I go with you."

The boy's narrow, dark face lit up. "My father says it is all right to go. He says a small thing like nearly drowning should not stop you from doing what you love."

Joe laughed. "Your dad's right. But if I'm taking you down, I want you to stay close this time."

"I will, I promise."

Joe nodded. "First, I gotta have something to eat."

Not a lot, since they would be diving again, but after working all morning, both of them could use an energy boost. Ron and Wally were still working below. They'd be coming up for their break when Conn and Joe went back down.

"We won't be long," Conn said to Hope, thinking how good she looked in her conservative two-piece swimsuit, trying *not* to think she looked even better in her tiny yellow flowered bikini—or better still, nothing at all.

Hope waited next to Michael on the diving platform when Joe and Conn came back up on deck. Since the men had promised to show them the site, they would be wearing air tanks instead of using the hookah, since the breathing lines attached to the boat were more confining.

As the four of them made the shallow descent, Hope stayed close to Conn, and Joe made sure Michael didn't stray. The water was clear, a crystalline aqua-blue populated with hundreds of exotic fish. Hope had been reading up on them: a small black grouper, a beautiful blue parrotfish, a yellow-tailed damselfish. The array of colors and odd-sounding names went on and on.

As they neared the bottom, Conn pointed to a small reef shark circling above the ballast pile, which stretched out in front of them like a lumpy carpet on the ocean floor. Hope wasn't afraid of sharks. At dive school, she had learned that they mostly just wanted to be left alone. The shark swam off into the tall sea grasses bordering the stones and disappeared.

Hope turned to survey the ballast pile, which was amazing—eighty feet of round, sand and algae-covered rock that had been lying on the bottom of the sea for hundreds of years. She could almost see the huge galleon whose hold it had come from, the ship's appearance boxy, its flat stern marked by rows of small, square windows, the top decks enclosed by ornate wooden rails.

There wasn't much coral in the area. She had read that coral, being a living creature, avoided shipwreck sites because of the contamination from the wreckage. But the stones sheltered an exotic array of sea life—ribbon-like neon gobys, jawfish, frogfish, and blenny. They lived among the rocks and scuttled out of sight as the group swam past. At the edge of her vision, a big barracuda darted through a hole in the boulders, disappearing in the darkness beneath.

Conn spotted something among the stones and left them a moment, finning away from the pile, over to the edge of the sand to retrieve the hand-held blower. A number of water-logged ship's timbers had managed to survive the years, Hope saw as he blew away a sheet of sand. They lay in haphazard, crisscross mounds on top of the ballast. Most had passed into eternity, along with the crew and passengers aboard the ship.

Closing in on the spot Conn searched, they all pitched in to lift away some of the ballast stones, which, with the buoyancy of the water, weren't as heavy as they looked. They filled the basket suspended by the crane, allowing them to see what lay beneath, giving them access to an amazing cache of oxidized silver coins that appeared to have once been contained in a barrel of some kind. All that remained were the barrel staves and the decayed container's valuable contents.

Through a combination of tugs on a floating buoy and hand signals to the video camera, the men had developed a communication system that allowed the divers to talk to the crew on the boat.

The crane swung the basket of stones out of the way, dumped the basket, which was then refilled with the heavy clumps of silver coins and hauled aboard the boat. Hope and

Conn moved along the ballast pile, stopping here and there to examine something that might prove interesting. At the edge of the pile, tall sea grasses and algae waved like long green tongues in the pull-and-tug of the tide.

Glancing down as she swam along, Hope spotted the glitter of what looked like gold, motioned to Conn, and swam excitedly toward it. Reaching down, she plucked up a shiny gold cob, then another. Conn swam over and gave her the thumbs-up sign, then began lifting and moving stones so they could see deeper into the ballast pile.

They were so busy hunting for treasure they didn't realize how far the two of them had swum from Michael and Joe, who searched the stones closer to the ship.

They didn't realize that they were not alone.

Hope spotted the intruders first—two divers, each wearing wetsuits and double tanks, down at the far end of the ballast pile. She nudged Conn and pointed, saw him tense. He was too far away to signal Joe, so he motioned for Hope to stay where she was, then turned and started swimming toward the men. Both of the divers took off, swimming rapidly into the sea grass and tall strands of leafy algae, disappearing around a mound of sand that had slid off the main shoal, down into the ocean.

Conn followed. Knowing she shouldn't but worried that he might get in trouble, she started making her way toward the place where he had disappeared.

As she rounded the protrusion of sand, the next few seconds seemed to happen in slow motion. She spotted Conn and one of the divers, but the other man had hidden behind a wall of waving sea plants and she could tell Conn didn't see him. Then she noticed the spear gun he lifted from his side and her heart seemed to simply stop beating.

There was no way to signal a warning. Hope swam madly as the diver lifted the weapon, aimed at Conn, and fired. Eyes wide in horror, she watched the spear slice through the water, saw Conn turn toward the danger an instant too late, and a scream lodged in her throat. Conn gripped his side and doubled over as the spear tore through his wetsuit and into his flesh, then streaked out the opposite side. The cloudy substance pouring into the water was blood, and a fresh shot of terror slammed through her.

By the time her gaze returned to the diver, the man was a dark speck moving off beside his friend through the water. Hope kept swimming toward Conn. He had turned around and started back in her direction, spotted her, and signaled for her to swim for the boat as fast as she could.

He was bleeding badly. Dear God, she wanted to stop and find some way to help him, but the urgency of his movements warned her there wasn't time. From the corner of her eye, she saw a dark shape cutting through the water and realized why. The reef shark they had seen before was returning, joined by another, larger shark angling in from a different direction.

The wild beating of her heart increased and her mouth went dry. The mouthpiece felt thick and uncomfortable, the air going in and out of her lungs seemed to burn. She was breathing too fast, she knew. She forced herself to take a slow breath of air and calm down. By now the two of them were swimming side by side, both of them finning through the water with all of their strength. Joe must have seen them racing toward him and realized something was wrong. He motioned for Michael to surface and this time the boy obeyed without question.

Joe waited for their approach, then fell in behind them, protecting their backs as they started to make the brief ascent. She saw him pull his dive knife out of the sheath at his waist as two more sharks began moving in.

Hope and Conn broke the surface of the water at about the same time and started swimming toward the platform. Michael was already there, pulling himself up to safety.

"We need help down here!" the boy shouted, and Pete and Andy came on the run. Ron and Wally bolted out of the galley and all of them rushed toward the diving platform. Andy hoisted Hope out of the water, while Wally and Ron hauled Conn out, and Pete reached for Joe.

Hope jerked off her mask and Ron helped her with her tanks while Joe began to carefully help Conn shed his gear, using his dive knife on Conn's wetsuit, splitting it open and making it easier to peel him out of it. Blood poured out of the wound in his side, mixing with the water on his skin, forming pink rivulets that soaked into his swimsuit and ran down his legs.

"We've got to get him to a hospital," Hope said, trembling. Her insides were tied in knots and a huge lump clogged her throat. "He needs a doctor. There's no way to know how badly he's injured until we can get him some medical care."

"King's the next best thing to a doc," Joe said. "Pete's gone to get him."

Hope turned back to Conn. "You need to lie down," she gently insisted, easing him down on his back on the platform, his hand still pressed over the wound to help stop the flow of blood. "The less you move, the better."

"We need to fly him back," Joe said. "I hope to hell the plane's on the island."

"I'll find out." Andy took off for the radio in the chart room.

"What the hell happened down there?" Joe asked Conn, relieved to see King thundering along the deck with towels beneath a thick arm and the first-aid kit in hand. Professor Marlin flapped along in his wake, worry lining his wrinkled face.

"Spear gun. My fault. Should have been more careful. I figured they were lookie-loos. I thought if I scared them a little, they'd leave and wouldn't come back."

"Any idea what they were doing down there?"

"Thieves, I guess. Two of them. I think they must have found something. That's probably why they shot me. They didn't want to give it back."

Hope looked down at Conn's pale face and her heart squeezed so hard she could barely breathe. Conn was injured. She didn't know how badly. Her chest was aching, her mouth dry as cotton. She wanted to cry, but didn't dare. For Conn's sake, she had to be strong.

"The treasure's been all over the news," Ron Keegan said. "They're saying the find might be bigger than the *Atocha*. They're talking about hundreds of millions of dollars. That much money's bound to bring every scum ball in a thousand miles out from under his rock."

King arrived just then and knelt at Conn's side. "Gimme some room, boys."

"Ron, you and Wally go back up and see when Chalko's gonna be here with that boat," Joe said.

They nodded and hurried toward the ladder, giving King room to work. Gently, the big man moved Conn's hand away from the wound and began to carefully examine the jagged tear in his flesh. "Looks like de spear went straight through. Don't look like it hit anything important, but you're bleedin' pretty bad."

He took a syringe out of the first-aid kit and shot some kind of painkiller into Conn's arm. A shot of antibiotics followed. "You feel better in no time. Try not to move."

Professor Marlin hovered nearby, careful to stay out of the way but obviously as worried as Hope was. As the drugs pumped through Conn's veins, King cleaned the wound as best he could, then took heavy gauze pads out of the first-aid kit, stuffed them into the jagged opening, then pressed pads against both the entry and exit wounds in Conn's side. He bound the bandage in place with wide strips of gauze, followed by adhesive tape.

"That should hold till we can get you to de hospital."

Conn's eyes slid closed and Hope reached out and took hold of his hand. It felt icy cold, colder even than her own.

"King's taking good care of you," she said, her voice rough with fear. "You're going to be all right."

His eyes cracked open and the edge of his mouth faintly curved. "You got that right, baby. You don't think a little fishing spear is going to . . . keep me away from you?"

Her throat closed up. She managed a wobbly smile, but her eyes filled with tears. She tightened her hold on his hand and blinked to keep from crying.

Overhead they heard the *whop whop whop* of a chopper. One of the television helicopters, cameras undoubtedly rolling. Apparently they had heard Andy's call for help. When Andy came out to tell them the chopper had come to airlift Conn to the hospital, Hope whispered a little prayer of thanks.

There was no time to change her clothes. One of the guys handed Joe a lightweight jacket and he draped the oversized garment over her shoulders, covering up her swimsuit. She heard the thud of a pair of flip-flops being tossed down on the deck. Joe helped her put them on as the pontooned helo settled in the water beside the boat and Pete brought the Boston Whaler around to ferry Conn over to the aircraft.

Though he never made a sound, Hope could see the pain etched into his face at the effort it took to climb into the Whaler. The brief, bumpy ride leached the rest of the color from his face as the Whaler transported him across the bouncy waves to the chopper, but finally he was settled inside.

Hope climbed in beside him, gripped his hand, and the chopper lifted away.

One of the reporters she recognized from their morning at The Villas knelt next to Conn.

"How you doin', Reese? You hangin' in there?"

Conn opened his eyes and looked up at him. "I don't have much choice."

"You know you owe us one for this." He gave Conn a toothy smile. "How about an exclusive?"

Hope had never disliked reporters until that very moment.

*   *   *

As the helo swept into the air, Joe made his way up to the bridge to speak to Captain Bob. "After what just happened, there's no way we can just leave this place unguarded, even if we're back by tomorrow night. I'm gonna call Markham, see if he'll anchor the Sea Ray out here with a couple of security guys until we get back from Jamaica."

"Good idea." The captain lifted his bill cap and raked a hand through his thatch of silver hair. "In fact, I think Conn may have made that call before he went diving."

Joe nodded, thinking that sounded like his friend. Conn liked to be prepared for whatever might come up. He probably figured leaving the place without security wasn't a good idea.

Heading down to the chart room, Joe phoned Pleasure Island to make sure Conn had made the necessary arrangements and got through to Eddie Markham. Briefly he explained what had happened to Conn and that there was undoubtedly more trouble ahead.

"How bad is he hurt?"

"We don't know yet."

"I'll call the hospital, see what I can find out. In regard to the Sea Ray, I'd planned to send Chalko out with a couple of men. They aren't divers, but I'll make sure they're in uniform. Maybe seeing them will serve as a deterrent."

"Thanks, Mr. Markham."

"No problem. By the way, I heard you got married. Congratulations."

"Thanks. Unfortunately, we haven't had time for much of a honeymoon."

"First chance you get, bring your wife out to the island. The two of you can have a couple of days at The Villas on me . . . sort of a wedding present."

Joe grinned into the cell phone. "Thanks, Mr. Markham. I'll definitely take you up on that."

"In the meantime, just phone Chalko and let him know what time the *Conquest* plans to leave."

"Will do." Joe hung up, ending the call. If he wasn't so

worried about Conn, he'd be moon-walking. Two days with Glory in one of Markham's luxury villas. He could imagine a hundred different ways he'd make love to her. But until he knew his best friend was out of danger, the honeymoon would have to wait.

Needing a little hand-holding himself, Joe called Glory on her cell phone to tell her what had happened.

"Oh, my God! Is Conn going to be all right?"

"King thinks so, but we won't know for sure until the doctors get a look at him."

"I can't believe someone shot him with a spear! I'm driving down to the hospital. I can be there in a couple of hours. Hope must be worried sick."

Joe felt a sweep of relief. He'd hated to send Hope off alone, but there was only so much room in the chopper. "That'd be great, honey. She could probably use a friend right now."

"I just know how I'd feel if you were the one who got hurt." Glory signed off, anxious to get on the road to Kingston, and Joe felt an unexpected tightening in his chest. He might not have known Glory long but he knew everything about the kind of person she was. Kind, generous, loving. Joe was absolutely sure about that.

"Do you think they are at the hospital yet?" Michael asked, walking up to where Joe stood in the chart room. The boy's gaze slid off in the direction the chopper had flown, and Joe could tell how worried he was.

"It won't take them long to get there. I'm sure Hope will call as soon as she knows something." Joe reached over and squeezed the kid's shoulder. "Conn's dealt with a lot worse than a little spear in the side. Ask him to show you the scar in his leg sometime."

"I saw it when we were diving. How did it happen?"

"Slug from an old Russian carbine. We'd just hit the beach. Chance encounter with a group of tangos who weren't supposed to be there. Conn took out five of them before he passed out."

"That is so cool!"

"So you see, a little fishing spear ain't no big deal." Joe settled an arm around Michael's shoulders. "In the meantime, while we're waiting for that call, why don't we go down to the galley and see what your old man's got to eat?"

Michael managed a halfhearted smile. "I guess I could eat something."

The kid could eat anytime, anyplace. Still, Joe could see nothing he said was going to ease the boy's worry. As they reached the galley, he discovered neither one of them was in the mood to eat.

Chapter 22

Hope sat anxiously in the waiting room at Douglas Memorial Hospital in Kingston. The room was sparsely furnished, just a beige vinyl sofa and a couple of matching chairs, a plain walnut table with a small brass lamp on top, and a table in front of the sofa stacked with dog-eared magazines.

A chrome-legged table against the wall held a stainless steel coffee urn, a bowl of crusty sugar, and a small pitcher of cream that was beginning to curdle. Hope had filled a small Sytrofoam cup but only taken a few absent sips before it went cold.

Sitting in one of the vinyl chairs, she clutched the jacket Joe had given her tighter around her shoulders, wishing she'd had time to change. At least the swimsuit had dried, so she was no longer cold in the air-conditioned room.

For the first time in her life, she wished she smoked.

She sighed as she paced the floor in the small, spartan waiting room. Only one other person sat in the room, a tall, thin black man in a loose-fitting flowered shirt whose wife had been rushed to the hospital with appendicitis. They had spoken briefly, then both lapsed back into silence.

Every time a nurse appeared in the hall, her gaze swung in that direction and the knot in her stomach tightened. She thought about getting another cup of coffee but her hands had started shaking and she was afraid she would spill it.

Then the door to the waiting room opened and Glory Ramirez swept in, tall, blond, and, for the first time, looking less that perfect.

"Hope! I came as soon as I could! I've been so worried! How's Conn? Are you all right?"

The barrage of questions threw her for a moment, but she heard concern in the younger woman's voice and felt an unexpected comfort in her presence.

"I'm all right. I haven't heard anything yet. The nurses said it would probably be a while."

Glory surprised her by pulling her into a hug. "I came to wait with you. I can only imagine how awful I'd feel if something happened to Joe."

Hope felt a thickening in her throat. Knowing Glory had been one of Conn's lovers, She hadn't wanted to like her. Now she discovered it was going to be very hard not to. "Thank you for coming."

They sat down on the vinyl couch and Glory took hold of her hand. "He's going to be okay, you know. I mean, Conn was a Navy SEAL. Those guys are really tough."

Hope felt the ghost of a smile. "I saw him in a fight once. He took on three men all at once and didn't even break a sweat."

Glory laughed and some of the tension Hope had been feeling began to ease. Glory was right. Conn was tough. He was going to be all right.

They sat there in silence for a while, both of them trying not to worry. Then the door of the waiting room swung open and a white-coated doctor walked in. Fear tightened her chest and all of Hope's optimism drained away.

"Is he . . . is he going to be all right?"

"You are Mrs. Reese?"

"Well, I'm—"

"Yes, she is," Glory cut in, flashing her a look that warned her to keep quiet.

"Then I will take you to see him." The doctor, East

Indian, black-haired, black-eyed, with the smoothest dark skin she'd ever seen, seemed to realize he hadn't answered her question. He smiled. "There is no need for you to worry. He is going to be just fine."

Relief hit her so hard, that for a moment she felt dizzy. Thank God Glory stepped forward and settled an arm around her shoulders.

"You heard what the doctor said—Conn's going to be fine. Go on, now. I'm sure he'll be anxious to see you."

Hope just nodded. Following the doctor down the hall, she walked past him into one of the hospital rooms and stood at the foot of Conn's bed. For a moment, he didn't realize she was there.

He was propped against the pillows, his hair mussed and his face deathly pale. "I need my clothes," he was grumbling to the nurse beside his bed. Hope could hear the slur of drugs in his voice. Hanging from a stand above his head, a pouch of blood dripped fluid into a length of plastic tube that fed intravenously into his arm. "You've patched me up . . . now I'm outta here."

Hope took a steadying breath and walked toward him. "You aren't going anywhere, hotshot. You're staying in this bed until the doctor says you're well enough to leave."

The hardness in his features softened. "Hello . . . sweetheart." He reached out and caught her hand, brought it to his lips. "I told you . . . I'd be fine."

The nurse slipped quietly away and Hope stood there looking down at him, her heart twisting with a mixture of relief and something she refused to name.

"How are you feeling? Are you in pain?"

Conn gave her a lopsided grin. "I'm pretty well . . . drugged up at the moment."

The doctor stepped in from behind her. "He was very lucky. Nothing vital was injured. Mostly he lost a lot of blood." Conn still looked pale beneath his dark tan, but she thought that he did look better than when he'd arrived.

"I won't be . . . diving for a while," Conn said, each word

thick and soft, "but the docs did a great job . . . stitching me up. If you hadn't come storming in here like the . . . wrath of God, I'd be out of here . . . by now."

Hope reached down and touched his cheek. "You're staying until they say you can leave, and that's final."

One of Conn's dark eyebrows went up. "You the one . . . giving orders now?"

She smiled, resisting the urge to touch him again. "I am today. And if you know what's good for you, you'd better obey them."

Conn's lips curved but his eyes were beginning to close.

"I will give you a moment alone with him," the doctor said in his heavily accented English, "then you will have to leave."

The doctor left the room and Hope sat down in the chair next to Conn's bed. She thought that he was asleep, but he opened his eyes and looked at her. "Thanks for coming . . . with me."

Hope swallowed. Wild horses couldn't have kept her out of that helicopter. It bothered her to think how worried she had been, how terrified for Conn. She didn't want to feel those kinds of emotions for a man. Until today, she wasn't even sure she could.

She managed to muster a smile. "Glory's here, too. It was really nice of her to come all the way down to wait with me."

"She's a good girl. Maybe Joe was right to . . . marry her."

"She loves him, Conn. You can see it every time she says his name."

Conn's intense blue eyes searched her face. He looked as if he wanted to say something, but didn't.

He sighed into the quiet. "All right . . . I'll stay tonight. But I'm gone . . . first thing in the morning."

"I guess that's as good as I'm going to get."

He gave her a sleepy smile that made something tighten in her chest.

"The boat's on its way to Port Antonio," she told him. "Maybe Glory will stay in town with me tonight and all three of us can drive back to the boat in the morning."

The nurse came in just then. "Sorry, time for you to leave, Mrs. Reese."

Hope's gaze sliced to Conn and she flushed. "They wouldn't let me in unless they thought I was your wife."

He smiled at her softly. "It's all right. I kind of like . . . the sound of it."

Hope ignored the little tremor of unease that slid down her spine. She reached over and combed her fingers through his hair, leaned down and very softly kissed his lips. "Get some rest. I'll be back first thing in the morning."

She started to back away but Conn caught her hand and tugged her toward him for a last soft kiss.

"Stay out of trouble, Sinclair," he whispered against her ear as she drew away. "I'll see you . . . in the morning."

Hope looked down at him, saw that his eyes had drifted closed. She remembered the soul-shaking emotions she had felt when she had seen him hurt and bleeding and thought that her troubles had only just begun.

Hope rented a room at a small motel called the Wanderer's Inn not far from the hospital, an inexpensive place with rooms that faced the parking lot. Glory had insisted on staying the night with her in Kingston, though Hope knew she would rather have driven back to Port Antonio to wait for Joe, no matter how late the boat got in.

The motel had a souvenir shop off the lobby. The shop was closed, but the desk clerk opened up for her. Hope bought a pair of cheap khaki shorts and an orange tee shirt with JAMAICA printed in bold letters across the front to wear over her bathing suit, the best she could do for now.

As soon as they got to the room, she phoned the *Conquest* to let the guys on the boat know that Conn would be all right and that he was being released in the morning.

She didn't miss the relief in Joe's voice—or the eagerness when she told him she was handing the phone to Glory.

The two talked longer than they should have, considering

the cost of a satellite call, but Hope figured Brad could afford it. Glory hung up, wearing a dreamy smile and chattering sweetly about Joe, and they left to get something to eat. When they got back to the motel, Hope called the hospital to check on Conn's condition one last time. The nurse said he was doing fine and sleeping soundly.

Fatigued clear to the bone, Hope crawled into bed and fell almost instantly into an exhausted slumber nearly as deep as Conn's.

Both women woke up early, Hope anxious to see Conn, Glory eager to get on the road back to Joe. Hope showered and dressed first. Desperate for a cup of coffee, she grabbed her purse and headed out the door for the pastry shop she had seen down the block when they checked in.

"I'll bring you a cup of coffee and something to eat," she called to Glory through the bathroom door. "I'll be back in a couple of minutes."

She wound up buying two pastries for each of them, a croissant and something that was gooey and raspberry-filled. As worried as she'd been about Conn last night, she hadn't had much of an appetite. This morning she was ravenously hungry.

She was on her way back to the room, crossing the parking lot, walking along the corridor that led to room 101, when she noticed a man rapidly approaching behind her. A second man, shorter and olive-skinned, raced up to join him. An instant later, she was shoved up against the wall, her back slamming into the batten-board siding, a thick hand wrapped around her throat.

She knew Kingston could be a dangerous place. She tried to rein in her fear, tried to calm her racing heart, noticed for the first time the tattoo of a spider on the back of the darker man's hand.

"We've got a little message for you, Hope," the other man said, the sound of her name sending a shock wave through her. "It's from your friend, Jimmy Deitz." He was American, she realized, with fair skin and blond hair shaved to the scalp. He was holding something in his hand. He held it up in front of her face and the long, shiny blade of a knife snapped out.

"You remember Deitz, don't you? Short guy, built like a tank? Paid to stick his nose into other people's business?"

Her stomach contracted. She thought of what had happened to Buddy Newton. Dear God, what had they done to Jimmy? "You must be mistaken. I don't . . . I don't know anyone by that name."

The darker man pinning her against the wall, the one with the tattoo rumbled a laugh. "You don't, huh? Well, from now on, he don't know you, either. He's done working for you or anyone else."

"That's right," Shaved-head chimed in. "Jimmy's retired. At least till his broken legs grow back together."

Her head spun and the bile rose in her throat. She tried to take a calming breath but it was impossible with the hand clamped around her throat. "I told you, I don't know what you're talking about."

"You're done with your little investigation," the blond man went on. "You and Jimmy both. That's the message. You're not writing any more articles for any friggin' paper. You're not meddlin' where you don't belong. You're stayin' out of other people's business or you're gonna end up dead. This is your last warning. You got it?"

The hand around her throat tightened, began to squeeze. The bag of pastries, still clutched in her nerveless fingers, dropped to the ground, the two cups of coffee inside the bag landing with a thud and tipping over on the sidewalk.

Hope tried to pull the encroaching hand away, tried to claw herself free. The knife flashed just inches from her face.

"You got it?" the blond man repeated.

She couldn't breathe, couldn't speak. Dark circles began to spin in front of her eyes. She tried to kick out but no longer had the strength.

The tattooed man squeezed harder, shook her till she thought her neck would snap. "You got it, bitch?"

She tried to swallow, couldn't, then frantically nodded. An instant before she passed out, he let her go and she collapsed down the wall, clutching her bruised and aching throat, desperately trying to breathe.

"Meddle again and you die," Shaved-head warned.

"Tell anyone this happened and you die," the tattooed man said. Leaving her slumped against the wall gasping for air, the two men trotted off down the corridor and disappeared around the corner of the building.

For several long moments she just sat there trembling. Then she finally mustered the strength to slide up the wall and back on her feet. Her purse still dangled from the strap slung over her shoulder. The donuts were forgotten as she swayed along the corridor down to the room and hammered on the door, too shaken to dig out her key.

"Glory . . . it's me."

The door swung open an instant later. "Did you forget your—ohmygod!" Glory eased her into the room and closed the door behind them. She guided Hope over to the bed and urged her down on the mattress. "God, what happened?"

Hope's trembling fingers moved toward her throat. For the first time she noticed the rip in the neck of her tee shirt and the splinters in the fabric that were scratching her back. Her throat still ached and she was shaking all over.

She swallowed, making her throat hurt. "It's a long story. A problem I had back home finally caught up with me." She went on to explain what had happened in the corridor and why, briefly telling Glory about Hartley House, the article she had written for the *Village Independent*, her ongoing investigation, and that the men had come here to warn her not to interfere again.

"How did they know you were here?"

"I don't know. The attack on Conn has been all over the news. The news crew was filming as Conn and I got into the helicopter. I'm sure that reporter mentioned the hospital they took him to. Or maybe they've been watching me from one of those boats."

Glory's dark eyes widened. "You don't think those are the guys who shot Conn?"

It had crossed her mind the instant she had seen the knife. "I don't know that, either. They didn't look much like divers. I guess they could have been down there to shoot me and not him, but if they wanted to kill me, they could have done it this morning."

"We'd better call the police." Glory got up from the bed, but Hope caught her arm.

"No police. These guys mean business, and this is Jamaica, not the States. We don't really know who we can trust."

Glory took a breath, let it out slowly. "Then we'll tell Conn. He'll know what to do."

"No!" Hope's hold tightened on Glory's arm. "He's not even out of the hospital yet. I don't want him worried. He's already got enough trouble as it is. Once he's recovered enough to handle it, I'll tell him myself."

Glory mulled that over. "All right, we won't tell Conn. We'll tell Joe. He's was a SEAL just like Conn. Joe can—"

Hope shook her head. "I'm through getting other people hurt. As far as I'm concerned, this is over. The detective I hired is out of commission. If I let the whole thing drop, they'll leave me alone and that'll be the end of it."

She wondered how they'd found out about Jimmy, then remembered he'd said something about not cashing the checks they were writing him. Maybe that had been the tip-off. She wished she could call, but if she did, she would only be putting him in more danger. A get-well note with a message inside would have to do.

Glory's gaze ran over her, taking in her disheveled appearance. "Conn's going to know."

Hope released a shaky breath. She hadn't thought of that. Getting up from the bed, she walked over to the mirror above the dresser. The woman staring back at her had tangled red hair, a rip in her orange tee shirt, and big red blotches, rapidly turning to bruises, all over her neck and arms. There were bruises on her back as well, she knew, though she couldn't see them.

"Oh, God."

"Look, here's what we'll do. I brought a few things with me in case I needed to stay. Nothing's your size, but I think there's a blouse in there that will work if you tie it up around your waist. The collar will help hide the bruising. We'll use some of my makeup on your neck to cover the rest. If we're lucky, Conn won't notice until you're ready to tell him."

Hope managed a smile. "Thanks, Glory. I really appreciate everything you've done." And she was thinking that maybe the smartest thing Joe Ramirez had ever done was to marry Gloria Rothman.

It was half an hour later by the time Hope was dressed in Glory's borrowed blouse, her bruises covered with a thick layer of makeup, her composure steady enough for them to drive back to the hospital.

Conn was wearing his swimsuit when she walked into his room, looking far too good for a man who was standing next to the hospital bed he'd spent the night in. As she had left the motel, she'd had Glory stop the car while she rushed back into the souvenir shop next to the office to buy him a short-sleeved shirt. It was pale blue, size extra-large, with the motel name embroidered on the pocket. But it buttoned up the front so he'd be able to get it on. His swimsuit would have to do until they got back to the boat.

"Hi . . ." he said with a smile when he glanced up and saw her.

Hope smiled softly, her heart kicking up in a way she wished it wouldn't. "How are you feeling?" She handed him the shirt, admiring his incredible chest, trying not to look at the bandage wrapped around his middle and wondered if she were somehow responsible for the injury he had suffered.

"Better. Still hurts like hell, but I refuse to spend the day drugged up like a dummy. How anyone could think that's fun I can't imagine."

Hope laughed. She helped him put on the shirt, moving slowly, trying not to hurt him. He didn't make a sound but his jaw was set and she knew his side must be throbbing like the very devil.

"Why don't you take something—even an Advil would help."

"I took four already. I'm not a martyr, you know. It's just that I've got things to do when we get back and I need to be able to think."

Knowing it was useless to argue, she simply stepped back to look at him. His tan was back in place, his eyes as blue as the sea and no longer glazed with pain, though she caught a tightening in the lines of his face whenever he moved.

"All right, macho man, let's blow this popstand."

He grinned. "You got it, babe."

The endearment washed over her. He was using them more and more often. She told herself she didn't like it, but it was a lie. She loved the soft way he said the words—and it scared her to death.

She took a breath, refusing to think about it now. Shoving open the heavy door, she held it while Conn walked out. No wheelchair waited in the hall. This was Jamaica. Life was less restricted here, the rules more relaxed. A few feet down the corridor, Glory stood waiting, tall and blond, her hair swept up in a ponytail, a big smile on her face.

"Hiya, handsome. I hear you need a ride."

Conn leaned down and brushed a brotherly kiss on her cheek. "Thanks for coming, Glory. I was worried about Hope being here all alone."

Glory flicked a glance at Hope, thinking of what had happened at the motel, but Hope shook her head. Glory looked at Conn and smiled. "I was glad to come."

"Joe called," Conn said. "I told him we'd be on our way as soon as I could bust out of this joint. He said all I had to do was pick the lock and knock off one of the guards."

"Well, hey," Hope said, "for you that's a piece of cake."

Glory laughed. "That sounds like Joe. God, I can't wait to see him."

"You ready to go?" Hope asked Conn.

He nodded. "All the paperwork's done. All we gotta do is make it to the getaway car."

Hope grinned. "The car's right out front." She let Conn lean against her as they moved down the hall, though she thought he could have made it on his own. "I think we're all more than ready to go home."

The double glass doors swung open and they walked out on the wide front steps. Hope froze, stunned by the array of newsmen waiting for Conn to appear.

"They weren't here when we came in," she said.

"Well, they're damn sure here now." Conn kept on walking.

As he slowly navigated the steps, one of the reporters shoved a microphone in front of his face. "Do you think they were after the treasure, Conn?"

"What do you think?" he said, and kept going.

"How much have you brought up so far?"

"No comment."

A woman reporter stepped forward. "Do you think the authorities will catch the man who shot you?"

"No," Conn said bluntly as Hope opened the door of Glory's rental car and helped him stretch out in the backseat as best he could. His jaw was clenched in pain and several reporters were yelling questions as she firmly closed the door. Hope hurriedly sat down in the passenger seat and Glory jammed the car in gear and hit the gas.

As they drove off down the block, she looked back at Conn but his eyes were closed, his jaw still set. They had paid the motel clerk an exorbitant price for two old, crummy rubber pillows, but watching him trying to get comfortable, Hope thought it was worth it. He slept on the drive back to Port Antonio and so far he hadn't noticed the neat makeup job Glory had done on the ugly bruises on her neck.

Hope shivered just thinking of it.

She remembered the words she had meant to say to Buddy Newton but never got the chance—*it isn't worth dying for.*

Hope intended to take her own advice.

CHAPTER 23

Conn felt like hell. His side ached like a red-hot poker had been shoved through his skin; he was weak and a little light-headed. He slept for a while, uncomfortably squeezed into the backseat of Glory's rental car, propped up on a couple of worn-out foam pillows. He hoped the sleep would help him recover his strength. He had work to do when they got back.

He was awake when the car pulled into the scenic little town of Port Antonio. He asked Glory to stop at Gilligan's and she wheeled the car up in front.

As soon as they had begun finding treasure, he had placed an order with the owner of the dive shop for a Divelink system. The underwater communication devices that allowed divers to talk to each other as well as the boat had arrived last week, just after they had left port.

Conn wished he'd had them the day he'd had the run-in with the thieves. Divelink masks could communicate up to a distance of forty-five hundred feet and even had an emergency signal that alerted other divers when a diver was in distress. If he'd had the equipment, maybe he wouldn't have wound up getting shot.

But the masks were extremely expensive and diving as

shallow as they were, he hadn't really thought they would need them. With the latest find, the danger element had increased. Now he was damned glad the equipment was there.

Hissing a breath, ignoring a hot stab of pain in his side, he got out of the car and started walking. Hope was immediately next to him, helping him up the few steps to the front door. An amused smile curved his lips. He could have made it without her, but he liked having her fuss over him.

He would never forget how worried she had been when he had been injured. He didn't think Kelly had ever cared that much.

But Hope cared. Conn was more and more determined to make her realize just how much.

"You should have let me come in and pick up whatever it is you need," she scolded. "You should be resting as much as you possibly can."

"Don't be a nag," he teased, smiling as he ran a finger along her cheek. She looked up at him with those lovely sea-green eyes and heat rushed into his groin. As impossible as it seemed, he went hard. Damn, now he ached in two places instead of just one. "This won't take long. We'll be on our way in just a few minutes."

The equipment looked good. After signing more than five thousand dollars onto the Treasure Limited credit card, he let Hope help him back out to the car. The owner, an Asian man nearly as short as Hope, must have seen the story of the assault on the news. He insisted on carrying the equipment out to the car, waited as Glory unlocked the trunk, then loaded the gear inside and closed the lid.

"You take care of yourself, now, Mr. Reese," the man said with a singsong accent.

"Believe me, I will."

Hope helped him into the backseat of the car and when she straightened, he happened to see her wince. "What happened? You get hurt yesterday, too?"

The color drained from her face. "It . . . it isn't that. I just . . . I think I pulled a muscle . . . maybe climbing out of the water in such a hurry. It's nothing to worry about." She tried to smile but failed, managed with the second attempt.

Conn frowned. She was lying. He wasn't sure why.

But he damned well intended to find out.

More reporters waited at the dock. Captain Bob had done a remarkable job of entertaining them without really telling them much. Hope spotted Joe pacing the bow of the boat when the car rolled into the parking lot. He scrambled along the deck, down the gangway, and raced madly toward them. Glory jammed the engine into PARK so fast Conn hissed at a sudden jolt of pain.

"Sorry," Glory said, swinging open the door, and then she was in her husband's arms.

Hope watched them a moment, the tender way he held her, the fierce possession in his eyes when he looked at her, and a lump rose in her throat. She wished Richard had loved her that way, loved her and the child she had carried. But Richard loved only himself, and the pain he had caused had destroyed any chance for her to love that way again.

As she climbed out of the car, Hope paused. For the first time it occurred to her that she had never loved Richard that much, though at the time she had believed she did. An image of Conn appeared in her mind—tall, strong, fiercely passionate, incredibly protective. He was a man a woman could love with all her heart.

Any woman but her.

He was watching her, she saw, as she turned to help him climb out of the back, looking at her with the same fierce possession she had seen in Joe's dark eyes. She could feel his gaze moving over her almost as if he'd touched her, feel the powerful attraction between them. Desire shot through her, and overwhelming need.

And love.

The unwanted thought rang in her head as clearly as the bell in the church on the hill. Dear God, she couldn't deny it any longer. She was in love with Conner Reese, and she simply could not be.

It was impossible. Out of the question. She knew what it would feel like if things didn't work out between them, knew that she could not survive that kind of loss a second time.

Two more weeks, she thought. *That's all there is for us. Two more weeks and I can go back to the life I lived before.*

By then, the final magazine article would be finished. She was no longer involved in the Hartley House story. She could go back to New York, return to her job at *Midday News.* She would be safe there, her heart and soul no longer in danger.

She took a deep breath. Two more weeks. The pain of leaving would worsen with each passing day, but the reward would be two more weeks of precious memories. And Conn needed her. She wasn't about to leave when he was still hurting.

She managed to muster a smile. "Let's get going, macho man. I think you said there were some things you needed to do."

Instead he reached for her, cradled the side of her face with his hand, tipped her head back, and captured her lips in a long, soft kiss. The bruises on her neck throbbed, but the pain disappeared beneath his gentle assault. His lips were so soft she sank into them, his kiss so deep and fierce she couldn't catch her breath. His tongue swept in, and she had to force herself not to melt against him.

If he hadn't been hurting so badly, she would have thrown her arms around his neck and kissed him the way Glory had kissed Joe, with every part of her body and even a little of her soul.

Instead she eased away. "If you don't stop, even with that hole in your side, we're going to be putting on quite a show right here in the parking lot."

Conn didn't laugh. There was something in his eyes as he watched her. The heat remained. He was hard, she knew, obviously as needy as she.

"I can think of better places, but, hey, if you insist . . ."

She laughed softly, eased an arm around his waist on the side that wasn't injured, and helped him cross the parking lot toward the gangway. News crews hovered there, turning toward them the minute they realized Conn was on his way.

The same questions were hurled at him: "Do you have any idea who shot you? Do you think they'll catch the men who did it? How much treasure have you found so far?"

Conn gave them the same responses, mostly "No comment."

At last they were safely aboard the *Conquest.* Hope helped him down to the chart room and he settled back on a padded bench along the wall.

"Glad to have you back," Andy Glass said.

"How you feeling?" Captain Bob asked.

"Never better," Conn said with a straight face that made all of them grin.

One after another, the crew came in to check on him. Michael had gone home with his grandmother, his adventure over and time to go back to school. But he left a note for Conn, telling him to get well quick.

The professor had also left the boat, asking Joe to relay his get-well wishes. He had a few more lectures to give at the college, and Andy said Professor Marlin's wife, Mary, and daughter, Virginia, were coming to Jamaica for a week-long visit. Hope prayed the older woman would have one of the rare, lucid periods the professor had mentioned and be able to enjoy these last golden hours with her husband.

Then Tommy Tyler walked in, cocky and grinning as usual, freshly shaved, his short red hair recently trimmed. "Hey, Conn. Sorry to hear what happened."

Conn carefully clasped the younger man's extended hand. "To tell you the truth, it's a little embarrassing. I was trained for that kind of stuff, you know? I can't believe I let some bozo sneak up and shoot me."

Hope reached over and touched his shoulder. "You weren't expecting to be attacked in your own backyard."

He cast her a look, the same one he had given her a couple of times earlier, but didn't say anything. She wondered if somehow he knew about the attack on her that morning, but she didn't think there was any way he could.

He turned his attention to the captain. "We can't afford to leave the site anymore, Bob. Not even overnight. There's too damned much money at stake. From now on, we'll have to have our fuel, water, and whatever supplies we need ferried out to the boat."

"Good idea," Captain Bob said. "I'd been considering that myself. Expensive, though."

"With what we're bringing up, it looks like we'll be able to afford it."

The captain nodded. "I know someone who can handle the job."

Hope talked to Tommy while the necessary calls were made, but her mind remained on Conn. She couldn't seem to stop worrying about him, wishing he were resting instead of taxing his strength.

"I wish I could have been here the day you found the ballast pile," Tommy was saying. "I've been working on another assignment. But I did get some great photos of the stuff the boat brought in to Jamaica. There was an armored car waiting to haul the gold to the bank. The magazine's gonna love it."

She tried to pay attention to the conversation but she knew Conn must be tiring. She was surprised when she looked up to see him standing right in front of her, a hard look on his face.

"We need to talk. Let's go."

Her stomach tightened. His jaw was clenched and she didn't think it was from pain. "All right."

They made their way down to his cabin. She noticed he didn't seem to need her help, though she knew he must be hurting. As soon as they stepped inside, he slammed the door.

"All right, what the hell is going on?"

She swallowed, felt the soreness of every bruise on her throat. "I don't know what you mean." She didn't. At least she wasn't completely sure.

"You're a really terrible liar, Hope." He reached toward her and she noticed a makeup smudge on the back of his hand. Very carefully, he used his thumb to remove another smear of flesh-colored cream from the side of her neck. He held it up in front of her. "Now, tell me what happened."

His tone was implacable, yet she didn't miss the concern. She moistened her lips and raised her chin. "I had a run-in with a couple of thugs this morning. I think they may have been the same guys who attacked us in New York. Or at least two of the three, since the third man is probably still nursing a broken arm."

"What did they do?" His jaw looked carved in stone, his legs braced slightly apart as if he intended to take on her assailants.

"Not much. Basically they gave me a taste of what it feels like to be strangled, then delivered a message. I had better stay off the Hartley House story or I'll wind up dead."

A muscle tightened in his cheek. "They found out Deitz was still working for you?"

She nodded. "They broke both his legs."

"Christ. How'd they find out?"

"I don't know. He told me once he wasn't cashing their checks. Maybe that made them suspicious."

"That's it? They came all the way over here to threaten you just because Deitz was still sniffing around?"

She glanced away for an instant and Conn's eyes darkened.

"What else, Hope? What else did you do?"

She sighed. "I wrote an article for a small, liberal newspaper in Manhattan called the *Village Independent*. The story outlined what had happened to Buddy, the things Deitz told me about the owners on each side of Hartley House wanting to buy the piece for a hundred-million-dollar development, along with my own suspicions. Apparently it was printed and somehow they figured out I was the one who wrote it."

"Dammit, Hope! Those guys could have killed you!" He towered over her, looking like he wanted to do it himself. God, she could imagine him commanding a small army of men without the slightest problem.

"Take it easy, okay? They didn't kill me. They didn't even break my legs."

"That isn't funny."

"Actually, I thought it was." She looked up at him. "I'm off the story, all right? I'm out of it completely. That's what they wanted. That's what they got. So I'm not in any more danger."

He released a frustrated breath but enfolded her in his arms. Hope let him, just slid her arms around his neck and did her best not to hurt him.

"It's all over, okay? I would have told you but I didn't want you to worry."

Conn eased back to look at her. "You're a real handful of trouble, you know that?" And then he kissed her, very tenderly, very thoroughly. She didn't mean to kiss him back quite so passionately. She knew what would happen if she did. But her mouth parted and his tongue slid in and her own tongue slid over his. Conn groaned.

"We can't do this," she whispered, drawing away. "We might reopen your wounds."

"There's a risk in everything." Conn kissed her again and her body began to melt at the same time her brain screamed a warning. There was a chance she'd been responsible for getting him shot in the first place. She wasn't about to be the one to hurt him again.

Ignoring a stab of regret, Hope stepped out of his embrace. "No way. It's too dangerous."

"I want to be inside you. I want it so much I can hardly think."

She knew he was aroused. She saw the need in his eyes, the hunger. Her own need stirred, urging her to ignore the damage she might do to Conn.

She looked at him and yearning swept over her. She wanted him as much as he wanted her. Maybe more. Taking his hand, she led him over to the bed, unbuttoned and eased the pale blue shirt off his shoulders, her gaze skimming over the bandage around the indentation of muscle over his ribs. Reaching down, she began to shove down his swimsuit. It was the same one he'd been wearing yesterday. Traces of blood stained the fabric, and her chest tightened.

Very carefully, she slid the suit down his long, muscular legs and helped him step out of it, then eased him down on the bed.

Conn reached for the buttons on her borrowed blouse. "Your turn now."

Hope shook her head. "Just lie back. Let me do this for you."

Conn's gaze bored into her. She pressed her hands against his chest, urging him back on the bed. As soon as he was settled, she began to take off her clothes, removing each piece slowly, baring her breasts first, letting the tension build. His eyes were hot and dark by the time she was finished. Naked, she started kissing him again, refusing to rush, driving him to even greater arousal.

He was beautifully built, his erection large and heavy, rising up from a nest of dark curls. She had never made love to a man this way before but she wanted to now, wanted to do this for Conn, wanted to know him in a way she hadn't known a man before.

With her hands and her mouth, she pleasured him, brought him to a shaking climax. And gained something unexpected for herself. An erotic pleasure that was nearly as satisfying as if their bodies had physically joined.

She was so completely aroused she didn't realize Conn's hand had moved between her legs, that he was giving her pleasure as well. Not until she climaxed with such stunning force that she cried out his name and slumped over him on the bed.

She felt his hands in her hair, stroking gently, tenderly caressing her cheek. "You're quite a woman, Hope Sinclair."

And she thought that Conner Reese was quite a man.

Chapter 24

Conn slept the rest of the afternoon, for which Hope was grateful. The crew finished refueling and resupplying the boat, getting ready to return to Pleasure Island. Joe had taken off with Glory as soon as the car rolled up, the two of them returning to her motel, no doubt, to spend the day in bed. They returned just before the boat was ready to pull away from the dock.

Conn was awake by then, standing next to Hope on deck, watching the newlyweds say good-bye.

"It doesn't seem fair," Hope said to Conn, unable to miss the glint of tears in Glory's big brown eyes. "I mean, you and I are sleeping together. I wish there were some way——"

"Hey, great idea." Conn smiled. "Wish I'd thought of it myself."

"Thought of what?" Hope watched him take careful steps along the deck to where Joe gave Glory a last good-bye kiss.

"I'll see you soon, honey." Joe cradled her face in his hands and gently kissed her again. "I love you."

"I love you, too, Joe."

Hope envied Glory the ease with which she spoke the words. She didn't think she'd ever be brave enough to say those words again.

"Wait a minute, you two!" Conn called out to them, snagging Joe's attention.

He grabbed Glory's hand as she turned to leave, looking grateful for the few minutes' respite. "What is it?"

"Hope and I were talking. We thought maybe Glory might like to come along. You guys could use Hope's cabin and she could move in with me."

Hope's eyes widened. Sleeping with Conn was one thing. Moving in with him was another. But when she saw the joy leap into Joe's face, saw the tears return to Glory's eyes, she couldn't bring herself to say no. And it wasn't as if the whole crew didn't know about her and Conn anyway.

"You're the best, Conn." Joe clapped him on the back and Conn winced. "Sorry." But Joe kept grinning, turning to sweep Glory into a hug. "Get your stuff, woman. You're coming with me."

Glory squealed in delight, threw her arms around Joe's neck and kissed him. She turned to give Conn a big, grateful hug, but he held up his hand and shook his head.

"A *thank-you* will suffice. Besides, Hope's the one who's giving up her cabin."

Glory squealed again, raced over and hugged her, her blond ponytail wiggling. "Thank you, thank you, *thank* you! You don't know how much this means. I'm so glad we're friends."

"I think I do know. And I'm glad, too." And she was. Very glad. Glory was a wonderful young woman. Hope felt lucky to have met her.

By morning they were anchored back over the ballast pile. A flotilla of boats still surrounded the buoy-marked search area but they seemed to be keeping their distance. She wondered if there was someone on one of the boats who was watching her, ready to carry out the death threat the men in Jamaica had made.

She shivered to think of it, took a calming breath. What she'd said to Conn was true. She was off the story. She shouldn't be in any more danger.

As soon as the sun was up, the divers went to work, only three of them now, rotating two at a time and working throughout the day. Conn was looking for two more men to join the dive team, hoping to put them to work sometime next week.

The boat was fully rigged out for the search, the men using the hookah lines to breathe, the mailbox and hand-blowers to move away the deep layers of sand. Dredges were used to lift and strain artifacts and debris from the ocean floor.

Ron Keegan brought up the first piece of treasure that day. He was wearing one of the Divelink underwater communications masks that Conn had bought. Hope, Andy, Captain Bob, and Conn were gathered in the chart room, listening to his voice coming over the speaker.

Hope could hear Ron's excitement when he found what the video cameras showed to be a cache of palm-sized gold disks and several fifteen-inch gold bars.

"This is fantastic!" Ron said. "They were being transported in some kind of a wooden chest, I think. Chest is long gone, but, man, this is beautiful stuff!"

In a single day, they brought up four gold bars, hundreds of oxidized silver coins, a silver ewer, a silver plate, and the gold hilt of a sword encrusted with emeralds. Just for fun, the guys brought up a couple of corroded cannonballs and the brass barrel of an ancient blunderbuss.

As pleased as Conn was, she could feel his frustration, his restlessness. He wanted to be down there, wanted to be one of the men searching for treasure. It wasn't going to happen, at least not for a while.

The search continued. The following day, Joe uncovered a length of gold chain that had once been part of an intricate belt. In the same area, he and Wally began finding other personal items, the kinds of beautifully crafted pieces they had found in the area to the north: a gold-and-emerald brooch, a gold crucifix inlaid with onyx, and pieces of an onyx rosary.

After four days of searching, the hold was full of gold and

silver, the safe filled with priceless antique gold jewelry. Conn had decided to fly the load to the bank in Port Antonio as soon as security arrangements could be made.

Still, there was no sign of the most valuable artifact of all—the golden Maiden. Of course, the statue might have been stored somewhere on the top decks when the ship went down, or it might be lying somewhere in the scatter pattern and not be found for years. Or never.

Hope was sitting on a deck box on the bow, working on the final article in her series, trying not to think how fast the time was approaching that she would be leaving, when she saw one of the boats in the distant flotilla racing toward them.

"Looks like someone's finally gotten brave enough to come over," Conn said as he walked up.

It was a boat she'd never seen, a huge white luxury yacht at least ninety feet long, the kind of boat that cost millions of dollars. Conn lifted the pair of binoculars looped over his neck and peered into the lenses. She heard him softly curse.

"Brad Talbot. I should have known. With all the press lurking around, I'm surprised he didn't get here sooner." He looked through the lenses again. "He's got a redhead with him and a couple of people who look vaguely familiar." He unlooped the strap from around his neck and handed the binoculars to Hope.

Sliding her sunglasses up on her head, she focused the lenses and trained the binoculars on the approaching yacht.

"I'm pretty sure the guy next to Brad is Regis Philbin. There's a blonde standing next to him. Looks like it might be Kelly Ripa."

Conn shook his head. "Talbot's nothing if not creative. If anyone can stir up media coverage, he can."

"Brad's definitely got connections. He thrives on who he knows and what they can do for him."

A muscle flexed in his jaw. "In a way, I'm glad he's here. I'm going to have a little chat with good ol' Brad. He's not the only one who can deliver a message."

"Wait a minute, Conn. We don't know he's behind what happened to me. We don't even know if he's involved."

"Well, just in case he is, the two of us are going to have a talk."

Hope caught his arm. "Please, Conn. Don't buy any more trouble."

Conn smiled darkly. "I never buy trouble, baby. I get more than I can handle for free."

Turning away from her, he sauntered off toward the chart room, favoring his right side only a little, leaving her at the rail to greet the boat when it arrived. As the yacht cut its powerful engines and settled into the waves, Talbot and his entourage climbed aboard a rubber Zodiac and one of the crew steered them over to the *Conquest*. The group disembarked, climbing out on the boarding platform, and Captain Bob went to greet them.

"Welcome aboard, ladies and gentlemen!" He helped each of them up the ladder, shaking hands as they stepped onto the deck. "Mr. Talbot, it's good to see you. Mr. Philbin—it's a real pleasure to meet you. I'm a very big fan. You, too, Ms. Ripa."

"It's just Regis and Kelly," Regis said, smiling.

The curvy redhead that Hope had seen through the binoculars came aboard, followed by a tall, thin man with salt-and-pepper hair. A cameraman stepped up on deck last, along to film the event to be aired on television in an upcoming show. He worked unobtrusively, documenting Brad's meeting with the captain and the presence of Regis and Kelly; then he turned the camera lens toward her.

"I'm just another reporter," she told him, and he turned the camera off.

"Where's Conn?" Talbot asked, glancing around, obviously eager to get his photo taken with the media's latest target.

"He's down in the chart room. I'll see if I can convince him to come up on deck."

Talbot frowned. He didn't like anyone who didn't obey his dictates. Hope smiled. Of course Conn wasn't crazy about it, either.

She found him poring over a detailed diagram they had made of the site, showing the exact layout of the ballast pile—the width, length, its longitude and latitude, and the precise location of each of the divers' finds. He looked up as she walked in.

"Okay, you've dodged them as long as you can. You can plead fatigue later, but you need to speak to them at least for a couple of minutes."

He didn't like it, she could tell, but he went with her, grumbling all the way. Regis and Kelly were friendly. They seemed like sincerely nice people. She even saw Conn crack a smile or two at something one of them said.

Talbot was another matter entirely. Conn believed it was possible Brad had something to do with the attack on Hope, and as protective as he was, he didn't take that lightly. He nodded a greeting and shook the man's hand, but his brief smile didn't reach his eyes.

The third man in the group, narrow-faced, tall, and thin, was Jack Feldman.

"Jack's the head of Talbot Security," Brad said by way of introduction.

"Nice to meet you," Feldman said to Conn, who nodded in return.

Brad tipped his head toward the yacht. "Jack's brought a team of professional divers, guys with military experience. They'll be stationed aboard the yacht. The *Wind Runner* will anchor with the rest of the boats so Jack can keep an eye on things while the divers keep the perimeter secure. I'll only be here a couple of days, then I'll be flying back, but Jack and his men will be staying. Jack will be handling underwater security from now on."

It wasn't a bad idea and Conn seemed to relax a little with Talbot's words.

"That sounds good to me. I hated to see my guys constantly having to look over their shoulder."

"If your thieves come back," Talbot said, "if anyone tries to steal anything down there, they're going to wish they hadn't."

Conn nodded. "This much treasure is definitely an entice-
ment."

Then Brad introduced the redhead who hung onto his arm.
"This is Mandy. Mandy, meet Hope Sinclair and Conner Reese."

She was petite, like Hope, maybe a little taller and wearing more makeup. "Nice to meet you." Mandy clung to Brad,
rubbing up against him, encouraging him to look into the
enormous amount of cleavage showing above her bathing
suit top, but her big blue eyes were hot for Conn.

She made a slow perusal of his body, taking in the width
of his shoulders, the powerful biceps beneath the sleeve of
his shirt. He was wearing shorts and Mandy didn't miss the
long muscles and sinews that lengthened and tightened
whenever he moved.

Hope's stomach knotted. An image of Richard popped
into her head. Richard had been handsome, too. In a different way from Conn, he'd been incredibly attractive. Other
women noticed, gave him the same come-on look the redhead was giving Conn, but Hope had trusted him, loved him,
believed he would be faithful.

God, what a fool.

Making a polite excuse, she turned away from the redhead,
leaving Conn at the woman's mercy. He cast her a look, but
she just kept walking. As she reached the ladder leading down
to the cabin she now shared with Conn, she heard Mandy asking to see the treasure, heard Brad and his guests chime in.

It was almost dark when Conn finally came down to the
cabin, the lines of his face tight with fatigue.

"Are you all right?" she asked, unable to stop herself.

"Thanks for throwing me to the wolves."

She kept her gaze carefully guarded. "I thought Kelly and
Regis were great."

"Nice people. I'm talking about Brad and the redhead."

She looked away, back down to the book she'd been reading, open and resting in her lap. "She seemed to like you just
fine."

Conn caught her arm and hauled her up out of the chair, knocking the book onto the floor. "I don't give a damn whether she liked me or not. I'm not interested in one of Brad's sleazy women. I think I made that clear before. The only woman I'm interested in is you."

She gasped as he pulled her into his arms and very thoroughly kissed her. Hope stiffened for an instant, then melted, kissing him as hotly as he was kissing her. She blinked when Conn firmly set her away.

"All men aren't like Richard. I know you don't believe it, but it's true. Someday, maybe I can convince you."

Someday. If she had that long to wait.

She didn't. "Too bad I'll only be here another couple of weeks. After that, I'll be heading back to New York."

He slowly straightened, making him look even taller than he usually did. "That doesn't have to happen, Hope. You could make other plans."

"I've got a job, Conn, in case you've forgotten."

"I haven't forgotten anything. But there are other jobs, other places to work."

She didn't want to talk about it, didn't even want to consider the possibility. "You look beat," she said, changing the subject. "Why don't you lie down and rest for a while? I need some air. Maybe while I'm gone you can get some sleep."

Conn said nothing, but his eyes were dark and hard. "You said you'd give this relationship a chance."

"I'm here, aren't I?"

"Your body's here. What about your heart?"

The question twisted a painful knot inside her. "I left that behind a long time ago. I tried to tell you that, Conn." She didn't say more and neither did he. Turning away from him, she walked out and closed the door.

Glory spotted Hope on the bow, the wind ruffling her shiny dark red hair. Even from a distance, Glory could see the tension in her friend's small shoulders. As she approached, she noticed a trail of tears had dried on Hope's cheeks.

"Hope, honey, what is it? Did you and Conn have a fight?"

Hope shook her head, raked a hand through her hair. "Not exactly. It wasn't really a fight. I just . . . I told him the truth, that's all. That in two more weeks I'd be leaving. I'll be going back to my job in New York. We both knew it would happen, sooner or later."

"What did Conn say?"

"He said I could make other plans, find a different job."

Glory bit her lip. "I guess you don't want a different job."

"It isn't the job. I mean, I like my work, but I could find another job if I had to."

"What then?"

"I just don't want that kind of involvement. I don't want to take the kind of risk you took when you married Joe. I couldn't handle it if things went wrong." There was something in Hope's face, something dark and troubled.

Something that made Glory's chest feel tight. "What happened to you, Hope? Someone must have hurt you really badly."

Hope turned away and stared out over the water. The sun was down, the water dark and still. For the moment none of the men were around and the deck was quiet.

"I loved a man once," Hope said, "or at least I thought I did. We lived together. We were going to get married."

"What happened?"

"A couple of months before the wedding, I got pregnant. I was so happy. Richard seemed really happy, too. I wanted a baby so much. I wanted a husband and family." She blinked a couple of times and Glory could tell she was fighting not to cry. This was obviously a very painful subject.

"Then what happened?"

"I got pregnant. It was an accident, but I thought it was wonderful. I thought Richard would think so, too." She took a shaky breath. Two weeks before the wedding, I came home early from work. I opened the bedroom door and there he was, naked in our bed, making love to my best friend."

The darkness in Hope's expression was nothing compared to the emptiness in her eyes. Glory had never seen anything like it. She was afraid to ask more but something told her Hope needed to say it, to get it out in the open.

"What . . . did you do?"

Hope swallowed and tears glinted in her eyes. "I looked at them and I felt sick inside, sick and betrayed. I turned and started running. Richard followed me as far as the front door of the apartment. He was yelling for me to stop, telling me he was sorry, but I just kept going. I ran into the elevator and when the doors opened in the lobby, I ran out. It was winter. The front steps of the apartment building were icy, and I fell."

She leaned forward, her hair obscuring her face. "Oh, God, I can remember the exact moment I hit the sidewalk, how cold it was, how my belly clenched in pain, and I knew. *I knew.* In that moment, I knew that I had killed my baby."

Her body shook with silent sobs as she stared back out to sea. Unconsciously, she wrapped her arms around her middle as if the baby were still inside.

Glory was afraid to touch her, afraid if she did, her fragile control would shatter completely. "Richard killed your baby, Hope, not you."

She turned, her eyes bleak and filled with tears. "Yes . . . Richard killed my child. My baby was only two months old, but I loved it. I loved it so very much."

The tears spilled onto her cheeks. Glory put her arms around her friend. "It's all right, honey. Sometimes bad things happen."

"I know."

"In time, you'll get past it. One of these days you'll have another child to love."

Hope straightened away from her, took a deep, shaky breath. "That isn't going to happen, Glory." She wiped away the wetness with a hand that trembled. "I can't trust enough to love. I can't take the risk that something like that might happen again."

Glory wanted to argue, to tell her that loving someone was worth any kind of risk, but Hope's bleak expression said it wouldn't do any good.

"You just need time," she said softly. "In time, you'll feel different."

Hope tried to smile. "I hope you're right." But it was obvious she didn't really believe it.

"Are you going to be okay?"

Hope nodded, her usual self-control settling back into place. "Thank you for listening. I've never told that to anyone before. Not even my sisters. Somehow I just couldn't."

Glory's throat closed up. She gave Hope a last long hug. "Thank you for trusting me enough to tell me."

Hope nodded and both of them turned toward the sea.

Glory's heart went out to her friend.

And to Conn. It was obvious he was in love with her. Glory prayed he would find a way to win Hope's trust. If he did, Glory was sure he would also win her love.

Conn watched Talbot's fancy leased yacht pull up near the *Conquest* the following day. Apparently, Brad's celebrity guests had flown back to Jamaica, but Brad was staying until tomorrow. The redhead came back with him, hanging on Brad's every word. Talbot must have noticed the heated glances she'd cast Conn's way the last time she was aboard. She was far more circumspect today, careful to keep her eyes firmly fixed on Brad whenever Conn was around.

He started along the deck to where his partner stood at the rail, watching as the crane brought up a load of silver bars. Next to Brad, Tommy Tyler madly snapped away on his digital camera.

"This is incredible," Talbot said to Tommy as the crane set the metal basket down on the deck.

"Yeah, and they haven't even really started digging into the ballast pile." Tommy snapped another shot.

"But there's still no sign of the Maiden."

Tommy grinned. "You'll make a ton of money even if they don't find it."

Conn walked up to the men just then. "Sorry to interrupt, but I need to talk to you, Brad."

Talbot smiled. "Sure. No problem."

They moved down the deck to a place on the stern where no one could hear them. Though a stiff breeze blew across the deck, not a strand of Brad's blond hair, cut short and perfectly groomed, ever so much as waved. His eyes, hidden behind his Armani sunglasses, seemed to take in his surroundings without the need to turn his head.

"A few days back something happened to Hope," Conn said.

"That so?"

"It seems a couple of guys roughed her up pretty good outside her motel room in Kingston, told her she had better keep her nose out of other people's business. It was a warning not to pursue the Hartley House story."

"I didn't know she was still working on it." Brad looked sincere. But then he was good at that.

"She isn't. Not anymore. She's out of it completely."

"Smart girl."

"It would be equally smart for anyone who might think of hurting her again *not* to try it. That person might end up with more trouble than he can handle."

Only Brad's mouth moved. "Now it sounds like you're giving *me* a warning."

"I am."

"What does any of this have to do with me?"

"Maybe nothing. Maybe something. Whichever it is, I don't want Hope getting hurt."

Talbot shrugged. "If she's off the story like you say, I don't see any reason for her to get hurt."

"Exactly," Conn said, his eyes hard on Brad's face.

The redhead sashayed up just then. "Well, here you are, you naughty boy. I've been looking all over. I'm getting lonesome, sweetie pie."

Brad gave her a slightly too-wide smile and slid an arm around her waist. "I can take care of that. We'll go back to the yacht. I'll have the chef prepare something special for lunch and have it sent down to my cabin. I'm sure I can think of something to keep you entertained until the food gets there." He reached up and squeezed one of Mandy's enormous breasts.

The redhead giggled and slapped his hand away. "Brad!"

Talbot turned to Conn, his smile still in place. "Let me know if you run across the Maiden."

"I'll do that," Conn said.

He watched Talbot walk away, the redhead plastered to his side. He hoped Talbot heeded his warning. He wanted Hope safe and he would do whatever it took to insure that she was.

He was still pissed at her. She could be a damned hard lady when she wanted.

But he knew it was partly his fault. He should have known convincing her to stay with him wouldn't be that easy. He would give her some time, let her mull over the notion for a while, but he wasn't giving up.

Conn wasn't a man who accepted failure.

He got what he wanted. And he wanted Hope Sinclair.

Chapter 25

A calm sea surrounded them in the darkness. A fingernail
moon hung over the water, casting a thin track of light. Sitting
in the galley, Hope chatted amiably with the men. King had
made a tasty meal of conch chowder and homemade bread
that the guys gave rave reviews.

Glory and Joe cuddled together on the opposite side of
the dinette, staring at each other as if there were no one else
in the room. They seemed so happy, so much in love. Hope
thought of the conversation she'd had with Glory and had to
admit that telling her secret to a friend, speaking the awful
words out loud, had somehow made her feel better.

It was a gift of sorts, something good she could take
home with her when she went back to New York.

Seated next to Conn as she usually was, she finished her
chowder and last bite of warm buttered bread, flicking an occasional glance in his direction. He hadn't said much during
the meal. She knew he was still brooding over the harsh
words she'd flung at him in the cabin.

She wished she hadn't said them.

Even more, she wished that they weren't true.

But the fact remained, she would be leaving and it would
happen soon. She had completed her last article, sent it in

over the Internet, and received praise for a job well done. In the next few days, she was bound to hear from her employer. Any day now, she would have to go back to New York.

She looked over at Conn, her chest feeling heavy. For the last few nights they had slept together in the narrow bunk, but they hadn't made love. She had lain there aching for him, loving him and desperately wishing she didn't. Part of her wanted to run from him again, get as far away from her unwanted feelings as she possibly could.

But now that the time to leave was drawing near, the other part wanted to stay with him forever.

She left him in the galley talking to Joe and headed up on deck. It was dark outside, only a sliver of moon, but the night was warm and clear, the stars a spray of diamonds overhead. She was thinking of Conn, the breeze tugging at her hair, when Andy walked up beside her.

"You got a phone call, Hope. It's that guy, Gordy Weitzman, who called you before."

A thread of unease slipped through her. She was off the story. She should have e-mailed Gordy. Then again, maybe the call had nothing to do with Hartley House.

"Thanks, Andy." He handed her the satellite phone and she pressed it against her ear. "Gordy?"

"Hi, Hope. It's good to hear your voice."

"You, too."

"Listen, I'm sorry to bug you, but that lawyer friend of yours called."

"Matt Westland?"

"Yeah. He was trying to get hold of you. I wasn't sure I should give him your number so I said I'd take a message."

"Listen, Gordy, I'm off the Hartley House story. Things were really getting rough."

A heartbeat passed. "I heard what happened to Jimmy Deitz. Wait a minute—are you saying his *accident* had something to do with Hartley House?"

"I'm not saying anything, Gordy."

"Wow. I didn't put two and two together. I guess I should have."

"Probably better if you don't."

"Listen, Westland called to tell you your friend, Mrs. Finnegan, inherited the property."

Her stomach instantly knotted. "Oh, no."

"'Fraid so."

"Tell me she's going to sell."

"Westland doesn't think so."

Hope started trembling. "Oh God, Gordy. Mrs. Finnegan's an old woman. She can't fight people like these. I've got to call her. Try to talk some sense into her."

"Maybe you should just stay out of it."

"I've been trying to. Somehow I can't seem to make it happen."

"Well, whatever you do, I wish you luck. Be careful, Hope." Gordy signed off and Hope stood there clutching the phone.

It was too late to make the call tonight. With a sigh, she headed for the chart room to return the phone to its usual spot. Conn was waiting when she got there, his eyes on her face.

"Who was it?"

She thought about lying, but only for an instant. As Conn had said, she was a very bad liar. "Gordy Weitzman. He called to tell me Mrs. Finnegan inherited Hartley House."

"The old woman at the funeral?"

"That's her."

"Christ, I hope she's planning to sell."

"Not according to Matt Westland, the attorney who's been representing the tenants."

He pinned her with a glare. "Don't even think about calling her, Hope. You're out of this, remember?"

"I have to call her, Conn. I have to try to make her see reason."

"No." She was still holding the phone. Conn snatched it out of her hand. "You're out of it, Hope. If I have to throw the goddamned phone overboard to keep you from risking your life, that's exactly what I'll do."

Her temper began to rise. "I just want to talk to her, Conn. No one's going to know."

"I'm telling you it isn't going to happen and that's what I mean." He handed the phone to Andy. "She's not to make any calls unless I say so."

Andy flicked a regretful look at Hope, then nodded to Conn. "You're the boss."

Hope made a sound of exasperation and marched toward the ladder. *Big, hulking, overprotective brute.* She didn't want to get involved again any more than he wanted her to, but there were things a person just had to do.

Sooner or later, the chart room would be empty. One call might save a woman's life. Eventually, she would get the chance to phone New York and when that opportunity came, Hope intended to take it.

The chance came sooner than she expected.

The day Brad Talbot left to return to Jamaica aboard the Pleasure Island plane, Conn sent a shipment of treasure with Brad and one of his security men to be delivered to the bank. Since then, the hold and the safe were filling up again.

With so much treasure aboard, Conn, Joe, Wally, and Ron were taking two-hour night shifts, patrolling the deck in case they had unexpected visitors. Conn had drawn the late shift, then returned to bed at dawn to catch a couple of hours sleep.

Hope wasn't sleepy. And she didn't want to lie next to him, feeling the heat of his body, wanting him and wishing she didn't, knowing all she had to do was reach out and touch him and he would make love to her.

Instead, slipping quietly out of bed, she left him sleeping and headed for the galley. Most of the crew was there, she saw, including Captain Bob and Andy Glass.

Hope cast a glance toward the chart room. With no one

around, this was the chance she needed. She could use the phone and put it back before anyone would know she had been there.

The cell sat in its usual place on the counter. She glanced around, hurriedly reached for it, and punched in the number for information. She dialed again, listened to the ring, and waited impatiently for someone to answer.

"Mrs. Finnegan?"

The old woman had always been an early riser. "Hope? Is that you, dear?"

"Mrs. Finnegan, I don't have much time. I called to talk to you about selling Hartley House. I know that isn't what you want to do, but it's too dangerous for you to try to fight these men any longer." Briefly, Hope explained what had happened to the detective she had hired and the threat she had received outside the Wanderer's Inn.

"I'm sorry to hear you were hurt. You shouldn't have called, dear. You mustn't involve yourself any longer."

"Please, Mrs. Finnegan, what you're doing is just too dangerous."

"I'm an old lady, dear. If something happens, it just does."

"What about the inheritance tax?" Hope asked in desperation. "What about the condemnation? Even if you could prove your case, you would have to have money enough to fix up the building."

Mrs. Finnegan chuckled over the line. "I have plenty of money, dear. I never said much about it. I live a modest life and that's the way I like it. Buddy knew the truth. He knew I'd have more than enough to pay the tax and do the needed repairs. He had already made arrangements to have the work done, so it won't be that hard."

"Mrs. Finnegan, you are risking your life."

"Like I said, I'm an old woman. I haven't got many years left and those I have won't be worth living if I have to give up my friends. We all talked it over. We're going to keep fighting for Hartley House."

Hope's eyes slid closed. There was nothing else she could

say, nothing she could do. "If I think of anything that might help, I'll let you know." Pressing the END button, she quietly hung up the phone.

Conn was standing in the doorway when she looked up, a hard look on his face. "Was that who I think it was?"

She felt the burn of tears. "Please don't be angry. I had to call her. I had to try."

Conn released a breath, crossed the room, and wrapped her up in his arms. "I know you did. You've got more courage than any woman I've ever met. That's one of the reasons I'm so crazy about you."

Hope slid her arms around his neck and just hung onto him. *I love him,* she thought. *I love him so much. Oh, God what am I going to do?*

He kissed the top of her head. "I don't suppose you convinced her?"

"I wish I had."

Conn sighed. "You tried, baby. That's all anyone can do."

She'd tried. Maybe Mrs. Finnegan would think over what Hope had said. God, she prayed the old woman would eventually see reason.

And that Adelaide Finnegan wouldn't end up like Buddy Newton.

The day slipped past. It was almost sunset, the distant sky streaked orange, pink, and blue, the sun a huge red ball mirrored by the sea. The divers were making their last dive of the day, Joe and Wally on the hookah lines.

Conn stood at the rail next to the crane, directing Pete to move the arm a little farther out over the ballast pile, when he spotted Andy running toward him.

"Conn! Hurry! You have to come quick!"

Worry hit him. Then he saw the grin on Andy's face. "What is it? What's going on?" Conn fell in behind him, both of them anxious to reach the chart room.

"They've found something. It's wedged beneath a thick layer of ballast, but Joe thinks it could be the Maiden."

Conn felt a jolt of adrenaline. As they entered the chart room, he could hear Joe's excited voice coming over the speaker.

"Man, I think this might be it! Whatever it is, it's gold and it looks like a big chunk of it."

Hope must have heard the commotion. She came down the ladder and walked toward him. "What is it?"

"We aren't sure yet. Joe thinks it might be the Maiden." He turned toward the ladder. "I'm going down."

Hope rushed after him. "What about your side?"

"It's been almost two weeks. I'll be fine."

"It's been eleven days, and you aren't all that fine."

He turned to look at her and the edge of his mouth faintly curved. "For someone without a heart, baby, you sure sound a lot like you care."

She didn't say anything to that, just kept dogging his steps toward the locker where he kept his dive gear.

"It'll be dark by the time you get down there. You'll just have to come back up."

Conn looked over at Pete. "Get me a couple of dive lights. And something that will sit on a tripod. I'll take the equipment down with me."

Hope caught his arm. "Are you sure you won't reinjure your side?"

He bent his head and gave her a brief, hard kiss. "I'll be fine, but thanks for the worry."

With a little help from Pete, he pulled on a wetsuit, put on his inflatable vest and an air tank, grabbed his fins and one of the new Divelink masks, and padded off toward the diving platform.

Hope watched him go. "Don't you think it's too soon for him to dive?" she asked Ron Keegan.

"If Joe's found the Maiden, Conn deserves to be there when they bring it up."

"I know, but—"

Ron squeezed her shoulder. "He'll be fine."

She supposed he would be. The bandages were off, but his stitches were still in, the entry and exit wounds still red, puckery, and swollen. She wished he wouldn't go.

She caught sight of Tommy coming up from below with his camera. He hurried along the deck to the dive locker and started suiting up. Finding a priceless treasure like the Maiden, a statue rumored to be worth as much as ten million dollars—maybe more—was something none of them wanted to miss.

Making her way back down to the chart room to watch the search on the video screen, Hope walked up to Andy Glass, who stood in front of the monitor. By now the sun had completely set. The water was pitch-black except for the lights the divers pointed in front of them.

Sea grasses waved in the cones of light, casting eerie shadows. A long, slippery eel slid out from a cave created by the ancient stones, sneaking off out of sight in the darkness. In the distance, at the edge of the video screen, she thought she caught a glimpse of one of Talbot's professional divers guarding the perimeter of the site, but the image was so far away she couldn't be sure.

For minutes that crept like hours, Hope watched Conn and the others lifting away the big, round, algae-covered rocks, loading them into the basket attached to the crane, digging deeper and deeper into the ballast pile.

Every now and then, the bright yellow glitter of gold glinted between the mossy stones, and her pulse kicked up. Then Conn lifted one of the heavier pieces of ballast away and all of the divers froze.

Conn's deep voice boomed over the speaker. "Well, folks, it looks like we've found the Maiden!"

In the chart room, a cheer went up. Captain Bob grinned from ear to ear. "It damned sure does!"

Even in the wavering light of the lamps, there was no way to mistake the incredible golden statue Conn held up in front of the camera, about eighteen inches long, the figure of a young, nude female with full, up-tilting breasts and wavy hair that spilled down to partially cover them.

The piece looked pre-Columbian, a fertility goddess, perhaps, a younger version of the rounded female figures Hope had seen in the South American section of the Natural History Museum. Except that instead of rough gray granite or shiny black onyx, the piece was formed of solid gold.

The divers slowly surfaced, bringing up the statue and their undersea lighting gear. Caught up in the excitement, Hope hurried up to the deck to watch the men come aboard. Conn and Joe broke the surface first, Tommy, Ron, and Wally just seconds behind. The divers pulled off their masks and set them on the platform next to where Conn had placed the Maiden. They slipped off their fins, climbed out of the water, and began to strip off the rest of their gear.

A few minutes later, Conn stepped up on deck holding the Maiden.

"You found it," Hope said, throwing her arms around his neck.

"We sure did, baby. She's beautiful, isn't she? Almost as gorgeous as you." He leaned down and kissed her, a deep, sexy kiss that ended far too quickly.

She was breathing hard when she broke away, Conn's hungry blue gaze fixed on her face. There was promise in those eyes and a warning that seemed to say, *You've been sleeping in my bed. Tonight I'm going to have you.*

Unconsciously, she trembled, wanting him, too.

They set the statue on the green plastic cloth they used to display their finds, and for the first time she noticed the emeralds embedded in the gold. The gems were a precious commodity often found aboard the galleons. Fisher had found three thousand on the *Atocha,* one of the reasons the treasure had been valued so high.

These glorious stones formed the eyes of the Maiden, beautiful gems that winked and glittered in the lantern light, almost as much as the gold. A huge stone glittered in the

Maiden's navel, two served as her nipples, and another sparkled at the juncture of her legs.

Joe grinned. "These guys knew where the real treasure was."

Glory laughed and playfully slugged him. "Joe!"

Conn was looking at Hope again, his eyes hot and dark. Too many days of sleeping next to each other without touching. Too many nights yearning for each other. It wouldn't happen tonight. His gaze said that was certain.

After everyone had the chance to see the statue and Tommy had taken dozens of photos, Conn took the Maiden below. Since the piece was too big to fit in the boat's small safe, it was placed beneath the tarp that covered the treasure in the hold.

"We'll be flying the statue to the bank in the morning," he announced a little later. "I've made arrangements with Eddie to use the plane."

"You're taking it there yourself?"

"Joe and I are both going. The professor is meeting us at the dock. He's over the top about this, as you can imagine."

He and Joe could handle the security, Hope knew, relieved that the incredibly rare artifact would be transported to a safe location.

"I thought you might like to go with us," Conn said, running a finger down her cheek.

Her heart squeezed. She would love to go with him. Their time together was coming to an end. She expected to receive a call at any moment. "I'd love to go," she said softly, wanting these last few days for herself, wishing she was strong enough to stay.

Conn glanced at the crew still milling the deck. "We've still got tonight to worry about. Ron, you'll be taking the first watch, just like before. Then Joe, Wally, then me."

"Sounds good, boss," Ron agreed.

"It's been a long day. Let's get some sleep."

But the heat in his eyes when he looked at Hope said neither of them would be sleeping anytime soon.

* * *

It was late when Conn stirred. He checked the clock on the nightstand. Not yet time for his shift to begin. Still, something bothered him, nagged at the edge of his mind. He'd always had a sixth sense for trouble and that sixth sense was gnawing at him now.

He slipped out of bed, pulled on a pair of khaki shorts, reached into a compartment under his bunk, and pulled out his 9mm Glock. He hadn't fired the weapon in years, but he always kept it close. He tucked it into the back of his shorts and quietly left the cabin.

On deck, his gaze searched for Wally. *He's probably walking the deck,* Conn told himself, hoping the man hadn't fallen asleep. He started toward the stern, then stopped as the unfamiliar smell hit him. The acrid sting of smoke slammed his senses into alert. Adrenaline rushed through him and every muscle went tense.

Not sure where the smoke was coming from, he started for the engine room; then a blaze of orange erupted behind him. Conn spun and started running, heading toward the ladder leading down to the galley. There were propane tanks in there. If the flames reached them—

"Fire!" he shouted. "Fire in the galley!" Careening down the ladder, he jerked a fire extinguisher off the wall and started spraying the flames. Orange and red tendrils ate into the cabinetry, blazed up the tiny curtains over the portholes. The dinette was burning, and flames licked at the floor.

Joe got there first, grabbed a dishtowel, and started beating away. Ron appeared, followed by Andy and King, who carried a second extinguisher. At the sight of his domain being destroyed, King swore foully.

"Everyt'ing was turned off when I left," the big cook said defensively, madly shooting a spray of white foam at the fire.

"I've got a feeling someone came in here after you left." Conn handed his extinguisher to Ron, who shot a stream of foam on the area burning around the dinette. While the men slowly brought the flames under control, Conn climbed the ladder to the deck, then pulled the gun from his waistband to check the load.

He punched out the clip, saw it was full, and shoved it back in, then spotted Hope racing toward the galley, her red hair sleep-mussed and her face pale.

"It's all right. They've got things pretty well in hand down there. I need you to help me find Wally."

She spotted the gun in his hand and her face went even paler. "This was Wally's shift?"

"Yeah."

She trembled at his worried expression. "I'll start on the top deck," she said, bringing herself back under control.

Conn just nodded. He returned the pistol to the back of his pants and began making a sweep of the boat, jogging off toward the bow, checking the port side, and finally the stern. No sign of Wally.

He made his way below, his worry building. Still finding no sign of the diver, he headed for the hold, certain now what he would find.

Or wouldn't find.

Tossing back the tarp that covered the treasure, he saw exactly what he had feared. The Maiden was gone. The gold disks were gone as well, but amazingly, the gold and silver bars and clumps of coins scheduled to be flown out with the statue in the morning remained.

"You knew what you were after, didn't you?" Conn said aloud. "And you were in a damned big hurry." They had taken only the Maiden and two gold disks they could easily handle but nothing that might slow them down.

Tossing the tarp back over the remaining pieces of treasure, he hurried back up on deck, more worried about Wally than he had been before.

"Conn! He's over here!"

The fear in Hope's voice sent a chill down his spine. He raced toward the bow of the boat, saw Hope kneeling next to Wally's unconscious body.

"He's badly hurt," she said, her voice shaking.

"Looks like someone hit him over the head."

"They dropped a tarp over him and covered it with rope. Everything's usually kept so neat . . ." She broke off, took a shuddering breath. "I can't get him to wake up."

Crouching beside the stocky diver, Conn examined the gash on his head. "Wally, it's Conn. Can you hear me?" The man didn't move. The cut over his eye trickled a faint trail of blood, and there was a huge lump on the back of his head. "Wally, you need to wake up now."

The diver groaned and moved a little. When his eyes slowly opened, Conn felt a rush of relief.

"What . . . happened?"

"Somebody wanted you out of the way." Conn turned to Hope. "He's probably got a concussion. We need to get him some medical attention."

"I'll go get Andy, get him to radio the island."

"We can take him in the Whaler if we have to, but the Sea Ray would make him more comfortable."

Joe and Ron walked up just then.

"What the hell's going on?" Joe asked, spotting Wally sprawled on the deck.

"We had visitors. They clobbered Wally and helped themselves to the Maiden."

Joe's jaw clenched. "Son of a bitch."

"I think they must have heard me moving around below. I figure that's why they set the fire. Create a diversion—give themselves time to get away."

"Well, it sure as hell worked."

Glory came running up just then. "Wally!" Kneeling beside him, she reached down and caught hold of the diver's hand, her eyes going to Joe.

"Looks like he's got a concussion," Joe explained. "Whoever hit him was after the Maiden."

"Did they get it?"

Conn grunted. "Unfortunately, they did."

"How many people knew we had it?" Joe asked.

"Everyone aboard. And of course, Talbot and Markham."

Joe shook his head. "God only knows who those idiots might have told."

"One thing's clear. This has been in the planning stages for some time. I'll take a look around, see what I can find, but my guess is they got the call telling them that we'd found the statue and they were ready. I figure they came by sea, but left the boat a ways away and rowed over in a dinghy of some kind."

"How many do you think?" Joe asked.

"Two, maybe three. They knew what they were doing."

"Ex-military?"

"Probably."

"Talbot. He's got four or five of those guys on his payroll."

"Maybe. But I've got a hunch these may have been the same guys who shot me. They were sniffing around, maybe trying to find the Maiden even then. That happened before Talbot arrived."

Joe looked off toward Pleasure Island. A few distant lights winked in the darkness from the tiny village on the south end of the shore. "Maybe it was Markham."

"Could be. I hate to say it, but it could be that someone on the *Conquest* was behind this. We can check the phone records, see what calls were made after the Maiden was found, but that'll take time and if somebody called from here, he could have used a radio."

"I don't think anyone on the boat would do something like that," Glory said firmly, still holding onto Wally's hand.

"I hope you're right. For now, the most important thing is to get Wally ashore so he can get the proper care."

Hope hurried up just then. "Chalko's on his way."

Conn nodded. "This is getting to be a habit and I don't like it."

Neither did Hope, he could see by the concerned look on her face, but the island was a sovereignty all its own. There was no police force to call, just the small group of security guards who worked for Eddie, not much more than rent-a-cops, no one they could really turn to for help.

They would have to help themselves, Conn thought, and that was exactly what he meant to do.

Chapter 26

A freak storm rolled in. There was just enough time to get Wally ashore before the unexpected squall hit the island.

Aboard the *Conquest,* the galley was a blackened shambles, the walls badly scorched, the floor burned clear through in one spot, the stove out of commission, plates broken, pots and pans melted and ruined. Already badly disheartened by the attack on their friend, the crew grumbled over their missed morning meal.

When Captain Bob informed them the *Conquest* would be heading back to Jamaica for repairs, the men practically cheered.

Unfortunately, the winds were still blowing up a gale, the rain dropping in sheets. The captain decided to wait until the storm blew itself out before setting off on the ninety-five-mile trip back to Jamaica. In the meantime, Conn quietly did his best to solve the mystery of who had stolen the Maiden.

Though he hated to do it, he searched the crew's quarters and even the captain's, but came up empty-handed. It was a relief to find nothing. He knew these men. Most of them had become good friends. He didn't want to believe any of them would steal from him.

Still, there was no way to know for sure.

And it worried Conn that the intruders had picked Wally's watch to commit the theft, not his or Joe's. How had they known which man would give them the least amount of trouble?

Conn figured if any of the crew were involved, it might be Pete Crowley. He had never trusted Pete, though he wasn't quite sure why.

It was still early in the morning. Conn found Hope standing in front of the windows in the chart room, staring out through a haze of rain at the turbulent sea. She looked more fragile than she usually did and his chest tightened. She had come to mean so much to him. It worried him to see her this way.

"You okay?"

She nodded, managed a smile, though it looked a little wobbly. "I'm fine. How's Wally?"

"Ron's got him resting in one of the villas while they wait for the storm to break so the plane can fly out. The weather's got everything shut down. The good news is there was a doctor vacationing in one of the units. He took a look at Wally, said he definitely has a concussion, but he thinks he'll be all right."

Hope's eyes slid closed. "Thank God." She stared back out the window, her gaze fixed on the gray sea.

Conn studied her petite, womanly figure. She had so much strength. It was amazing that she didn't seem to know. "As soon as the storm breaks," he said gently, "the *Conquest* will be heading back to port."

She turned and looked up at him, and he thought he could drown in those lovely green eyes. They had made love two times last night but already he wanted her again.

"What about the Maiden?" she asked.

"I spoke to Talbot, told him what happened. He's royally pissed, as you can imagine."

"Then you don't think he's behind the theft?"

"It was never the money for Talbot. It was always the publicity. The statue would have given him even more of what he wanted. Which is not to say Jack Feldman or one of his men couldn't have been the ones who stole it."

"I take it Feldman and his crew will be guarding the site while the *Conquest* is away."

He nodded. "We don't have any other choice. Feldman's going to anchor over the site until I can make arrangements to get another salvage boat out here and a couple more divers. Joe and Ron can come back with the other boat."

"You could certainly use the help."

"We've already brought up the stuff that wound up on top of the ballast pile when the ship went down. Whatever else is down there is going to be harder to find."

"What about the treasure that's still aboard?"

"After what's happened, I don't want to send it back on the boat. I talked to Eddie. I told him we need to fly the stuff back to Jamaica and get it in the bank. I told him I'd be bringing it in personally. We can stay in one of the villas until the plane leaves."

"What about finding the Maiden?"

A muscle tightened in his jaw. "That's the question, isn't it? Once we're ashore, I plan to do a little looking around. The men who took the statue may have come from the island. With the storm keeping everything grounded, they may not have been able to get it off."

Hope made no reply. He knew she understood how much he wanted to find the statue.

So far, he didn't have much of an idea where to look.

There was a break in the storm late in the afternoon, a brief hole in the weather that allowed the Sea Ray to come out and pick them up, along with the treasure, and ferry them back to shore. Hope said good-bye to Captain Bob and Andy, Tommy Tyler, Joe, and the crew, feeling a sense of loss so strong it made her heart ache.

The call from *Midday News* had come through less than

an hour ago. Artie Green had phoned personally. Her job was waiting, he said. It was time to go home.

Hope fought not to cry.

She would be leaving the Caribbean, leaving Pleasure Island. Leaving Conn before she weakened and agreed to stay with him.

She couldn't afford to do that. She didn't have that kind of courage. Each day she fell more deeply in love with him. If something went wrong, if things didn't work out, she simply could not bear it.

Glory approached her last. Blinking back tears, Hope gave her a good-bye hug, uncertain if she would ever see her friend again.

"You're leaving, aren't you?" Glory said softly, her blond ponytail streaming in the wind. "I can see it in your face."

Hope took a shaky breath, let it out slowly. "My boss called a little while ago. My last article for *Adventure* has been completed. If the weather is good enough for the plane to fly out, I'll be leaving in the morning."

Glory's dark eyes misted. "Have you told Conn yet?"

Hope shook her head, fighting tears. "I knew the call was going to come, just not exactly when. I've been meaning to tell him, but then they found the Maiden and things got so mixed up. I'll have to tell him tonight."

Glory reached over and caught her hand. "Are you sure about this, Hope? Are you sure you're doing the right thing?"

"I'm not like you, Glory. If I stayed with Conn, I'd be afraid all the time, afraid of loving him more and more and then losing him."

"Conn isn't like that. I think if he really loved a woman, it would be forever."

"But you can't know that for sure, can you, Glory? And I'm not willing to take the risk."

"You can't know anything for sure, Hope. And Conn is worth the risk."

Hope said nothing more. The two women hugged again

and Hope left to join Conn. She tried not to think of what Glory had said, but the words haunted her, dared her to set aside her fears and take a chance on loving again.

Hope steeled herself. She wasn't ready yet, wasn't sure she ever would be.

With fresh resolve, she picked up her bag, pasted on a smile, and walked to where Conn stood waiting at the rail.

"Ready?"

She nodded.

His eyes remained on her face, searching out her feelings, trying to read her troubled thoughts.

"Are you all right?"

She forced her lips to curve. "So much has happened. I'm just tired, is all."

He eyed her a moment more. "The treasure's all been loaded. Let's go."

She felt his hand at her waist, strong and sure as he guided her to the loading platform and into the sleek white Sea Ray.

Chalko smiled and nodded a greeting, which both of them returned. As soon as they were safely aboard, the black man shoved the throttle into reverse and backed away from the *Conquest;* then the speedboat leapt ahead.

The swells were still high, the troughs frighteningly deep. Gray clouds were closing back in and she could see the dark haze of rain beginning to sweep over the south end of the island. As the Sea Ray roared away, she took a last look at the big salvage boat rolling in the heavy seas, feeling homesick for a place that shouldn't seem like home but did, a place that held memories she would never forget.

Tonight she would have to tell Conn she was leaving. Her eyes filled with tears. It was going to be the hardest thing she had ever had to do.

The drenching rains resumed as if they had never stopped. The Island Jeep waited at the dock, its clear plastic windows rolled closed to keep out the worst of the downpour.

A second Jeep held two security guards, who jumped out in the rain as they saw the speedboat approach. They waited at the dock until the Sea Ray's lines were secure, then jumped in to help unload the treasure.

It didn't take long to transfer the valuable artifacts into the waiting Jeep. Conn helped Hope into the Jeep Chalko drove, then climbed into the back. With each of his movements, he could feel the bulge of the 9mm Glock riding in the waistband of his pants. It had been a while since he'd fired the weapon. Still, it was amazing how familiar the pistol felt in his hands.

Following the Jeep that carried the treasure, Chalko drove along the paved road leading from the dock back to the main office of The Villas. The island's private airport sat off to the right. As the Jeep rolled past, Conn noticed The Villas' twin-engine Beech, its wings securely tied down. Another, smaller aircraft, a Cessna Turbo 210, rested on the tarmac a few feet away.

"Who's that other plane belong to?" Conn asked Chalko.

"One of Eddie's guests. I think his name is St. Giles."

"When did he get here?"

"His plane landed just before the storm hit. He is scheduled to fly out in the morning, if the weather is good."

Conn sat back as Chalko drove along the road, fidgeting a little as he followed the other Jeep, forced to go more slowly than he liked.

St. Giles. The name rolled around in Conn's head. He knew that name, though he couldn't quite remember where he'd heard it. Something told him it was important that he remember.

When they reached the main building, another uniformed guard waited in the lobby. He helped the other two men carry the gold and silver bars, silver coins, and a box containing gold-and-emerald jewelry into the building, on its way to the safe in Eddie's office.

Conn smiled darkly, figuring the treasure would be safe. If Eddie were behind the theft, he could have taken the stuff last night. Of course, if the rumors were true, the Maiden was far more valuable than all the other pieces put together.

If the thieves could find a buyer for it.

Chalko stopped in front of the luxurious villa Conn and Hope had stayed in the night of the party, got out, and carried in Hope's luggage.

"I put the rest of your things in the bedroom," the black man said, referring to the articles she had left for safekeeping instead of taking them on the boat.

"Thank you, Chalko. I appreciate all you've done."

There was something in the way she said it, something that made Conn uneasy. It was time they talked. Tonight he would make certain they did.

In the meantime, he had pressing responsibilities, and a single name kept nagging him. "You ever heard of a guy named St. Giles? Seems like I know the name, but I can't remember where I heard it."

"Isn't he the guy who found the emerald cross, the first piece of treasure off the *Rosa?* I think he's that friend of the professor's."

In an instant, the pieces all slid together. *Julian St. Giles.* He had found the gold-and-emerald cross with the initials on the back that the professor had tracked to the *Rosa* passenger list. "That's the guy. He's a collector in Jamaica. I think he's also a dealer. Damn, I need to use the phone."

Striding toward the bedside table, Conn lifted the telephone receiver and dialed the office, then asked the receptionist to place a satellite call to Professor Marlin and rattled off the number of Marlin's cell. Earlier, Conn had phoned him with the news that the Maiden had been stolen and his partner had been devastated by the theft.

He wasn't going to like Conn's suspicions any better.

"Doc? It's Conn. I need to know the name of that collector friend of yours."

"Why, his name is St. Giles. Julian St. Giles."

"That's what I thought. Any chance he'd be interested in buying the Maiden?"

"You must be joking. Of course the man would be interested. Any collector who's ever heard of it would be interested in such a fantastic piece."

"What I need to know is whether St. Giles is capable of raising that kind of money. Would he or one of his clients have the roughly ten million it would take to buy the Maiden?"

"I don't believe ten million would be nearly enough, my boy, but yes. Julian is well known in the art world. His reputation is spotless. He deals with only the most discriminating buyers."

"Thanks, Doc. That's all I needed to know."

"But what does Julian—"

"Gotta run, Doc. I'll let you know if anything turns up."

Conn hung up the phone, hoping none of Markham's people had been listening in on the call.

"What's going on, Conn?" Hope walked toward him across the bedroom. She had just stepped out of the shower and was wearing one of The Villas' thick white terry cloth robes. Covered from neck to foot, she was still the sexiest woman he'd ever seen.

Conn reined in his thoughts, telling himself he could make love to her later. "I've got a hunch Eddie Markham may be involved in the theft of the Maiden. As soon as it's dark—which won't be much longer—I'm going over to his house and see what I can find."

"What makes you think it's Markham?"

"That was St. Giles's plane we passed at the airport. Eddie must know St. Giles is on the island and that he'd be someone with an interest in the Maiden, but he never mentioned it. I think St. Giles is here to buy the statue. He was probably planning to fly it out tonight, but the storm's got him boxed in."

"What are you going to do?"

"Stake out Markham's house, see who shows up. Maybe I'll get lucky."

"If you're going to Markham's, I'm going with you."

Conn shook his head. "No way. You're going to stay right here, out of danger."

"I'm going, Conn. You can't see the front and back at the same time. You're going to need my help. Besides, all we're going to do is watch the house."

"You aren't going, and that's final."

She gave him a too-sweet smile. "Have it your way, then. I'll just sit right here, waiting for you like a good little girl until you get back."

He knew that look. She planned to follow him the moment he left the villa. "You little witch. I suppose the only way you'd stay here is if I tied you up. Since that is something I'd rather do under far more intimate circumstances, I guess I'll have to take you with me."

"Very sensible."

And he was only going to watch the place. It was probably a total waste of time. Grumbling about hard-headed women, he waited as she walked over to the closet and pulled out a pair of jeans and a dark blue shirt.

She was dressed and ready to go a few minutes later, a pair of sandals on her small, slim feet.

"You're going to get wet, you know."

"I've been wet before. Besides, it isn't that cold."

Conn went over and pulled a short-sleeved black knit shirt out of his bag, stripped his tee shirt off over his head, and pulled the knit shirt on instead. The darker colors would blend better with the night. He was glad to see that Hope had also figured that out.

"Put this on. At least you'll be able to see." He tossed her a dark blue bill cap to help shed the rain and dragged a black one down over his forehead.

This time of year, the sun still set fairly early. As soon as he felt sure they wouldn't be spotted, they slipped out the back door and headed for the big, plush villa that Eddie Markham called home.

It sat on a rise overlooking the sea, white plaster walls, red tile roof, bigger even than the rest of the units in the de-

velopment. Waves crashed on the beach below the house and
rolled toward the huge front windows overlooking the sea. A
small, private dock allowed boats to come and go at their
leisure.

Markham lived an expensive lifestyle. And though The
Villas had begun to prosper, they hadn't been as lucrative an
endeavor as Eddie had hoped. He'd been ecstatic when they'd
found the treasure. The money from the sale of the Maiden—
money he didn't have to split with anyone else—could set
him up for at least the next few years.

"I'll watch the front. You take the back," Conn said to
Hope as they neared the house, figuring that if St. Giles appeared, he would likely come straight to the front door of the
house. Eddie had no reason to think Conn suspected him. As
far as anyone could guess, the thieves had come off one of
the numerous boats anchored around the wreck site.

And the truth was, they very well could have.

If he hadn't accidentally discovered St. Giles's presence
on the island, Conn wouldn't have linked Emperor Eddie to
the theft.

But once in a while fate cut you a break. Maybe this was
one of those times.

Chapter 27

One thing Hope discovered—stakeouts weren't the least bit of fun. For hours, she had been huddled beneath the broad, flat, variegated leaves of a huge philodendron plant, a small bit of shelter from the seemingly endless onslaught of rain.

She had been staring through the windows of Eddie's study for so long her vision was beginning to blur. So far, all she'd caught was an occasional glimpse of him. By now, he had probably gone to bed.

Every half-hour, Conn had come to check on her. She knew he was worried about her safety and her discomfort out in the elements, but each time she assured him that she was all right. She could do this one thing for him before she said good-bye.

Her chest squeezed at the thought. She wasn't sure how long they would be out here in the darkness before Conn gave up and they went back to their villa. As miserable as she was, she would almost rather stay out in the storm than face the storm of his wrath once she told him that she would be leaving.

Her heart set up a painful throbbing. God, it hurt to love someone. But it hurt even more to lose them. Leaving was the answer. For her it was something she just had to do.

Something stirred in the darkness behind her. Hope crouched lower beneath the leafy foliage, all but disappearing in the rain. Her pulse quickened. Conn hadn't been gone that long. It had to be someone else. Then she heard the soft whisper of his deep voice next to her ear.

"Someone just showed up out front. Portly fellow wearing a hat. Could be St. Giles."

She turned back to the window. "Look—they're walking into the study now." Eddie Markham led the way, followed by a heavyset man in light brown slacks and a white, short-sleeved knit shirt. His hair was beginning to gray and there was a bald spot on the back of his head.

"What are you going to do?" Hope asked softly.

"I'm going in. I want you to go back to the villa and wait for me there."

She shook her head. "I'm not leaving. Don't even think about trying to make me."

Conn swore softly. "All right, dammit, then stay right here. Don't get any closer. If anything happens, I want you to head out of here as quickly and quietly as you can. Get back to the villa and call the *Conquest*. With the weather the way it is, the boat hasn't been able to leave. Tell Joe what's going on. Tell him I'm at Markham's. He'll know what to do."

She wished Joe were already there, or that Conn would wait until he came, but she knew he wouldn't.

He's a SEAL, she told herself. *He knows how to handle these things.*

And he was carrying a weapon. A big, ugly, lethal-looking gun he undoubtedly knew how to use.

Hope watched him slip soundlessly away. It was amazing how quietly he moved. One minute he was crouching there beside her, the next he was gone. Nothing moved in the darkness, not a leaf or a blade of grass. Not a sound reached her ears, yet she knew he was out there, silently making his way toward the house.

Her heart was galloping so hard it hurt. The palms of her already rain-slick hands were beginning to feel hot and clammy. Inside the study, she could see the two men talking. Markham walked over and pulled the drapes, obscuring her view, and silently she cursed.

There didn't appear to be anyone else in the house, though by now Conn was probably inside. She needed to get closer, find a way to see what was going on.

Moving as quietly as she knew how, Hope made her way around the perimeter of the terrace, keeping low, the ground wet enough to hide the sound of her footsteps. Once she reached the house, she flattened herself against the plaster wall near the window. She couldn't see inside, but she could hear the two men talking, and there was no way to mistake what was going on.

"Don't worry. They'll be here any minute. Would you like a glass of brandy while we wait?" Eddie's voice, jovial, confident.

"No, thank you. You're certain they have it? That it's the Maiden and not something else?" British. Undoubtedly St. Giles.

"They've got it. And it's definitely the Maiden. Once you've seen it, assured yourself it's authentic, I'll expect you to transfer the money."

He nodded. "We can do it from here, over the Internet, just as you suggested. Fifteen million transferred to your personal account in the bank on Grand Cayman."

"As soon as I've verified the money is there, you can take the statue and leave. You won't be able to get off the island until the weather clears, but I understand you have someone with you who'll be able to keep the statue safe until your plane can leave."

St. Giles moved a little and so did Hope, allowing her to see the men through the split in the curtains. The collector smiled. "Forest is quite a capable man. He'll be here any minute."

Adrenaline shot through her. Another man was coming. She prayed Conn was able to hear the conversation.

It was only a few minutes later that two more men arrived

at the house. The front door must have been left unlocked in anticipation of their arrival. Eddie invited the men into the study, two nondescript males, both around five-foot-ten, one of them black, probably Jamaican, the other fair-skinned with light brown hair. The second man carried a cardboard box that appeared to be quite heavy. He set the box on a carved wooden table near the center of the study.

Eddie greeted them briefly, addressing the black man as Brunet, the white man as Williams, and instructed the latter to open the box he'd brought in. He did so carefully, lifting out the heavy statue and setting it down on the table.

The Maiden. Hope felt a rush of excitement just looking at the beautifully formed, glinting chunk of gold.

"My God." St. Giles walked toward the Maiden like a man in a trance. His hand trembled as he reached out to touch the statue, run his finger over her long, wavy hair. "She's the most beautiful thing I've ever seen."

Eddie flashed a satisfied smile. "She's yours, St. Giles. All you have to do is come up with the money." He turned to the other two men. "If you gentlemen will step into my office, we can finish our transaction and you can leave."

While St. Giles examined the statue, viewing it from every angle, lifting it and checking to be certain it was authentic, the other men followed Eddie into a small room off the study that served as an office. The men returned a few minutes later, apparently satisfied with the compensation they had received for their work.

Everything seemed to be moving along as planned. Hope figured Conn would wait until the men who brought the statue were gone before he stepped in to retrieve the Maiden. She was standing there worrying about him, afraid of what would happen when he appeared, when she felt the hard steel barrel of a pistol pressing against her ribs.

"Enjoying the conversation?" The upper-class British accent slid through her like a knife.

She had forgotten about St. Giles's man. She had wrongly assumed he would arrive at the front door like everyone else.

Her pulse raced, her mind as well, trying to think what to do. She took a steadying breath, turned to look up at him, and gave him a phony smile. "I take it you're Forest."

The edge of his mouth faintly curved. "I see my reputation precedes me." His face looked hard in the thin ray of light seeping out from between the curtains. She noticed that his gun never wavered.

"Since I don't believe we've met, why don't we go inside where we can be properly introduced?" The gun nudged her forward.

Hope scrambled to think of an option, or a story she could tell that he might believe, but it was obvious there were no options, other than to do as the gunman said. And she thought that he wasn't the sort of man to believe anything but the truth.

"There's a door 'round the side." He prodded her again, the gun pressed firmly against her. "Let's go."

Well, at least I'll get out of the rain, Hope thought grimly, making her way along a path that led to a heavy wooden door on the east side of the house. Forest rapped on the panel a couple of times and the black man named Brunet let them in.

Forest urged her forward with the barrel of the gun. In the light of the hallway, she saw that he was tall, his skin slightly weathered. He had hard, carved features and thick black eyebrows, yet he was attractive in a brutal sort of way. With his clipped British accent, a sort of bad-guy James Bond, she thought, wishing she could find the courage to smile at her faint attempt at humor.

"Ah, Forest! There you are. Do come in." They followed the sound of St. Giles's voice down the hall and into the study. The collector's face went white when he saw that his associate was not alone.

"As you can see, I've brought a visitor," Forest said.

"Your timing could certainly have been better," grumbled St. Giles.

"Well . . . Ms. Sinclair . . ." Eddie Markham walked toward her, his expression cold and unpleasant. "Under different circumstances, I'd say it is good to see you. Unfortunately for all of us here, it is anything but."

"I found her outside, peeking in the window," Forest explained, the gun now pointed at her heart. "From the looks of her, she's been out there quite a while."

For the first time, Eddie noticed her clothes were drenched, and dripping all over his highly polished wooden floor. "Get her a towel, Williams. She's ruining my ungodly expensive parquet flooring."

Williams left the study and returned a few minutes later with a thick white towel, which Hope used to blot some of the water from her face and clothes.

"I don't like this," St. Giles said, pacing back and forth. "What the devil was she doing out there?"

Eddie fixed her with a glare. "Unfortunately, I think I know." He checked to make certain Forest still had her securely in the sights of his weapon and walked toward her. "Where is he, Hope? Is he inside the house? I don't believe you came here by yourself. Where is my illustrious partner?"

Hope swallowed the lump of fear that rose in her throat. "I don't . . . I don't know what you're talking about. I spotted St. Giles's plane at the airport and put two and two together. I figured you might have the statue." She managed a confident smile. "If you did, I thought maybe my silence would be worth a price."

"Very astute of you. But there is no way in hell Reese would have willingly let you out of his bed."

Forest caught her arm and dragged her closer. She felt the pressure of the gun barrel against the side of her head.

"Where is he?" Eddie asked. When she made no reply, he walked over and opened the door to the study. "I know you're out there, Reese. If you want your lady to keep on breathing, you had better come out and join us."

Hope stood frozen, heart thundering, praying Conn would stay hidden. Forest worked the slide on the pistol, cocking the weapon, then returning it to her temple. She heard Conn's softly muttered curse.

He stepped out of a darkened room into the hallway, both of his hands in the air, the pistol dangling from one of his fingers.

"Move forward," Forest instructed. "Very slowly."

Conn made his way several feet into the study.

"Set the pistol on the floor and kick it out into the hall." Conn obeyed, using the edge of his foot to shove it across the wooden floor. "Now close the door."

He did it slowly, the door making a soft click as it closed. Then he turned to face the group gathered in the study.

"Quite a little party you've got going here, Eddie."

"Yes, isn't it? A few more guests than I'd planned, but then I've always been good at improvising."

"I don't like this," St. Giles said for the second time, his voice a little shaky. "I'm a businessman. I didn't expect these kinds of complications."

"Take it easy, St. Giles," Eddie warned. "You and I are going to complete our transaction just the way we planned. Then you and Forest can take the statue and leave." He flicked a glance at Williams and his companion, Brunet. "For a little additional compensation, my friends here will take care of the *complications*."

Conn stiffened, his gaze swinging to the men and back to his partner. "You're willing to kill for the damned thing, Eddie?"

Eddie made a faint shrug of his shoulders. "I've never killed anyone. When necessary, troublesome people may have occasionally disappeared, but that was never my concern."

"You're the law here, Eddie. Even if you sell the statue, there's not much we can do. Take the money and let us go."

Eddie lifted an expensive cloisonné vase off the carved wooden table in front of him, held it up and examined it in the lamplight. "I wish it were that easy. I'm not about to spend the next twenty years looking over my shoulder, worrying about you and Talbot."

He nodded at Williams, who pulled a pistol from the back

of his pants and leveled it at Conn. "You two will have to come with me."

Conn flicked Hope a glance, telling her to trust him, to let him pick the time to make his move. She gave him a faint nod. Conn was a SEAL. She trusted him to get them out of this mess in one piece.

"St. Giles, you come with me," Eddie commanded.

The collector cast a nervous glance from Conn to Hope and back to Eddie, uncertain what to do. Before he could take a step forward, the study door slammed open, crashing back against the wall, jerking all of their attention in that direction.

"Nobody move!"

Hope's eyes flew wide at the sight of Andy Glass standing in the opening, feet splayed, gripping Conn's pistol in both hands. Andy's eyes looked huge behind the lenses of his glasses, and the gun trembled wildly.

Dear God, does he even know how to use the damned thing?

"I heard what you're planning, Mr. Markham, and I won't let you do it. I was wrong to get involved in this in the first place." He adjusted his grip on the gun. "There was just so much gold, and I wasn't going to get any of it. Just a measly bonus. I have a wife back home, a couple of kids. I thought, hey—it's just money. What would one missing piece hurt?" The gun wavered. Andy took a firmer hold on the weapon. "But I'm not about to let you hurt these people. These people are my friends."

Hope's heart twisted. Andy Glass was not a criminal. But gold tempted even the best of men.

Then everything happened at once. Conn eased back toward Andy and reached for the gun. At the same instant, Andy made some kind of move forward; Williams saw it and fired. Andy screamed in pain and pulled the trigger on the pistol, then hit the floor, clutching his leg.

"Get down!" Conn shoved Hope to the floor, shielding her with his body, as Williams returned Andy's shot. Then Conn was up and running. He hit Williams with a body block that sent the man flying into the wall, his gun discharging again. Hope saw Eddie Markham go down. Conn moved again. She didn't see exactly what he did to the Jamaican, but when she turned, the man was lying unconscious on the floor.

Markham was down and not moving. From beneath Eddie's body, a stream of blood poured out on the floor.

St. Giles crouched beneath a table, his face as white as the walls. Andy lay there, making little groaning sounds. Conn's weapon lay on the floor a few feet away. He reached down for the gun, but Forest's deep voice stopped him.

"I wouldn't do that if I were you."

Conn slowly turned, holding his hands out in front of him. He cast a look at Hope, saw that she was trembling but seemed all right, and focused his attention on the collector.

"Looks like it's your call now, St. Giles. You can have your man kill all of us and take the statue, or you can turn around and leave. Sooner or later, the statue will be for sale and you'll have another chance to buy it. The question is, are you a businessman, like you said? Or a murderer, like Eddie?"

St. Giles was visibly shaking as he climbed out from under the table. "Are you saying you won't press any sort of charges?"

"You were only a buyer. We're going to need buyers for the stuff we're bringing up from the *Rosa*."

"I'm not . . . not a murderer." He glanced at the man who worked for him, sending a silent message. "We'll be gone as soon as the weather is good enough for the plane to leave." He tipped his head toward the door of the study. "Come, Forest. It's time we were on our way."

Forest waited for his employer to leave, then backed out behind him, still pointing the gun. When he reached the hallway, he stuck the pistol into the waistband of his slacks beneath the loose hem of his shirt, turned, and walked out of the house.

Hope surveyed the bloody carnage around her and felt a

sob rising in her throat. She must have made some kind of sound because an instant later she was wrapped in Conn's arms.

"It's all right, baby. It's over. Everything's going to be okay."

She nodded, her throat closed, tears burning her eyes. She clung to him for several long moments, thought of Andy, injured and bleeding, took a deep breath and walked on trembling limbs over to where he lay on the floor.

"My leg," Andy said. "Oh God, it hurts."

Using the towel Williams had brought her, Hope made it into a pad and pressed it against the wound to stop the flow of blood. Conn walked to the phone on Eddie's desk and called the front desk.

"We've got a situation here. Send over your security guys and someone who knows something about first aid."

The operator said something and Conn said, "That's right, Markham's house."

He hung up the phone and turned to Andy, whose face was contorted in pain. "How did you get here?"

"I took the . . . Whaler. I figured I'd be back before anyone noticed it was gone. Eddie . . . he was supposed to pay me tonight . . . for helping him steal the Maiden." Andy looked up at Conn. "The night he threw the party I was complaining about not getting a share of the treasure. He called me later and we made a deal."

"You told them to come during Wally's shift."

He nodded. "I told them where to find the statue." Tears welled in his eyes, making them look wavy behind the lens of his glasses. "I've never stolen anything in my life. I don't know what came over me. I almost got both of you killed."

Conn laid a hand on the smaller man's shoulder. "That was a very brave thing you did tonight, Andy. You probably saved our lives. I think we ought to just call it even."

Andy looked up at him. "I don't understand."

"Does anyone else know you were involved in this?"

"Only Eddie."

Conn looked over at the body lying in a pool of blood on the floor. "Markham's dead. We've got the statue back. Let's just get you fixed up and let that be the end of it."

Andy's mouth hung open. "You mean . . . you're not going to press charges?"

"No charges, Andy."

Andy reached out and gripped his hand. "Thank you, Conn. I'll never forget this. Never."

"Money makes men do crazy things. Gold's the worst. Maybe I should have cut a different deal with Bob and the crew from the start. Next time, I will."

Andy said nothing, just eased his head back down on the floor. Hope kept him still and kept pressure on the wound while Conn went over to check on the other two men.

"Are they still alive?" Hope asked.

"They're fine. Just a bad headache when they wake up." Conn walked over to the window, ripped two of the gold-tassled drapery cords down from the curtains, then walked back and used them to tie the men up. They were conscious by the time the security guards arrived. Conn instructed the guards to take the men back to the main office and lock them up for the night.

As the guards were removing their prisoners, Chalko arrived. "The desk clerk said someone has been injured?" He looked down and saw Andy.

"Is that doctor still on the island?" Hope asked.

"Yes, I will take your friend there." For the first time Chalko noticed Eddie.

"I'm afraid there was an accident," Conn told him. "Eddie got into an argument with the men your people just took out of here. Things got heated. Shots went off and Eddie was killed. It wasn't an intentional shooting."

Chalko didn't ask anything more, and Conn didn't volunteer. There was no real law on the island. Conn wondered what would happen to the place, now that Eddie was gone.

"The rain has stopped," Chalko said. "The storm is breaking up. The pilot says as soon as it is light, he will be able to fly out."

Conn just nodded. He needed to phone the *Conquest* and talk to Joe, tell him what had happened. In the morning, the plane would be flying both Wally and Andy to the hospital in Kingston—and carrying two prisoners to the Kingston jail. He needed Joe to help with security.

A second trip would be required to transport Eddie's body. Conn and Hope could fly the statue and the treasure in then.

"I guess Williams's shot killed Eddie," Hope said. "What do you think they'll do to him?"

"Who knows? They don't have jurisdiction over the island. As messy as this is, I'd just as soon stay out of it. I'll tell them it was an accident, an argument that got out of hand. They'll do what they do and that'll be the end of it."

"Ironic, isn't it? Andy betrays you, then gets shot trying to save you. Eddie tries to steal the statue and take the money for himself and winds up getting killed."

"Maybe that says something about doing what's right."

"Maybe it does."

Conn took a last look around. "Let's get out of here."

"Let's," Hope said, starting for the door. "I can't wait to get home."

Conn caught her arm and turned her to face him. "Which home are you talking about, Hope? The home that includes me? Or the one in New York?"

Chapter 28

The rain had stopped but the wind still howled. Palm leaves scratched against the windows of the villa, and the steady drip of water reached into the quiet of the bedroom.

Wet and miserable, Hope had showered as soon as they got back, changed into fresh clothes, then blow-dried her hair. She felt weary and desolate, and exhausted clear to her bones.

Conn was in the bathroom now. She could hear the shower running, then the soft roar of the spray came to an end as he turned off the nozzle and stepped out onto the Spanish-tile floor.

Hope pulled the thick white terry cloth robe a little tighter around her. The moment she had been dreading was only seconds away. Conn had said nothing on the ride back from Eddie's and neither had she. Even after they reached the villa, the two of them had barely spoken.

Still, somehow he had figured out what she meant to do.

He walked out of the bathroom, wearing only a pair of navy cotton pants, no shirt, no shoes, his dark hair damp and glistening, almost black in the soft light of the bedroom. The faint shadow of a beard made his face look hard as he walked over to where she stood and reached down to take her hand. "I think it's time we talked, don't you?"

She only nodded. Her throat was aching. She felt the sting of tears but blinked them away. They sat down on the sofa in the living room, Conn still holding her hand.

"Go on. Say it. You're getting ready to leave."

She nodded, took a shuddering breath. "I'll be going as soon as the plane can get me back to Jamaica. My boss called yesterday. I wanted to tell you, but everything got so mixed up."

"How can you go back when you still might be in danger?"

Hope moistened her lips. "Artie and I talked about Hartley House. He says Mrs. Finnegan has agreed to sell. I told him I was glad. Too many people have been hurt already."

"What happened to change her mind?"

"I'm not sure. Artie said as far as he knew there haven't been any more incidents. At any rate, he wants me back and tomorrow I'm going."

Conn's hold tightened on her hand. "I don't want you to go, Hope."

"I have to, Conn. We both knew this would happen, sooner or later."

"There are other jobs. You just finished writing a magazine series. Plans can be changed. I love you, Hope. I want you to stay here with me."

I love you. For a man like Conner Reese to say those words . . . The lump forming in her throat went tighter. Tears burned her eyes. "I can't stay with you."

Conn took a deep breath, released it slowly. "This isn't the night I would have chosen. This isn't the way I pictured it happening, but I don't have time to wait."

He went down on one knee in front of her, still holding onto her hand. He lifted her fingers to his lips and very softly kissed them. "I love you, Hope Sinclair. I want you to stay and make a life with me. I'm asking you to marry me."

"Oh, God." She started crying then—big, deep sobs she couldn't hold back that made her tremble all over.

Conn sat down beside her and pulled her into his arms.

"It's all right, baby. Please don't cry. You're supposed to be happy when a man asks you to marry him."

She only shook her head. "I can't marry you, Conn. I can't marry anyone."

"If you love me, you can. Money isn't going to be a problem. We'll figure a way to work out the rest."

She bit her lip, fought back a fresh round of tears. "You don't understand."

Conn straightened on the sofa, raked his dark hair back with his fingers, but his eyes remained on her face. "I know about the baby, Hope. Glory told me. She knew she was breaking a confidence but she loves you. She wants you to be happy. She wanted me to know what happened."

Her chest was aching. She couldn't seem to catch her breath.

"I can only imagine how much losing that child must have cost you. But what happened is past. I'm not like Richard. I won't let you down." He moved closer, bent his head, and very softly kissed her. "I can give you that baby you wanted, Hope. My baby. Say you'll marry me."

She leaned toward him, her eyes glistening with tears, and buried her face against his shoulder. If she hadn't already known she loved him, she would have known then. She could read the pain her words inflicted and it hurt her as badly as it was hurting him. She wasn't sure she could bear it.

But losing him now would be easier on both of them than losing him after they were married. She trembled as she eased back to look at him. "I'm not ready yet, Conn. Maybe in time . . ."

His expression subtly shifted, hardened. "Either you love me or you don't, Hope. If you do, then marry me."

"I told you, I'm not ready for marriage. Not after what happened. Not yet."

"If I thought it would make any difference, I'd give you some time, but I don't believe it would. I married one woman who didn't love me enough to stay with me. I won't make that mistake again. I won't wait for you, Hope. Don't expect it of me. If you love me, you'll marry me."

"Sometimes loving someone isn't the only thing that matters."

"It's all that matters to me. If you leave, if you walk out that door, if you're not willing to commit, don't expect to come waltzing back into my life whenever you please."

Her eyes slid closed. God, it hurt so much. "I can't stay, Conn. I don't have the courage. I—"

"That's it, then? You're saying tonight is all we have?"

She swallowed, every cell in her body aching for him. "Yes . . ."

His features looked carved in stone. "Then tonight, you're mine." Conn hauled her to her feet and into his arms, and his mouth crushed down over hers. It was a hard, bitter, savage kiss, filled with the pain of loss and despair. And yet she wanted it, craved it. Needed it like the air she breathed. She kissed him back the same way he kissed her, with all the pain she was feeling, all the regret.

She loved him. But she was a coward.

She loved him. But she could not stay.

She felt his big hands on the sash of her robe, jerking the ties, pulling it open. His mouth found her breast and he suckled her there, took her nipple into his mouth, bit the end. The robe fell away as he shoved it off her shoulders, down over her hips, into a pool at her feet. Then he was lifting her up, carrying her into the bedroom.

She could feel the warmth of his skin, the movement of the muscles across his chest. She trembled as he set her down on the edge of the bed, turned to strip off his pants. Returning to the bed, he kissed her, explored her mouth with his tongue, teasing and coaxing, making her burn.

"I want you to remember, Hope. I want you never to forget." His mouth was a hot brand moving over her, leaving a scorching path along her throat, over her shoulders, the flat spot below her navel. Kneeling in front of her, he parted her legs, kissed the insides of her thighs, then he found the entrance to her core and his mouth settled there.

Heat enveloped her. Fire roared over her, burned through her, lifted her, scorched her until she dug her fingers into his thick dark hair and shattered in a powerful climax.

Conn came up over her, entering her roughly, plunging deep, impaling her with a single hard thrust and filling her completely. "I love you," he said. "I want you to remember."

Hope swallowed back tears, knowing she would never forget. With each deep stroke, he imprinted himself upon her. Each time he withdrew, she knew an ache so powerful she whimpered. And yet there was pleasure, intense and powerful. Deep and burning. She knew he felt it, that it was there, mixed with the pain.

The ache continued to build. She loved him. But she could not stay.

His beautifully sculpted body shifted as he moved. Powerful muscles rippled as he surged deeply inside her. She looked into his face and the pain she saw staggered her, made her weep his name.

His pain was hers; hers became his.

They clung together, overwhelmed by emotion, driven by despair. Conn surged into her again and again, and though she silently wept, she couldn't resist the pleasure.

The first climax hit her so hard she shook. It was followed by another, even more intense. Conn's own release hit equally hard, both of them trembling, their bodies locked together, covered by a sheen of perspiration.

He was still hard when he withdrew, his muscles taut as he rose above her on the bed.

"I love you, Hope. Say you'll stay."

She bit her lip, tears streaming down her cheeks. She only shook her head.

Conn stared down at her for a long moment more, his blue eyes full of longing. Then the emotion disappeared from his face as if it had never been there. He turned and walked out of the room.

Chapter 29

Horns blared on crowded Sixth Street far below Hope's apartment window. Taxis fought to reach the sidewalk in front of the building where frantically waving patrons huddled in their heavy wool coats. Hope had been back in the city for nearly a week. It felt like a year.

It was the eighteenth of March. Gray clouds hovered over the tops of tall buildings. An icy wind whipped against doors and blew papers into the streets. God, she missed the heat and the sun. She missed the blue-green waters and sugary white-sand beaches. Mostly she just missed Conn.

Since the day of her return, she had thrown herself into her job. She had stayed long hours in the office, volunteered for extra assignments, anything to block memories of him. Nothing had worked. She thought of him day and night, couldn't sleep, could barely force herself to eat.

Her friend Jackie Aimes had stopped by as often as she could, but Jackie was involved in a serious relationship with the man she had met some weeks back. Besides, seeing how happy she was only made Hope feel worse. Jackie was worried about her and so was her family, who had begun to call on a daily basis.

She knew they could hear the brittle edge in her voice, the

tears she couldn't quite hide no matter how hard she tried. She was working on a feature for the *Living* section of the paper about a local grammar school being remodeled and all the problems it entailed, but it wasn't challenging enough to hold her interest. Unable to resist, she had phoned Mrs. Finnegan to find out why the old woman had finally decided to sell.

On the other end of the line, Mrs. Finnegan's voice sounded defeated and weary. "It was Skolie, dear."

"Buddy's dog?"

"Yes, that's right. They abducted him. Stole his leash right out of the dog-walker's hands. I received a ransom note the following day. They said they would send him back to me in little pieces if I didn't agree to sell." She made a tired, sighing sound into the phone. "Buddy loved that dog. It was just too much."

"Oh, Mrs. Finnegan."

"I've signed the first few papers. I'm sure there will be more. We have to be out in sixty days."

"I'm so sorry," Hope said.

That had been two days ago. After all that had happened, Mrs. Finnegan and the tenants of Hartley House were still going to lose their homes. She hadn't believed her mood could possibly get worse.

Then this morning, her sister Charity had arrived completely out of the blue, smiling and excited, having traveled all the way from Seattle to New York to impart her thrilling news.

"I know I should have called," she said as Hope pulled open the apartment door. "But I wanted to surprise you. I wanted to tell you the good news in person. Call and I— we're going to have a baby!"

Hope had looked at her sister's radiant complexion and the wide smile on her face and simply burst into tears.

She started crying and couldn't seem to stop. Until that moment, Hope had always been the one to take charge. Now she sat back and let her middle sister take over, let Charity brew tea for her, prop pillows behind her back on the sofa, cover her legs with a blanket.

"You have to tell me everything," Charity demanded. She was three inches taller than Hope's five-foot-three, with straight blond hair that reached her shoulders, beautiful and sweet, and not yet showing the baby she carried.

"I should be happy for you," Hope said between fits of tears. "I mean, I *am* happy. It's just that . . . just that . . ." She broke off, unable to finish, and simply shook her head.

"All right, that's just about enough. You are going to start from the beginning and tell me what's going on. Then we're going to figure all of this out."

Hope sniffed into her Kleenex. "We can't figure it out. Even if I went to see him, it wouldn't do any good. Conn told me if I left, not to come back."

"If he loves you, he'll want you back. The question is, are you sure you love him?"

Hope started crying.

"Okay, okay, you love him." Charity reached down and stroked Hope's hair. "Really, really a lot, right?"

"Yeah. Really a lot." She accepted the fresh tissue Charity held out to her, blew her nose, and dabbed at the wetness on her cheeks.

"Tell me all of it, Hope. I want you to go all the way back to Richard. I have a feeling that was where your problems really began."

And so that was just what she did. For the next half hour, Hope spilled out the pain of loving someone and suffering his betrayal, the crushing disappointment and feeling like a failure. Then she told her sister what she hadn't told her before.

"That day I found them together . . . I was two months pregnant with Richard's child. I saw them and I don't know . . . I just seemed to go a little crazy." She told Charity about running away, about how she had slipped on the ice on the front steps of the building. "I lost the baby, Charity. Dear God, I wanted that child so much."

She cried for a while, and Charity cried with her. They talked about what had happened and she cried a little more, but now that she had told Glory and her sister, and Conn knew the truth, it didn't seem to hurt quite so much.

"Conn said he would give me another baby. Why did I have to be such a coward?"

Charity reached down and caught her hand. "Hey, it's okay. When I left the Yukon, I never thought I'd see Call again. I thought he was still in love with the memory of his first wife. The truth was, Call was afraid, just like you."

"What if I married Conn and it didn't work out? What if things went wrong? What if he doesn't really love me the way I love him?"

"What if he does?" Charity asked softly. She squeezed Hope's hand. "What if he gave you a child and loved you just the way he said? Wouldn't that be something worth risking everything for?"

Hope inhaled a shaky breath. "Funny, all week, I've been thinking that same thing. What if Conn is the one man who would really love me for all of my life?"

"Do you think he's that kind of man?"

Hope's eyes filled with tears. "Yes."

"Then you have to tell him. Tell him that you'll marry him."

She only shook her head. "I can't. He said he wouldn't wait. He said if I walked away, not to come back. His mother ran off and left him when he was a little boy. His wife never really loved him. She left him just like his mother. Now I've done the same thing. He'll never be able to trust me. And if I went down there and he turned me away, I couldn't . . . I just couldn't bear it."

Charity didn't say more, just got up from the sofa, marched over and picked up Hope's address book off the desk and started thumbing through the pages.

"What are you doing?"

"If you don't want to call him, I will."

Hope sat up on the sofa. "Are you crazy?"

But Charity just started dialing. And despite her reservations, Hope didn't stop her. Instead, she tossed back the blanket and walked up next to her sister.

"Hello, I'd like to speak to Conner Reese. Is there any chance he's there?"

The only number Hope had was the satellite phone on the *Conquest.* The boat was in Jamaica for repairs. Conn was probably not even aboard.

"Thank you." Charity flicked Hope a look. She held the phone a little away from her ear so that both of them could listen.

Hope's heart leapt as a familiar deep voice came on the line. "Hello."

"Hi, is this Conner Reese?"

"This is Conn."

"My name is Charity Sinclair. We've never met but I believe you know my sister."

She could feel the sudden tension on the line. "Has something happened to Hope?"

"No, no, it's nothing like that. She's fine. Well, actually, she's not fine. She's completely miserable. You see, Hope is desperately in love with you."

He grunted. "I think you must be talking about someone else."

"I'm telling you the truth. My sister loves you. I was kind of hoping . . . well, that you might come up to New York and talk to her."

"No way. Not a chance. Hope left me—I didn't leave her. I won't play games, Charity. And I don't want a woman who doesn't love me enough to stay with me."

"But—"

"Hope has to trust me or it would never work out between us. She has to look inside herself and know with absolute certainty that I'm not going to fail her. That I can be the man she needs me to be."

Charity bit her lip. She glanced over at Hope. "At least let me tell her you still love her."

"Sorry. That's something Hope has to figure out for herself. Tell her the boat will be in dry dock for a few more weeks. I'll be working aboard her for at least that long. Tell her if she figures out what she wants, she knows where to find me."

"She won't come, Conn. She's afraid you'll turn her away."

Hope thought she heard a dirty word. "Tell her I'll give her a sign. I'll hang a light on the bow. If she's welcome, the light will be on. If the light's not on, she'll know it's over."

Conn said good-bye and hung up the phone, and Hope sank down on the chair in front of the desk.

"You have to go," Charity said firmly.

"If he still wanted me, he would have said so."

"In his own way, he did say so. You just weren't listening." Charity clamped her hands on her hips. "Dammit, I've never known you to be such a coward."

Hope managed a smile. "I was always a coward. I just hid it well."

Charity walked over to the window, looked down on the traffic below. "None of us wants to get hurt, Hope. But in a way, Conn's right. If you can't trust him not to hurt you, if you don't have complete faith in him, then you shouldn't marry him. Think about it, Hope."

Conn stood on the bow of the *Conquest*, his hands braced on the rail as he stared out into the darkness. A thousand times he had thought of the phone call he had received from Charity Sinclair. A thousand times he wished he had said something different, wished he had told Hope he loved her.

And yet he knew in his heart he had done the right thing. If Hope couldn't trust him, if she believed he would cheat on her like Richard, or hurt her in some other way, then he didn't want her.

The night was quiet. He could hear the water lapping against the dock, the groan of the ropes on the boat in the next slip over. Then the sound of footfalls intruded, approaching along the deck as Joe walked up beside him.

"You've been out here quite a while. The guys have a hot card game going on down in the galley. I thought maybe you'd be interested."

Conn raised an eyebrow. "You're playing cards tonight?"

Joe gave him a sheepish smile. "Actually, I'll be spending the night with Glory at our apartment. I just thought you might want to play."

"Thanks, but I'm not in the mood."

Joe's gaze followed Conn's back to the darkened water. "I know what she meant to you, man. I know how you must be hurting."

"Even I didn't know how much she meant to me. Not until she was gone."

"It's probably not the right thing to say, but maybe Hope was never really the one. With Glory and me, we knew—practically from the moment we met. We knew we were right for each other. Maybe you're supposed to find someone else."

Conn just stared out to sea.

"Why don't you fly back with me to the wreck site tomorrow? We'll do a little diving, a little treasure hunting. Maybe it'll take your mind off Hope."

Conn ignored him. "Damn, I forgot to turn the lights on. Do it for me as you leave, would you, Joe?"

Joe sighed. "It's been two weeks, Conn. She isn't going to come."

A muscle jerked in Conn's cheek. "Just turn on the god-damned lights!"

Standing in the darkness of the Port Antonio dock, Hope heard men's voices coming from the bow of the *Conquest,* but she was too far away to hear what they were saying. All she knew for certain was that there was no light hanging on the bow. All she knew was that Conn didn't want her.

She could feel the tears beginning to build, feel them spill over onto her cheeks. She thought she had cried herself out in New York. She wished she could find a way to regain her tough facade, but during the weeks with Conn, somehow she had lost it for good.

Turning away from the boat, she started walking, moving briskly, anxious to get away, trying to outrun the pain. As she raced along the boardwalk, something caught her eye. A flash of light behind her illuminated the darkness, arresting her where she stood. Slowly turning, she looked back at the boat. The bow of the *Conquest* was awash in light, a sea of tiny white bulbs that lit up the night. White lights flickered from the rigging, strings of lights dangled from the crane. More strings draped across the railings.

There were lights everywhere, lights that said she was wanted, that she was still loved.

"Hope!" She saw him then on the deck, his big hands braced on the rail. "For God's sake, don't move!" He raced for the gangway, ran down to the dock, turned, and started running toward her.

Hope made a strangled sound in her throat, dropped her bag, and started running back to him. Conn caught her in his arms, lifted her against his chest, and just held her.

"I can't believe you're really here." A faint tremor ran through him, and her arms went around his neck.

"I was so afraid you wouldn't want me," she whispered against his ear.

"If you hadn't shown up by the end of the week, I was coming to New York to get you."

Her eyes slid closed. "I love you, Conn. I love you so much. I was a fool to leave."

Conn set her on her feet and captured her face between his hands. "That's right, you were. Don't do it again." And then he kissed her. The sweetest, fiercest kiss she had ever tasted.

"I love you so much," she said again and smiled up at him through her tears. "When are you going to marry me?"

Conn threw back his head and laughed with pure joy.

Then the laughter slipped away. "Are you sure, baby? Are

you sure this is what you want? If we get married, it's got to be forever."

Forever. It was the most precious word she'd ever heard. "I've never been more certain of anything in my life."

Conn kissed her. "Then how about we get hitched tomorrow?"

Hope threw her arms around his neck. "Tomorrow is perfect."

EPILOGUE

Six Months Later

Life is nothing if not bizarre, Hope thought as she nestled in her husband's arms in their big king-size bed. Still pleasantly sated from their recent bout of lovemaking, her mind sifted through the amazing events of the past six months.

In the end, she and Conn hadn't been married that Sunday, but decided to wait until some sort of wedding plans could be made. Hope quit her job at the newspaper, and two weeks later they said their vows in a small ceremony in the lush tropical gardens of the Sans Souci Resort in Ocho Rios.

The wedding was a lovely affair, attended by both of Hope's sisters and their husbands; her father and stepmother; Jackie Aimes and her fiancé; the crew of the *Conquest;* and a handful of Conn's Navy SEAL friends, including Joe and, of course, his wife, Glory.

Hope had worn a gauzy white wedding dress and orchids in her hair, while Conn had looked incredible in his dark blue suit and white shirt. They had honeymooned in a suite at the resort on the cliff overlooking the sea, and Hope had never felt more certain that she had married exactly the right man.

A week later, they had returned to the boat in Port Antonio so Conn could get back to his job, and Hope had received an unexpected wedding gift.

They had been standing in the chart room next to Andy Glass when Captain Bob walked up. He handed Hope a manila envelope covered with cancelled postage stamps. It was addressed to Hope Sinclair, c/o the *Conquest,* General Delivery, Port Antonio, Jamaica. But it had apparently taken a circuitous route, being forwarded through both Montego Bay and Kingston.

"Mail's not the greatest around here," the captain explained. "One of the guys at the post office said it had been sitting there for a while and decided to bring it over."

Hope studied the envelope, turning it over in her hands. "There's no return address." She tore the envelope open, reached in, and pulled out the three-and-a-half-inch floppy disk she found inside. "Look at this." She checked both sides, but there was no label on it.

"Is there a note or anything?" Conn asked.

She turned the envelope upside down and shook it, and a single slip of paper fell out.

You were right about everything. This is the best I could do. Maybe it will help.

"It isn't signed," she said. "I wonder who it's from."

"Why don't we see what you got?" Walking over to the computer, Conn shoved the disk into the slot and clicked on the A-drive. There was only one file listed on the disk menu.

"*Phillip Jersey Personal Citibank Account Records,*" Conn read. "Who's Phillip Jersey?"

Hope stared down at the screen. "Oh, my God! Phil Jersey is the building inspector who condemned Hartley House. Hurry, open the file."

Conn clicked the mouse, and a list of Phillip Jersey's checking account deposits and debits flashed up on the monitor.

"This looks like something off his personal computer," Hope said. "The record goes from December tenth through

January sixth—the week before and the weeks right after the condemnation. Look at this. Over that period, there are five ten-thousand-dollar deposits put into the account."

"Let's see if the account shows who the checks came from." Conn clicked on the deposit line, and the name Martin Reyes popped up. "Ever heard of him?"

Hope's pulse started pounding. "Oh, my God, I actually know who he is. Martin Reyes works for Wells, Powell, and McGuiness. Richard and I attended a couple of benefits the firm sponsored. At one of them, there was a mixup with the seating, and Martin Reyes and his wife wound up sitting at our table. He was kind of an underling. I think he worked in the controller's office."

Conn checked the other four deposits, and Reyes's name came up each time.

"Interesting. If I recall, Jimmy Deitz said Wells, Powell, and McGuiness is the law firm involved with both properties abutting Hartley House and also Americal Corporation, the guys who want to buy it."

Conn looked at her and smiled. "Baby, I think you may have found exactly what you've been looking for. I think you've just been given the ammunition you need to save those folks at Hartley House. Who sent it, do you think?"

Hope looked down at the note. "Someone who didn't want to get involved." Hope tapped the paper. "Someone who was very close to retirement and didn't want to jeopardize his pension." She looked at Conn. "I think this came from the guy who took over my story. *Midday News* figured he would just sit back and do nothing, that he wouldn't give them any trouble." She grinned. "But once a reporter, always a reporter. I think this came from Randy Hicks."

Conn reached down and popped out the disk. "We'll send a copy of this to the district attorney's office. Combined with the way Buddy died, Jimmy Deitz's 'accident,' and all the other stuff that's happened in the last few months, I don't think they'll be able to sweep this under the carpet any longer."

He pulled Hope into his arms. "But that disk'll have to go

in the mail. You've made your last trip to New York for a while."

Hope just smiled. "Too cold for me in New York." She looked down at the envelope that had circulated over half of Jamaica. "But I think we'd better send it Federal Express."

That had been six months ago. After the D.A. had received the disk, an investigation had quietly begun. The paper trail was easy to follow, and the wheels of justice began to turn. To save himself, the building inspector sang like a bird. Martin Reyes, the accountant who had signed the checks, incriminated everyone from his immediate boss to the senior partners in Wells, Powell, and McGuinness. They, of course, were also happy to make a deal.

It included the name of their client—a senior senator from New York State named Arthur Kingsley, who stood to make millions. Kingsley rolled over on Brad Talbot, saying Talbot and his henchman, Jack Feldman, had been behind the fire at Hartley House and the attack on Buddy Newton.

The politician went down beneath a hail of verbal gunfire that called for his resignation and looked as if it might wind up putting him in jail, at least for the next several years.

Jack Feldman made his own deal, giving up the names of the thugs who had beaten Buddy Newton to death.

Unfortunately, after hiring the best attorneys in the country, who made a series of brilliant legal moves, Talbot managed to extricate himself, since he had no financial gain in the deal, just expectations of a long list of paybacks.

Still, for the most part, Hope felt that justice had been served.

It was Sunday morning. As the two of them lay in bed, Hope thought how happy she was. They had rented a beautiful apartment in Jamaica until they could find exactly the place they wanted to purchase for Conn's diving resort, still not quite certain where they wanted to live. Glory and Joe had overcome the problems they faced with Glory's parents and seemed even happier than they had been when they first got married.

Unconsciously, Hope's hand came to rest on her stomach. For the past few weeks, Conn had been trying to convince her to stop her birth control pills. He wanted a child as badly as she did, and, of course, her biological clock was ticking. Last night, she had discarded her monthly pack.

She trailed a finger along Conn's chest and his muscles tightened. "Charity is having a baby. I wonder when Patience and Dallas will decide it's time to start a family."

Conn chuckled. "Dallas runs a ranch. He'll need sons to help him. I imagine they won't wait too long."

Hope trailed her finger a little lower. "I stopped taking the pill last night. With a husband like you, I don't imagine I'll have long to wait for that baby you promised."

She could feel the smile that broke over his lips. Conn came up on an elbow, bent his head, and very softly kissed her.

"Not long at all," he said. She didn't miss the love in his eyes or the hot look that followed.

She and her sisters had always done everything together. Why should having babies be any different?

They were all three married now, and each of them had had her own adventure. Hope slid her arms around Conn's neck as he kissed her, certain the future would be the greatest adventure of all.

Author's Note

Though this book is purely fiction, the vast amounts of treasure carried by the galleons is true. The treasure aboard the *Atocha*, found off the Florida coast, was valued at over four-hundred-million dollars. In the two hundred years Spanish galleons sailed to Spain laden with gold and silver, over two thousand ships went down. Only ten percent of those ships have been found. Eighteen hundred treasure-laden vessels remain lost at sea.

I hope you enjoyed Hope and Conn's adventure. If you haven't read Charity and Patience's stories, MIDNIGHT SUN and DESERT HEAT, I hope you'll look for them.

Wish you love, luck, and adventure.

Kat